Between the Lines

T. GEPHART

Published by T Gephart
Copyright 2020 T Gephart
ISBN: 978-0-6487943-4-9

Discover other titles by T Gephart at the retailer of your choice or on Facebook (www.facebook.com/pages/T-Gephart/412456528830732), Twitter (twitter.com/tinagephart), Goodreads, or tgephart.com

Cover by Hang Le
Editing by Insight Editing Services
Formatting by Elaine York, Allusion Publishing
www.allusionpublishing.com
Proofread by Rebecca, Fairest Reviews and Editing Services

Between the Lines

I figured since it started with you, it should end with you.
Not sure if I would've discovered the world of my delicious
firefighters and kick-ass women without you,
but I'm glad you were along for the ride.

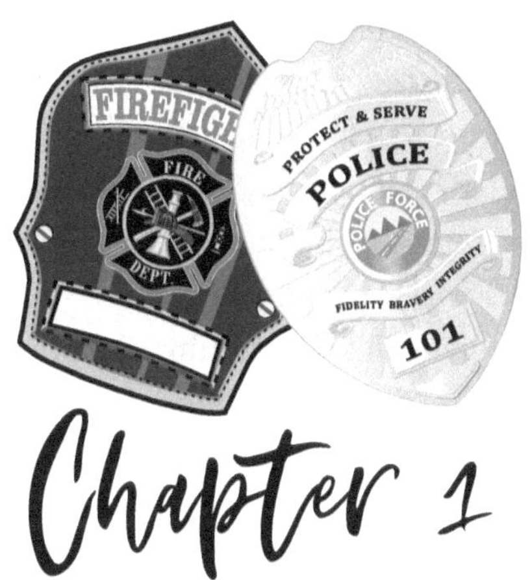

Chapter 1

Tessa

NEVER LEAVE A *fallen soldier behind.*

It had been drummed into me since before I could walk, service and sacrifice hardwired into my DNA like my brown eyes and dark hair. Not that I had much of a choice when both my parents were retired military, each of them having done stints deployed in warzones. Mom was Air Force, and Dad, a Marine, and it didn't matter they'd long hung up their uniforms, they lived—and held their two daughters—to the same standard.

"Okay, so here's what's going to happen." My eyes panned across the room, cataloging intel as I memorized the layout. "You're going to start on the south perimeter and work your way in. I'll keep eyes on you and be your backup. If it looks like it's getting hairy, I'll come in and pull you out."

"I don't know, Ricci," Miller hesitated, the fear in his eyes very real, "maybe we fall back, get some more recon."

A frustrated breath blew out my lips, my commitment to my partner and my last name keeping my feet rooted in their place. "Grayson," I used his first name, hoping it would ease some of the tension, "you can do this. It's been two months since Maxine left and you said that meeting someone new was what you wanted."

Spending Saturday night at a club with a friend was never a hardship, but *Vault* was the shiny new thing in the Meatpacking District and filled with pretentious assholes. I also despised Maxine, and as much as I hated seeing my friend going through the heartbreak, I was glad she was gone.

He was visibly deflated, scanning the offerings of beautiful women but lacking any of the confidence he'd had when we'd walked in. And when you're a cop in New York City, confidence wasn't something that was usually in short supply.

"Miller, you're a good guy. You're smart and good-looking, and any woman would be lucky to have you. Don't try and find someone to date, just go have a conversation. Let them tell you how great you are, because you obviously don't believe me."

He shrugged, sinking his hands into his pockets. "Maybe it's too soon? And speaking of getting out there, why aren't you? I know you didn't wear that dress for my benefit." His eyes floated down my mostly exposed body. "Not that I don't appreciate the effort."

My balled fist punched him in the arm, laughing as I tossed my hair back. "Just because I have to keep myself regulation appropriate most of the time, doesn't mean I don't like reminding the world I'm a woman. And you're welcome, just don't stare at my tits too long and make it weird."

Miller's lips spread into a smile, shaking his head as he looked back at the crowd. "Fine, I'm going in. But if I give you the signal, you pretend I'm like your baby daddy or something like that and get me the hell out. I'm out of practice, and these women look like they'd eat me alive."

"Only if you're lucky, Miller." I gave him a not-so-gentle shove. "And I'll extract you from hostile territory the minute you put out the distress call."

Like a proud parent on the first day of school, I watched as my amazing partner, Grayson Miller, took the first tentative steps into the crowd. I knew he would be okay, which was why I agreed to go to *Vault* in the first place.

While our station was in the Hell's Kitchen precinct, over the bridge in Brooklyn was where we called home. I lived in a tiny cubbyhole my dad told me I was paying way too much for, with Grayson living in a cupboard remarkably similar about a few miles away. It was dumb luck that we got along so well, our friendship evolving from the minute we'd been paired up by the department. And while there'd never been a romantic attraction between us, I would, without a doubt, take a bullet for him. So I guess standing around a nightclub while he tried to get lucky wasn't such a big deal.

And as much as we hated coming into the city on our time off, Manhattan was definitely the place for our latest mission. Not only were there more options, but no one seemed to care what we did. And if you were looking to hook-up rather than hunt for a relationship, being somewhere no one gave a shit was preferable.

"Hey, beautiful." Some dude in a suit sidled up next to me as I watched Grayson from a safe distance. "What's someone as sexy as you doing alone in a place like this?"

I tried not to laugh, wondering if his old man had given him pointers. Because surely that little gem didn't work after 1985. Turning, I noticed that while his *line* might have been tired and old, he wasn't. He was good-looking, late twenties to early thirties, and his suit was incredibly well-tailored. It fit him just right, showing off his attributes in the best possible light, which is why I assumed he was wearing it.

"I'm not alone." I smiled, deciding I wasn't interested in the distraction. The night wasn't about me, and even though it had been a while since I'd had a hook-up of my own, I needed to stay focused. "Better luck next time."

"So, where's your date?" Suit man didn't take the hint, glancing around us and probably expecting some angry possessive meathead to make an appearance.

"Why? Am I a piece of luggage that can't be left unattended?" I asked, slightly irritated. "Or are you angling for a threesome and want to see if he's up to par?"

Suit man's eyes blinked wide in surprise, probably not expecting the last part. And I'll admit, it was added purely for shock value. Because if I had to tolerate a stupid question then I might as well entertain myself.

His silence spoke volumes, his mouth opening and closing with no real comeback. It was clear that looks were all he had going for him, which was a shame because I might have welcomed a little intellectual sparring. Foreplay was mental for me as much as it was physical.

"Nothing?" I shrugged, already bored. "Better stay in the shallow end of the pool then, have a good night." I grinned, leaving him with what I thought was some helpful advice as I went looking for Grayson.

It wasn't ideal that I'd lost my line of sight, praying he hadn't gotten himself into too much trouble, or was looking for a bailout while I'd been occupied.

"Ricci!" I heard my name, a female voice calling me from the direction of the bar. My head swiveled, torn between continuing to look for my partner or acknowledging whoever wanted my attention. My eyes flicked back to where Grayson had disappeared, squinting as I tried to find him in the sea of people.

"Ricci!"

My name again, the choice made for me as I felt a tug on my arm. "Hey, I thought it was you. I can't believe the law is in my house and didn't say hello." Her eyes floated over my dress before returning to my face. "Oh, so I guess you're here on pleasure rather than business."

Her smirk was predictable, the fiery redhead not known for being subtle. I grinned, lifting a shoulder in a shrug. "I'm trying to blend in, Raelle. Advertising I'm a cop is probably bad for business."

"Please," she scoffed, waving her hands. "You think Marcus would let *anything* illegal go down in here? You guys wouldn't even be able to cite someone for littering in this place. But it's good to see you enjoying the spoils of our fine city. Let me know if you want me to set you up. There is a day trader, that is hotter than should be legal, sitting at the bar primed for a good time. And trust me, in that dress," her finger swirled in my direction, "there isn't a man in this place going to assume you're a cop."

Well, if anyone knew what the men in the club were thinking, it would be Raelle. As the sultry bar manager for the hottest new club, she was living up to both of those reputations. She was beautiful with an unapologetic sexy vibe, unashamed to flaunt what she had while working the bar like she'd been born to do it. Guess that was how she'd noticed me in a crowd of sweaty, gyrating bodies, her eagle eyes spotting that I wasn't looking to score like everyone else.

"I'm just here to help Miller get over his cheating ex, not really interested for myself."

It wasn't a lie either, my expectations of finding anyone remotely engaging were at an all-time low. Not because the men in the club weren't attractive, that wasn't the problem. But because I was tired of dealing with guys who were intimidated by the badge or my attitude. Even in a city as big as New York, it was hard to find someone who was secure enough in his own manhood to deal with me. And despite sometimes feeling like I was "too much," I refused to compromise. At least for the current week. A cheeky hook-up, with a guy who didn't know who signed my paycheck, could very well be on the agenda at some point in the future if my hormones took over.

"Miller looks like he has it handled." Raelle lifted her brow, my partner shooting us a sly smile as he came into view. He'd acquired some company since he'd disappeared, an enthusiastic brunette on his arm as they made their way to the bar. "Let me know if you guys need anything else. Presley likes to keep our first responders happy."

And with a nod, she headed back to the bar.

The "Presley" in question was the owner of *Vault*. Who, in addition to being smart and ambitious, was the sister of one fireman and engaged to another, both who served in our precinct. We'd also looked out for her when she was dealing with a crazy-ass ex, so her feelings of gratitude were a little more than just the run-of-the-mill *liked to keep us happy*.

My eyes glanced over to where both Raelle and Grayson had migrated, the long bar of *Vault* getting a lot of action from the thirsty crowd. My partner—like the rest of the people vying for drinks—seemed completely oblivious to me and my look of satisfaction, glad it hadn't taken long for our mission to have been achieved.

Of course, all that had happened so far was two people of the opposite sex sharing a friendly conversation. But even if that was all that transpired for the night, it would be a massive step in the right direction, Miller's smile hinting it had been the ego boost he'd needed.

Meant I could relax a little too, the need to intervene hopefully lowering by the minute. Not sure what I wanted to do with my newfound reprieve from responsibility. Dancing wasn't really my thing, and finding a distraction of my own wasn't on the agenda either. Which left only one other option, drinking.

While I vowed to stay sober and alert, a drink or two wasn't going to kill anyone. And considering we were in a bar, it would probably help me look less like I was on a stakeout and more like the general population.

I was making my way over to the bar—the end opposite Miller so I didn't cramp his style—when I noticed a couple of familiar faces sitting in a nearby booth. They had a waitress looking after them, laughing animatedly as she seemed to be taking their order.

Great.

Leighton and Tibbs were here.

While their appearance didn't really surprise me—the two of them comprising of the previously mentioned brother and the fiancé of the owner—I had hoped I'd be spared the interaction. And not because I had an issue with firefighters in particular. In fact, Leighton was a total sweetheart, and one of the nicest guys you'd ever meet.

But Tibbs.

Yeah, he was something else.

I'd seen him perform acts of unparalleled bravery and his commitment to the FDNY and competency in the face of danger was something I admired and respected.

But once he took off that uniform, he was a complete manwhore.

A *beautiful* manwhore, delicious in every way that mattered, and I'll admit I'd been unable to take my eyes off him when we first met. God, I remember that day, his smile, the way he strode into the room with such confidence, my heart beating a little faster every time he'd look in my direction.

But beautiful or not, he was nonetheless a manwhore.

He was unapologetic about it too, the smug smile on his face confirming he knew his amazing six-two athletic frame would probably be cozied up to some bar bimbo by the end of the night. They'd take one look at his gorgeous hazel eyes, incredible body and sexy smile and would willingly be his next conquest.

And what I hated more than *anything* was that I even cared.

What did it matter who he went to bed with or how many women he *entertained*? On the list of my concerns, it should've ranked dead last. But regardless of not wanting to have anything to do with Tibbs taking up my mental space, I couldn't help that thoughts of him and his stupid sexy face and body featured anyway.

It was ridiculous, an irritation that chaffed me like a blister that wouldn't quite heal. And if there was any God at all, I hoped his next hookup gave him a scorching case of genital warts and his dick would fall off.

Sure, it was irrational. Because while I'd admit—begrudgingly—that he was gorgeous and probably knew exactly what to do with that sexy body, he was the last person on earth I would sleep with. One, because I refused to be another number on his list of used-and-discarded. And two, because even if I lost every single ounce of sense I had and went *there* with him, he'd probably turn me down.

Yep, even the manwhore had a type, and apparently, I wasn't it.

I should have been thanking my lucky stars, grateful that even though I'd entertained the idea one time—before I knew how incredibly gross he was—that I'd been spared the indignation and embarrassment. But it didn't matter, it still stung. It hadn't even been a *real* rejection, our interactions never getting past a platonic capacity.

Nope, I was an idiot, holding a grudge because he did the one thing I'd demanded. To be treated like a person instead of a vagina. I wanted no special treatment, to be one of the guys. And he excelled at it. Hell, half the time I was positive he'd forgotten I was a woman, trash talking with me like I was one of the men in his crew.

Gah, I hated I still thought about it. And hadn't let the stupid—and unhealthy—fantasy of him go.

But if not for his questionable choices when it came to dating and women, he would've been *exactly* the kind of guy I'd want.

Strong, determined, hardworking—and someone who treated me like an equal. Throw in his amazing body and gorgeous face and he was perfect. Hell, I'd even been tempted to ask him out in the beginning, attracted to him in more ways than just physical.

But *perfect* doesn't exist. And Tibbs was a crotch hound that I wanted no part of.

My eyes floated back over to where he was sitting, covertly appreciating how hot he was even though it would be a cold day in hell before I'd ever admit it out loud. I wasn't in the mood to deal with him *or* his lady friends, so avoiding his vicinity was my prime objective. With any luck, Miller would give me the signal he didn't need me anymore and I could head home.

If I stayed, and he saw me, Justin Tibbs would find a way to ruin my night. Because as much as I liked to look at him—and I liked it very much—I hated there was a part of me that was still attracted to him. Even though I knew it was never going to happen. And then have to watch him give it away so effortlessly to other women.

It was easier when we were part of a group, the buffer giving me a chance to ignore him or at least distract myself from the spectacle. But with Miller occupied, I was out of luck, and didn't know if I had the energy or the inclination to be polite.

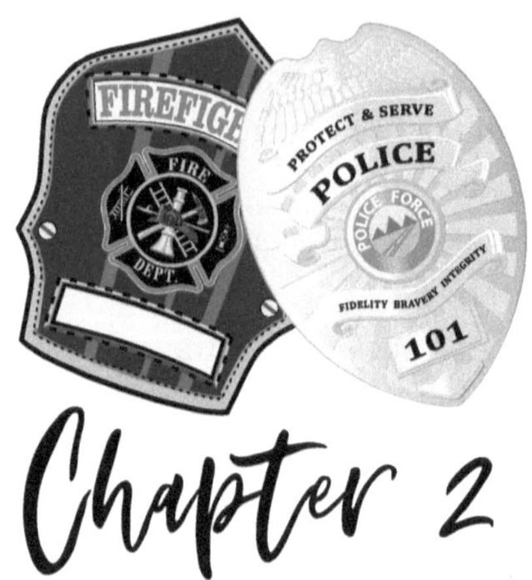

Chapter 2

Justin

"WIPE THAT SMUG look off your face, I know you were with my sister. There was no need for you to go *to the bar for beer*, Denise would have happily delivered them." I shook my head, Leighton returning to the table with a couple of beers. And unless he'd gone to get our drinks in Queens, he'd taken way longer than required. It didn't take much to work out where he'd been.

"You have an issue with me saying hello to my future wife?" He eased back into the seat, not even trying to hide his smirk. "It would've been rude of me not to."

"Yeah, yeah, whatever." I rolled my eyes, knowing he'd been doing a lot more than saying a fucking hello. And not that I wasn't ecstatic my best friend and my sister were going to be tying the knot sometime soon, but the idea of them getting busy wasn't what I wanted in my cerebral cortex. She was *still* my sister, and I really didn't ever need to imagine that.

Leighton laughed, taking a slow pull from his beer. "You know, I half expected you not to notice. Where did those women who were in your lap go? You run out of North's deodorant?"

"Fuck you. North has nothing to do with it." I flipped him off.

It had started as a joke, me stealing North's deodorant from his locker whenever we got back from calls. The guy couldn't go two steps without some woman throwing herself at him. It was like he had some magical superpower that could attract ladies without even trying. I mean, sure he was decent looking, but he was no more special than any of us.

Our jobs in the FDNY demanded we stay in shape, so most of us got a decent amount of action. And since Leighton *and* North were both out of rotation, it meant more for me.

And not sure if it was the added opportunities or the lack of competition, but things had been relatively good with the ladies. Except for the current situation, which had been fruitless.

"Meh, they were predictable." I sighed, bored they'd just been more of the same. "I think I might be coming down with something. I swear, five minutes in and I was already losing interest."

It was unlike me to turn down attention, especially when it came in such a delightful package. I reveled in it, getting off on hero worship and appreciation, believing that having a healthy ego was nothing to be ashamed of. If anything, it drove me to be better. Pushing myself to compete against the guy I was yesterday so I was constantly a better version of myself. And yeah, maybe the adulation was one hell of a sweetener.

So why I had turned down the fine-looking women who were more than happy to give me what I usually wanted was a mystery. Hell, it even surprised me.

"You think that maybe you're seeing everyone in healthy and loving relationships and possibly want it for yourself?" Leighton raised a brow as he leaned in and whispered, "You know, I hear it's contagious. Good thing it's pretty fucking awesome too."

I rolled my eyes, knowing that me wanting to be tied to a ball and chain was definitely *not* the reason for my lack of interest.

"Jesus, Leighton. You hear yourself? This is *me* we're talking about, not *you*. I love you, brother, but you sucked at playing the game. It was only a matter of time before you ended up taking the walk down the aisle. Now, North, that was the one that came out of left field. Not that I'd blame him with a woman like Quinn, but everyone knows that shit is the exception and not the rule. So, going to have to pass on giving some girl the key to my balls."

It wasn't like I had issues with long-term relationships per se. My parents had been married for forever and were still into each other. As were Leighton's parents. So, I knew it worked out sometimes. Which was why I'd consider it when I was like forty or something. Hell, the chief was edging close to fifty and had recently tied the knot and had a new baby. And considering what a shitshow his first marriage had been, it was proof there was no need to rush it.

"Well, whatever your deal is, make sure you don't say any of that shit in the best man speech at my wedding. Especially about North's wife." Leighton laughed, shooting Presley a smile as she walked by, almost ignoring me completely.

He was so whipped.

It hadn't even been ten minutes since he'd come back to the table, but by the way he was looking at her, it was like it had been a fucking week.

"Christ, Leighton." I shook my head, rolling my eyes as Presley gave him a stupid love-struck grin of her own. "If you want to go hang out with her, go. I don't need a sitter."

Leighton shook his head, watching as Pres disappeared from view. "Nope, she's working. Besides, this conversation about your balls is so riveting. Not sure I want to miss it."

My grin widened as I flipped him off. We'd known each other since we were eighteen, moving into an apartment in Hell's Kitchen and gone through the academy together. He'd been the only roommate I'd ever had until he moved out and shacked up with my sister. And as much as I liked having the apartment all to myself, I kinda missed having him around. He was more than my best friend. And while he was soon going to officially be my brother-in-law, he'd been family for longer than I could remember.

"Fine, stick around." I pretended like I wasn't thrilled he wasn't going to ditch me in favor of Presley. "But do me a favor and dial down the commitment talk. I'm happy for you, and for everyone else who's . . ." I waved my hand around trying to find the right word, "giving up their freedom, but it's not for me. I must be just getting the flu or something. Or maybe yesterday's warehouse fire took more out of me than I thought."

Yesterday had been a shitshow.

We'd barely clocked on when the first call came in, and they didn't stop until we were done twenty-four hours later. A five-car collision where miraculously no one died, two domestic disputes, and a gas leak—just to name a few, and all before dinner. So, when we were faced with a warehouse burning out of control close to midnight, we'd been running on vapors.

Still, there was no other job I'd rather be doing, even though it could be physically and mentally exhausting. Which was why after twenty-four hours of duty it was important to let off some steam. Recharge in the best way I knew how in the forty-eight before heading back in. Not sure why my usual methods weren't up to scratch.

"Maybe you should—" Whatever else Leighton said was completely lost on me. It was like I could hear he was talking, but the words receded into background noise.

Holy.

Shit.

My eyes snagged on what was probably the hottest brunette I'd ever seen, which was saying something because, trust me, I'd seen plenty.

She was toned, a body that clearly saw the inside of a gym on the regular, with the length of her hem giving me a *really* good view of her legs.

And fuck did I like what I saw.

Her killer heels boosted her height, but even without them she wouldn't be short. And while it was hard to tear my eyes away from her legs, the rest of her was pleading to be discovered.

Jesus.

The curves of her body leaned more toward athlete than model, every muscle radiating strength and power like it was begging to be unleashed.

And I liked it.

The fact I could put my hands around her and not feel like I was gonna break her was a turn on I hadn't realized I wanted. And if all she had was a smoking hot body, that probably would've been enough. But she was gorgeous as well. Long, straight, dark brown hair that spilled over her shoulders like an oil slick and a pair of dark brown eyes that were staring right back at me.

She looked . . .

Hell, did I *know* her?

When I didn't look away, her eyes narrowed, a silent conversation I didn't understand happening between us that got me on my feet whether I wanted to or not.

And trust me, I wanted to.

"Heading to the bar," I mumbled to Leighton, not daring to break eye contact with my mystery woman. I wasn't risking her leaving and losing her forever.

Nope.

Not happening.

My body moved through the crowd unable to shake the feeling that we'd met before. And fuck, if I'd been stupid enough to date her and *not* called her back, I'd beg—on my hands and knees—for her forgiveness.

She didn't flinch, standing her ground as I closed the distance, and I liked the heat in her eyes. It was somewhere between lust and hate and I'd be lying if the combination wasn't doing it for me in some sick twisted way.

Oh, we knew each other all right. And while I didn't know the circumstances, we'd definitely *not* slept together. Because while I'd made some questionable calls in my life, there is no way I'd have slept with her and not wanted a second taste.

It didn't take long until I was standing in front of her, moving through the crowd quickly with a desperation crawling up my skin I didn't quite understand. Those beautiful eyes were filled with so much trouble I had to fight the urge not to just bend down and kiss her.

"I know you." It wasn't a question, not bothering with the hello because it was time I didn't want to be wasting. My mouth lowered, skating the shell of her ear as I whispered, "And you know me too, don't you?"

Her hand pushed hard against my chest, her eyes flaring wide. "What the hell are you doing?"

So far, the only one who'd done any touching was her. And while I wasn't in a hurry to stop her from putting *whatever* she wanted on me, the edge in her voice had me slightly concerned.

"I'm not doing anything." I lifted my hands, proving they were behaving. "But I'm also not wrong. I might forget a name, but I never forget a face. And yours isn't one I'd be able to get out of my memory even after a lifetime."

She laughed, tossing her head back before her eyes settled back on me. "Really? You that bored tonight? C'mon, Tibbs, I haven't got time for your bullshit."

Tibbs.

So she *did* know me.

Hearing my name on her lips just made me want to hear it again.

Moaned.

Repeatedly.

But while we'd established she knew who I was, I was still coming up empty on the circumstances, and why she was so pissed off. Granted, I wasn't exactly the most reliable guy around, but I was respectful. Annnnnd always made sure any woman who was with me didn't regret it in the morning.

"I'm not here because I'm bored, sweetheart. So why don't we start with your name, beautiful, since you already know mine."

Backing down wasn't an option. Neither was ignoring that as much as she wanted to pretend to be irritated, she hadn't asked me to leave, nor had she done so herself. And while the details of her identity might've been foggy, her ability to kick some serious ass was not in question.

She radiated confidence.

And power.

And if she wanted out of the conversation, I'd have already been handed my balls.

Not sure I *didn't* want that to happen, to be honest. The idea of her chewing me out kinda made me hard. Her attitude was as attractive as the rest of her, and I wasn't dumb enough to walk away, especially when it was so incredibly familiar. And so goddamn delicious.

Confusion flashed through those beautiful brown eyes as she met my stare, and whatever she'd thought I was going to say, that hadn't been it.

She leaned in, her voice stroking me in all the right places. "Are you fucking with me, Tibbs?"

My eyes closed, unable to stop myself from savoring the treat that was hearing my name and the word, *fucking,* in the same sentence. And the only reason why I didn't beg her to say all of that again was because I wanted to hear what else she had to say, hoping it might include some other dirty words as well.

"I'm not fucking with you," I almost choked out. "I—"

"Heeeeey!!" Leighton's voice came up behind me, the bastard wearing a beaming smile as he slapped me on the shoulder. "Ricci! What's happening? Damn it, Tibbs, why didn't you invite her over already. We've got a booth if you want to hang. Unless you're here with your friends, don't want to cramp your style."

"Ricci?"

The name fell out of my mouth as it tumbled around in my brain, unable to piece it together. Because the only *Ricci* Leighton and I knew was a cop from our precinct and while she was totally cool . . .

"Wait! *Tessa* Ricci?" I asked again wondering how much I'd drunk. It was only a few beers, right? Not enough to be hammered.

My gaze steamrolled over her body again, trying to reconcile the new information.

Jesus.

Fucking.

Christ.

"Yes, it's me." She rolled her eyes at me before turning to Leighton and giving him a smile. "And thanks, but I'm probably going to bail soon. I was Miller's wingman, but I think he's got it handled." Her head tipped to the far end of the bar, her partner— also in civilian clothes—having what looked to be an in-depth conversation with some girl.

"Come on, have a drink with us," Leighton offered, ignoring me and my inability to say anything other than just her name. "It's not every day we're all off shift together *and* in the same place."

"You're so beautiful." My eyes widened, the words spilling from my lips before I could stop them.

Actually, *beautiful* was underselling it. She was by far the most gorgeous woman I'd ever seen. And how I'd not noticed before was a mystery I couldn't work out.

Leighton coughed, elbowing me in the ribs. "What he means is—"

"No, seriously." I cut him off, not in any way confused as to what I *meant* to say. "You're fucking stunning."

My eyes raked over her, absorbing every cell. I couldn't believe she'd been hiding that ridiculously hot body underneath a cop uniform for the last three years. And wow, I was suddenly becoming a huge fan of the NYPD. Hell, even the few times I'd seen her out of uniform, she'd never looked like that.

I'd always thought she was pretty, sure. I mean, I hadn't been blind. But what I was seeing in front of me went so far beyond fucking pretty, it wasn't even funny.

Her eyes narrowed, the smile tightening on her face. "You know, if that was supposed be a compliment, you shouldn't sound so surprised when you say it. It negates the sentiment."

She probably had a point, but if she'd expected me to keep the surprise from my voice after discovering all of *that*, then she didn't know me well enough.

Actually, she didn't.

Something I was definitely going to change.

"My apologies." I put my hand to my heart, my lips edging into a grin. "So, Ricci," *Lord, I was still reeling from the shock,* "enjoying your night?"

Her brow arched, again like she was expecting something different. But I wasn't a complete moron, and unless I wanted to totally blow it, I needed to play it cool.

Not that it was going to be easy.

Oh hell, no.

It was diffusing a bomb wearing oven mitts level difficult. But I never backed away from a challenge, and I was looking forward to finding out which wires needed to be cut.

"It's been okay." Her shoulder barely lifted, not committing to a full shrug.

And I don't know why, but the indifference was sexy. "Well that shit won't do. Presley finds out someone has been in one of her clubs and having just an 'okay' time, shit will hit the fan. Someone will get fired for sure."

Total bullshit.

Well, Presley *would* be pissed about someone having an ordinary time, but no one would be joining the unemployment line because of it. At least not that I knew of. She was a hard-ass—especially when it came to me—but she wasn't totally heartless.

"So, I think it's in everyone's best interest if you come back with us and at least pretend to enjoy yourself."

If I'd been hanging with anyone *other* than Leighton, I might have reconsidered. I didn't need the competition. And judging by the eyes on her from a suit hanging at the bar, my feelings of her being the most beautiful woman in the room weren't mine alone.

But Leighton was neck-deep in love with my sister and even if he wasn't, would never tangle with a woman I was interested in. And if he hadn't guessed I was interested yet, I'd be confirming it very, very soon.

She glanced over at Miller, her partner still busy with his date. "You going to continue to be weird, Tibbs?" Her eyes swung back to me. "Because I don't have the bandwidth to deal with you tonight."

I leaned in, looking for any excuse to get closer. "Well then, let's go see exactly what you do have the bandwidth for."

Weird was the last thing she was going to have to worry about.

Nope, not even close.

And by the end of the night, I was positive I wasn't the only one who was going to be looking at the situation very differently.

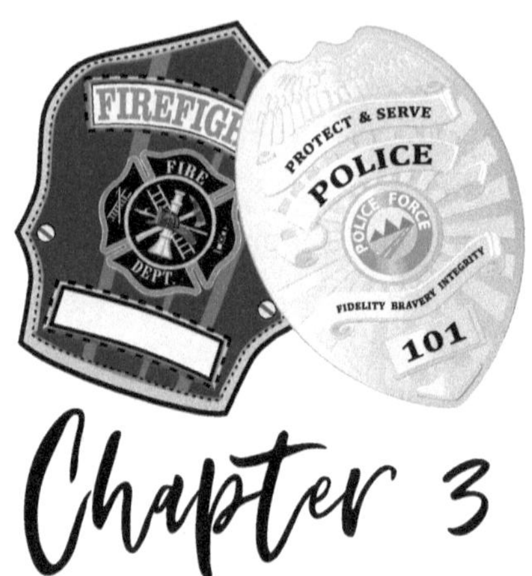

Chapter 3

Tessa

IT WAS EITHER curiosity or boredom that had me agreeing to hanging out with Leighton and Tibbs. Because common sense surely wasn't responsible.

Not because I thought they were terrible company—well Leighton wasn't at least—but because I didn't particularly think any good would come of it.

Tibbs had either been drinking heavily or had a brain injury. Because the way he'd looked at me when he'd first approached had been the same sexy eyes he usually reserved for his ho parade.

Smoldering.

Illicit.

And dancing with so much heat I was surprised he hadn't been rocking a full erection.

I'd seen the "look" firsthand, watched as he charmed his way into other women's pants like a lion moving in for the kill on a savannah. But had *never* been the recipient of it. And maybe part of me—the stupid part, obviously—was intrigued.

He hadn't known it was me.

At least not initially, eyeing me up and down like I was a snack and he hadn't eaten in a while. It was both thrilling and unnerving, hating myself for whatever small—microscopic— segment of my brain thought it had been a good thing.

Man. Whore, I reminded myself. In case I was the one with the brain injury and actually entertaining the idea of doing anything with Justin Tibbs other than Mirandize him.

"So, Miller is still trying to get over Maxine?" Leighton asked, pointing to the vacant booth they previously occupied. "What happened with the two of them? Last time we spoke, he'd been thinking of proposing."

I shuffled in, sliding my butt along the black leather semicircle seat as Tibbs followed close behind, forcing me all the way to the other side. He didn't even give Leighton a chance, filling the space next to me and keeping his body just far enough from mine so our thighs weren't pressing together. It seemed weird that he wanted to sit in the middle, but since I didn't like being caged in, I wasn't about to complain.

"Well, finding out she'd been screwing a bartender from TGI Fridays probably made him change his mind," I bit out, the idea she could cheat on a guy as amazing as Grayson still making me mad.

It was unlike me to share business that wasn't mine, and I absolutely hated people who gossiped. But exposing Maxine for the deceitful piece of shit I'd always suspected and was later proven to be, was too big a temptation. Plus, it was Leighton and Tibbs, and they'd probably hear it from someone at the station anyway. It wasn't exactly a big secret.

"Ouch," winced Leighton, flagging over a waitress as he planted his ass on the curved leather bench next to Tibbs. "Poor Miller. Still," he glanced over to where my partner was still happily entertaining the brunette, "looks like he's found something interesting to take his mind off her. At least for a few hours."

"Yep," I agreed, my eyes deviating to the bar briefly before returning to my male company. "Small mercies. He's a good guy, he deserves someone equally great."

"What about you?" Tibbs asked, a grin twitching at his lips.

My eyes widened. The idea of me and Miller dating was so freaking foreign I couldn't even believe he'd suggested it. Yeah, we were good friends, but he was more like a brother to me. No. There was no scenario where Grayson Miller and I would ever be romantically involved. Even if we didn't work together.

"Umm, he's my *partner*, moron. Not only is that the worst idea ever, but it's not even like that with us," I scoffed, wondering if he would've even suggested it if he hadn't seen me in a dress.

Tibbs chuckled, rolling his eyes. "Not you and Miller, Ricci. Jesus. I meant you and *someone else*. You dating anyone?"

Wow.

Why did he even care?

It could've just been small talk.

And since I'd so easily volunteered information about Miller's relationship status, I couldn't really think it was too personal to talk about my own.

Or he could want to know for more devious reasons. Like to amuse himself with the fact that I was single.

Deciding I wasn't going to willingly give him any advantages, I turned to face him, our legs accidentally making contact. "What about *you*, Tibbs? Dating? Wait . . ." I paused, tapping my finger against my lips. "You can't really call it *dating* when you're only with them for a night."

It was a cheap shot and I was better than that, annoyed at myself for sinking to that level. Not only because it was none of my business, but because as long as it was consensual, who the hell cared how many people he slept with.

Leighton laughed, coughing into his hand as the waitress approached us. "So, Ricci, you want a beer? Cocktail? Tibbs, want some Neosporin to go with that burn you just got?"

"I'll have an old fashioned." I smiled sweetly, knowing my little jab was going to earn me some recourse. "Thank you."

"I'll have a beer. Stella. Thanks, Denise." Tibbs winked at the waitress who seemed thrilled just to have his attention. And if he was annoyed by what I'd said, he wasn't showing it.

"I'll just take a soda, Denise." Leighton grinned. "And thanks again."

Denise didn't bother writing down our order, nodding wordlessly but giving Tibbs an appreciative smile before she sauntered off.

"So, you really want to know about my dating habits, Ricci?" Tibbs popped a brow, not moving his leg which was still pressed against mine. "Or there something else you want to make assumptions on." He didn't even try to hide his grin, like he was pleased I'd basically called him a whore.

"More an observation than an assumption, Tibbs." I met his smirk with one of my own. "But if it makes you feel better to talk it out, then go ahead. We've got at least ten minutes before our drinks arrive, you'll just have to find something else to talk about for the other eight."

Last thing I wanted to hear about was Tibbs with women, but I wasn't going to be the first one to flinch either.

Tibbs laughed. "Tell me, Ricci. Do they teach you how to be so judgmental in cop school or you learn that on the job? You know, if I didn't know better, I'd say you were jealous."

"Oh plllllleeeeasssee," I scoffed, unwilling to accept there was any validity to his statement at all.

Like none.

Because I couldn't be any less jealous if I tried.

And jealous of what exactly? Of those women he treated like disposable razors? Like that was something to aspire to.

"Wow, no wonder you guys need to ride around in a truck. Your egos wouldn't fit in a regular sized vehicle." I rolled my eyes, choking back the laugh.

And to think I'd been attracted to him; I'd reallllly dodged that bullet.

Leighton pointed his finger at me, shaking his head. "Hey, don't include me in this shit. You two want to insult each other, have at it. But don't be bringing the uniforms into it."

"Yeah, Ricci," Tibbs chuckled as a smug grin edged at his lips.

"You're just as bad, Tibbs." Leighton raised his brow, challenging his friend to say different.

Tibbs pinned his buddy with a hard look but the smile he was fighting told a different story. "Where's the loyalty, brother? I need better friends."

Leighton planted his feet on the floor, coughing out a laugh as he stood. "And on that note, I'm heading to the bathroom. Play nice, kids."

He shot us a grin as he walked off, leaving me alone with Tibbs while he disappeared into the crowd.

Great.

"It would take a lot longer than ten minutes."

"What?" My head whipped back around, Tibbs still wearing his smug grin.

"*Anything* to do with me and women," he qualified.

"Oh really? Like ten *real* minutes? Or using guy measurements?" I asked, unable to stop myself. It was such a bad idea to continue . . . and yet . . . "You know that's why so many women have trust issues. *More than ten minutes, bigger than six inches.* . . blah, blah, blah. Believing in alternate facts doesn't make them true."

He coughed, his eyes darkening while he sucked in a full breath. "You know, all this talk, Ricci, I feel the need to defend my honor."

"And do what, Tibbs?" I was almost afraid to ask.

He was kidding, right? He wasn't seriously suggesting that we . . . What the hell *was* he suggesting?

"You're not dating anyone. I'm not dating anyone." He waved his hand nonchalantly. "And you made some very serious accusations."

"I never said I *wasn't* dating anyone," I pointed out, wondering why out of everything he'd said, that was what I was focusing on.

He leaned in closer, dropping his voice even though it was competing with the music. "Are you?"

"No," I answered honestly.

"Neither am I."

It shouldn't have mattered one way or another, but those words made my skin tingle. And the way he was looking at me made it even worse.

I hated it.

Hated that for some stupid reason I was still attracted to the jerk, especially knowing all I knew. And what? I should be grateful that he suddenly showed interest in me because I was wearing a goddamn dress?

Hell.

No.

I was smarter than that.

I was, wasn't I?

"What do I care?" I volleyed back, hoping he wouldn't see through my bravado.

His gaze dipped to my lips but didn't drop any further, moving back to my eyes. "You're not even a little bit curious?" he asked, his voice dangerously seductive.

"No." I sucked in a breath, doing my best to keep my voice from wavering even though inside I was hot and confused. "Why don't I just go home now and be disappointed. It's how the night will end anyway and at least then you can still live in your own delusion and I can save myself the time."

"A beer, old fashioned, and a soda." Denise had returned, lowering the drinks from her tray one at a time onto the low table in front of us. "Anything else I can get you?"

It was perfect timing.

Punctuating that it was definitely time to leave because I was on a very slippery slope with Tibbs.

"Thanks." I stood, picking up the tumbler and downing the drink in one big gulp. It burned, the rapid injection of whiskey heating my throat and making my eyes water. But sipping it and sticking around wasn't an option either.

"We're good, Denise, thanks." Tibbs waved her off, keeping his eyes glued to me.

"Well, I should—" I didn't get to finish my sentence, Tibbs already on his feet, wrapping his hand around my empty glass.

"Go?" he asked, leaning in a little closer, a grin taunting me. "You running from me, Ricci?"

I wasn't sure if it was the alcohol or the fact that Justin Tibbs—a guy who'd never given me so much as a second glance— was hitting on me, but it suddenly seemed funny. "Oh, Tibbs. You really want to go there?" I laughed, arching a brow as I threw back a taunt of my own.

I'd never run from anyone or anything, and I sure as hell wasn't going to start now.

"I'll go anywhere you want to take me, Ricci. Anytime. Any place. To do anything you have in mind." His head tipped toward the exit. "Where are we heading?"

He was kidding of course, radiating his usual cockiness, because for the most part, women really *did* fall at his feet. And I totally understood it too, not blaming the poor souls who were captivated by his spell. They couldn't help it; he wasn't only incredibly nice to look at but could be ridiculously charming as well.

But unlike those other women, I knew better. Besides, I'd inherited the willpower of my father and the stubbornness of my mother which mixed for a lethal combination. Not sure which of my awesome parents gifted me my sarcasm but that was another trait I was thankful for. Especially when I shot Tibbs a cocky grin of my own, making him falter a little.

"Do you need to go tell Leighton?"

He looked at me puzzled, narrowing his eyes as he tried to make sense of my question. "Tell him what?"

"That you're leaving." I dropped a hand to my hip, resting it there casually as I continued. "Not sure what your arrangement was, but I wouldn't want your bestie to be mad at you."

His eyes widened, the confusion all over his face. "I'm leaving?"

I rolled my eyes trying to look bored. "Seriously? Did you not just say you'd go anywhere I want to take you? Or was that just idle chat?"

He swallowed. Hard.

Either he had been playing some game—knowing the chances of me saying yes were remote—or he hadn't meant it. And I was really curious which of those reasons was responsible for wiping that confidence from his face.

I liked it.

Tibbs on edge, and knowing I'd been the one to put him there.

"Ricci, I—" He stopped, taking a minute before sucking in a breath. It was all he needed, finding whatever confidence he'd lost as his eyes heated. "I'll text him. Did you drive?"

"No. We'll grab a cab. Send your text, and I'll let Miller know he's without backup. You ready?" My head tilted toward the exit.

"I'm always ready," he leaned in and whispered, his breath tickling my neck. "Let's see you put your money where that mouth is."

It was a staring competition.

A game of chicken.

A chess match, where one of us had to flinch, and it sure as hell wasn't going to be me.

I had no idea if he genuinely thought he was going to end up sleeping with me, *or* he was calling me on my bullshit and refusing to be the first one to blink. And part of me was excited to find out which. I was clearly more jaded or bored than I first thought, the thrill of playing our little game making my skin tingle.

Lowering my eyes for a minute, I quickly typed a text to Miller, asking him to confirm he was fine before I bailed. He'd looked solid the last time I'd glanced at him at the bar, but I wasn't going to desert him either, even if I had a point to prove. Luckily —or unluckily, depending on how it all panned out—he responded quickly that he was doing great and was relieving me of my duty. He didn't even ask questions, thanking me for the ride along and letting me know I would get a full debrief tomorrow. Good to know, but I wasn't sure if it would be reciprocated.

Tibbs seemed done with his little text exchange too, sliding his phone back into his pocket as I tossed mine into my purse, the grin he was wearing a little sexier than I would have liked.

"Good to go?" I asked, arching a brow, knowing it was time to raise the stakes.

He lowered his hand, his eyes searching for permission before pressing it tentatively against my back and throwing in a few extra chips of his own. "Soooooo good, Ricci. Let's go."

I didn't ask him to lift his hand, not entirely hating the pressure as he followed me toward the door. Marcus, the head of security, watched as we left, giving us a curt nod but not saying anything. It wasn't his style, the man who was a slab of granite with zero emotion flicked his eyes back to the club as we stepped out onto the street.

"Your place?" Tibbs asked, raising his hand and flagging a cab. He looked pleased, biting back his grin as he kept his palm pressed to my body. I liked the way it felt, my skin tingling under his touch. It was hard not to lean into it, refusing to give him the satisfaction even though I wanted more of it.

The cab stopped in front of us, my answer given as I tossed out my address to the driver while we slid into the backseat.

I wasn't sure exactly what I was doing.

But there was no way I was going to lose.

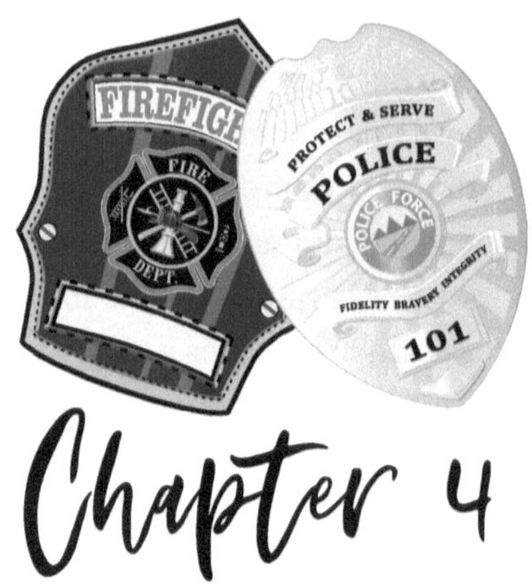

Chapter 4

Justin

S HE WAS PLAYING me.
Had to be.

Because as hot as Ricci was—and baby, she was incredible—there wasn't a chance she was going to take me home for hot sex with no repercussions.

It didn't work that way.

Not with girls like her.

So instead of ending the night how I'd prefer—both of us naked and me touching that fine body of hers—I was walking around a field of landmines, just waiting to see which one went off.

It made me hard.

The element of danger attached to it making my balls draw up tight. And I couldn't have wiped the smile off my face if I'd tried.

"You live in Brooklyn?" I asked as we crossed the bridge, watching as the city was left in our rearview. I'd assumed she lived around the precinct, the commute from the outer borough to Midtown, not one I'd sign up for.

"You sound surprised. Not everyone can afford that Manhattan rent. Even out in Flatbrush, it's more than I'd like."

She was right about that. Real estate surges had made housing prices ridiculously expensive, but that wasn't why I was surprised. It was that I'd never really asked, or even bothered to find out. We'd hung out—had a drink or two along with other members of our crews—but it never occurred to me she didn't live in my neighborhood. Not that it mattered either way, it was just curious that I'd known her for a few years and something as basic as her address had been a mystery. Especially since she'd obviously known mine.

"You stalking me, Ricci?" I asked casually, pretending like the thought didn't thrill me a little. "Guess it's hard to issue a restraining order on yourself. But if it helps, know there will be no formal complaint lodged by me."

She rolled her eyes, her lips twitching into a grin. "Don't flatter yourself, Tibbs. We have your address on file from when you made the report against Presley's ex-boyfriend. But if it makes you feel better, I'll leave an anonymous tip that you're running a meth lab out of your Hell's Kitchen apartment. That'll get you all kinds of *sexy* attention." Her brows lifted at the suggestion.

"Stop teasing me, Ricci," I chuckled, pretending like hearing her whisper the word "sexy" didn't turn me on more than it should. It didn't even matter what context it had been in, my eyes flicking to her mouth and wondering what it would be like to kiss her.

Bad idea, Tibbs. Especially when the attempt might be met with being tazed and a face full of pepper spray. And strangely those odds didn't make me any less hard.

Her fingers reached up and tossed her dark hair off her shoulder, radiating the same confidence and control I'd seen her rock a million times before in her PD blues. If she was edgy or uncertain, she sure wasn't showing it, pulling out some bills from her purse to pay the driver as we slowed to a stop.

"Here, let me." I pulled my wallet from my back pocket, grabbing some cash and handing it over before she had the chance.

She eyed me hard, the annoyance radiating off her skin. "You didn't have to do that."

"Since when do I do anything I have to?" I asked, cracking open the door and stepping onto the sidewalk. She wasn't far behind, shuffling off the seat and managing to get out of the car without letting me see what kind of panties she was wearing.

Impressed—and a little disappointed—I waited for her to adjust the hem of her dress; her fingers curled around her keys as she led me to the front exterior door.

With no words exchanged, I followed her inside the main foyer and then up two flights of stairs. I hung back a little, unable to peel my eyes from her amazing ass as her athletic legs climbed with what seemed like no effort. She could probably run those steps even in those heels, the confident flex of those muscles sexier than any porn I'd ever seen.

Oh, and I still had no idea what the hell we were doing, finding myself inside her apartment as she turned on the light and locked the door behind us.

"So." She anchored a hand on her hip, tipping her head to the side like she was inspecting me.

"So," I echoed back, keeping a foot or so distance between us and not hating the attention. "Now you have me here, what are you going to do with me?" I had a list in case she needed it, and all of them involved me touching her.

Her lips pressed into a pout like she was giving it some serious consideration, holding her arms across her chest enhancing what was already a sensational pair of tits. "Why don't you take your clothes off."

So that's how you're going to play it, huh?

The suggestion was not one I was expecting, but I wasn't backing down either. I'd come all the way from Midtown knowing I was probably thirty minutes away from being tossed out on my ass. And if she thought that me getting naked in her living room was going to bother me, she picked the wrong person to play the game.

"As you wish," I added with an exaggerated flourish, folding myself at the waist as I bowed like she was royalty. Then straightened, my fingers not taking much time to unbutton my shirt and pulling it apart at the middle.

There was only the slightest reaction, her eyes darkening as she watched me pull off my shirt with no hesitation. It dropped to the floor, my fingers moving to my belt, keeping our stare locked as I unhooked it and then moved to the fly of my pants.

She chewed on the corner of her lip, not saying a word as I continued to strip, pushing my pants down my legs before kicking off my shoes and pulling off my socks. If this turned out like that time Leighton and I went camping when we were eighteen and the son of a bitch stole my clothes, I was going to be pissed. I'd had to walk back from the lake completely naked, saved from catching an indecency charge on account it was dark and we were in the fucking woods.

I was positive I wouldn't have the same amount of luck this time around if I ended up walking home with my dick hanging in the breeze. My fingers hesitated at my boxer briefs just waiting for her to call time out.

Any minute now. My thumbs hooked in the waistband when I heard the sharp intake of air.

"Should I stop?" I asked, willing to play it all the way to the end. After all, I wasn't shy, and if she wanted a free peep show, I had no problem giving her one.

Spending a lot of time in the gym and working with the fire department gave me the kind of body that backed up the arrogance. So yeah, she might be doing it for sport, but she also didn't hate what she saw either. That was pretty fucking obvious, her eyes rolling over my skin like she was measuring me up for a suit.

"Ricci?" I pulled down the elastic just enough it hadn't slipped into dick pic territory yet. But another inch and it was going to be anything other than decent. "I'm not in the habit of sexual harassment. So if you want me to keep going, I'm going to need a verbal confirmation."

There was a line.

And fucking dare or not, I wasn't going to cross it.

Not with her.

Her dark eyes tangled with mine, her lips parting slightly as she sucked in a breath.

"You were just going to get naked because I asked?"

And ladies and gentleman, we have a winner.

I fucking *knew* it.

"That's usually how it works." I adjusted the waistband of my boxer briefs so all the good bits stayed hidden, but didn't make any moves to put the rest of my clothes back on.

"Just like that . . . I say take them off and you do?"

I wasn't sure if it was curiosity or disbelief that had her repeating the question, the look on her face unreadable.

It was fascinating.

She wasn't horrified, and sure as hell didn't look offended. In fact, what seemed to be mostly getting under her skin was there was a guy willing to get naked in her living room and she couldn't understand my motivation.

Hmmmm.

Interesting.

"You're concerned I'm too compliant?" I asked, raising a brow. "Or is it my virtue? You trying to save me, Ricci? Worried random women are taking advantage of me?" I finished with a laugh.

Because if *that* was what she thought, it was motherfucking hilarious.

Her lips twitched, like she also thought it was funny but didn't want to give me the satisfaction of a reaction. It was kind of sexy. The ridiculous amount of control she had over herself gave nothing away.

She strolled over, her hand extended like she was going to touch me but instead grabbed my chin, pulling it down so our eyes met. "Did you come here thinking I was going to fuck you?"

And if her control was a turn on, the casual way she said *fuck* was on a whole other level.

Jesus.

"Nope." I didn't even have to lie, knowing sex hadn't been on the table. "But I'm also not a pussy. And I was curious."

She was so close, her lips just barely out of reach. And even though kissing probably wasn't on the table either, I couldn't help but wonder what her mouth would taste like. Had she'd always been that hot? How the hell could I have not noticed.

"Basically you're telling me you have shitty impulse control and an inability to back down." Her eyes darkened, one of the corners of her mouth edging into a grin. "Just *how* far would you have gone, Tibbs?"

Her voice was low, stroking my name like I wanted her hands to do to other parts of my body.

"Pretty fucking far." I didn't hesitate, because she wasn't wrong. I *did* have issues with impulse control and backing down. And even more importantly, I didn't see either of them as a personal flaw.

Her hand moved from my chin to my chest, her fingertips hovering over the skin but not making contact. I had no idea what she was doing, or why it felt so good, but if she wanted to do it all night, I wasn't going to be the one to say no.

She tilted her head, bringing her mouth to my ear and whispered, "What if *I* got naked?"

"Fuuuuucccccck."

It was a curse and a fucking prayer, the jolt running down the length of my cock so strong I thought I was going to come. No one had even touched it yet, just the sadistic mind game and the idea of her naked, enough to get me off.

Until she laughed.

The control she'd previously had locked down, completely gone as she giggled her fucking ass off. Meanwhile I was still turned on and mostly confused.

"You are too easy, Tibbs. You thought you had me with your little striptease. I didn't even have to take a thing off."

Goddamn it.

She'd won.

Fuck.

Fuck.

Fuck.

And she wasn't wrong either. I'd been prepared to stand around with my dick in my hand in an effort to make her crumble and all she had to do was whisper in my ear.

"You play so fucking dirty, Ricci." I leveled her with a stare even though I wasn't half as pissed off as I was pretending. "I thought cops had more integrity than that."

Her hands pushed roughly against my chest. "And I didn't know you'd be such a sore loser. So I guess we both learned something new."

And even though the touch wasn't sexual, I liked it, holding her hands still against my skin. "Yeah. Maybe we did."

She smiled, and it wasn't the fake kind either, her whole face lighting up. And if I thought she'd been beautiful before, she just elevated to another level. "You can put your clothes on, Tibbs. I've had my fun."

"Oh, so that's how it is?" My hands settled on her waist, holding her still as I gave her a grin of my own. "I'm just here to amuse you? Wow, heartless as well as cruel. And while we're at it, why don't you explain to me why I've never seen you dressed like this." My eyes flicked down to her dress and the smoking body it was hiding underneath.

"It takes a special kind of talent to make the way *I* dress to be about *you*," she sighed, shaking her head. "Could you be any more conceited?"

I shrugged. "I mean, I could but I feel like the effort is wasted since no one else is around to see it."

And then the laughing stopped.

Her beautiful smile dropped, and whatever easiness I'd been feeling leaving along with it. So fucking fast too, the air cooling between us in an instant as she took a step back. "You should get dressed; I'll get you an Uber."

"Wait a minute." I reached for her, my fingers curling around her arm before she got too far. "We were talking shit and having a good time a minute ago, what just happened?"

Because I know I didn't imagine it. And while Ricci and I had always been cool, it felt like maybe we were getting to know each other a little better. I liked it. Even if I was still bewildered how beautiful she'd obviously always been, and I'd been clueless.

"Nothing happened. Just get dressed."

She almost had me convinced, except I wasn't stupid. "Just tell me already. I know you're pissed off." And if I could be guaranteed it wouldn't earn me a knee in the balls, I'd have told her she was just as hot pissed off as she was when she laughed. But that currently wasn't the point, and as we'd already established, I had a problem not pushing an issue.

"I'm not pissed off, I'm bored. We've both had our fun, but I'm on duty tomorrow."

The mask of indifference slipped back over her face, her tone giving nothing away. Maybe I'd been mistaken and read it all wrong. "O-kay, I'll get dressed then." I lifted my hands, taking a step back. "What shift you working tomorrow?" I switched gears, testing to see if small talk was going to be shot down too.

"Four to twelve."

She watched as I reached for my pants and pulled them on, following my hands as I zipped and re-did my belt.

"At least you don't have to deal with the early morning, that's got to be nice."

Next was my shirt, the fabric slipping over my shoulders before my fingers got busy with the buttons. It had been a lot more fun taking it off but—whether she wanted to admit it or not—I still had her attention.

"Yeah, I'll go organize your ride." She made a move to get her phone, my hand on her arm stopping her.

"I can get my own ride, but thanks. Besides, it would be too much like you leaving money on the dresser beside the bed, and I don't want to feel cheap."

The shadow of a smile returned, and I liked that she hadn't totally frozen me out. Funny how a couple of hours ago I wouldn't have given a shit what she thought. Not that I didn't appreciate the NYPD, but if one of them didn't like me, I wasn't going to lose any sleep over it. But yeah . . . with her, I cared.

"I wouldn't want you feeling cheap." She reached down and handed me my shoes, the words thankfully lacking animosity. We hadn't totally regained whatever ground we'd lost, but I was hopeful.

Figured if she wouldn't tell me why she was pissed, maybe I'd settle for changing her mood. Because given a chance, I'd like to revisit that smile.

She didn't even try to hide that she was watching, barely blinking as her eyes stayed locked on me. Something other than standard interest smoldered behind those beautiful dark lashes, clear I wasn't the only one feeling the newfound attraction.

"Last chance, Ricci," I asked, adjusting the rest of my clothes. "You sure you don't want something else before I leave?"

It was risky, but I couldn't help myself, the chance to play a little longer too tempting.

She coughed out a laugh, anchoring her hands on her hips. "Nothing you can give me, Tibbs. But if I ever get desperate, I'll let you know."

It was my turn to laugh. Because regardless of what was coming out of her mouth, her eyes were saying something else. And I had a hunch the desperation she might feel would be an entirely different kind.

"Suit yourself." I shrugged, already planning my next move. "Guess I'll see you around."

"Yeah, guess so," she murmured, walking with me to her front door. "Enjoy the rest of your night."

I leaned in, smelling the sweetness of her perfume or shampoo or whatever it was that made her seem so delicious. "Oh, I intend to, Ricci." And without bothering to hide my smirk, I strolled out of her apartment.

There wasn't a chance I'd forget any of it.

How hot she was.

How hungry her eyes were.

Or how much I liked her smile.

And if she thought we were just going back to professional courtesies, she was mistaken.

Not a chance, sweetheart.

Not even close.

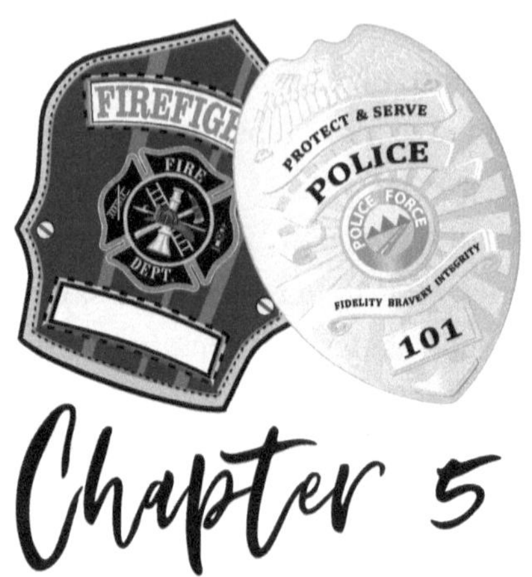

Chapter 5

Tessa

M E AND MY big ideas.

Invite him to your apartment, Tessa, let the guy get almost naked. Because that was going to solve all kinds of issues. Ha! What a fucking dumbass. Me, I mean. But he wasn't too far behind.

So predictable too. Him, I meant. Or maybe me too. But *seriously*, he suddenly pays me two ounces of attention and I was supposed to what? Fall over myself?

Not.

Fucking.

Likely.

Granted I did enjoy messing with him.

And watching him take off his clothes was a treat I couldn't have even hoped for. But if he thought we were going to be anything other than acquaintances then he was delusional. And sure, I might have encouraged him a little, genuinely letting my guard down and enjoying the mental tug-of-war. But that was all it was.

Entertainment.

Because I was bored.

That had to be the reason why—because I'd clearly lost my goddamn mind—I thought he was sexy. And why my stupid disobedient hands had wanted to touch him so badly. He definitely lived up to the hype. His body deserved all the adulation I'd heard about it and more. It needed a parade, and a key to the city, and a monument in Columbus Circle. The idea of what that body was capable of not really hypothetical when the display teased with dirty promises. Ones I'd have very much liked to find out.

Pity his mouth was attached to it.

Two things.

One, he'd probably been bored too.

That had to be the reason he'd said all those things about me being beautiful or whatever, because he'd never so much as sniffed in my direction. I was a substitute, a way to pass the time, a method to amuse himself. Which to be fair, I couldn't totally be mad at because that was what I'd been doing too.

And two, if I was dumb enough to think there was a legitimate connection and maybe that spark/attraction/voodoo was real, he'd have probably slept with me and then forgotten me just as quickly. And how fun would *that* be next time our paths crossed on the battlefield? Or worse, if someone found out.

Nope.

If I wanted to have a meaningless fling with a hot guy it would be with someone I didn't have to meet in the field. Or worse, see in the future casually over drinks and watch while he gargled another woman's tonsils.

I definitely had my father's temper.

Which was why I was actually doing Tibbs a favor by not even entertaining the idea of the two of us hooking up.

Assuming that was what he wanted.

And I wasn't sure he did.

Gahhhhhhhh.

Why the fuck did I even care? Why was I even wasting a second, let alone a whole freaking morning—after an equally long sleepless night—thinking about it. It was done, dusted, over. And while it had been mildly amusing, I probably wouldn't see or hear from him again for who knows how long.

In fact, he'd probably gone right back to the club, found some other woman, and gone to take his clothes off in *her* apartment. And I'd bet *she* didn't ask him to stop when he got to his underwear. I probably could've waited until he had them off before I called his bluff, because he looked pretty committed to going all the way. No harm in looking, right? It wasn't like I had my service weapon against his head, forcing him to do it either; he'd offered. And yes, it would have totally been wrong, using him in that way. Sexist. Degrading. And if the situation had been reversed, I'd have been horrified. So I was a hypocrite, but at least I was honest.

Still. . .

No.

Hot or not, he was off-limits. I didn't want to be someone's flavor of the month, didn't need to be stationhouse gossip, and didn't want to complicate a relationship which was just fine the way it was. I'd just keep my stupid sexy thoughts to myself— because the safety of my imagination was totally okay—and use them when I was alone.

And horny.

When I needed to get off.

"You're dropping your left," my dad shouted from behind me. "You want to end up with a fist to the face?"

I spun, the sweat pouring off me as I lowered both my gloved hands. "I don't think the bag is going to swing back. I'd say I'm fairly safe."

He shook his head, steadying the heavy bag that hung from the ceiling truss. "You do something, you do it properly. You train at full intensity so if there's ever a reason, you haven't learned bad habits. Now, lift your hands again and show me what you got, Baby doll. I know I didn't raise a woman who walks into the gym because she wants to look good in lycra."

I laughed, because as much as my dad was a hard ass, he loved his girls fiercely. He wasn't even afraid to show it, hugging me whenever I walked into his gym and telling everyone how proud he was. I'd assumed he'd always wanted a son, but they were words he'd never once said. Instead he raised two daughters who could change their own motor oil and throw one hell of a right hook. And he totally worshiped my mom, showing me exactly what a good man looked like.

Without argument, I lifted both fists and fixed my stance. He nodded silently, holding the bag and grinning as I alternated between jabs and upper cuts. "Just so you know," he chuckled from behind the vinyl, "if you ever want to turn pro, I'd have no problem being your manager. Just don't tell your mother I suggested it. She'd serve my balls up on a platter."

I was fairly sure that the only thing on earth my dad was afraid of, was my mother when she was mad. And for good reason too. Because as tough as he'd trained both me and Emilia—my sister—to be, that fierce DNA we got from our warrior mother. I think that was why he bought the boxing gym when he retired from the Marines. He needed to keep sharp and fit, and have a place to hide out whenever they had a disagreement.

"Your secret is safe with me, Pops." I laughed, enjoying the exhaustion in my muscles and the distraction from my previous thoughts. It had been the reason I'd come to the gym in the first place, hoping some time beating the shit out of something might eradicate what I knew were nothing but bad ideas. Sexy ones, but bad nonetheless.

When Dad was satisfied my form was up to scratch and I'd sweated a third of my body weight onto the mat, he told me to go hit the showers. "You're working today." He waved me off when I told him I was still good. "Don't want you out there with nothing left in the tank. Shower, refuel, and recover," he instructed, his concern hovering between father and trainer. "And make sure you tell Miller I'm still waiting for him to get his ass back here too."

"Dad, last time he was here you put him in the ring with Terenzio. He had to ice his ribs for a week." My poor ill-prepared partner's visit to my dad's gym still giving Grayson PTSD.

"So?" he scoffed, shaking it off like it was no big deal. Terenzio weighed at least two hundred and fifty pounds of pure muscle and could headbutt a bus and still be standing. "I didn't see you scared to get in the ring after him. And Terenzio didn't take it any easier on you."

That was true, my own ribs needing some time with the ice. "Yeah, except you'd trained me to take the hits, and I knew what was coming. Poor Grayson thought it was going to be a friendly spar, you can't blame the guy for not wanting a repeat."

"Well that wouldn't be a problem if he came back." He winked, shooting me a grin. "Go on, get out of here before my next client arrives. He hits like a five-year-old and I don't want to embarrass the poor asshole by calling him a pussy in front of you."

Accepting the towel my dad handed me, I wiped off before giving him a hug. "Thanks for the workout, tell Mom I said hi."

"Will do, Baby doll. Make sure you come visit soon. Emilia is deployed for another two months and your mom misses having her girls home."

I nodded, promising to call and visit more often before heading to the locker room.

The shower stalls weren't fancy, but the water was hot and felt nice on my tired muscles. The room was also spotless with amazingly soft towels, probably because the women's locker room didn't get a lot of action. Most of the people who came through the door rocked the Y chromosome, those of my fellow sex preferring the shiny new Active Fitness chain that opened a few doors down. But I hated group fitness classes, couldn't stand wheatgrass, and preferred to be trained by someone who had more experience than a three-month online course. And I liked that my dad didn't pull any punches, pushing me just as hard as any guy who walked through the door.

Ironic that Tibbs was similar in that way, or at least he had been. And now I was slightly worried things might change. And well, I couldn't have it both ways, could I? Be grateful he didn't see me as a "girl" and complain he didn't want me as a woman. Because that would be psycho.

After I was clean—and hoping to leave all thoughts of Tibbs down the drain with the soapy water—I dressed and headed back to my apartment. There were still a few hours before I needed to be in Midtown to report for duty, and other than a quick message to assure me he was alive, I hadn't heard from Miller. And since I was no longer hitting something, I could use the distraction.

Yep.

Anything other than think of Tibbs.

Because unfortunately it wasn't only his ridiculously hot body that I needed to avoid, it was the sexy, witty, fun side that I'd suddenly discovered as well.

"Are you going to see her again?" I asked Miller as we walked to our cruiser. "Or you going to keep things casual. If you're taking a vote, I say play the field a little longer."

Grayson had told me that Ariel—the woman he'd met last night—had been more awesome than he could've imagined.

They laughed and chatted at the bar, and finally went back to her place where he totally forgot about his cheating ex-girlfriend. He didn't tell me he'd slept with her, but judging by the smile on his face when we'd turned up to the station, I assumed he had.

He shrugged, getting that stupid look on his face when he got hung up over a girl. "I don't know, Tessa. I kinda feel like we have a connection. She gets me."

"Goddamn it, Miller," I breathed a breath of frustration. He'd called me by my first name which usually meant he was serious. And considering last night was supposed to be a fling, I didn't like where the conversation was heading. "You've known her for a night, how much of a connection could you have? You can't fall in love with her. There's a rule, six months before you can even consider being in love with someone else. You are in complete violation."

That was Grayson though. He fell in love hard and fast, which was why he ended up with a broken heart. Still, I'd hoped he'd hold out a little longer, waiting until the second or third date before declaring they had a "connection."

He laughed, shoving my shoulder before moving to the driver's seat. "Oh, yeah? What code are we talking about? Because I'm fairly sure there is no such rule."

"Just promise me you're not going to move in with her or anything," I slipped into the passenger side of our car, "and for God's sake, do not propose."

"Jesus, Ricci. I know I work fast but not that fast. I promise I'll talk to you before I make any life-changing decisions." He settled into the seat beside me, buckling up before hitting the ignition.

The captain had kept us mostly busy and we hadn't really had time to chat. But we were heading out to a domestic dispute and I figured I could use the time on the drive over to convince him not to declare his undying love. It was going to be a challenge but I had to at least try.

"Good. I'll be like your sobriety sponsor but for relationships. You have to do all ten steps before you can say the L word. And no cutting corners." I smiled as we pulled out of the lot.

"Yeah, yeah." Grayson grinned. "And where did you run off to last night? Nothing take your fancy?"

We hadn't discussed my exit, or that I hadn't left alone, his news taking precedence. It was preferable, if I was honest, not excited to tell him I'd gone home with Tibbs even though nothing had happened. "I wasn't feeling it." I chewed on my lower lip, feeling guilty for not coming clean. "And I was tired."

He nodded, not questioning my motives because he had no reason to suspect otherwise. "Well, thanks for coming out with me anyway. If you ever need the favor returned, I'm your guy. I'll even play the jealous boyfriend." He lowered his voice before turning to me. "*Hey asshole, get your hands off my woman.*"

"Great. I'll remember that." My eyes rolled, not convinced by his fake meathead routine. "And by the way, my dad thinks you should come back to the gym."

Miller shook his head, not even letting the idea settle. "Not happening, Ricci. I like my kidneys too much and would prefer them not to be tenderized."

We laughed about my old man on the way to the address, pulling up to the curb when we arrived at the apartment building. The call had come from a neighbor, a couple apparently fighting so loudly there were concerns it had gotten physical.

"101," I confirmed with Miller, having already been let into the building by the neighbor who'd called us. "Both have priors so let's not take any chances."

You could never tell what was going to happen when you knocked on someone's door. Especially if they hadn't been the ones to call you. But with domestic disputes, there was always that element of uncertainty.

Did they have a weapon?

Would they even open the door?

Were there kids involved?

And so many variables that we literally had no idea what we were walking into. At least with a drug bust or a burglary, the bad guy was clearly defined. But the last thing you wanted to do was draw a weapon in someone's home and potentially hurt the person being abused, or worse, someone's child.

Miller rapped on the apartment door, no noise coming from the other side, and announced us.

"Hello?" The chain bolted to the wood obscured most of her face, but it was clear the woman had been crying. "What's happened? Is George okay?"

"Ma'am, can we come inside and have a chat?" Miller asked, his shoulders still tense even though the situation didn't present as hostile. "You're not in any trouble but we want to make sure you're fine."

His voice was low and soothing, completely non-threatening. I liked that he used his brains as well as his badge and gun, not everyone on the force shared his philosophy.

My eyes scanned the exterior, glancing down the hall and then over to the stairwell we'd just climbed. The last thing we needed was the other party involved blindsiding us. And until we were sure he was no longer on the premises, we had to operate on the assumption he still was.

The woman—Kiera Castle—hesitated, unlatching the chain and opening the door once Miller had shown her his badge. She didn't say anything though, letting us into the apartment while keeping her mouth shut.

"We had a call that there were some loud noises coming from this apartment," I started, careful not to use any accusatory words that might spook or antagonize her. "Is there anyone else in here with you?"

"It was the T.V.," Kiera lied, the screen in question completely dark and by the looks of it, not even plugged in.

I nodded, pretending like I believed that shit and glanced around the small living room. "Did George say when he was coming back?"

George Phillips wasn't only her boyfriend, but the other name on the lease. And while it seemed he'd "stepped out" and wasn't around, he'd been arrested once before for assault as well as possession. Probably the reason he'd ghosted, either high or strung out.

"I don't know. He . . .he went to get cigarettes. He might be gone awhile," she coughed out, possibly a little high herself. "But I promise I'll keep the noise down so there's really no reason for you to be here."

This wasn't Kiera's first rodeo, having an assault charge of her own. Which meant she wasn't saying anything, maintaining her right to remain silent, and clearly not our biggest fan. "Are you sure you're okay?" I asked, not seeing any visible signs of battery but needing to ask all the same. "We know you guys were arguing."

She shook her head, refusing to admit anything. "I told you it was the tube. George isn't even here, he's gone. So unless you have a warrant, you need to leave."

Annnnnnnnd there we had it.

Without any evidence of a crime, and Kiera unwilling to file a complaint, there wasn't a lot we could do. Unfortunately, that's the way it went more times than not. Our hands were tied and other than reassuring them that we'd be back, we had to leave and hoped no one ended up hurt or worse.

Miller let her know she could call us if her recollection of the evening changed or if something happened later when George returned. He left her a card with a number but I had a hunch we wouldn't be getting that call.

"She's lying, and I hate that we're probably going to be back here sometime soon." Miller shook his head as we walked back to the street.

"Hopefully we don't need to come back with a body bag. But what can we do? We can't search the place without a warrant."

It sucked, but that was the job. And while there were parts that were truly horrible, I couldn't imagine myself doing anything else.

We were almost back at our cruiser when I noticed a figure leaning against our car. It was Tibbs, his delicious body wrapped in jeans and a sweatshirt, and a grin that spelled trouble widening across his face.

"Ricci, you working the beat? Who did you piss off?" His head tipped in greeting to Miller but he made no attempt to move from his perch.

"Not that it's any of your business, but we were responding to a call. You loitering, Tibbs?" I asked, my heartbeat kicking up a beat.

Having just gotten him out of my head, his appearance both excited and annoyed me.

Mostly annoyed.

Or . . . NO, I was annoyed.

Definitely.

He casually moved away from the car, waving his hand in the direction of the street. "You know I live a block away. I was just taking a stroll."

"Really?" I asked, my head tilted curiously. That was one hell of a *coincidence*. He was *right* in front of the address we'd just come out of, around the same time we were leaving? I mean, I wasn't a bookie, but I'd guess the odds weren't high.

"Yep. I like to breathe in that fantastic fresh air." He took an exaggerated breath, rubbing his hands down his chest. "And it's such a great night for it."

"Are you high, Tibbs?" Miller asked, laughing as he looked on, confused. "We need to call Cap or Chief to come and collect you?"

Of course Miller had no idea it wasn't drugs that were responsible for his ridiculous behavior, but some new-found obsession Tibbs obviously had for messing with my head.

Tibbs gave us both a reassuring—not that I felt it—smile before addressing my partner. "All good, Miller. How was last night? Sorry if pulling Ricci away left you without cover, you seemed like you had it handled though."

Shit.

Shit.

Shit.

Firstly, I hadn't even mentioned to Miller that I'd *seen* Tibbs last night, let alone had a conversation with him. And the last thing I wanted him to think was that we'd been discussing his personal biz. Even though, I guess we had. But only because Tibbs and Leighton had seen him with a woman and asked about Maxine, not because I was trying to gossip. And secondly, I didn't want *anyone*—including Miller—thinking we went home together. Okay, so maybe we did, but NOT like that. And nothing sure as hell happened.

Right on cue, Miller turned to me, his eyebrows flirting with his hairline. "Oh really? Yeah, my night was great. Doesn't sound as interesting as yours and Tessa's though. Maybe you guys should fill me in."

"I took him back to my place, made him strip to his underwear, and then tossed him out," I chuckled. The irony that everything I'd said was the truth wasn't lost on me. "So not a lot to tell."

Tibbs laughed, amused by my retelling. "And how much did you think about me after I left?" He leaned in closer, his voice more seductive than necessary. "Be honest."

He.

Was.

Such.

An.

Asshole.

Not only was he taunting me—very deliberately, I might add—while I was at work, but he was doing it in front of Miller.

He wanted a reaction. Some kind of continuation of the game we'd played last night because he was still rotated off and was bored. And that it aggravated me, I'm sure was a bonus.

"You guys need a minute? I'll just go check in with dispatch." Miller tried unsuccessfully to hide his smirk as he unlocked the cruiser and hopped in.

Traitor.

"Why are you here, Tibbs? And why are you trying to make it sound like something happened last night? Are you that hard up for action that you need to fabricate it?" My hand went to the butt of my gun, if for nothing else to remind him I had one and choosing his words wisely would be advised. Hell, if it wouldn't get me paperwork, I'd have pulled it out and beat him over the head with it.

He didn't even blink, not at all perturbed by the evil stare I was giving him or the weapon my hand was resting on. His ever-present cocky grin just got wider. "And why are you trying to make it sound like *nothing* happened? I thought you and your partner share everything. You didn't let him know who you went home with? Ricci, is there trouble in paradise between you and Miller?" He mock gasped. "I always thought you guys were rock solid."

"I didn't tell Miller because there was nothing to tell. You and I both know that last night was . . ." I paused, trying to remember what possessed me to invite a guy I was extremely attracted to but knew there was no future with to my apartment. I wasn't drunk, so that wasn't an excuse. Poor judgment? Lack of entertainment? In need of a distraction? Yeah, any of those would do, but I wasn't sure any of them fit.

"Nothing," I finally added, not able to find another word. Because really, that's exactly what it had been.

"You need to expand your vocabulary, Ricci, but it's cool. It's fine if you want to deny that getting me back to your apartment was the highlight of your night, I'll survive. But unlike you, I can admit that I kinda liked being there with you. And I think we should maybe do it again. This time I vote you take *your* clothes off. Only seems fair."

"Are you insane, Tibbs?" I spat out, wondering if maybe we shouldn't haul him in for a 72-hour psych hold. He couldn't be serious? And if he wasn't, he was taking messing with me to a whole level that wasn't appreciated. "You do realize I have handcuffs and a gun, right?"

He leaned in, keeping his voice tight between the two of us. "Ricci, kinky stuff like that is a turn on. So if you want to cuff me, you'll get no objections from me."

And that was how my career would surely end.

Police brutality charges filed against me because I beat the hell out of one of FDNY's finest. Because as much as he was an ass, he was an amazing firefighter so of course it would *seem* unprovoked.

Damn it, Ricci.

Why didn't you just go home alone last night?

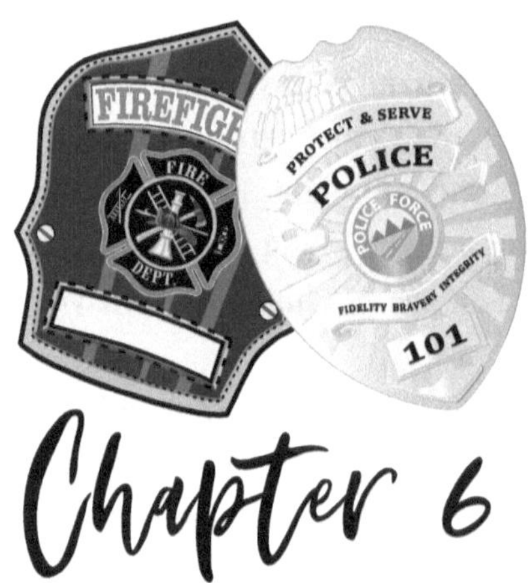

Chapter 6

Justin

SITTING AT HOME and listening to a police scanner wasn't what I'd usually call a good use of my time. It had its advantages from time to time—like if there was something going on in the neighborhood. But other than that, I usually left it to conspiracy theorists and nerdy teenagers who hadn't discovered fucking yet. But knowing Tessa Ricci was going to be on duty was too much of a temptation, especially since I hadn't been able to stop thinking about her all night.

It wasn't just her hot body either, although, Jesus, I hadn't been able to get that off my mind. Never going to be able to unsee it, that was for sure. And it was going to feature heavily any time I felt the need to jerk off. Which surprise, surprise, was a lot since last night.

But more than just her body, was an interest I couldn't quite shake. The fascination with her, and finding out what made her tick, rated high on my list of priorities.

I knew surface stuff, about as much as you can know about someone you'd seen casually. But as far as I was concerned, I was going in completely blind, not having a clue about the woman she really was.

And that was going to change.

The sooner, the better.

Which was why the minute I heard Ricci and Miller were responding to a possible domestic situation literally a block from where I lived, well, I saw that as a sign.

Didn't have to wait too long either, the two of them emerging from the apartment building not long after I'd arrived. And thankfully not tossing someone in the back of their squad car either. Because trying to sweet talk Ricci when she was making an arrest wouldn't have gone well.

She was crazy pissed off, her beautiful brown eyes tossing out so much hostility I was caught between concerned for my personal safety and really turned on. I liked that about her, the fact she wasn't scared to get aggressive. That she didn't feel it necessary to constantly play nice. It was one of the few things I actually knew about her. Seen her in action when she disagreed with a point of view, and the fucking balls she had to stand her ground to defend it.

I liked it.

Completely different to the party girls I usually entertained, no one ever giving me the level of pushback and sass, she did. And after what felt like months and months of more of the same with those other women, the intellectual sparring with Ricci was as much as a turn on as the rest of her.

Hell, I wanted it.

Wanted her to debate me on anything, and watch her as she tried to prove me wrong. The idea of a heated discussion making me just as hard as kissing that smart, argumentative mouth.

She hadn't said anything, her lips tightening into a firm line while she narrowed her eyes. And while I wasn't sure it wasn't going to be me tossed into the back of that squad car, I could barely contain my excitement.

"You're thinking about it," I grinned, positive her idea of cuffing me was vastly different from mine.

Still wasn't sure I didn't want it, because that was exactly the sick puppy I was.

"Maybe Miller was right, you *are* high," she chuckled, her eyes widening in disbelief. "Wow, okay. Look, you're not on duty so what you do in your own time is your own business. But I'd be worried if you have a piss test tomorrow, that shit will show up for sure."

Deflection.

Denial.

And dead wrong.

"I'm not high, Ricci. And maybe my method needs work, but there's no denying an attraction between us. So why don't we see where it takes us?"

I wasn't prepared to wait around and leave that shit to chance. Plus, I'd not had more than a passing interest in a woman in what had to be forever. So if there was one I couldn't get my mind off, that was something that shouldn't be ignored.

"What the hell was that, Tibbs? Did you just ask me out?" she coughed out, the surprise genuine as she looked me dead in the eyes.

To be honest, I'd expected the shock, but I wasn't going to let that sway me. "Yes, Ricci, I'm asking you out. Getting naked is totally optional, but I thought we might get to know each other a little better first."

She shook her head, huffing out a breath before turning back to her car where her partner was waiting. "Tibbs, I haven't got time for this."

"Wait," I fought the urge to grab her arm because, hello, she had a fucking gun and I didn't completely have a death wish. "I'm serious. I know you think I'm messing around—and maybe I am a little—but not about us getting together. I promise I'll be a good boy. You can even pick where we go and what we do."

It was a concession I knew I was going to need to make. And I was cool with letting go of some of the control if it got me what I wanted. Who cared how it happened as long as the end result was the same.

Me and Ricci, and the endless possibilities.

And until she told me—minus the sarcasm—that she wasn't interested, I was operating on the assumption that I wasn't the only one feeling that spark.

That hadn't been indifference I saw in her eyes last night, and that laugh and smile hadn't been manufactured either. So, either she'd missed her calling on Broadway, or I was reading it exactly right.

"Tibbs," she hesitated, and I was taking it as a good thing that she hadn't automatically shut it down. "Look, I need to go back to work. Just . . . I don't know, stay out of trouble."

"That wasn't a no, Ricci." I waved my finger at her, unable to hide my fucking delight. She could've totally said it. Told me that it was never going to happen, but she didn't. And that meant at the very least she was thinking about saying yes.

Which reinforced what I already knew.

Tessa Ricci *was* interested.

"Go home, Tibbs." And call me crazy but the hostility that *had* been in her voice was noticeably lacking. "I have Cap's number and I don't want to call him on his day off."

"Whatever you say, Officer Ricci." I bowed, tipping my chin to Miller who was looking on at the exchange with a grin. I had no doubt she was going to get twenty questions the minute her ass was in that car and I didn't even regret it. "You enjoy the rest of your night. Hopefully Midtown behaves itself for you."

"Yeah, considering how it started, I don't like my chances," she answered with a chuckle. And with the flick of her chin, she turned toward her car.

She was chaos.

Dialed in, with the explosion just ready to happen at any moment.

And it was the sexiest thing I'd ever seen.

Even in her PD navy blues, her hair tied back regulation tight, with barely a lick of makeup, she was fucking beautiful.

How I'd never seen it was a mystery, but you can pretty much guarantee I was going to notice everything about her from here on out.

"Given anymore thought to your spare room?" Evans was already busting my balls, the kid having asked, hinted, begged, and whined about needing to move out of his mom's place since Leighton started playing house with Presley.

No shit, he didn't even let the dust settle, pleading his case about how awesome it would be if he moved in.

"I'll cook *and* clean," he added. "And I'll never be late on my half of the rent. And—"

"Dude, you're coming on waaaaaay too strong. No wonder you can't keep a girlfriend, you're so fucking needy." I waved my hands, needing a break from his endless petitioning. "And I already told you, I haven't decided yet if I want another roommate."

I'd been dragging my feet on finding a replacement mostly because I wasn't sure I could live with anyone else. I'd been lucky that the apartment in Hell's Kitchen actually belonged to my grandparents, so the rent was ridiculously generous considering the location. They'd long made the move down south to Boca, so they were happy to have the place lived in. It generated some passive income, keeping them flush in bingo money, and not have to worry about tenants trashing the place. Plus I took care of all the maintenance so they didn't get those pesky calls whenever a faucet seal needed replacing, so all in all, it was a sweet deal that suited us both.

"C'mon, Tibbs. What are you going to do with that place all to yourself? You won't even notice I'm there."

Leighton smirked as he rolled one of the hoses, enjoying it way too much considering his departure had caused the thorn in my side to start with. "You do sound a little desperate, Evans," he chuckled. "Maybe you should talk to the rookie, I hear he's planning on moving out."

Evans sighed, the kid not helping his case with the amount of drama he was showing. "Are you kidding? Rizzo's mom still makes his bed and irons his underwear. He's not moving anywhere unless she comes with him. And you both suck, assholes."

Flipping us off, Evans disappeared back into the stationhouse, leaving Leighton and I out in the bays to finish checking gear. "Remember when he was too busy trying to kiss ass to be mad?" I tipped my head in the direction he'd just gone, a laugh escaping my throat. "When did he get so moody?"

"They grow up so fast. One minute it's all eager to please, then the next it's *go fuck yourself*. Kinda makes me proud," Leighton added, wiping a fake tear from his cheek. "But seriously, are you holding out on letting him move in because you like watching the kid squirm? Or are you looking for a better offer? Because he would pretty much lick your balls if you asked him, and I'm positive you aren't going to get that from anyone else."

We both laughed, only half sure Leighton was joking. "I don't know," I shrugged. "But I am thinking of adding their willingness to lick my balls to the interview questions for any prospects. Sounds like something I might enjoy after a hard shift."

It had been a slow call day which had given me a lot of time to think. Usually not a good thing—and not something I enjoyed all that much—but a particular brunette had occupied my thoughts, and I couldn't stop grinning.

Granted, nothing had actually happened, and as far as us going out, well, I hadn't even gotten her number yet. But as sure as I was standing there, cataloging shit for the engine, it was going to happen.

What a shame I'd missed the conversation she must've had with Miller, the idea of her talking about me when she got back in that car making me stupidly excited. And while I was sure she put her own *spin* on it, she couldn't deny the facts. And there'd be a greater chance of me tossing in my turnouts and becoming a swimsuit model than Ricci lying to her partner.

I was still lost in my own head when I heard the chief yelling at me from the doorway. "Tibbs, PD are here to see you."

It was like God had somehow answered a prayer I hadn't yet asked for, amused she hadn't been able to keep away either.

I liked it.

That she felt that compelling twist in her gut as much as I had.

Unable to wipe the smile from my face, I glanced over at Leighton before heading into the stationhouse. He rolled his eyes, clearly not sharing the same enthusiasm I did. Obviously I'd told him about Ricci, because unlike her, I didn't hide anything from my best friend. He'd been skeptical about our connection, the bastard questioning me if maybe I hadn't imagined her interest. *Yeah, I hadn't imagined shit.* But he was supportive like he always was. Good thing too because me and Ricci were happening, and I didn't need the negativity.

"Hey." I tried to contain my surprise as I strolled in, the two officers waiting for me in the breakroom.

And of those two uniforms, neither of them was the hot brunette I'd been thinking about.

Interesting.

"McKinley, Deets," I walked over and shook their hands, not wanting to be rude even if I was more than a little disappointed.

If it wasn't Tessa, why the hell did PD want to see me?

Last time I checked I hadn't parked illegally or had any outstanding warrants, and as far as everything else, I was a model fucking citizen.

"Tibbs, how are you doing? Mind if we take a seat?" McKinley took the lead, pointing to a chair before nodding to the chief. He'd hung around which meant he either knew what was going down or suspected it wasn't a social call. And not sure I was good with either of those scenarios.

"You boys want to tell me what's going on?" I pulled out a chair and parked my ass in it, watching as the chief silently did the same.

It was never a good thing when Mack—the chief—was quiet. It could only mean bad things. Or he was so mad he hadn't formed the words yet, and again, not something I wanted to be on the receiving end of. I'd take his high-volume furor any day of the week and twice on Sundays rather than his muted, simmering rage.

Jesus.

It must be bad.

"Mack, what the fuck? Is it Presley? My parents?" It hadn't been that long ago my sister had been terrorized by a shithead she used to date, and I wondered if the somber mood wasn't connected with that. Though surely they would've involved Leighton—her fiancé—if that were the case?

"Relax, Tibbs." Mack reached out and cupped my shoulder. It wasn't just the concern in his tone but in his touch that unnerved me. And I swear if someone didn't start talking in the next three seconds, I was going full-scaled nuclear.

"No one's hurt, and we'd like to keep it that way."

"We're here . . ." McKinley paused, swallowing. "To do a wellness check."

"What. The. Fuck?" I coughed out, convinced he had to be joking. "A wellness check? On me?"

He had to be kidding.

Had to be.

Because there was absolutely nothing wrong with my fucking mental health and I was the last person who needed—

"Ricci mentioned she saw you loitering around the street last night, said your behavior was erratic. We know sometimes the pressures of the job—"

"There's nothing wrong with me," I barked out a laugh. "And trust me, as much as I appreciate the concern, it is completely unnecessary."

Oh, she was fucking good.

I was so fucking impressed she'd had the balls to pull it off, I wasn't even pissed she had the chief and two of her buddies convinced I was on a ledge. Hell, I didn't think she had it in her, assuming she followed regs like they'd been hand delivered by Jesus Christ himself, worried about the waste of police resources.

Who knew she was such a bad girl?

"Tibbs, there's no shame in needing a timeout." This time it was Mack, the compassion genuine as he kept his voice low.

"Mack, I know, and if I needed *anything*, you'd be the first person I'd come to," I reassured him. "This is just Ricci messing with me, like I was messing with her last night."

"Last night? So she did see you on the street?" Deets asked, shooting a look to McKinley I didn't like.

"Not like that, guys," I rolled my eyes. "I heard dispatch on the police scanner, I knew where she and Miller were, so I turned up. It's this stupid game we're playing. Seriously, call and ask her."

A look passed between McKinley and Deets and I could tell they weren't buying it. Which was why Ricci had sent those two instead of some of the other officers we knew.

"C'mon, this is *Tessa*." I hoped using her first name illustrated the point. "You think if she honestly believed I needed a wellness check she wouldn't have done it herself? Or waited a whole twenty-four hours? She'd have either brought me into the station last night or been on my doorstep this morning; we all know she has issues delegating. The only reason you both are here is because she wanted to jerk my chain a little. And kudos to her, because for a second, I thought I was in some real trouble." I couldn't stop the laugh making its way up my throat, unable to feel annoyed or angry even though it would probably be justified.

But whether she wanted to admit it or not, her little stunt proved she'd been thinking about me. And I couldn't see anything in that situation which was a negative.

In fact, it kinda turned me on a little.

And yeah, I knew I had issues.

Considering the evidence in front of him, McKinley nodded before excusing himself to make a call. He knew Ricci probably better than any of us, and had to admit that I wasn't wrong. Deets joined him, probably curious for the whole story as well which left me alone with the chief.

"You want to tell me why you were listening to a scanner and messing with Tessa Ricci, Tibbs? Because if that little nugget of knowledge is supposed to convince me you're not having an episode, I'm not sure it's hit its mark." Mack's voice had lost some of the concern, the hard edge I was more familiar with returning.

"Relax, Mack. I promise it wasn't as shady as it sounds. But we . . ." *hooked up? Spent the night? Messed around?* None of those really fit and made it sound fucking indecent which it hadn't been. And I wasn't about to trash her reputation. "We met up at Presley's club a couple of nights ago, when Leighton and I were hanging out. Anyway, we started messing with each other, letting off some steam. And I don't know, we just sort of connected. I swear, Chief, it's mutual. I'm not about to stalk a member of the NYPD. Apart from the legal ramifications, I'm not that kind of a guy."

He nodded, knowing that while I could be a pain in his ass, I wasn't a fucking deviant who would ever hurt anyone, let alone a woman. "So you two are playing some stupid game like a pair of middle schoolers?"

"Yeah, I guess so." I grinned, wondering if that meant I got to pull on her hair. I'd like that, and wouldn't object to her pulling mine.

Mack shook his head, pushing up from his chair. "I swear, I don't get paid enough to deal with this shit. But since your issues are stupidity and immaturity, there's no reason for me to be involved. Last time I checked, no one walked into oncoming traffic purely from being a dumbass. Tell McKinley and Deets I'm in my office if they need me. I expect you are fine in getting this situation squared away without any input from me."

And with some choice words sworn under his breath, he disappeared out the door.

With both cops in the hall, I was curious as to what my diabolical little hard ass was telling them. Surely she'd come clean, let the poor guys off the hook since she'd already had her fun. Though it did already get me thinking about payback.

I was just about to head back into the bays, let McKinley or Deets come find me when they were done, when the door opened. And this time, it was exactly who I wanted to see.

"That wasn't as satisfying as I thought it would be." Ricci folded her arms across her chest, leaning on the jamb. "You didn't even get mad. What the hell is wrong with you?"

My feet planted on the floor, moving to where she was standing, barely containing my grin. "Your captain going to give you paperwork? Can't say he'd be too happy wasting the city's resources to further your own agenda."

"To be fair," she took an exaggerated breath, the air rushing past those beautiful lips. "You were acting like a crazy person last night on the street. Miller was ready to call in the wellness check right after we left.”

“Yeah? You know, if you wanted to see me, Ricci, all you had to do was ask. I think I made myself pretty clear on wanting to see you.”

I wanted to kiss her.

Like pull her into my arms and *really* fucking kiss her.

Irrational, since we clearly hadn’t moved to a place where that would be welcomed, but I wanted to, all the same. My hands rolled into fists at my side to stop me from doing something stupid, the urge to touch her driving me a little insane.

“And what would we do? When we saw each other?” Her voice was low, seductive, which probably hadn’t been her intention, not that my cock gave a shit. Her eyes didn’t leave mine as I moved closer, the gap between us barely platonic.

“I have ideas,” I breathed out, wondering when some asshole either of us worked with would burst into the room and ruin our moment. It was only a matter of time, and I was far from being ready to wave her goodbye. “Give me your number and I’ll show you every last one.”

I wasn’t sure what I wanted more.

To kiss her, to touch her, or the promise that I’d see her again.

But all of that would have to wait.

“Give me your phone.” She held out her hand, her face completely impassive as I grinned like I’d won the fucking lottery, digging out my cell from my pocket.

Her brow rose as it dropped into her palm, adding her number as I looked on. “This better be *your* number, Ricci. I like this little back-and-forth we have going on, but I’m not in the mood to get hauled in by McKinley and Deets for real.”

She laughed, the sound warming my chest as she handed it back, her name and number still displayed on the screen. “I never took you as someone with trust issues, Tibbs. But if it makes you feel better, I'll stand here while you call it."

I shook my head, believing that she hadn't slipped in the digits for a local pizza place or worse, the number of her ex-boyfriend. "You'll be hearing from me."

It was a promise, the need to see her again so visceral that I couldn't even understand it considering she hadn't even left yet.

"See you around, Tibbs." She turned, not giving any indication on how she felt about it either way.

And fuck me, if that didn't just make it more interesting.

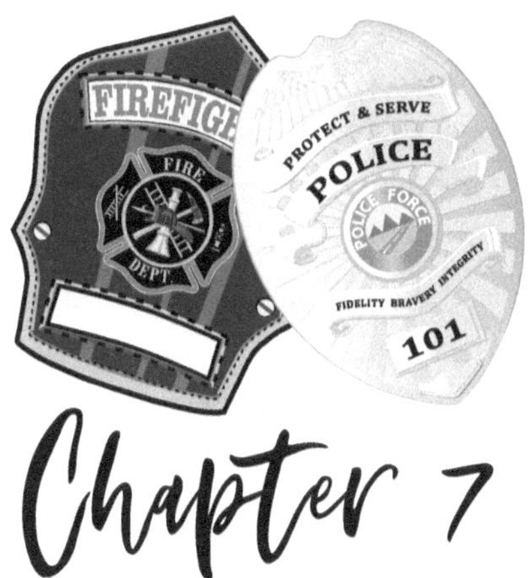

Chapter 7

Tessa

"**H**OW DID HE take it?" Miller was waiting for me outside the West 38th Stationhouse.

We'd tailed McKinley and Deets on their way over, hanging back because I assumed at some point they were going to have questions.

"He wasn't even mad," I huffed out in disbelief, shaking my head. "It was almost as if he was pleased."

It usually wasn't my style to recruit the help of others when I wanted to prove a point, fairly capable of getting it done myself. But if I'd walked into the firehouse—citing the need to do a wellness check on Tibbs—the ruse would have lasted at most two minutes. Three, if he was taken by surprise.

Instead we'd told McKinley and Deets—two uber-concerned, strait-laced cops who'd transferred from upstate—that Tibbs had behaved a little erratically the night before.

Technically, it wasn't a lie, the moron hanging around the street while we attended a call like a stalker. And wouldn't you believe that I hadn't even needed to suggest they go pay him a visit, the pair of them volunteering to make sure our buddy in the FDNY was doing okay.

So maybe I felt a little—like a tiny bit—bad that their well-meaning concern had been unfounded and unnecessary. McKinley giving me an earful on how wrong it was to joke about someone's mental health. And sure, I was going right to hell, because the idea that someone having a genuine hard time was not a joking matter. Usually I'd be the last person to ever try to minimize anyone's struggle or trivialize it in any way.

I'd seen the fallout from trauma on the job.

Heard both my parents talk about their friends who dealt with PTSD.

But Tibbs.

Uhhhhhh, he just brought out the worst in me.

And while I did feel guilty about it, and possibly remorseful, I was slightly annoyed that the only irritation had come from the two officers and not from Tibbs himself. It didn't speak volumes of my personal character, the stupid prank something I'd expect from a cadet straight out of the academy rather than someone like me.

Still, right or wrong, good or bad, I couldn't make myself regret it.

"I know you explained it to me, and I'm not trying to be an asshole. But seriously, what the hell happened the other night? You and Tibbs? He's the last guy in the city I'd imagine you with."

I'd had no choice but to tell Miller the whole sordid tale last night after our little run in with Tibbs on the street. He had questions, naturally, and then wanted to know how much I'd had to drink.

It was true, as couples went, we were unlikely.

Mostly since he'd never so much as looked in my direction, let alone shown any interest. And I'd never breathed a word to anyone about my earlier attraction to the guy who Miller assumed I saw as a buddy. And I didn't disagree. The idea of the two of us becoming more . . . well, I wasn't convinced that maybe I wasn't the one who needed the wellness check.

Realistically, even if we did—and that was a really big if—go out on a date, that would be as far as it went.

One date.

Possibly two, because he would try to sleep with me, and there was no way I would after only dating him one time.

So maybe we'd go out two times. And then he'd realize I wasn't going to fall into his bed or offer to give him a blowjob in a dark corner, and he'd get bored. Because there was no way he was interested in me in any way that was long term.

Sure, he might have found me attractive, having seen me out of uniform and looking more like a *regular* woman. But I wasn't delusional. He probably saw a *lot* of beautiful women who were a whole lot more available than I was. And as much as I would *love* to believe Tibbs wasn't anything special, he kinda was.

He was charming, and funny, and smarter than he pretended to be. And if you could overlook that cockiness, you saw he was actually really sweet too. Of course he was also a gorgeous guy with an amazing body who was outstanding at his job. And yes, I will admit, that firemen are kind of hot.

"Tibbs and I are just friends, Grayson." I rolled my head to look at him, only calling him by his first name when I was serious. "And I'm sure that's all we'll ever be. He's just discovered that I have a pair of tits and a vagina, and he's not sure what to do about it. But I'm under no delusions that I'm going to be his next girlfriend. Does he even have girlfriends? Pretty sure he is a serial one-nighter with commitment issues, and the last thing I need in my life. But, and I'll say this only to you, because I don't trust anyone else not to take it the wrong way. I like hanging out with him. He makes me laugh, and I love how he isn't scared to speak his mind around me. Even if most of it is inappropriate.

Maybe we end up being just better friends. Surely that can't be a bad thing?" I ran out of steam, all the thoughts that had been going through my head finally spoken out loud.

Because as much as I was attracted to Tibbs, I knew there was no real future for us. There couldn't be. Not when the only thing we really had in common was we wanted to sleep with each other.

Ahhhh yes.

I said I *wouldn't* sleep with him, not that I didn't want to.

Miller shrugged, putting the car into drive and pulling away from the curb. "Tessa, if you want to date, screw, or just get to know, Tibbs, you're not going to hear judgment from me. But thinking he isn't going to want you as his girlfriend is the biggest load of horse shit I've ever heard. Do you honestly think he's going to spend time with you, get to know the real Tessa Ricci and decide, *nah, I don't want any of that?* Wow, you are even more delusional than I thought."

Miller was good for my ego, but that's what best friends were for. They built you up even when you didn't believe it yourself, and trust me, there was nothing wrong with my self-esteem. "And yet, you've resisted," I pointed out, the idea of the two of us ever dating so laughable I could barely say it without choking.

"Meh, I was scared of you initially. It made it easier for me to fight the attraction. Then you became more like my sister, and well, I ain't into that." He laughed. "Sucks to be you though, because I'm a fantastic boyfriend. If you'd just been less intimidating at the start, you might have had a chance. Unfortunately now, it's too late."

"Wow, no wonder I'm looking at Tibbs," I sighed drily. "Girl gets that kind of rejection, and she's just not sure what to do."

All jokes aside, I hadn't exactly been lucky in the love department. It was hard to find a guy that wasn't scared off by the job or the badge. And more times than not, it didn't last long.

And for what it was worth, I wasn't all that sad about it, believing that I deserved a lot more than a guy who could only stick it out a week or two before running. I assumed if I was ever going to find someone for the long haul, he'd have to be some beefed-up Special Ops guy who didn't care his wife carried and had a mean right hook.

Still, Tibbs . . .

What was the harm in indulging the distraction? As long as I played it smart and kept it casual, there'd be no reason why I couldn't have some fun. At least until my Special Ops guy showed up and took me to his bunker.

Luckily for me, the rest of our night was so busy, Miller and I didn't have time to talk about Tibbs. We'd been on call after call, limping into the station shortly before midnight, ready to hand over to the next shift.

"You want to grab a late dinner/early breakfast before we head back over to Brooklyn?" Miller offered, yawning as he grabbed his keys. "I know it's counterproductive since I should go to bed and sleep when I get home, but I need a coffee in the worst way."

I completely understood the predicament, the desire to refuel especially after a long eight hours at odds with the need to power down and get some decent sleep. But since I usually laid awake for a few hours anyway, I saw no issue with spending part of that time with Miller and carbs.

"You want to get one to go and then eat at that place near my apartment? They have 24-hour breakfast and I would love some waffles."

With our plan in place, we hopped into Miller's Honda Civic and headed back to our side of town. Since we lived so close and worked the same hours, we usually carpooled, seeing no point in taking two cars. We didn't even stop for coffee, Miller deciding to get one with breakfast, talking about the plate of bacon and eggs he had in his future like it was his dirtiest fantasy.

Brooklyn didn't have the same vibe as Manhattan; it was so much more laid back. And while I'd absolutely love to live in the city—if I could get a decent price for my kidney on the black market—I didn't mind being a little farther out. It helped that Grayson lived there too, the two of us spending more time together than most couples.

We pulled into a parking lot, the place mostly deserted except for a beat-up truck and a shiny new sedan. Since we were still in uniform, I liked the idea of it being mostly empty. Not that I wasn't unbelievably proud of being a cop and serving the city, but inevitably it—the uniform—attracted attention. Most times it was great, citizens giving you their appreciation and thanks. But not everyone was a fan.

Miller pulled open the glass door, a bell at the top announcing our arrival. The waitress didn't even blink, sashaying her way to us and shooting us a smile. After an over-excited greeting—I assumed it had been a slow night for her—we were seated in a booth with a pair of menus.

"I want the biggest serving of waffles you have," I didn't even bother looking at the other options. "And coffee. Oh, maybe some hash browns on the side."

"And I'll have the big breakfast, extra bacon, and a coffee as well," Miller followed, having already decided what he wanted before we'd even left Manhattan.

"I like it, you know what you want." The waitress smiled. "I'll put your orders in right now and get you those coffees."

"Soooooooo . . ." Miller deliberately left the sentence trailing. "Where you and Tibbs going on your big date?" His brows lifted suggestively in case I hadn't gotten the hint with his tone.

"You know, he might not even call me. Maybe he just collects numbers and scrolls through his phone whenever he needs an ego boost," I deadpanned, not believing for a second Tibbs wouldn't use the number at least one time.

"We already established you're awesome and he's going to fall madly in love with you," Miller yawned, suppressing a grin. "Not sure Tibbs is the only one who likes getting that ego boost, Ricci. Sounds to me like you guys would make a perfect pair."

"Oh please, I'm *nothing* like Tibbs. NOTHING. And if you know what's good for you, you'll take that back." The threat had barely settled when my phone lit up with an incoming call.

Like the devil had been summoned, I had no doubt of the identity of the unknown number.

Tibbs.

Unless that Saudi Prince was calling me back, offering me another chance at forty-two million if I'd just give him my bank details. But I'd say the smart bet was on the fireman probably still on duty in Midtown.

"Aren't you going to answer that?" Miller gameshow waved his hand at my buzzing phone. "Wouldn't want him to think you were dodging his calls."

Rolling my eyes, I swiped the incoming call and lifted the phone to my ear. "Hello," I said curtly, wondering if he'd literally been waiting until I was done with work, or he called everyone at ridiculous o'clock in the morning.

"Ricci," he cooed into the phone, his voice thick like he'd been sleeping. "Do you always sound so pissed off on the phone or is that venom just reserved for me? Got to tell you, if you're trying to turn me on, it's working."

Wow.

Really, Tessa?

This was what I wanted?

So apparently I was attracted to guys with God complexes who got off on my distaste. And here I thought *he* was the one with the problem.

"What do you want, Tibbs? A bedtime story?" I breathed into the phone. "Or did you think I'd be in bed by now, hoping

I'd tell you I was naked between my sheets and dreaming about you."

He coughed, clearing his throat. "Fuck, Tessa. You have to warn a guy before you say something like that. At least let me get somewhere private where I can enjoy it."

"I'm not in bed, or naked, or dreaming of you, Tibbs," I yawned, purposely ignoring how much I liked hearing him say my name. It wasn't the first time, but somehow it felt a little different. "But I am hungry and tired, so if you were looking for cheerful, you're gonna be shit out of luck."

"Not looking for anything other than to check your schedule. Figured I'd catch you before you went to sleep. I know how insane your days can be, especially when you have to head into work later."

Unlike the FDNY, who worked twenty-four on, forty-eight off, NYPD worked eight-hour shifts, five days straight. And depending on which rotation you were on, that workday didn't always land during regular business hours. Currently Miller and I were rocking the four to twelve. Which meant mornings were usually a flurry of getting laundry done, groceries, working out, dealing with regular everyday shit, and then going to work when most people were heading home.

Factor in sleep, and downtime was limited. It also meant catching up with friends or dating was also left for those two prized days off, whenever they landed. Guess my schedule and constant rotations probably hadn't helped my love life either.

It was surprisingly more considerate than I'd expected, my eyes narrowing as I waited for the extra sexual innuendo or *whatever* Tibbs usually added.

"And?" I asked between the pause.

"And?" Tibbs chuckled. "And what? I said you could pick the place and activity so the *and* is pretty much on you. Unless you want me to take the lead, Ricci, and then I can do that."

Still nothing.

Almost as if it were just a regular guy asking me on a regular date, which couldn't be right because there was nothing *regular* about Tibbs.

Miller's gaze flicked to me, only hearing one side of the conversation and trying to piece it together with limited information and my animated reaction. "What?" he whispered, waving his hand as I sat in stunned silence.

"Justin." His name felt weird in my mouth, unsure if I'd ever called him that. "I know we've both been having fun with this, but are you *seriously* asking me out?"

It was unlike me to call the time-out, not liking how exposed it made me feel. For all I knew, he was going to laugh his ass off, the, *"Jesus, Ricci, you really thought I was serious?"* ready in his mouth. But I was tired, and confused, and completely lost on the rules of engagement. And if that gave him the upper hand, then I'd deal with it accordingly. Redirection was always a possibility, and I could work within parameters when I knew what they were.

Currently, with Tibbs, I had no idea.

"Umm, yeah, what did you think I was doing?" His voice was liquid, no hint of the humor or ridicule I'd been bracing myself for.

Why? I wanted to ask, the question swallowed because there was no way I'd ever show him that much vulnerability. Instead it hung around my neck, feeling like a woolen scarf that was wrapped around too tight.

Shaking off feelings I really didn't understand, I decided I was overthinking it way too much. So what? He was asking me out—one time—and we'd already established it was probably just to get into my pants since he'd noticed I was a woman. Big deal!

Annnnnd I knew he had the ability to be charming, he'd just never directed it at me. Again, nothing new to see here. Why I was even concerned about what his intentions were, was a mystery. Because we'd be back to regular scheduling—i.e. being smart asses and largely ignoring each other—probably within a week.

"Well, if I can pick whatever." I cleared my throat, deciding that I could at least control the tempo. "How do you feel about meeting me on Friday? You'll be off, right?"

"Yeah, I'll have Friday and Saturday off. You?"

"Same," I nodded, the universe having a sense of humor in that we shared the same two scheduled days off.

"Must be fate," he chuckled before turning serious. "So, Friday, what are we doing? And please don't disappoint me with dinner and a movie, Ricci. The stars are literally aligning for this to happen, I don't want to waste it on some mediocre bullshit."

"Like anything you'd do with me would be mediocre," I scoffed, the excitement bubbling in my gut more than I would have liked. "Please, Tibbs, I could take you to get a root canal and I'd still blow your mind. Keep Friday free, I'll text you the details. Oh, and I hope you're up for getting sweaty."

Sadly, not the kind he probably had in mind.

There was a low hum of approval, his voice getting a little husky. "Oh, I'm up for anything you've got, Ricci. I'll be counting down the days."

Ironically, so would I.

"Good, I'll see you then." My smile widened, my pulse quickening from the thrill. "Bye, Tibbs."

"Later, Ricci."

The call ended.

"That look," Miller pointed to my face, his grin matching mine, "usually means trouble. What the hell are you going to make the guy do?"

"Put him through his paces," I sighed, watching as our waitress approached with two loaded plates we were going to demolish. "Let's see what Justin Tibbs is made of."

And I was going to enjoy the hell out of that.

Chapter 8

Justin

LIKE SHE PROMISED, Ricci had sent me the address of a gym in Queens. Why she wanted to go there was beyond me. But if it made her excited to see me workout, then who was I to deny her. And given the chance to see her in some lycra while she squatted and lunged, or needed a spot, yeah that was something I'd rather die than say no to.

Didn't even need to think about saying yes, accepting her eleven o'clock suggestion without hesitation, and wondering if she had plans for the rest of the day. I liked she wanted to get started early, giving us hours to fill with nothing but each other.

I couldn't even remember the last time I was excited to go on a date, let alone actually done something *other* than fucking. Not that I was a complete jerk, I'd taken women to dinner or breakfast, sometimes even lunch. But typically it was before or after—the fucking usually the main event.

I hadn't been interested in more. Not thinking "the one" even existed, and not at a point in my life where I wanted more. It was easier to play it cool, and made for a lot less hurt feelings.

And for the most part—given my odd hours and the demands of the job etc.—it just worked. No one complained either, the girls who I'd been filling my time with lately, just as happy to forgo the pretense, which was why I hadn't even bothered to try.

But Ricci was different.

For starters, she was nothing like those other girls, and was about thirty times more interesting. And while I absolutely wouldn't turn down sex if that was on offer, I was good with whatever. I meant it when I said she could pick what we did—I didn't care. And as long as I got to spend time with her—and got to know what was going on behind those dark brown eyes—then I couldn't be any happier.

She was infectious, compelling in a way, I didn't fully understand. She was smart, called me on my bullshit, which pushed me to be better. I'd never had that, not with anyone who wasn't my family at least. It was exciting, and so refreshing, I couldn't wipe the grin from my face. It wasn't just about getting physical, but knowing her on *every* level. And while that compulsion might've been new, it wasn't something I'd even think or want to change.

The rest of the week seemed to take forever.

Forever.

And while I wanted to call her and see if we could move up our date, I resisted. Last thing I wanted to do was come on too strong, like Evans trying to land my spare room, and I didn't need to give her an excuse to cancel.

Okay, so maybe I texted a few times. But that didn't count because I texted everyone, and it didn't constitute conversation. They were fillers, impassive Post-It notes of communication that basically let everyone know you were still alive. So technically it was allowed. Hell, if I'd had Miller's number, I'd have texted him too just to prove the point. And since every single one of those interactions with Tessa had been platonic, it wasn't even close to crossing the line in what could be perceived as flirty.

My thoughts, on the other hand, had.

Repeatedly.

But again, completely acceptable considering no one else was in my head and I was going to think whatever the hell I wanted.

And dirty thoughts about Tessa Ricci was currently my favorite hobby.

So when Friday finally came I was about ready to jump out of my skin. It was as if someone had added some extra days to the week, or at least a few rogue hours that weren't necessary, positive time had slowed to a crawl. But good things came to those who waited, and I was being as good as I knew how.

It was just before eleven when I pulled around the back of *High and Tight*, the venue of our morning date. It was unremarkable in every way, lacking the flash and appeal of popular city gyms, and looked like it reeked of used jockstraps and Icy Hot.

But, whatever. I wasn't some stuck-up asshole who needed a chai latte chaser after a lifting session, so if Ricci thought that shit would scare me away, she was going to be waiting awhile.

I grabbed my gym bag from the trunk of my Impala, checking my phone one last time to make sure she hadn't canceled. It hadn't even occurred to me that she might stand me up, my muscles twitching as I considered the possibility.

She wouldn't, I rationalized, believing she wouldn't waste my time on some elaborate plan and then not turn up. And not wanting to waste a second more with the mental debate, I locked my car and headed inside.

There was a reason *High and Tight* looked like a reject from the movie *Rocky*, the gym less tailored to *"bro, do you even lift?"* and more in line with *"the next heavyweight champion of the world."* It was a boxing gym. Completely no thrills, with a full-sized ring in the middle, hosting a bunch of guys whose deltoids looked like the needed their own zip code. They didn't even look up, each of those freaks of nature continuing with their workouts while I stood in the doorway.

"Hey!" Ricci's voice snagged my attention, swiveling my head to see her standing in front of me.

Jesus.

Fucking.

Christ.

My lungs burned with the need for air while the windbags seemed to have forgotten their purpose. And every single one of my muscles seized like one of those meatheads had punched me square in the gut.

Dressed in a pair of tight black shorts that looked like they were painted on, the fabric curved around her thighs and ass in what could only be described as spectacular. I was given a front-row seat to the view when she turned, glancing back to the ring when someone called out. Equally impressive was the tight black sports bra she was wearing, the amount of toned skin on display making me feel like I was going to stroke out.

"Hey," I coughed, unable to keep my eyes from widening as I scanned the length of her body like there was going to be a test on it later.

Fuck, she was hot. So toned and tight, and so fucking defined she looked like she belonged on an Olympic podium collecting a gold medal. I couldn't even reconcile what I was seeing, her body so strong and powerful, yet so undeniably feminine it almost didn't seem real.

She'd been sexy as hell the other night in the club—that tight dress making me hard in all the right places—but the current version was more than just a nice body. It was conditioned to perfection, demanding respect more than adoration. And fuck me if I didn't want to give her both.

"So, you want to work out?" I lamely asked, leaving whatever game I thought I had in the parking lot. I seriously had to fight the urge to get on the floor and thank God for the gift that was Tessa Ricci.

Hell, no wonder she kept that locked down most of the time. If word got out, there would be assholes boosting cars and mugging old ladies all over Midtown just hoping she'd be the one to slap on the cuffs. And this asshole would be the first in line.

She didn't miss a beat, completely unaffected by my mumbling bullshit as she grabbed the gym bag from my shoulder. "Let's get your stuff stashed and then we can start."

Yeah, okay, let's do that. I nodded, words proving too much of a challenge as I let her lead me to a set of old-school metal lockers that were bolted to the wall. Fuck, she could have taken me to a walk-in freezer and racked me like a side of beef and I probably wouldn't have complained. My eyes unable to move from the curve of her ass even though I knew I needed to look away.

"Tibbs?" Her raised brow hinted that it probably wasn't the first time she'd said my name. "You still with me?"

"Um, yeah?" I answered, sounding just as indecisive as I felt because, honestly, I had no idea where I was.

Did I die on the way over? Was I dreaming and this shit was a product of my overactive imagination? Because as real as it seemed to be, I was struggling keeping my spirit in my body and my tongue in my mouth.

"Look," I decided to come clean. It was either that or risk her thinking I had a brain injury. Which to be honest, I wasn't sure those shorts hadn't given me an aneurysm. "You're going to need to give me a minute. Because as it stands, you are without a doubt the hottest woman I've ever seen. And yes, I've seen plenty of hot women, which I'm only mentioning so you know my data pool was large and varied, and my assessment is reliable."

She looked down at her body, clearly not seeing it the way I did. "You'd see more skin on the dance floor of your sister's club,

Tibbs. But if this is too much for you, maybe we should put a pin in it, and you can head home."

"No!" I yelled so loud some of the meatheads actually turned around. How they'd been able to work out while Ricci looked like a female gladiator ready to lead the resistance was beyond me. Still, not something I was going to point out. "If you think I'm walking out that door right now, you are insane." I tried to keep the crazy out of my voice even though I was feeling slightly unhinged. "I'm good. Solid. Ready to do whatever it is you want to do. I am not going anywhere."

It was a promise.

A vow.

A sworn fucking oath, because even though I had no idea what her plans were for me, I knew I wanted them.

"O-kay, but if this gets too much," she waved her hand in front of herself like she was a set of shiny new steak knives, "you can bail at any time."

I'd rather die, I didn't say, nodding my head, not trusting my mouth not to get me into trouble.

Like a zombie I followed her to the center of the gym, watching as she hoisted herself up onto the ring in a set of perfect fluid movements that were almost poetic. It was definitely not her first time. She sat casually on the middle rope, waving for me to join her as I tried to do the same.

I wasn't a little guy.

Six-two and having spent a decent amount of time in the weight room, I was far from average. And it was a good thing too, because when you attended a fire you needed to be strong and fucking agile, and have the stamina to cut it on the lines for hours if that was what it took.

So even though I was physically bigger—in every conceivable way—than Ricci, I was struggling not being dwarfed by her fucking aura.

She owned it, a confidence that couldn't be taught, radiating out of her as I squeezed through the center ropes and planted my feet on the main part of the ring. And that right there—that unshakeable self-assurance—was even sexier than her amazing body.

"You going to fight me, Ricci?" I laughed, my eyes following her as she moved into the corner of the ring.

"Yep," she answered with no hesitation, reaching down and grabbing a roll of gauze. "And you're going to fight me too. But we need to wrap first. I don't want to hear it from Mack if you hurt your hands and then can't hold the hose. I like the guy, but he's scary when he's mad."

Wait.

What?

Yes, Mack was absolutely a scary motherfucker when he got pissed, so it came as no surprise that even Ricci didn't want to take the big guy on.

What I was having a problem with—or more to the point couldn't get my head around—was the other part.

I had been joking. Assuming that if she wanted to glove up and smack me around a little, I was up for the punishment. I could take a hit, and chances were my mouth had probably helped her with the motivation. All good.

But me hitting her?

Not fucking happening.

"I'm not fighting you, Ricci. You want to punch me, then go for it. I'll even block if you want me to participate. But I have *never* hit a woman, and I sure as hell am not starting with you."

It had to be a test, some fucking pop quiz to see if I really *would* do whatever it was she wanted. And while I was game for almost anything—seriously, I could count on one hand the number of my hard passes—I was NOT taking anything remotely close to a swing.

"You're not hitting a woman, Tibbs. It's sparring. You know boxing is a sport, right?" She rolled her eyes, taking the gauze and wrapping it around her hands.

She'd clearly done it a million times before, the fluid, quick flicks working efficiently as they covered her knuckles.

What the hell was happening?

Was she moonlighting as an MMA fighter? Sure would explain the body and the confidence, not that any of that would change my stance.

"Ricci—" I was just about to launch into all the reasons why it was an incredibly bad idea when I was cut off.

"Baby doll! I thought you weren't coming in until tomorrow." The commanding voice boomed as footsteps made their way to the ring. The guy had to be in his fifties but was still plenty in shape, his eyes flicking to me before switching back to Tessa.

Baby doll huh? The guy either had an allergy to breathing or knew Ricci fairly well.

"Dad," *well I guess that answered that,* Tessa smiled at the guy in question. "I was going to come say hi later. Tibbs and I were just going to get some time on the mat."

"Hello, sir." I held out my hand, wondering if he'd somehow be able to know I'd had impure thoughts about his daughter. Mind reading wasn't really a thing, right? Because if it was, and he could, I was in some serious shit. "I'm Tibbs, pleased to meet you, Mr. Ricci."

"Tibbs? You on the force too?" He grunted, taking my hand and giving it a bone-crushing squeeze. Yeah, he might not be able to read my mind but something told me he could probably guess what I'd been thinking.

"FD," I responded, thankful he let go of his grip without dislocating my fucking fingers.

"Fireman," he nodded in what I hoped was approval. "You looking to train?"

My "no" drowned out Ricci's "yes" as his brow knitted in confusion. "Well which is it? Because we're not running a daycare."

Wow, we needed to get Tessa's old man and Mack together, they'd be a barrel of fucking laughs.

"Tibbs is worried about hitting a girl." Ricci grinned, saying it like it was a personal flaw.

Tessa's old man—who hadn't yet introduced himself and I was beginning to think that was intentional—laughed, sizing me up before meeting my eyes. "Is that true?"

Why the hell was me doing the *right* thing suddenly bad? And what kind of asshole would want a guy to hit his daughter?

"I don't hit women, sir." I didn't flinch, making no apologies for my stance.

He laughed again, louder this time, as his head tipped to Tessa. "You think you're going to hurt her? Buddy, I don't know what spaceship you crawled out of, but I'd be more worried about what she'd do to you."

Old man Ricci was at least an inch shorter than me, but he acted like he was a hundred feet tall. I was positive he didn't know how to back down, a trait he'd passed down to his kid probably around the same time he taught her to fight.

I got it. Not all families were the same, and while some—mine—went camping in summertime, others—hers—trained for caged death matches.

"So let me get this straight," I glanced over at Ricci who had finished with the gauze and slid on a pair of bright red boxing gloves. "You *want* me to hit her." Because *that* made sense.

He curled his lip, tilting his head to the side. "You want to date my daughter?"

Well, so much for easing myself into the situation. And I wasn't sure what would be easier. To shut my mouth and fight—fuck, I could barely even think it—Ricci, or admit to her hard-ass old man that I wanted to date his daughter.

Please, God, do not let this be a trick question.

"Yes, sir, I do," I answered, because . . . fuck, I really did want to.

"Then wrap your goddamn hands and stop being a pussy."

"Okay." I held up my palms, my limit for being polite reached at being called a pussy.

"Dad," Ricci snarled. To her credit, she looked genuinely annoyed. But I didn't need her or anyone else fighting my battles, especially when it came to proving I wasn't a coward.

"It's fine, Ricci. I've got this." I turned to face her dad. "You don't know me, which is probably why you're making assumptions. But let me set you straight on a few. I'm not some jerk-off who is going to turn and run because you don't like me. And regardless of what you think, I'm not going to do something I don't want to do. Also, I am not—and never will be—a pussy." I left off the *fuck you* because I knew it wouldn't be helpful.

"Ya done?" he asked, looking bored. Completely saw where she got *that* from.

"Yep, pretty much." I nodded, not willing to back down.

"Tessa is probably one of the most talented fighters I've ever had the honor to train. And if I thought you had the potential to hurt her in any way, I'd take you out myself. But you want to date her, then you better have a pair of beachball-sized testicles because a woman like that is not a walk in the park."

"Dad!" Tess interrupted.

"Don't *Dad* me, Baby doll. He needs to hear this." He waved her off before giving his attention to me. "I want you to see what she's capable of, see how strong she is, how meticulous she can be when focused. So you can't pretend you didn't know what you were getting yourself in for. I've seen her make men double her size pee their skivvies, because boxing is about what's up here," he rammed a finger against his temple. "Not what's here." He held up his fists. "You want to know her, then know *all* of her.

Not just the pretty parts. Or go find yourself a Fifth Avenue Barbie and save yourselves both the trouble."

Well, fuck.

Was I actually considering it?

Yeah.

Yeah, I was.

"Where's the gauze, Ricci?" I held out my hand, my brain still not on board even though it was clear my body was.

Her gloved hand tossed me a roll, grinning excitedly as she moved to a shadow boxing warm up.

Of all the shit I ever thought I'd do, getting into a boxing match with someone I wanted to fucking date would have to rank dead last.

Was I still going to do it?

Obviously, I was.

My wraps weren't as clean or as tight as Tessa's, her old man handing me a pair of boxing gloves before stepping out of the ring. He—like his kid—seemed way too thrilled about this shit, which just made the situation even more fucked up than it already was.

And if that weren't enough, we'd seemed to draw a crowd. The gaggle of *Apollo Creeds* gathering around the outside of the ring like the Pope was about to give a blessing.

Awesome.

Just fucking awesome.

"Three, three-minute rounds. No headshots and nothing below the belt," Tessa's dad called from the sidelines. "Go ahead and shake."

Ricci tapped the top of my gloves, shooting me a grin before back-walking on the balls of her feet to what I assumed was her corner.

One hell of a first date. And for the record, there wasn't a chance she was having *any* say in the second. And to think

I'd told her dinner and a movie was out, those two pedestrian options were looking pretty fucking awesome right about now.

Backing away—without the fancy footwork—into my corner, I waited for her dad to ring the bell.

Ding.

Ding.

We were barely out of our corners when I felt the first punch make contact. I hadn't even seen it, the blow to my kidney coming out of nowhere as I took the full force of the hit without having a chance to brace.

"Jesus," I cursed out, managing to maneuver out of a second hit, but not so lucky on the third. She was quick, agile and lethal, each punch explosive as it made contact, and that wasn't me being generous either. She was hard and fast, and I needed to pull my head out of my ass if I didn't want to end up on my knees.

Going against everything I ever believed—and praying to God for his forgiveness in advance—I let loose with a few decent jabs of my own. She was quick, but I had a bigger reach, able to land a couple of decent—*fuck, who the hell was I anymore?*—hits on her while she continued to do damage.

She barely blinked, accepting the impact of my punches without so much as a whimper and moving me around the ring like we were line dancing.

At first, I was definitely pulling my punches. Holding back the power because even though I'd clearly lost my mind and was participating in the stupidity, I hadn't turned into a complete degenerate. But as the fight went on—and after enough body shots to rattle my molars—I was ashamed to say, I completely forgot.

How had it not been three minutes yet? My gloves managed to deflect the last of her offensive attack before her dad finally rang the bell.

She was a hurricane, rolling onto the shoreline, fucking shit up and then retreating with zero shits given to the carnage she'd left behind.

Both of us were breathing heavy, backing away into our respective corners, taking the small reprieve that wouldn't be sufficient for my head or my body.

I was so fucking appalled.

So horrified and yet so incredibly turned on that I was going to need years of therapy before I'd ever be right again.

"Ready?" her dad asked from the sidelines, the bell ringing before either of us had given our answer.

Two more rounds, I reminded myself as I pushed off from the ropes. Just six lousy minutes and it would all be over.

Learning from my past mistake, I decided to draw her in rather than the other way around. But no, what I hoped would give me more time, did absolutely nothing as she controlled the tempo even though I'd landed the first punch.

She was a machine, each of her fists hitting their mark even though I was actively trying to stop her. Oh, I got in a few decent shots—*seriously, I was going to burn in hell for eternity*—as well. But while mine had power behind them, they lacked the precision and finesse of hers. And I could tell that she was also starting to hurt.

"Shit, Ricci." I made the mistake of dropping my hands for a second, the left right combo hitting me square in the gut. Guess that was what I got for letting down my guard, my internal organs begging me not to make that mistake again.

"C'mon, Tibbs, please tell me you're not tired already?" she taunted, her lips edging into a smile just as my fist made contact with her ribs.

It didn't feel good, both of us wincing as she did the same to me.

Ding.

Ding.

That bell, the saving grace, as we limped to our corners.

One more.

Three more minutes.

All I had to do was last three more minutes.

And I swore on what was left of my kidneys that I'd never make fun of those stupid erectile disfunction ads ever again. Because hey, now I understood how those assholes thought three minutes felt like three years. Didn't mean I supported their case of limp dick, but at least I got it.

My back rested on the ropes as I caught my breath, glancing across the ring to Tessa who watched as I pulled off my T-shirt. She was glistening, the sheen of sweat coating her skin while she stared at me with wild eyes and messed up hair.

Her tongue darted across her lips, her gaze following the lines of my chest before dropping to the waistband of my shorts.

It was hot.

So fucking hot, and I had to remind myself that her dad was *literally* watching us, which meant pulling her panting mouth into a kiss would not be a good idea. That, and we still had one more round to go and I didn't trust her not to take advantage.

Man, she was messing with my head.

And I wanted more of it.

I didn't even hear old man Ricci's warning when the third-round bell rang, my feet hitting the mat automatically as I moved forward. She did the same, engaging me first before I returned the favor.

With no idea—and not really caring—who was winning, we traded blows fairly evenly. And by the time the final bell rang, I'd never felt so relieved in my whole life.

Unable to stop myself, I pulled her into a hug. "You are incredible," I whispered against her hair, feeling the vibrations of her laugh against my bare chest.

"For someone who doesn't hit women, you sure held your own."

"Thanks, Ricci, that backhanded compliment is going to keep me up for the next week," I chuckled, still a little disgusted with myself but mostly ridiculously impressed by her.

"Break it up, you two." Tessa's dad magically appeared by our side, becoming the biggest cock block of all time. Not that I would have done anything. Well that was a lie because given a chance I would have definitely kissed her.

"You ain't bad for not having any formal training." It was as good of a compliment as I was probably going to get from him, and I was okay with that. "But Tessa got more technical points so . . . she wins. Don't feel too bad though, almost everyone had money on you not making it past the first round."

"Thanks a lot, guys!" I raised a gloved fist, saluting our audience who actually looked disappointed I wasn't lying face down on the mat.

Tessa was beaming, sliding off her gloves as she moved farther away. I didn't like that. The distance. With the hug I'd given her not long enough.

I hadn't really thought about it, and clearly neither had she, my arms around her feeling like the most natural thing in the world. But whatever moment had existed was gone, and she'd backed off when we'd been separated. And I was going to have to find a new reason to touch her.

"Get cleaned up, kids. You're both going to need some ice." Tessa's dad smiled, nodding to me before sticking his hand out. "And the name is Enzo. If you ever want to stand a chance in the ring against her, you should show up once in a while."

Then with the brief shake, he left us to go yell at someone else.

"I'll show you where the showers are." Tessa moved to the ropes, unwrapping her hands. "We can ice up at my place."

And whatever disappointment I was feeling, no longer existed. She was taking me back to her place, and I wasn't wasting the opportunity.

"Lead the way, Ricci."

Chapter 9

Tessa

"**L**IFT YOUR SHIRT."

He was perched on the edge of my sofa, his brow raised in curiosity.

"This seems to be a bit of a habit for you," he chuckled, lifting his T-shirt before pulling it all the way off. "Bringing me back to your apartment, asking me to get naked."

I rolled my eyes, pressing the ice pack against his toned torso. "You can say no, Tibbs. And don't pretend you don't enjoy it."

He didn't even wince, his pleased grin getting wider as I waited for him to take over. "So do you like to beat the living shit out of *all* your first dates? Or am I special?"

I hadn't really thought it through.

Assuming that he would show up to the gym but turn around and leave when I suggested we got in the ring. It was what I'd been expecting to be honest, with no man ever taking me up on the challenge. And then, after he left, his whole fascination with us dating would be over, and we could just move on. Or go back. Or just be done with the awkward stage we seemed to be in.

I'd wanted to force his hand, to prove that he wasn't *really* interested. Or that whatever attraction he thought he was feeling didn't go beyond the surface.

But . . .he surprised me.

Not only did he *not* turn around and walk away, but he went toe-to-toe with me on every round. He hit me hard too—which usually wasn't a positive—except that it proved he respected me as an athlete and trusted me to handle myself.

And that respect, that trust—it was a turn on.

His hand replaced mine, holding the ice pack in place as I slipped off my T-shirt and iced my own ribs. "You want some Advil?" I asked, settling on the sofa and watching him do the same.

"Nah, I took some Motrin in the car on the ride over here." His eyes dropped down to my sports bra briefly before lifting back to mine. "But if that food doesn't get here quick, another fight is probably going to break out."

I laughed, my muscles protesting a little as my chest expanded. "You want me to kick your ass again? Wow, Tibbs, you really are a glutton for punishment."

We'd showered and changed at the gym before getting into our own cars and driving back to my apartment. On the way home I'd ordered enough burgers and fries to feed an army from a place nearby that delivered because we were both starving.

"Yeah, I guess I am. Which reminds me, you didn't answer. You do this to every guy, or just me?"

I'd deliberately sidestepped his early question because I wasn't really sure how to answer. I didn't really want to admit what I was feeling. That part of me really liked him and it had been a strategy for avoiding disappointment. He thought I was strong, confident, and I didn't want to shatter that illusion. Besides, I wasn't exactly sure what was happening between us. And other than that really—and I do mean *really*—nice hug on the mat, it had all been pretty friendly.

"You thought that was a date?" I deflected, chuckling as I tried not to stare at his chest. He was in amazing shape, those muscles definitely not decorative. I wanted to rub my hands on them, to trace the curve of his body with my tongue, to—*Not helpful, Tessa. You are not sleeping with him even if he is hot and doesn't scare easily.*

"Of course, Ricci, I piss out blood on *all* my first dates." He laughed. "And don't even try and pretend like that didn't count. I asked, you accepted, we went somewhere together. It was a date."

"I assumed you'd chicken out." I shrugged, giving him at least part of the truth as I moved my ice pack to the other side. "No date has ever fought me before. I thought you would leave."

He tossed his ice pack onto my coffee table leaving his hands free as he turned toward me. "Did you not see what you were wearing? Umm, yeah, I wasn't going anywhere. But just so there's no confusion, I don't hit women. Ever." He stopped, looking at my raised eyebrow and the ice against my body. "Okay, besides that. Which—I'll add—I only did because it was obvious you were a professional and knew what you were doing. Not to say that it isn't going to totally mess with my head, but even if I hadn't fought you, I wasn't walking away."

"I'm glad." It had come out of my mouth before I'd had a chance to stop it, my body leaning in closer.

"Yeah?" he asked, his fingers moving to the ice pack against my skin. He hesitated, but only for a second before removing and replacing it with his hand. His palm was warm, making my skin shiver from the sudden change in temperature. "You're so hard to read, Ricci. But I really like that about you." His head edged closer, his other hand moving to my chin. "What do I have to do to get a second date?"

"Pretty presumptuous of you considering this one hasn't ended yet." I lifted my face, my hands finally getting what they wanted as my fingers moved to his chest.

He closed his eyes, sucking in a heady breath as I traced his abs and then moved on to his pecs. "Mmmmm, I'm not going to pretend I'm not cocky, Tessa." *God, I loved the way he said my name.* "And I'd say the chances are better than average that this one is going to turn out pretty fucking great."

His lips pressed against mine, my mouth opening automatically as he kissed me. He took the advantage, sliding in his tongue as his hand moved to the back of my neck and pulled me closer.

It was soft yet demanding, his mouth dominating mine while not overwhelming me with his body. The hand that had been pressed against my side slid up my torso but didn't even try to grab my tits, the slow glide of his fingers making my skin pimple.

I whimpered, scooting my body closer while he stayed on his side of the couch.

I wanted to straddle him, to climb into his lap and kiss him hard while our bare skin rubbed against each other. I wanted to feel if he was hard, to thread my fingers through his dark brown hair and watch his beautiful eyes while I rocked against him.

My core felt like it was on fire, my lips hungry as he gave me more.

"Fuck, you're sexy," he whispered against my lips. "If all I had to do was take a beating to be able to kiss you, I'll do it fifty times over."

"You're so sick," I chuckled between kisses, loving the way his mouth felt against mine. "I don't know what the hell I'm even doing with you."

"It's because you're sick too," he answered, pulling me closer. "Normal people don't hit each other for fun. And I could tell that you were getting off on it."

He was right.

I had been turned on.

"Stop fucking talking, Tibbs, or I'll stop kissing you." My butt lifted from the couch, moving to his lap like I'd wanted to in the first place as I wrapped my arms around his neck.

"*I'm* kissing *you*, psycho." His hands moved to my hips pushing them down as he ground against my core. "And I'm not stopping."

He didn't, bucking up under me while our tongues tangled and our bodies pressed against each other. The thin cotton of my sports bra was the only barrier between me and his chest, my nipples hardening from the friction.

It was hot and raw, and way more intense than I'd imagined it. He knew exactly how much pressure to apply, showing complete mastery over my lips while his hard-on worked against my clit even through our clothes.

I was just about to reach between us and unzip his jeans when a loud buzz broke through the room. It was coming from the intercom by the door, my hand frozen just above his waistband as we stopped and looked at each other.

"Food," I groaned, almost forgetting we'd been waiting for a delivery. "I need to let them up."

His hands anchored on my hips stopped me from moving to the door. "Wait." He leaned forward, kissing me again but much gentler than before. It was slow and seductive, only pulling away when the buzzer sounded for the second time. "Okay." He released me, my feet hitting the floor as I clamored off his lap and ran to my intercom and unlocked the external door.

That last kiss—the more gentle one—was oddly unnerving, the feel of him still on my lips as I opened my apartment door and waited for the delivery guy.

I felt him behind me, his hands handing me my discarded T-shirt. "Wasn't sure how big a tip you wanted to give him," he chuckled when I looked down and realized I was just in my sports bra and leggings. "Unless you like punishing all the guys in your life, in which case, leave the T-shirt off."

My grin widened, tossing the shirt aside as I waited. I wasn't shy and it thrilled me a little that he thought something as utilitarian as a sports bra was an instrument of seduction.

"Umm," the delivery guy's eyes widened as they dropped to my chest, "Tessa?"

"Yep, that's me," I smiled brightly, handing him the tip money I'd placed on the side table by the door. "Thanks so much," I held out my hand for the bags of food.

He hesitated, unable to pull his gaze from my chest until Tibbs cleared his throat from behind me. Then he thrust the bags at me, turning around and almost running down the hall without so much as a goodbye.

"You're such a sadist." Tibbs shook his head, biting back his grin. "That poor kid is just trying to do his job."

"Hey, this isn't sexy." I waved my free hand around my chest before closing the door. "It's functional and comfortable, and it's hard to work out effectively when you're wearing a bulky T-shirt."

"Ricci, you need to adjust your definition of sexy. I'd say me and speedy Pete," he pointed to the door, "are probably in agreement that we don't give a fuck how functional and comfortable it is, it's going to make us hard. And yeah, I get that it isn't its purpose and you assume that makes us pigs. But that doesn't make it any less true."

I shook my head, unable to suppress the laugh. He could be such a jerk, but he was so honest about it that it was kind of adorable. And yeah, I knew how it sounded, and it still didn't change anything.

"You going to be able to eat while I'm lounging around in my workout clothes." I lowered my voice, intentionally trying to sound sexy.

He nodded, taking the bags of food from me and pulling me closer. "Yeah, I'll be fine. I'll still be hard and thinking dirty thoughts, but I'm starving. So unless you're going to let me eat you . . ." His brow rose, smirking cheekily until I shoved him roughly in the chest. "Well, then burgers it is."

It was funny how if he'd said that to me a week or so ago, it would have totally grossed me out. The idea of him casually offering me oral sex so flippantly, not something I would have found endearing. But the more I got to know Tibbs—and it was still early days—the more I saw that was just his sense of humor. He was a little crass, and cocky, and mostly inappropriate. But he wasn't hostile or predatory, and up until recently, never so much as breathed a word to me that would've been out of line.

And more than all of that, he was honest. Completely unapologetic about who he was and owned it, and that was incredibly sexy.

"Let's go eat burgers, pervert." I pulled him toward my kitchen table.

If it was supposed to be awkward sitting down and eating fast food with someone you'd been dry humping not even half an hour earlier, I didn't feel it. Both of us demolishing our food while we sucked down a couple of sodas. He didn't even make a wiseass crack about my appetite, guys usually shocked I didn't nibble on a salad like a pet hamster.

It was only after we were done—and about a million calories consumed—that I wondered what to do next. Going back to kissing him sure sounded like a good option, but it also attracted a level of danger to it as well. I didn't sleep with guys on first dates, even if technically I'd known Tibbs for a while. And I didn't trust myself not to break my own rule if we went back to doing that, considering how hot it had made me the first time.

"How long have you been boxing?" Tibbs surprised me, clearing the wrappers from my table, apparently not feeling the same level of conflict I was.

Conversation.

I could work with that.

My back straightened in my chair, feeling slightly relieved I hadn't had to make the choice. "My dad had me and Emilia in gloves before we could even walk. He was a Marine. *Is* a Marine," I corrected. "You never really stop. Anyway, it was important to him that we knew how to handle ourselves. Said it taught not only strength but discipline. And since we were military brats, shit like that was just normal to us. I didn't even know not all girls got into the ring with grown-ass men until I was maybe sixteen."

Tibbs didn't balk, not seeming surprised as he waved his hand for me to go on. "Dad trained religiously when he was younger and even entered some amateur bouts. But we moved around a lot so he didn't really have the time to dedicate to the sport. Mom was Air Force so two active duty parents meant we did and went wherever the government told us to. So when he finally retired, he bought that old boxing gym in Queens and started training fighters. I think he always loved that part more, teaching someone how to properly throw a punch and take a hit. Guess that's why he'd been so hardcore with me and Emilia, he didn't have anyone else to impart his knowledge." I laughed, remembering how intense his drills had been. "Emilia was let off the hook when she enlisted in the Marines. Though she said all of Dad's training had been a godsend when she did the Crucible on Parris Island. And the academy for me was like a cakewalk."

"I bet." He eased back into his chair, a relaxed smile crossing his lips. "Presley and I had a more," he paused before chuckling, "regular upbringing. Milk and brownies when we came home from school, meatloaf on Thursdays—that kind of thing." He snapped his fingers suddenly like he'd remembered something. "There was that *one* time when they shipped us off to summer camp with the Israeli Secret Service. It was kinda rough, but they taught us how to kill a man with a pinkie finger, so I guess it wasn't all bad. But I think all middle-class white kids from Long Island did that, not sure if that makes me all that special."

"You're ridiculous." I laughed, my heart skipping a beat. It was both endearing and adorable, his attempt to compete with my unconventional childhood almost hysterical.

"Easy there, Ricci," he warned, biting back his grin as he tried to look serious. "I just told you I can kill a man with this," he wiggled his pinkie finger on his right hand, "I'd be a little more careful with those insults."

Any concerns I had of spending time with Tibbs after that kiss were very firmly put to rest. He didn't even try to kiss me when we moved to the couch, both of us grabbing newly chilled ice packs and reapplying as we continued to talk.

He told me all about growing up with Presley, and then how he and Leighton joined the academy and became firefighters. And I filled him in on all the places my parents had been stationed, how crazy it was to constantly be moving.

"You always wanted to be a cop?" he asked, his head rolling toward me.

I nodded, the need to serve my country something I couldn't have escaped even if I'd tried. "I felt I could do better work here, at home. I am so proud of my parents and my sister, but there is so much that needed to be done in our own neighborhoods. And I wanted to make a difference."

He rolled his eyes, groaning dramatically before throwing his hands up in disgust. "You had to take it *there*. Now how am I supposed to make fun of you being a cop when you make it sound so honorable? Jesus, Ricci. Lie. To. Me. Tell me what you really wanted to do was give assholes speeding tickets and eat donuts."

"Ooooooooooo I could totally eat a donut right now," I moaned, closing my eyes as I seductively licked my lips.

He stood quickly, the ice pack dropping to the floor as he held out his hands. "If getting one lets me hear you make that noise one more time, then we're leaving right now. There's got to be a million donut shops in Brooklyn. Hell, we'll drive back to Manhattan if we have to."

I didn't hesitate, letting my own ice pack drop as I linked my fingers with his and let him help me to my feet. "I know this amazing place that isn't far. There's a great Sushi restaurant nearby as well if you want to get dinner later."

And before I'd even realized what I'd suggested, I'd planned to spend the rest of the day with Tibbs. I hadn't even asked him. Not even considering that he had other things to do and maybe didn't want to spend his whole day off hanging with me.

"Sounds good to me." He pulled me closer, pressing my body flush against his as he dropped a single soft kiss on my lips. "But this still counts as just one date, and I want a second."

"You sure?" I breathed against his lips, wanting more than he'd given me but knowing it would invite trouble. "You could be sick of me by the end of it."

He shook his head, his eyes moving to my mouth like he'd had a similar thought. "Not a chance."

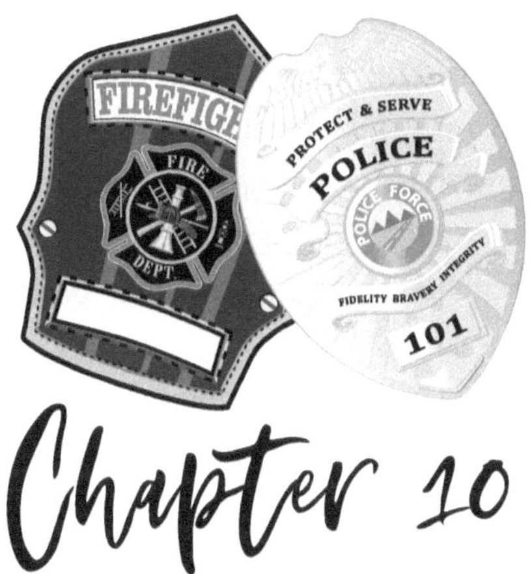

Chapter 10

Justin

IT WAS LATE when I got back to my apartment.

Eleven? Maybe even midnight? And if at some point during the day I'd glanced at a clock, I'd probably have a better idea.

But I hadn't.

Hadn't wanted to either, too busy to worry about unimportant shit like what position in the sky the sun was occupying.

The day had been . . . well, fucking awesome. Granted, it started a little strange, my trip to Queens not what I'd been expecting. But honestly, I'm not sure if given a choice, I'd have changed a thing.

Obviously, Ricci was hot.

I didn't need to do three rounds in a boxing ring to work that out. Although, I will say that I had developed a very unhealthy obsession with sports bras in the last twelve hours.

Her body was amazing.

Every inch of it was conditioned and toned, and if she was the last female body I ever saw, I'd die knowing I'd seen perfection.

Well, I'd seen *most* of it.

And while the thought of her naked made me so hard my dick hurt, I was taking my time getting to that part. She fascinated me in a way I couldn't quite explain, everything about her so interesting that I could spend literally hours and not get bored. Which is exactly what happened, and why I was limping into my Hell's Kitchen apartment at some point late in the night or early in the morning.

I'd been a good boy too, keeping my mouth and hands away from her most of the time because I knew exactly what would happen if I didn't. And once I went there—really went there—it was going to be hard to stop.

Jesus, it had almost taken an act of God to stop me when we'd been making out on her couch. Everything about her turning me on so fucking much, that if she'd touched my cock I'd have probably come in her hand. And she'd looked like she'd been considering it, her fingers dangerously close to the fly of my jeans.

There was no way I'd have been able to tell her no and try to be the guy who says we should wait. Yeah, that was a superpower I didn't possess, along with being unable to levitate and stop bullets with my bare hands. Same skillset, and none of them in my wheelhouse.

So knowing my limitations, I figured I'd just do my best to avoid it. And not because I *didn't* want to sleep with her. Ha, because, yeah *that* guy existed. No, I was torturing myself because I didn't want her to think sex was the *only* thing I wanted. And for a guy who usually only wants sex, I was just as surprised as anyone else to come to that realization.

"Fuck," I groaned, my body tight as I collapsed onto my mattress. I was going to need more Motrin—possibly a priest—and when I eventually got out of bed, I was definitely going to hurt.

But it was totally worth it.

As was the entire day I'd spent with her.

We'd spent hours in her apartment, talking about everything from our families to arguing about which New York slice was the best. She was delusional, because there was no way *Juliana's* in Brooklyn was better than *Joe's* in Greenwich. And when we weren't in her apartment—talking and trying to avoid putting parts of my body on hers—we were wandering around her neighborhood, eating donuts and ordering sushi.

And if I believed there was a chance I could spend the night and *not* touch her, I'd have offered to crash on her couch just so we got more time. But I'd reached my limit of being good and fatigue didn't do wonders for my willpower.

Which gave me two choices.

Either toss myself out—because she hadn't done it yet—and head back into the city. Or ask her to handcuff me to her coffee table and roll the dice the wood was strong enough to hold. It looked like a cheap import; I didn't like my odds.

"Ricci," I murmured, rolling onto my side as I closed my eyes and flicked through memories of the day like it was a movie. "You're going to be trouble."

It was just after ten a.m. when I found myself in my car, heading back over the bridge to Brooklyn.

No, not to Tessa's apartment because that would make me a stalker.

To Quinn and North's.

Sure, I possibly liked the idea that I was sorta in the general area and could potentially stop by since I was in the neighborhood. But I also needed someone to talk to and I didn't have the stomach to head to Presley and Leighton's and see my sister with messed-up sex hair. Those two had been fucking like fiends, positive they were going for some kind of record. And while I accepted they were adults and it was none of my business, I was already suffering a severe case of PTSD from hitting Ricci, I didn't want to add to my therapy bill.

"Tibbs, to what do we owe this pleasure?" North opened the door, his cute little daughter hanging off his arm. Ava was almost one and kept the big guy on his toes, but seeing him married with a kid still shocked the shit out of me.

"I have a question." I smiled at Ava who grinned and then waved. "How soon after you met Quinn before you slept with her?"

"Umm, hello to you too, Tibbs," North's hot wife and the woman in question appeared from the kitchen looking confused.

"Oh, hey, Quinn," I coughed out, thinking I should've probably asked if North was alone before launching into my investigation. "This is purely for scientific purposes, not because I get off on knowing when you did it."

North handed Ava over to Quinn, the two of them sharing a look I wasn't sure was a good thing. "Can you give me a minute alone with Tibbs, beautiful. If you don't see me kill him, you still have plausible deniability."

Quinn chuckled, giving him a quick kiss before whispering, "You better tell me everything after he leaves."

"Always." North put his palm to his heart, watching as his two ladies walked out of the room. "Any last words, Tibbs?" He tipped his head to the side, sinking his hands into his pockets.

"I told you, dude. It's not like that." I tried to reassure him, wondering why he would assume the worst. "I just know that before Quinn you could have *any* woman you wanted, *whenever* you wanted, and then you were just with her."

He pointed to the couch, gesturing for me to take a seat before shaking his head. "Well, yeah, that's what happens when you are in a relationship. You don't fuck anyone else."

"But did that happen right away? The relationship? Or did the fucking come first? Or was there no fucking so that's how you knew you were in a relationship?" My butt sunk into the cushions, watching his eyebrows shoot up at my question.

"You've had girlfriends before, Tibbs. You really need me to explain how this works?" North laughed, scrubbing his face with his hand.

"I know I've had girlfriends, North. But I was never really invested. And honestly, I wasn't really sad when it ended." I swear, I thought he was smarter than that. "Let's just say—hypothetically—that you met someone that wasn't like any woman you'd ever met." I waved my hand, building a picture. "And she's hot. Ridiculously hot, but more than that, she's great. Really great. And like the biggest smart ass, but you really like that too. And slightly crazy but you—"

"Jesus, Tibbs," North cut me off. "Did you find this girl on Craig's List? Because the way you're talking, I'm pretty sure you're going to end up with a toe tag."

I laughed, because dying at the hands of Ricci probably wouldn't be a bad way to go. "Relax asshole, I didn't find her on Craig's List. And she's a cop, if she was going to kill me, she'd know better than to leave the body."

His eyes got wide, sucking in a breath. "Holy shit, Tessa Ricci?"

How the fuck did he guess?

As far as I knew the only two people who had that kind of intel were Leighton and Miller, and neither of those guys would have told North.

"What?" I coughed out, wondering if maybe I'd accidentally said something myself. "We're talking *hypothetically*. That means that the situation probably doesn't even exist."

"Thanks for the English lesson, dumbass, I know what the word means. And I also know that two uniforms came in earlier in the week because apparently there were 'concerns'," his fingers made little air quotes, "about your mental wellbeing at her request. Then I hear that it was just some stupid prank between the two of you. But last time I checked, you and Tessa Ricci weren't exactly besties."

Okay, so maybe he was smart.

"So hypothetically—"

"Really?" he chuckled. "You want to keep pretending we are not talking about Ricci? Should I call her and ask her what she thinks? Or you just going to admit that you're into her and you don't want to screw it up?" He eyed me hard, folding his arms across his chest as he waited for me to answer.

"It's Ricci," I admitted, thinking if I was going to go to the trouble of seeing North and asking his advice, I might as well tell him all of it. "But what we talk about stays between you and me."

He nodded, agreeing. And if there was one other person I trusted other than Leighton, it was North. "Tibbs, I'm not going to say anything to anyone. Just tell me what's on your mind."

I scrubbed my face with my hands, blowing out a breath. "It's more than just attraction, North. And I don't want to screw it up."

It was the first time I'd admitted it out loud and accepted that there was a possibility that I liked this woman more than just a little bit. And I'd totally understand if North laughed, because honestly, the idea of me wanting more than just sex wasn't something I was expecting. Hell, two weeks ago, if he or anyone else suggested it, I'd have told them they were crazy. I'm fairly sure that was exactly what I'd said when Leighton made some joke about it the very night I'd noticed Ricci at the bar. But I guess the universe was funny like that, and whether I'd planned it or not, things were happening.

"Have you talked to her?" he asked, surprisingly serious and without cracking jokes. "Told her how you feel?"

Ha!

Did I talk to her?

Well wasn't that a fucking prickly question.

I pinched the bridge of my nose, wondering if anyone else got themselves into the kind of dilemmas I did. "See, that's just it. We spent the whole goddamn day talking. Talked about everything. Her family, mine. Work. And pretty much everything else except religion and politics. But as far as the stuff you're talking about, nope."

"Well," he shrugged, "Do you think she feels the same way? I mean, we all *know* Ricci, and have hung out with her. So is this more just hanging out?"

I got why he might have thought that, because we had "hung out" before. But that kiss on her couch, yeah, not even close to what we'd done before. "We kissed, North. And not like how you'd kiss your grandma. So as far as whether she's feeling the same way I am or not, I don't know, but it's not like before."

It wasn't.

And I might not have any idea what the hell I was doing but I knew that.

"Okay." North rolled his palms down the front of his pants. "I knew the minute I saw Quinn that she was different. First it was attraction, because unlike you and Tessa, I didn't know her. But all it took was five minutes talking to her in that coffee shop and I knew I had to see her again. She was different, so I was different. That's *how* I knew. And Tibbs, the fact we're even having this conversation tells me things are different with you. So, tell her."

His advice was solid, and while I expected nothing less, it was still reassuring to hear it. "Thanks, dude. I'm going to give her a call. I'll get out of your apartment so you can tell Quinn all my secrets."

"Good man!" North slapped me on the back and grinned. "But if you think she hasn't been listening the whole time, you clearly don't know my wife."

"It's more efficient that way." Quinn's voice came from the other room.

We both laughed, amused she hadn't even tried to pretend she hadn't been eavesdropping. But that was Quinn for you, unapologetic. A lot like Tessa. And damn if that wasn't attractive.

I said goodbye to North and Quinn, leaving them to play happy family and headed back to my car. I had a choice to make, and all three of my options had the potential to suck.

One, I could call Tessa, knowing she had another day off, and tell her I was in the neighborhood and risk her telling me she didn't want to see me.

Two, show up unannounced, not giving her the opportunity to turn me down but potentially think I was a stalker with boundary issues.

And lastly, three, go home, obsess about it some more, and wait for her to call me. But it could be a while and with our conflicting schedules, who knew when we'd get the opportunity again to hang out. Or she might not even call at all, thinking I would.

I shook my head, slipping into the driver's seat of my Impala and picking up my phone.

"Tibbs?" She answered on the second ring.

"Hey, I'm at North's but I want to see you." I put the car into drive, hesitating before easing away from the curb. "You going to call the cops if I show up on your doorstep?"

She laughed, sighing softly into the phone. "You think I'd let anyone else have the glory? Tibbs, please, you should know me better than that. I *am* the cops, if anyone is arresting you, it's going to be me. How soon can you be here?"

I felt myself smile, grinning like an idiot just from hearing her voice. "Depends, you going to cite me for speeding if I do it? Or is there some way I can talk myself out of a ticket."

"Just get here, wiseass. But try and keep the moving violations to a minimum."

Which meant I could break *some* laws.

"Got it, be there soon, Ricci."

"I'll be waiting, Tibbs."

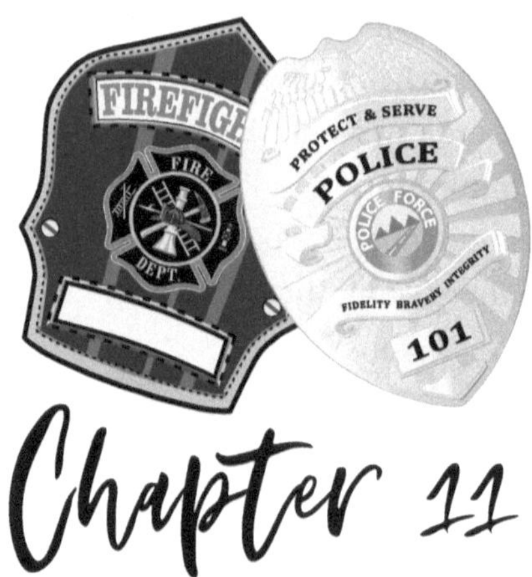

Chapter 11

Tessa

IT HAD BEEN twelve hours.

That was it.

Twelve hours since Tibbs had left my apartment and I invited him right back.

"Such a bad idea," I said to myself as I paced. "This is such a bad idea."

But for all my audible protesting, I couldn't get behind the sentiment. I didn't really believe it was a bad idea, wanting to see him as much as he apparently wanted to see me.

We'd shared one—really intense—kiss.

And for the rest of the day he'd kept his hands and lips mostly to himself.

If it were anyone else, I'd assume he had a change of heart—or just wasn't that into me—and was moving himself into the friend category. But in all the time I'd known him, he'd never wasted his time or his effort. And he didn't usually change his mind when it came to sex. I'd even overheard him say that sex was like pizza, and even bad pizza was still worth having. So either he'd suddenly taken a vow of celibacy—abandoning all his previous thoughts and feelings—or his lack of action was deliberate.

I knew where my money was.

For whatever reason, he'd decided that he *wasn't* going to try to sleep with me. At least not yesterday. Which was amusing and adorable all at the same time.

"Hey." He grinned, pushing his keys into his pocket as I opened the door. He'd buzzed minutes before, my stomach in knots as I'd waited.

"Hey, yourself." I stepped aside so he could walk into my apartment. "Did you forget something yesterday? Why the sudden need—"

He didn't let me finish, answering with his lips against mine. It was hot and desperate, my hand moving quickly to close the door before threading in his hair. He felt so good, his body pressed against mine as he kissed me, a small whimper making its way up my throat.

"I needed to do this," he mumbled between kisses. "I thought about it every second since I left, and it was driving me insane."

I didn't even care that I was right, too busy kissing him back to have time to gloat. I'd wanted it as well, desperate for another kiss even though I knew it would be hard to stop.

But it wasn't hard, it was impossible, my mouth opening and giving him access as he reached for my ass and lifted me off the floor.

"You're driving me crazy," I moaned, closing my eyes as he carried me toward the couch. It was where the madness had started, and I had a hunch, where it would continue.

"Tessa," his mouth moved to my neck, fevered kisses tracing the length of my throat, "I'm—"

"Stop talking, Justin." I felt his hard-on against my stomach, the pressure between my legs building. "I want more."

Yesterday, I'd had every intention of resisting him. There was still an attraction, sure, but I was positive I wasn't going to be another conquest for him.

Even though he was charming, and funny, and so goddamn sexy.

Then, I entered into negotiations with myself, reasoning that maybe if it were on my terms, it would be okay. What was the harm? And when did I start defining myself by the people I slept with?

And also, why the hell was I so judgmental?

"Say my name again," he begged, his fingers wrapping around the hem of my T-shirt as he laid me on the soft cushions of the couch. "Say it, Tessa."

"Justin," I moaned, arching into him. He felt so good, his mouth moving expertly from my lips to my neck, making my skin tingle everywhere he kissed.

His body hovered over mine, his knee between my legs as an arm braced the back of the couch. The other hand moved up my side, pushing up the fabric of my top and exposing my bare skin.

My fingers were busy as well, grabbing his T-shirt and pulling it off, our kisses interrupted by the need to get us both out of our clothes.

"Mmmmm." His lips dropped to the edge of my sports bra, kissing the band along my chest. "This thing is so fucking sexy."

It wasn't in me to argue again, because I really didn't care. My mind was unreasonably busy focusing on what his hands were doing and how good his mouth was making me feel. "Tibbs, that—"

"*Justin*, call me Justin," he groaned, pressing his thigh right against my clit.

My hips rocked, unable to stop them as the pressure built between my legs. "Right there, Justin. Oh my God, right there."

I wasn't even embarrassed, too desperate to release the pent-up frustration I'd been nursing since he left me the night before. I'd thought about that first kiss all night, dreamt about it and woke up wet just from the memory. I wasn't sure if I'd get the opportunity again so I was making the most of it.

"Yes, Tessa." His voice raw as he moved his leg, building more friction. "I'll give you whatever you want, baby. God, you look so beautiful like this."

My hands locked on his hips, pulling him down so his whole body was against me. His thigh was good, but I was taking him at his word that he'd give me whatever I wanted. And what I wanted was more of him.

"Jesus, Tessa," he chuckled as he pressed the hard ridge of his cock against my core. "Better?"

He didn't make a move to undo my pants, or me his, our bodies moving against each other as we found each other's mouths.

My leg wrapped around his hip as his hand went to my ass, both of us chasing a high as I felt my pants get wetter. It was so hot, and I was so turned on, making out with Justin Tibbs feeling better than the last real sex I'd had.

"I want to make you come, Tessa. I want to see what you look like when you unravel." His other hand moved to my sports bra, palming my breast as I felt him get even harder between my legs.

"Okay," I shuttered out on a shaky breath, completely on board with making me come. It was a fantastic suggestion and one I was immediately a fan of. "Fuck, Justin, right there."

"Mmmmmm, yeah, right there works for me too," he panted against my neck, my skin feeling electric under his breath.

It wasn't just me who was desperate to come, his cock straining against the fly of his jeans as he rocked against me. I loved that he was so turned on as well, the desperation in his hips as he chased his release while wanting to give me mine.

He felt so hard and thick, the length of him impressive. And as much as I didn't want to stop what we were doing, I was desperate to touch him. "I want to feel you," I breathed, trying to make the words come out right as we writhed against each other. "I want to touch your cock, Justin."

"Fuuuuuuucccckk," he groaned out, reaching down and steadying my hips. "You have any idea how hot that sounds? You're going to make me come, Tessa. And that's not happening until after you do."

My hand pressed against the fly of his jeans, moving my palm against his length. "But I want to feel you, wrap my fingers around you, squeezing you as I jerk you off."

I was never shy about asking for what I wanted, especially not in bed, unwilling to lay there and not participate. And what I wanted at that moment, was to touch Justin.

His mouth pressed against mine, swallowing the rest of my argument as his hand dropped between us. The weight against me lifted, the telltale sound of a zipper being lowered, breaking the silence.

Excitement flooded me, my fingers reaching down to meet his and discovering it was *my* jeans he'd unzipped. "I wanted—"

"Yeah, and I heard you. But I said I'm making you come first, and that's what I'm going to do."

Waiting for me to nod, he slid his hand against my cotton panties as a hard breath blew from between my lips. His ability to maneuver a situation to get his way was impressive to say the least.

"Justin." His name escaped my mouth as his fingers breeched the edge of my underwear. The softest touch made contact with my clit, my body bowing off the couch.

It felt so good, the pad of his thumb rubbing tight circles against me as I sucked in shaky breaths. He was teasing, the movements slow and controlled with a level of discipline I wasn't aware he possessed.

"More," I breathed, circling my hips in an effort to get more friction, but he didn't deviate, keeping his rhythm and ignoring my desperate thrusts.

It was delicious, the slow burn inching up my spine as my nerve endings sizzled. He was drawing it out, taking his time as he kissed my neck, dropping his mouth to the tops of my tits, alternating his kisses between my body and my mouth.

I wanted more, needed more, and wanted to touch him too. And since he was distracted, I was able to use it to my advantage.

Unable to stop my hands any longer, they undid his button and then his zipper. He moaned as I palmed him through the cotton of his boxer briefs, my fingernails grazing against his shaft as I slid under his waistband.

"Tessa," he warned, his kisses only stopping to hiss out my name.

But I was already committed, wrapping my hand around and giving him a firm, tight tug.

"Jesus," he cursed out, his hips thrusting as I slid up and down again.

We were still mostly clothed, only our T-shirts laying on the floor, reminiscent of the day before. I wanted us naked, to feel and see all of him, but couldn't make myself stop long enough to make it happen. And clearly it wasn't a priority for him either, his hand buried inside my panties and his fingers doing the most amazing things to my pussy.

"You're terrible at following orders, your captain must *love* you." He tried to laugh, the words coming out strained as I continued to stroke him.

My hips circled against his touch, wanting the release so much and not wanting it over. "I only follow orders that make sense—yours don't."

We stopped talking, neither of us capable of forming sentences any longer as hands and mouths launched a full-on assault. I teetered, my fingernails clawing at the edge of a cliff as he gave up the teasing and thrust two fingers inside of me.

That was all it took.

My body convulsed as I came hard, my grip on his cock tightening as I somehow managed to continue to stroke him. I wasn't even sure if that was what I was doing, my movements—like my body—a jerky mess.

"Tessa," he cursed out, a stream of yeses following my name as he pulsed, jets of cum spilling onto my stomach.

Fingers loosened their grip, my body twitching as we both rode our orgasms, pressed together in a heated, sticky and panting mess.

"That wasn't the plan," he chuckled against my ear, his lips making their way back to my mouth as he eased off me. "I just wanted to kiss you again."

"Well, I'd say you did that." My fingers reached up and traced his face. "And we established a while ago you have terrible impulse control."

"Me?" he scoffed. "You started this, Ricci. I was trying to be a gentleman."

And there it was, proof that for whatever reason, he'd been trying not to sleep with me. Even with the kissing, and the touching—he hadn't tried to turn it into sex.

"Why?" I asked, curious as to his motivations and what about me made things different.

He shook his head, kissing me softly. "Because I want a second date, Tessa. And another one after that too."

"You want to date me?" I hadn't meant to sound so surprised, but the idea of Justin Tibbs dating *anyone*, let alone me, wasn't something I'd thought I'd ever see. "Tibbs, are you sure that's what you want? And don't just say it because you think that's what I want to hear. I'm a big girl, I can appreciate this for what it is."

I was fully aware of what I was getting involved in. And while I really liked the friendship that was blossoming, I was under no delusions it was anything more. I hadn't even seen Tibbs with the same girl—let alone a girlfriend—in at least two years. And I'd rather he just be honest with me than pretend in an effort to save my feelings.

It was his turn to be shocked, scooting up to a sitting position as he looked at me. "Umm, why would you say that? What did you think I was doing here?"

"I thought . . ." I bit my lip, wondering if being honest was the right way to go. Because honestly, I wasn't sure. "I don't know."

It was confusing.

And mostly because I was confused as well. I'd been so sure that I wasn't going to cross the line with him and what did it take me? A day? Two? Barely a week since he tried to pick me up in a bar to us dry humping in my apartment. And as much as I thought I had amazing powers of resistance—my will power unsurpassed—I knew it was only a matter of time before I slept with him. I was attracted to him. And he was obviously attracted to me.

But a relationship.

A *boyfriend*?

To even suggest either of those things would be ridiculous because even *he* hadn't said that. He'd said *date*, and there was a better-than-average possibility that word meant totally different things to both of us. And I wasn't going to make myself look even stupider than I already felt.

"So if you don't *know*, can you accept that maybe I do?" His brow scrunched like he wasn't totally convinced either. "I want another date, Tessa."

A *date*.

There was that word again.

My lips lifted in what I hoped didn't look like a fake smile, the sentiment not quite there. "Sure, Tibbs. I'd like that." *It wasn't a lie, wanting to see him again.* "Why don't we get cleaned up and talk about it some more," I offered, still not sure of the definition.

He smiled, looking down at my belly and seeing the mess he'd made. "Yeah, we should definitely get cleaned up first. You want to go get a shower? I can wait."

"Suuuuuuuure." I nodded, grabbing my T-shirt off the floor and wiping up the mess. "There's beer in the fridge if you want it and I have the premium cable package." I picked up the remote, watching as he adjusted himself and zipped up.

It was weird.

Even though it had been exactly what I'd wanted, the after was definitely strange. But I seemed to be the only one feeling it, Tibbs walking over to my kitchen sink, washing his hands and drying off with a paper towel before returning to the couch.

"I'll be fine, Ricci. Go get cleaned up. Then we'll go out for lunch. But this time we're going to my hood, no offense."

He was so cool, calm and collected. As if he fingered women to orgasm every single day right before heading out to lunch.

Shit.

Well . . . maybe he *did.*

There I was, wondering why I'd been different, but maybe I hadn't been. I'd assumed he took women home, screwed them and then left, but I'd only been guessing. Because unless I'd been stalking him and peeking through his curtains—creepy—how the hell would I know?

Okay.

Okay.

Okay.

So jumping to conclusions wasn't going to be helpful or productive. And since what had happened between us had been purely consensual, and I'd pretty much initiated the touching part, I couldn't very well be angry about it. Hell, even if I'd wanted to, I couldn't, still feeling the buzz of the endorphins.

"Okay," I said again. Out loud though, agreeing—with myself—that there was no point overthinking it. "We'll go to Midtown. I'll be quick."

I shuffled off the couch, gripping my dirty T-shirt against my body as I headed to the bathroom.

His hand snagged on my forearm, pulling me back to him, his shirt still MIA as he wrapped his arms around me. "Hey, you okay?" He dropped a soft, sweet kiss on my lips, nothing like what he'd been giving me before.

"Yep, all good. Just hungry." I kissed him back, partly because I didn't want him to think I was freaking out a little, and partly because, well, I *really* liked kissing him.

"Well then hurry back so I can feed you." He reached down, grabbed my ass and gave it a squeeze. "Something tells me I don't want to see you *hangry*."

I nodded, pushing away from his chest as I tried to laugh. "Yeah, it's not a pretty sight." And with a flick of my hair, I disappeared into my bathroom.

Shit.

Shit.

Shit.

I held my breath, only exhaling once I'd locked the door and turned on the shower.

It was fine.

I could totally do the casual thing, maybe it was a friends-with-benefits situation, and really would that be so bad? He was a nice guy, even if he did have a tendency to sleep around. But I wasn't the morality police last time I checked. And if what he did with his hands was any indication of what he could do in bed, I was seriously doing myself a disservice if I *didn't* sleep with him.

He was a nice guy.

He was also crazy sexy.

And while I think he was probably allergic to monogamy, he wouldn't lie to me.

I was more than due a little harmless fun, and if I had to pick someone who could do that, then Justin Tibbs was the perfect candidate.

"Yeah, it's totally fine," I reassured myself as I stripped out of my clothes and hopped under the spray. "As long as I maintain control and not get too attached, it's going to be totally fine."

And for what it was worth, I honestly believed that.

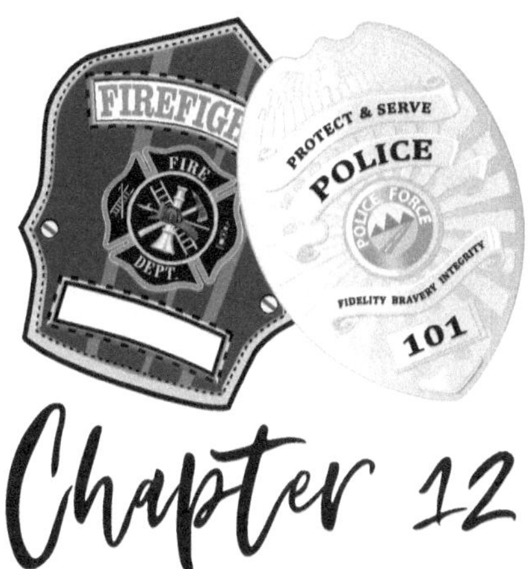

Chapter 12

Justin

THERE WAS SOMETHING about Tessa Ricci that made my game plan go out the window. Literally, I had walked into her apartment with one agenda—talking and not having sex—and ended up with my hands down her panties.

I swear, it hadn't been intentional. I'd taken what North had said on board and was going to tell her that I wanted to . . . I don't know, get to know her better for starters. Completely hands off too, because I was serious about liking her. She was so fucking intriguing, and fun, and that mouth . . .well, I could sit and argue with her all day and never get bored.

But.

But I'd taken one look at her and whatever the hell I'd meant to say or do was tossed to the side and I had no choice but to kiss her. I said I had no choice because I just didn't. My mouth and hands had their own agenda, and me being *a nice guy and telling her how I felt* wasn't on it. And while I knew I'd screwed up a little, it hadn't been a complete shitshow.

No sex.

Which considering how sexy she looked was a fucking effort, and clearly I possessed a level of restraint not even I was aware of.

I'd made her come though, that couldn't be helped.

And yeah, she'd made me come too because again, hello, she's fucking hot.

But sex had definitely not happened, so I was going to call it a win on that technicality and move the hell on.

"You decided where we're going?" Tessa emerged from her bedroom wearing a pair of jeans that looked like they were molded to her ass. Her top was tight too, the plain black T-shirt curved her body so nicely I had to mentally stop my eyes from ogling her tits. "Tibbs!" She jingled her keys. "Stop checking out my boobs and tell me where you want to go eat."

"For the record," my feet moved closer, unable to stop myself from wrapping my hands around her waist, "only teenage boys and perverts check out boobs, Ricci. Men—like myself— appreciate them. And they're fantastic, you're welcome." I tipped my head to the front of her top in a show of approval.

What I'd seen so far—through her sports bra and her top— was nothing short of spectacular. But I was desperate to see what they were really like, and to get those tight little nipples hard when I sucked on them.

Which I would.

Later.

She rolled her eyes but didn't seem annoyed, not even mentioning where I had my hands. "I'm not sure that's a compliment, Tibbs, but whatever. Where are we going? Or do you want me to follow you?"

"Follow?" I asked, wondering if she meant out the door.

"In my car." She motioned with her hands like they were on a steering wheel. "I assumed since you live in Midtown, I'd drive mine over so I can drive back after."

Which would make sense except I hadn't thought about her leaving and wasn't looking forward to saying goodbye.

"Okay, so here's a radical idea. Why don't you pack a bag and spend the night at my place?" Her eyes widened, opening her mouth to shoot down the idea before I'd even finished. "And no, not like *that*, Ricci." I laughed, genuinely not having meant her spending the night in my bed. Although, I wouldn't exactly say no.

No.

Focus, Tibbs.

"I have a spare bedroom, silly," I quickly added. "Leighton's room is still vacant and since you work right *there*, you can just leave in the afternoon from my apartment and not have to fight traffic over the bridge. We could just hang without having to watch the clock. See?"

It was clearly not what she was expecting, the surprised look only intensifying before she cleared her throat. "You want me to spend the night in your spare room?"

"Sure. Didn't you have fun last night?" Leaving her in the morning had sucked and not because I wanted to sleep with her. I'd just genuinely didn't want to say goodbye. So given the chance to remedy that little issue, I was going to take it. And since I hadn't handed Evans a key like he'd been begging me to do, I had all kinds of options. See, sometimes it paid to be an asshole.

She eyed me suspiciously, most likely assuming there was some other agenda. "Come on, Ricci, what are you worried about? You've already proven you could kick my ass if I get out of line." And as weird as that was to admit, it was a definite turn on.

There was something to be said about being with a girl who knew how to handle herself, and Tessa Ricci exceeded that on every level.

"You do realize we have an entire day to fill, Tibbs." She waved her hands in front of her. "Lots of time between now and bedtime."

I laughed, wondering if she liked arguing just because it got her off. "We could've been halfway to Midtown already. Just go and pack a bag, I thought you said you were hungry?"

Her brow arched in possibly the sexiest wordless protest I'd ever seen, but she turned and headed back to her room. It was too early to call it a victory, but it was promising.

A few minutes later, my argumentative badass emerged with a black backpack strapped to one shoulder. She'd been efficient, either getting her bag together in what I thought was record time for a woman, or that was her spare ammo and I was in for trouble. I wasn't even nervous to roll the dice, excited for what the day was going to deliver and hoping I'd be able to make her come again at least one more time.

Oh, I knew I was supposed to be good, but I was also a realist. And if she put her hands on me in any way that was sexual, I was going to have to reciprocate. Also, there wasn't a chance in hell I wasn't going to kiss her again. And since kissing is what usually started that downward spiral, there was a good chance we'd be back there again.

"You just going to stare or we actually leaving?" She cocked her head to the side, gesturing toward the door.

"Jesus, you really are cranky when you're hungry." I laughed, sliding her backpack from her shoulder and relocating it to mine. "Okay, Ricci, let's go before you bite my head off."

My car was parked around the corner on a side street, the shiny black paint of my Impala greeting us as we got closer. It wasn't as flashy as Leighton's Mustang, but hadn't come with the ridiculous price tag either.

"You know this would be a lot cooler if it was a '64," she bit back her grin as she slid into the passenger seat. "It's kind of a *dad* car. You know, when they're not having a full midlife crisis, but they've decided to upgrade from the minivan."

"Says the woman who's driving a Toyota Corolla," I scoffed, flipping her off at her lack of love for my wheels. "Driving an old lady car means you forfeited the right to comment on the cool factor of my car."

"It was my mom's car and she is *not* an old lady," she warned, waiting for me to get into the driver's seat before continuing. "And I got the car almost brand new because my mom barely drove it. It meant I didn't have car payments on top of rent, so I don't give a shit what it looks like."

I shrugged, pretending to be unconvinced. "How it was acquired wasn't up for debate. And doesn't change the fact I could smoke most people at a set of lights while your four cylinder is all excuse-me-sir-let-me-come-through."

She rolled her eyes, pointing to the road extending beyond the windshield. "Yet here we are, stationary."

"You're going to regret that." I laughed, hitting the ignition and revving the engine. "FYI, if we get pulled over, I'm totally throwing you under the bus and saying you made me do it."

"Do what?" she asked as I eased away from the curb.

"This." I planted my foot, the RPMs hitting the red as we entered traffic.

Yeah, it was childish, but I had the reputation of my car to uphold. And considering we still hadn't hit the main road, there was enough asphalt in front of us before I had to slow down for traffic.

Ignoring my flirtations with the speed limit, she laughed as I lane changed without decelerating, my foot only easing once I was convinced my point had been proven. "Not a dad car, Ricci. Unless you meant, *daddy*." My grin widened as we got closer to Manhattan.

"Wow, that was soooooo bad, Tibbs." She shook her head. "You're lucky you're hot or you'd be spending your nights getting quality time with your hand."

"You think I'm hot?" I asked, the revelation pleasing me more than it should. Obviously I wasn't an idiot and knew she was attracted to me, but hearing her say it out loud gave me a special kind of thrill.

Her eyes darted to me like she hadn't realized what she'd said until I'd repeated it back to her. But allowing her to take it back wasn't an option, and I wasn't going to let it slide either. "Go on, Ricci, tell me how hot I am."

"Tibbs, don't pretend like you don't know you're good-looking. You don't need me to tell you." She dismissed me with a wave.

"Hang on a second, when did you get to decide what I need to hear?" I argued back. "You think only women need to be told they're beautiful and guys should just assume? Wow, someone is sexist."

Honestly, I'd never really given a shit whether women thought I was hot or not. Not outside its ability to gain their interest and attention. I worked out because I liked the way it felt and it made my job easier, with the appreciative glances a really cool fringe benefit. But with Tessa, I really wanted to know.

"Fine," she huffed out a breath, conceding defeat. "You're beautiful, Tibbs."

"Not like that, wiseass. Say it like you want me to believe it." I laughed, loving watching her squirm. "Make me *feel* it, Ricci."

She threw her hands up, turning so she could face me while I continued to drive. "Justin," her voice purred, my name sounding sexier than it ever had, "you are so fucking hot. So beautiful. So . . ." Her hand dropped to my thigh and she gave it a squeeze. "Sexy, I'm not sure how I'm going to be able to keep my hands off you."

Between her low husky voice, the words, and the proximity of her hand to my crotch, I was already hard. And hell, if I wasn't all kinds of conflicted because I had no idea if she was kidding. "Don't play with me, Tessa. Not about that."

It was a warning, my limit to continue to play the game reaching its maximum as we got closer to my apartment. And fuck if I wasn't already thinking about all the ways I wanted her hands on me.

She swallowed, the comedy from her routine evaporating as my hand slid from the wheel and pressed against hers, holding it where it was.

Her hand moved higher up my leg, "I *meant* everything I said."

Fuck.

That was almost worse.

Knowing she meant it while I was unable to act on it, was a different level of hell. I was immediately pissed at myself for starting the conversation while driving, my responses limited unless I wanted to wreck my car and possibly end up in an emergency room. Not one of my smartest moves. "We're eating and then discussing this further," I coughed out, unwilling to let it go.

She played with her bottom lip, rolling it with her teeth as she nodded.

It felt like forever before we finally pulled into the parking lot behind my apartment, my hands barely getting the car into park before I popped open the door. I needed to kiss her, and while I didn't trust myself completely, not having her mouth was no longer an option.

I was at the passenger side door before she'd even got her seatbelt off, pulling her out of my Impala and pressing her against my chest. "You're so beautiful, Tessa," I moaned against her mouth. "So. Fucking. Beautiful."

"Not so bad yourself." I felt her smile against my lips. "I thought we were discussing this *after* food?"

"You going to write me up for not following procedure? Wouldn't be the first time." My hands dropped down and gave her ass a squeeze.

"I don't like paperwork." She returned the kiss, her hands doing some exploring of their own. "But we aren't going to make out in the streets like a pair of deviants. Don't really think it's a good look considering we both work in this precinct."

Well, she had a point. And while I didn't care what anyone thought about me, I didn't want anyone—either from my stationhouse or hers—talking about her. It was tough enough being a cop in the city, but female cops had it even harder. So she wouldn't be catching any additional heat because of me.

"Right." I nodded, slowly removing my hands from her perfect ass and lifted them away. "Guess we're eating then."

Pushing the disappointment away, I walked her up the stairs to my apartment. It was risky, the chance that the privacy would lead me astray, but we had her backpack to put away. Last thing I wanted was to give her any reason to leave, so making sure she understood that the night came with no expectations was my prime objective.

"You need anything before we leave?" I asked, tossing the bag on the floor of Leighton's old room. He'd left most of his bedroom furniture since Presley's place was kitted out. So other than needing to throw some sheets on the bare mattress, it was ready for a sleep over.

Her eyes floated over the room, looking around before turning back to me. "You were serious." It wasn't a question, more an affirmation that I'd taken her by surprise.

"I don't make a habit of saying things I don't mean." I gently brushed the hair from her face. "So yeah, I was serious."

I wanted to kiss her, her lips so close that all I had to do was reach down and take them. And without the worry about who was around to see, I was free to show her exactly how much I wanted her to stay the night.

My mouth hovered, brushing against hers lightly as I teased us both. Her breath came out in fast pants, her hand wrapping around the base of my T-shirt as she pulled me closer. "I'll spend the night, but only if I get to stay in your room." Her voice raw, unwavering as she told me what she wanted. "What do you think of that?"

Think?

She was giving me entirely too much credit if she thought I could function let alone think after that, my brain taking a vacation as my mouth closed the distance. I was trying my fucking hardest to be good, but denying her what she wanted wasn't an option either. "Just my room or in my bed?" I asked, wanting to clarify because there was a big difference.

"Your bed, Justin," she mumbled against my mouth, pushing me against the wall.

I loved her strength, her lean toned body pressing against mine and knowing I didn't have to worry about breaking her. "Yeah? I can take you there right now if that's what you want."

So much for being good.

It was overrated anyway.

Plus, North had never answered me on how long he'd waited before he'd had sex with Quinn, so for all I knew I was holding off unnecessarily.

My hands were all over her, tracing her curves over her clothes and imagining what she'd feel like naked. I wanted to know, to feel her against my body as I continued to kiss her with nothing between us.

"Tessa," I breathed, unable to stop kissing her as my mouth moved down her neck. I needed more leverage, spinning her around so it was her back against the wall with my body caging her in. "Baby, I'm so fucking hard right now and thinking straight isn't an option for me. So if you want this to stop you're going to have to tell me."

I wanted her.

Wanted her in so many ways I couldn't even decide where to start, but I needed to hear her say it was what she wanted too.

Her hand reached down between us, pressing the heel of her palm against the straining fly of my jeans. "No stopping, and this time I want more than just your hand."

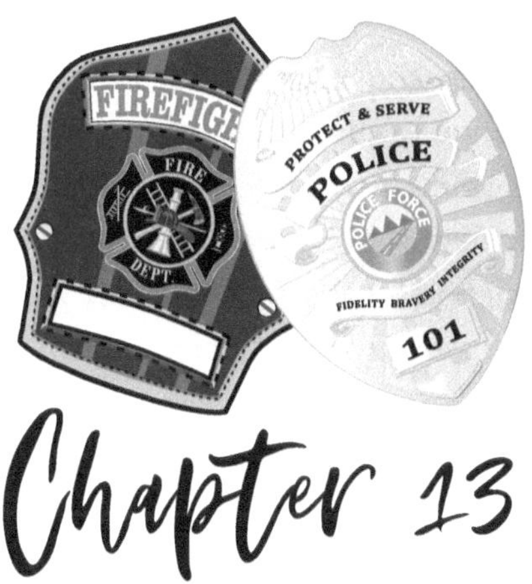

Chapter 13

Tessa

IF THERE HAD been some ambiguity as to whether Justin wanted to sleep with me, there wasn't anymore. And thank God for that, because for all my earlier protests about not wanting to be another woman in Tibbs' highlight reel, I really wanted him, too.

He was crazy hot, his body and mouth knowing exactly how to make me feel good. If it turned out to be a one-time thing, I still didn't think I'd regret it, feeling more turned on and ready to explode than I had in an entire year. Maybe I'd been doing it all wrong, and long-term serious relationships were overrated? In any case, I wasn't going to overthink what would probably be the best sex I was ever going to have with a guy who, for all his cockiness, was still really sweet.

By some miracle we'd navigated our way to his room, stripping and kissing the entire way, and leaving a trail of discarded clothes in our wake. Not once did he stop touching me, blindly guiding us to his bed until my back hit the mattress.

"Jesus, you have the most amazing body." His eyes roamed over every inch of my skin while he kneeled on the bed above me.

"I'm trying to take this slow, but I really don't think I'm going to be able to."

He looked huge above me, the hard angles of his toned chest and abs more defined as he sucked in slow, deep breaths. I'd seen him with his shirt off, held his cock as I jerked him off, and even with all of that, he was still more impressive than I'd imagined.

"It's not *my* body that's amazing." My hands moved across his chest, the tips of my fingers rippling over each muscle. "I totally see why you're so cocky now; no false advertising here."

Every part of him was spectacular but he didn't give me a chance to continue my appreciation, following me down onto the mattress and covering me with his body. "I'm glad you like what you see. But right now it's kinda gone beyond looking, baby, and I need to taste you."

His mouth pressed against my skin, kissing and licking my neck as his hands snaked down. I loved the way it felt, the greedy kisses followed his hands lower and lower as my breathing got quicker.

"So. Fucking. Hot." He punctuated each word with a kiss, wrapping his fingers around my thighs and spreading them open as he lowered his mouth.

I couldn't even think, his tongue flattening against my core before I fully registered what was happening as a heated moan spilled from my lips.

"Jesus, Justin." My back arched, leaning into him as he alternated between kissing and licking. "That feels so good."

Good was an understatement, my body tingling as my mind took a mental vacation. I'd had men go down on me before, and most of the time it was pretty good. But Justin was on a whole other level, his mouth doing things to me that I didn't even know were possible. It had started slow and languid, picking up speed and intensity before backing off right when I thought I couldn't stand it anymore.

It was like he could read my body, sensing all my cues and giving me just enough to make me feel crazy but not so much to send me over the edge.

Insanity.

Delicious.

Incredible.

Insanity.

"Oh God." My breathing increased, the heat traveling up my spine as he inserted first one finger and then two, pumping as his mouth continued its assault. I wasn't even sure I was still in my body, everything feeling so hypersensitive it was entirely possible my spirit had evacuated.

"Please, Justin, please," I begged, clawing at his shoulders and needing more.

"Mmmhmm," he mumbled against my core, refusing to let me come as he continued to tease. "I love it when you beg."

He was enjoying it, thrilled beyond measure while I was slowly losing my goddamn mind. "Justin, if you don't—"

"If I don't what?" he asked, thrusting his fingers in deeper as his thumb circled my clit. "I think I'm doing exactly what I should be."

The sadist smiled, dropping his mouth back between my legs as I felt myself explode.

"Oh God, oh God," I panted, my fingers gripping his hair as my body shook. It was too much, the waves of pleasure unrelenting as his tongue slowed, showing me mercy.

"You're so beautiful when you come." He moved his mouth back up my body, keeping his fingers buried inside me as he kissed up my torso. "I could get off just from watching you."

His voice was desperate, raspy, and dripping with so much need it made me feel powerful. I liked it, knowing he was on a hair trigger and I'd been the one to cause it.

"Nope, I want to be the one who gets you off." I pulled at his body, pressing my tits to his chest as I rubbed against him. He was rock hard, a groan escaping his lips as I slid my slick center up and down his shaft.

My legs wrapped around his waist, keeping him caged as I rocked my hips. Each glide up and down got him harder, his cock pulsing against me as he sucked in hard ragged breaths.

"Tessa," he breathed out on a growl. "Either I put on a condom right the hell now or I'm going to fuck you without one. I've never done that before, but I swear, if you don't stop, you're going to be my first."

It was tempting, the idea of him plunging into me bare so freaking appealing. But I resisted, knowing it was the sex endorphins talking and I wasn't in the right mind to be making those decisions.

I kissed his neck, my hands sliding down his chest as I circled my hips. "Please tell me you have one, I need you inside of me."

He cursed, a string of "fucks" dropping from his lips as his hand reached between us and steadied my hips. "I'm serious, Tessa. You're driving me crazy and I want you so fucking bad."

"I want you too, Justin." His eyes darkened as I said his name, both of us panting as he reached into his nightstand and pulled out a condom.

His body lifted off me, shuffling to his knees as he tore open the packet and slid the latex down his shaft. He didn't waste time with theatrics, back on me the moment he was covered and teasing my opening with his cock.

The heat in his gaze intensified as he slowly sunk into me, my name halfway between a gasp and a moan as it spilled from his lips.

"Yes," I begged, the sweet friction intoxicating. "More."

"You feel so good," he gritted out as he withdrew and then plunged back in. "So. Fucking. Good."

My head nodded, my ability to speak lost with each thrust of his hips.

If I thought what he'd done with his mouth and his hands had been amazing, it wasn't even close to how hot and wet he was making me with his cock. And either I'd forgotten how awesome it could be or it had never been that good.

"God, you're beautiful. You've been all I could think about since that night at the bar." His lips dropped to mine as he took my mouth, the taste of me still on his tongue. "I want to go slow with you, Tessa, but I just can't." It was an apology, the precursor as his muscles tightened and he unleashed.

It was raw, primal—the two of us in a tangle of sweat-soaked limbs as we battled to set the tempo. I wasn't even sure who was in control, our bodies rocking as we clawed at each other like savages.

"Justin," I warned, fairly positive I was either going to come or lose my goddamn mind. "Don't stop, please don't stop."

"Never," he ground out. "Not when I can feel how close you are."

With one last push he sent me over the edge, my fingernails digging into his back as my whole body seized.

Yes.

Yes.

Yes.

I wasn't sure if I was saying it or just thinking it, everything tingling inside as wave after wave of euphoria washed over me.

"Fuck, Tessa," he cursed, sucking in a hard breath as he thrust into me. And that was all it took, his cock pulsing inside of me as he too found his finish, both of us panting out of control.

I couldn't move.

Partly because Justin was plastered on top of me, and partly because I was positive my legs no longer worked. Something in me had probably short-circuited, every nerve in my body feeling like it had been electrocuted.

Speaking was also out of the question, my vocabulary reduced to a series of whimpers as I kissed him.

"So much for lunch, huh?" Justin chuckled, pushing himself up on his arms and lifting off me. "I promise I'll still feed you."

Food was the last thing on my mind, the confliction of feelings and emotions tumbling in my head as I laid underneath him. I'd always suspected he'd be good in bed, but he was so far beyond that.

"It better be good, Tibbs," I warned, slightly concerned he wasn't going to be as excited to have me spend the night since we'd already had sex. "Because if you dragged my ass into the city for a mediocre burger, I'm going to be pissed."

Would he even want me to stick around? Want more? Or was the thrill of the chase over and he'd be looking for an excuse to push me out the door. And even with the uncertainty of where I stood, I didn't even regret it, too buzzed from how good it had been.

"Relax, Ricci, you're in Manhattan now. Nothing mediocre about anything here." He leaned down and kissed me gently. "We can go out or order in, it can totally be your choice."

He didn't seem any different, and either was pacing himself or he wasn't in a hurry to get rid of me.

Interesting.

"Let's go out," I offered, curious to see what the rest of the day had in store. And considering we'd never really discussed what the hell either of us were doing, I wasn't exactly sure if the sex was a one-time deal or if it was something that would happen again. I knew what I wanted, and that was for it *not* to be over.

There was no way I could deny the magnetic pull of Justin Tibbs, something I'd been fighting for a long time. And even though I'd tried to talk myself out of it, there was no way I could pretend that sleeping with him wasn't amazing. I wouldn't feel bad about it either, willing to accept the outcome and deal with it like an adult. After all, he hadn't promised me anything, and I walked into it knowing exactly who he was.

"Perfect," his grin widened, "let's get cleaned up and then we'll head out."

With the decision made, he gently pulled out of me and rolled to his side. His lips lingered on my shoulder before planting his feet on the floor and lifting himself off the mattress. "Wanna get a shower with me?" His brow lifted suggestively as he held out his hand.

Guess it *wasn't* just a one-time deal for him either.

"Surrrrrrre." My lips twisted in a grin, not even pretending I didn't know what plans he had for inside that shower. "Let's go shower."

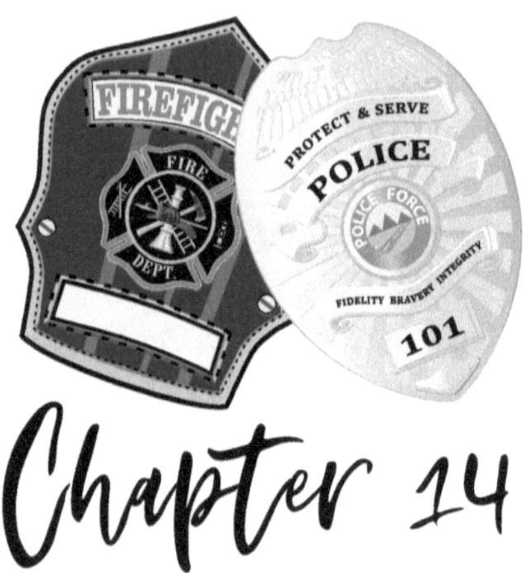

Chapter 14

TESSA RICCI'S BODY was perfect.

Seriously, there wasn't one thing about it I'd change. Everything from her tight abs and ass, to her amazing tits and toned legs.

And touching her was my new favorite hobby.

While my efforts to not jump right into bed with her had been commendable, I had to admit, I wasn't that strong. And who wrote the rules that a ridiculous physical attraction meant all we'd ever be was fuck buddies?

I'll tell you who, nobody.

All of it was complete bullshit, and while I absolutely wanted more than just sex with Tessa, there was no reason we had to deny ourselves either. And judging by the way she touched me, I'd say we were pretty much on the same page.

Neither of us could keep our hands off each other in the shower. The washing took a back seat as I made her come with my mouth and hands at least two more times before finally shampooing her hair. And when it was her turn to wash me, she gave me a blowjob that was as close to a religious experience as I've ever had.

Jesus.

That mouth.

It was almost unhealthy how much I was obsessed with her and that fucking mouth. Even when she was giving me shit, I loved it, hungry for every stupid thing that came from between those gorgeous lips.

Once we were both dressed and decent, we left my apartment and headed out. It hadn't even seemed weird, my hands gravitating to her as we walked to Gino's, finding myself pulling her closer to me as we said hi to Vera and got seated at a table.

"This is the best you got?" She smirked, glancing over the laminated menu.

Like us, Ricci and her station had more than their fair share of Gino's. The family-owned pizza place liked feeding first responders; we appreciated good food at decent prices, and they always made our orders a priority. Hell, they could have a pie from their oven to our stationhouse in less than ten minutes, and whenever one of us walked in, there was never a wait time. Which was why even though there were fancier places I would've liked to take her, we'd ended up at Gino's. We'd already blown way past lunchtime, and if we didn't eat soon, I was worried one of us was going to turn to cannibalism.

"Listen, we could have totally gone to that new Italian place in the Village, but you distracted me in the shower. You've only got yourself to blame." I could barely contain my grin.

"Me?" she scoffed, "I think you'll find it was *you* who started that. I was just minding my business, trying to get clean and you were—hands everywhere—intent on making us even later. And for the record, Tibbs, this isn't even close to lunch." She chuckled as she tapped her watch.

"Yeah, you tell yourself whatever you need to, Ricci. We'll just pretend you didn't put on that show with your tits and the bodywash. Not sure how I was expected to ignore that?" I laughed, shrugging like I hadn't enjoyed every single second of it.

It didn't even feel like a date, the conversation and the atmosphere so effortless it was like I was hanging out with Leighton. And that was rare, usually feeling like I needed to impress a girl or watch what I said or did, but with Tessa there was none of that. There was no pretense, no bullshit, and even though we'd had sex, she was still the same wiseass cop I'd always thought was pretty awesome.

"What are you smiling at?" she asked, lowering her menu. Not sure why we were even bothering with the charade, I was almost positive we were both getting pizza. "You have a weird smirk on your face, and I don't trust it." Her finger pointed accusingly at my mouth.

Yeah, whatever we were doing sure as hell wasn't just dating.

"You have issues," I chuckled. "You've clearly spent too much time with criminals and deviants if you think a smile is a bad thing." I dropped my own menu, folding my arms across my chest. "I'm smiling because it feels good, Ricci, no ulterior motive."

Part of that was a lie.

Sure, it felt good to smile but it was more about how *she* made me feel. And since I didn't fully understand it myself, I didn't want to go ahead and advertise it. Besides, the last thing I wanted to do was change how easy it was between us.

She shrugged, not fully buying my explanation. "Whatever, just as long as you don't expect me to participate. Because, hello, that's just fucking weird."

I laughed.

Couldn't have stopped myself even if I'd tried, loving she said whatever the hell she was thinking. There were no games, and that was so fucking refreshing I couldn't believe how much I didn't want it to end.

"Hey Tibbs, Ricci." Brooke, our waitress, lowered two plastic tumblers of water in front of us. "Ready to order or you need some more time?" She turned to Tessa before adding, "And by the way, I love your hair like that. You should wear it down more often."

Tessa—who apparently had no issue smiling for Brooke—grinned. "Thanks, but Cap will have my ass if I show up for a shift with it down. Uniform regulations."

Brooke nodded in sympathy. "Uniform regulations suck. Not to say I don't get it, but seriously, it's just hair, right?"

"Right," Tessa agreed.

It would have been easy for her to correct Brooke and let her know why those regs existed. That apart from uniform regulations being in place so we looked professional and represented our units in the best way possible, it was also about safety. But Tessa didn't go out of her way to make people feel bad, even if she knew she was right. It was something I'd noticed but never paid much attention to, her tendency to let things slide rather than make an issue. Funny how I'd never really appreciated it before.

"Tibbs?" Tessa asked, her raised brow hinting it hadn't been the first time she'd said my name.

"Huh? Sorry, wasn't paying attention," I admitted, not wanting to give her anything but the truth. "What were you saying?"

Tessa rolled her eyes, shooting Brooke a grin like they were sharing some inside joke. "I said, I'm getting the cheese pizza and a serving of mozzarella sticks. Did you want a beer or soda?"

She hadn't even asked me what I'd wanted to order. Getting the cheese pizza because she knew I was a purest and didn't like extra toppings screwing up my pie, and the mozzarella sticks because who didn't like fried cheese dipped in marinara? It was what I usually ordered when we came in as a group, and I guess she'd been paying attention.

"Beer, draft," I offered, a warm feeling spreading across my chest as I handed Brooke back the menu. "Thanks."

"Make that two. Thanks so much, say hi to your uncle in the kitchen for us." Tessa smiled, also handing back her menu.

Could it really be that easy?

Because if little things like remembering my order made me feel like a rock star, then how awesome was it going to be when she actually did something big? No wonder Leighton and North had been so hardcore, selling the virtues of relationships. Clearly, I'd been doing it wrong because this was nothing like I'd ever had.

"So," I rubbed my hands together, itching to reach across the table and touch her some more. "What are your plans for the rest of the week? I know you have work for the next five days. But what about the mornings before you start?"

I wasn't willing to wait until the weekend to spend time with her, knowing that with our schedules it wasn't going to be easy. I'd take a few hours when I was rotated off before she had to head in if that was all I could get, the idea of not seeing her, surprisingly depressing.

Yeah, that wasn't going to work for me. And fuck pretending it did.

"Well, usually I like to head to my dad's gym, laundry, grocery shop." She shrugged not fully understanding what I was asking. "The usual. Why? What did you have in mind?"

"I really want to see you. You think we can make that happen?" I stopped fighting the urge and laced my fingers in hers. Why the hell had I even been resisting it in the first place? Being with her—touching her—felt good. And even though no one would assume we were a couple just because we were together—cops and firefighters had a tendency to hang out—I wanted to clear up the misconception she was *just* a friend.

Her beautiful brown eyes lifted as they connected with mine, her teeth playing with her bottom lip. It was the first time I'd seen her hesitate, the flash of uncertainty not making me feel good.

"Sure, we can see each other." She nodded, her voice missing the confliction she'd given me with her eyes. And I wasn't sure exactly which one of them to trust.

Had I been more honorable, I might have tried to find out. But she'd already agreed, and I wasn't going to be stupid by trying to extrapolate the whys.

Fuck it.

We'd work it out as we went along, because I didn't like the alternative.

"You could try and sound a little more enthusiastic, Ricci." I leaned in closer, hoping I'd make her smile again. "I thought we agreed I need to be told how awesome I am."

Her lips twitched at the edges, fighting the grin. "You're so needy, Tibbs."

Usually I couldn't wait to get back to work, the two days off rotation dragging ass until I could head back to the station. It wasn't only because I loved my job—which I did—but I honestly loved the crew I worked with, as well. There wasn't one of them I'd trade, and even on a bad day, there wasn't anywhere else I'd rather be.

But it was hard to get out of bed when morning came, Tessa's warm body still curled up against mine when my alarm went off.

After Gino's we'd wandered around Midtown for a while just like we had in Brooklyn. There'd been no real plan or direction, her body gravitating toward mine as we walked. I'd barely even noticed that I'd had my arm around her the whole time, my hand anchored on her hip as we slowly made our way back to my apartment. Not once had there been an awkward silence or strained tension, the natural cadence of our conversation ebbing and flowing with no fucking effort.

But once we got inside, all bets were off. Neither of us able to keep our hands off each other as we left a trail of clothes on the floor, barely making it to my bed before we fucked like animals.

It had been fast and desperate, the need to be inside her so intense I thought my balls were going to explode. I loved that I didn't have to be careful with her, her groans of approval as I muscled her around the bed making me even harder.

But I could do slow and deliberate too, something I was able to demonstrate once we finally got underneath the covers. I'd pulled her on top, mesmerized by the sway of her perfect tits while she slowly circled her hips as she rode me.

If I'd died when I closed my eyes, I'd have gone a happy man. There was nothing I felt I needed to prove, nothing I'd rather be doing, and loving the delicious ache in my muscles from satisfying what had to be the most beautiful woman I'd ever seen. The warmth of her body pressed against mine made me feel like I was a fucking god as I fell asleep, the smile on my face both physical and metaphorical.

Only when it was time for me to slide out of bed and leave her, that the sense of disappointment settled in.

She looked so peaceful, her wild brown hair splayed out on my pillow, her body automatically rolling to my side of the bed once I'd vacated it. I wanted to crawl back in, to wrap those limbs around me and kiss her slowly until she opened those gorgeous brown eyes. I wanted to run my fingers down her back, feel the softness of her skin underneath my calloused hands, watch in awe at the strength in her muscles as she stretched and flexed.

It was the reason I was almost late, making it to the station just in time to stuff my backpack in my locker before Mack started his briefing.

"Nice of you to join us, Tibbs." The chief shot me a pointed look. "You need me to wait until you get situated? Get you a coffee? Roll out the red carpet?"

"Nah, Chief, I'm all good," I laughed, sinking into a seat as I shook off the sarcasm. The chief had a tendency to be prickly in the mornings, but not even his surly mood was going to ruin mine. "Carry on." I waved my hand, watching as he swore under his breath before continuing.

It wasn't until the briefing was over that North and Leighton cornered me.

"Didn't hear from you yesterday. What kept you so busy?" Leighton grinned like he already knew the answer.

"Really, North?" I glared at him, assuming he'd been the one who'd talked. "I figured you and Quinn would discuss me and Ricci, not start a phone tree."

North laughed, holding up his hands. "Hey, I didn't tell him shit. I was just standing here because I wanted to watch you squirm. You just copped to that all on your own."

Fucking Riley North.

It wasn't the first time the asshole had tricked me into admitting shit I hadn't planned. But since it was out there, I wasn't going to hide it either. "Fine, I was with Tessa." I lifted my chin, liking the way those words sounded as they came out of my mouth.

"Wow, Tibbs," Leighton wiped a fake tear from the corner of his eye, "I'm your best friend and you told North before me? I thought I meant something to you?"

The bastard was grinning, trying to stifle a laugh as he pretended to give me the third degree.

"Yeah, yeah," my hand shoved his shoulder roughly, "Well, you know now. And I like her, we're going to be spending a lot more time together."

"Has she been informed?" North chuckled. "While I'm glad you finally got your head out of your ass and worked it out, it is customary for you to tell the girl involved she's in a relationship."

The two of them were so fucking smug. Grinning like assholes and completely amused by the news that I had finally found a woman I really liked. And if I hadn't had the most awesome night ever, it might've bothered me. And considering I'd already made plans to go see her as soon as I finished my shift, I just couldn't work up a shit to give.

"Yes, she fucking knows." I rolled my eyes as I flipped them off. "Anything else? Or should we go get some work done before Mack tears us a new one?"

North shrugged. "I'm good, Leighton?"

"Yep, me too." Leighton nodded.

"Awesome, now let's get moving before one of us ends up in Mack's office."

As much as I loved the chief, the idea of sitting down and getting yelled at for a solid ten to fifteen minutes didn't fill me with joy. Besides, I was already itching to check my phone to see if Tessa had woken up and I didn't want to do it in front of an audience.

North tipped his chin in agreement and then headed out the door, leaving me with Leighton who I was positive had more to say.

"Hey." I got in first, figuring I owed him at least a partial explanation. "It wasn't personal me going to talk to North. It's just I know you and Presley don't get a lot of time together, and to be honest, I didn't want to walk in on you fucking my sister."

Leighton laughed, slapping me on the back before cupping my shoulder. "Dude, firstly, do not talk about Presley like that. You know I love you, man, but you cheapen my relationship with your sister like that and I'm going to have to teach you some manners." The bastard grinned, but I didn't think for a second he wasn't serious. "And I don't care that you went to North instead of me, I'm just glad you spoke to someone. Tessa is amazing. Not only is she a kickass cop, but one of the coolest women we know. I'm fucking ecstatic for you. I'm glad you're done playing the field and found yourself someone to make an honest man out of you. I was starting to worry."

That was the thing about Leighton, he was just genuinely pleased for other people's happiness, and why he'd always been such a good friend. I couldn't have asked for a better man to marry my sister, or as a brother to be in my corner.

"Thanks, buddy. Being with her feels like the most natural thing in the world," I confessed. "It doesn't even feel like we're dating, she's just so awesome. I'm not even sure how the hell I've known her all this time and didn't realize. She was right there, dude, right in front of me." I shook my head, unable to comprehend how many times we'd hung out and I'd never given her a second thought. "I feel bad for saying it, but thank fuck Miller's chick cheated on him. If she hadn't been out at the bar trying to get him laid, some other lucky asshole would have her."

"Yeah, funny how things work out, huh? Guess some things are meant to be." Leighton folded his arms across his chest looking pretty smug.

"Do not start with the fate talk, asshole. I'm not that far gone," I warned, refusing to believe there was some predetermined plan for anything, especially not my life. And if there had been, I could have used the intervention with that crazy chick I'd dated when I was nineteen.

Leighton laughed, punching me in the arm. "Why don't we wait and see before you start making wide sweeping statements. Now, if we're done proving that I was right, we should go start testing those radios."

I didn't bother arguing, secretly hoping he *was* right. I'd never really worried about losing a woman or the possibility of ending a relationship. Hell, half the time I was more concerned with trying to make sure I didn't get into one. But the thought of not having Tessa in my life was something I couldn't even contemplate.

Nope.

I didn't want casual with her. And I was going to enjoy spending as much time as possible with the most amazing woman I'd ever met.

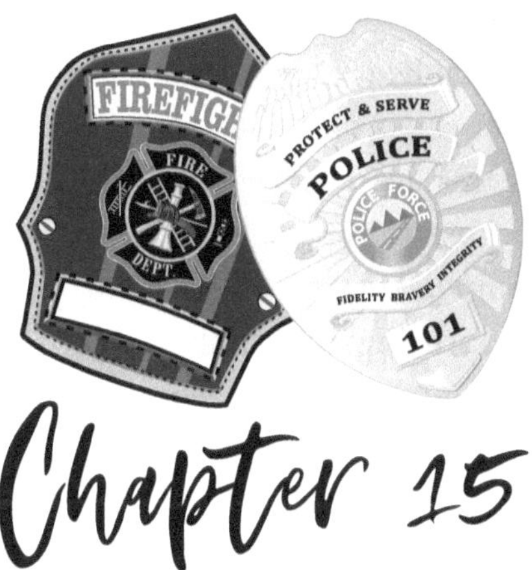

Chapter 15

Tessa

"SO, YOU AND Tibbs?" Miller coughed out before clarifying. "*Justin* Tibbs, the firefighter we've known for years who you said would be the last guy on earth you'd date."

While Grayson had known Justin and I had been spending time together, he had no idea we'd gone beyond just hanging out. "Okay, Okay." I shook my head, the memory of saying those words not that far in the past. "But that was because I thought he was a manwhore with no redeeming qualities. And since getting to know him better, well . . . he is kind of cool."

Kind of cool was an understatement, Justin Tibbs was more amazing than I could have even imagined. He was funny and smart, and didn't back down from a confrontation. The last part was important, especially considering most men found me "difficult" to handle. He didn't even blink, my "intense" personality not seeming to be a problem for him, which was probably the most attractive thing about him. And considering the man was hot with a body that was so sexy it should be illegal, that was saying a lot.

"Really?" Miller's head turned to me, his brow raising. "So he *isn't* a manwhore? Because I seem to remember you being pretty adamant that he was."

He was right about that. I hadn't exactly been silent on my opinion, my partner and best friend often subjected to my views on who Tibbs chose to screw. And most of those views hadn't exactly been complimentary.

"Well, I was being incredibly judgmental, wasn't I?" I argued, knowing my bias might have been more than a little slanted by my unresolved feelings for him. Hey, I wasn't perfect and never claimed to be, so yeah, part of my distaste *might* have been peppered by jealousy. "After all, how is it my business how many women he slept with? It wasn't like he was in a relationship and he was cheating on anyone. And I've not heard one of them complain or torch his house, so I assume he didn't lie to them either."

I wasn't thrilled that he'd probably slept with more people in a month than I had in my entire life, but I couldn't hold that against him either. We'd both made choices, and neither of us was an authority on who was right. And while I was being slightly defensive with Miller, I wasn't wrong either.

"That's true, he either has the most impressive penis these women have ever seen, and they're hypnotized by his magic dick. *Or* he isn't a complete asshole." Grayson agreed, neither of us having ever witnessed a girl going full psycho on him. Hell, most of them stayed friendly, casually waving hello with a smile when they saw him in the aftermath. It was something I'd often wondered about but hadn't let myself delve too deeply into. Because . . . yeah, I'd been jealous. Sue me.

"Yep. Not a complete asshole." I nodded, refusing to make any comments remotely connected to Tibbs and his dick. I loved Grayson, but talking about Justin's cock while in a squad car felt a little like crossing a line.

Miller shook his head, chuckling. "You've already slept with him, haven't you?"

So much for not crossing the line at work.

"What?" I scoffed, trying to laugh it off. "What are you talking about? I said we went to my dad's gym and we hung out over a couple of days. I never said—"

"Save it, Ricci," he lifted his hand, cutting me off, "I know you, and you and him have definitely done the deed. It's written all over your face."

I could have tried to deny it. Or even pretended to be indignant about it, reminding Grayson that it was no one's business who I slept with. But squad car, uniform and inappropriate workplace conversation notwithstanding, he did know me better than anyone. And even I had to admit I had a stupid, dopey grin on my face just thinking about that crazy fireman.

"Fine, we slept together. It was amazing. You want the minute-by-minute replay, you pervert?" I shoved his shoulder as I chuckled.

"Ewwww, um no," he coughed out. "I'm still trying to get my head around you liking the guy and *not* thinking he's a douche. I don't think my poor innocent brain could cope with whatever depravity the two of you are involved in."

My brows rose, settling into my seat as my grin widened. "Good, because it was *pretty* depraved. His place in Midtown has a secret dungeon room. Lots of kinky shit."

Grayson's eyes widened in horror, tightening his grip on the wheel. "Jesus, Tessa. While I think you're probably kidding, there's a part of me that can't be sure. And I'm going to have to look at the guy now and fucking wonder."

"That's what you get for bringing up his magic dick." I shrugged, a strange sense of contentment spreading across my chest. I was glad I'd told Grayson about Tibbs even if I wasn't entirely sure what kind of relationship I'd entered into. And it wasn't like me not to be sure of something.

It wasn't like I was Type A anal, needing a plan for every scenario. I loved being spontaneous and thought some of the best decisions were the ones you made with your gut on a moment's notice. But I'd never been with a guy and not known if he was my boyfriend or just someone I was sleeping with. I'd done both with some irregularity, but I usually had it worked out before we'd had sex.

With Tibbs, not so much.

It didn't feel like a regular fuck buddy situation, but I'd never slept with a guy like Justin Tibbs before either.

"So this something serious then?" Grayson asked the very question I didn't think I could answer. "I'm not trying to be a downer, but we see those guys all the time. And I know you can take care of yourself, Tessa, but I don't want you to get hurt either."

I sighed, trying to forget there was a chance that things wouldn't always be awesome between me and Justin, and it wouldn't be as easy as a regular break up. We worked in the same precinct, there would be cross over. I'd have to see him even if I didn't want to. "I don't know, Grayson," I admitted, shaking my head. "I just really like him. I don't have to pretend when I'm around him. I don't have to filter or tone myself down."

It was something I always considered whenever I met someone new. Whether I eased them in, letting them get comfortable before they got to see the real me. Or just threw caution to the wind and said fuck it. I hadn't even contemplated the choice with Tibbs, it was just us. And God, that was fucking sexy.

Grayson nodded, knowing firsthand there were no guarantees. He'd had his heart broken more times than was fair, and every single time he'd sworn it had been different. "You know what, Ricci. Good for you." He shot me a grin. "You keep doing whatever makes you happy and if he turns out to be a prick, we'll get Vinnie's cousins to take care of him."

"Vinnie's cousins are in construction." I laughed, the joke that one of our coworker's family had mob ties, not a new one.

"Exactly," Grayson agreed. "And a lot of problems can be solved with enough concrete, Ricci."

I laughed, glad Miller had been able to lighten the mood. "Deal. I'll be sure to let him know next time I see him."

"Why you guys gotta be up in my business all the time? I'm not doing anything wrong!" Madison whined, wriggling in the backseat. "I've got bills to pay, are you two assholes going to keep my lights on and food in my fridge? No, no you're not. So why the hell can't you just let me earn an honest living?"

Miller shook his head, shooting me a look as I peered over my shoulder at the disheveled redhead trying to twist her wrists out of the cuffs. Not sure how many times we'd told her that there was no way to get out of them without a key. And considering it was the third time in a month we'd picked up Madison Norris for prostitution, you'd think she'd know the drill.

"There's lots of jobs that don't involve you accepting money for sex, Madison. And what the hell is with the meth? You know we're going to have to add possession this time too." Miller was annoyed, more because he knew that Madison wasn't necessarily a bad person, but she couldn't keep clean. We'd tried to get her help, given her flyers for programs and clinics, and even let her off with a warning a couple of times. But it always ended the same way, the thirty-year-old sucking dick in an alley somewhere or screwing some guy in a parking lot.

"I told you it wasn't mine," she pouted, giving up trying to remove her metal bracelets and sitting up straighter in the seat. "You know I only do cocaine. I mean, I smoke, and occasionally I celebrate with some Molly, but that doesn't even really count.

But I've never touched Meth, that stuff will make ya crazy. I don't even know how it even got in my pocket. Someone must have planted it. Come on, guys, you know I don't lie."

She was right about that. For all her faults, she always copped to whatever the hell she was doing. She might have disagreed on whether or not it should be legal, but she never denied it.

Miller shrugged, probably guessing like I did that there was more to the story. "Well, once we get to the station you can try and get it straightened out," I offered, conceding that it could have possibly been one of her "dates." Not that it would make much difference, she was still probably going to be spending time behind bars at least until morning.

We'd just cruised past the fire station on W 38th when the external lights lit up, the bay doors opening as the engines got ready to go out on a call. Tibbs was probably already in his turnouts looking ridiculously sexy, and I had to fight the urge not to smile as I tried to imagine myself peeling them off him. I'll admit I wasn't immune to the allure of the uniform, but thinking about him in it was what really did it for me.

"Someone's lit something on fire," Madison tsked, shaking her head. "I hope those boys are being safe, especially now North is a daddy. I swear I'd give that man as many babies as he wanted, either him or Tibbs. I ain't that picky."

It wasn't a surprise she knew the guys or their names, especially since it had been on more than one occasion they'd been called when she'd OD'd. And for as much as Mack pretended to be a hard ass, he—like us—tried to do what he could for the people in our community. It was also not a shock that she had a thing for Riley North. Being married with a baby hadn't changed his popularity with the ladies, and even I could appreciate how good-looking he was.

But hearing her mention Tibbs made my gut twist. Not because I thought he'd ever been with her—it would be a cold day in hell before Tibbs would ever have to pay for sex. But just the idea that someone else wanted to have his babies.

I didn't even know if Tibbs wanted kids.

Hell, I didn't even know if *I* wanted kids.

But I didn't want to imagine him having them with someone else. In fact, I didn't want to imagine him doing *anything* with someone else. And considering I hadn't even established if we were exclusive or not, that was probably a problem.

"You don't want to have babies, Madison." Miller's eyes shot to me, probably reading my expression. "Too much responsibility. They cry all the time and cost a fortune. And considering you just told us you're already having trouble paying your bills, I'd say adding another mouth to feed isn't a wise choice."

I wasn't sure if he was actually trying to convince her that parenthood wasn't for her or change the focus from her sleeping with Tibbs, but I had to admire his effort.

Madison sighed. "Yeah, you're probably right. Besides, I hear those little fuckers rip up your vagina."

Miller and I both laughed, and I was glad the conversation moved away from Madison procreating with the guy I had complicated feelings about to her vagina.

There was *one* thing Madison and I could agree on, and that was hoping Tibbs, North, and everyone else came back safe. It was always a risk, something Miller and I faced too. But I knew they would be careful, his cockiness and bravery backed up by training and experience. And if ever there was a time I was in a burning building needing help, there wasn't anyone else I'd trust with my life.

It was only after we got Madison processed back at the station that Miller pulled me aside. "I thought you were going to jump in the back and go a few rounds when she mentioned having a baby with Tibbs." He chuckled, laughing now there was no danger of a police brutality charge on his watch. "I don't know what is more shocking to me. That Madison was considering having babies or how jealous you were at the suggestion."

"Fine," I admitted, throwing my hands up in the air and moving him away from where other officers could hear. "I was jealous. You don't have to be so pleased by it. If anything, it proves I'm human just like everyone else."

"Nah, I hear they program shit like that into AI now and I've seen you work out. I'm still not convinced you're one of us." His shoulder nudged mine. "Let's get back on the road, Ricci. You can even text your boyfriend while I drive, and I'll pretend not to notice."

I rolled my eyes, more at myself than Miller, because he wasn't wrong. I did want to text Justin, maybe even talk to him, and I'd never been one of those girls. "Fine, let's go."

When I'd gone to Midtown with Tibbs, I'd left my car back in Brooklyn which meant Miller had to drive me home. He didn't even mention the overnight bag I had with me, ignoring the obvious as he said goodbye and that he'd see me later.

I showered and then crawled into bed, falling asleep pretty much as soon as my head hit the pillow. I didn't even dream, my mind flatlining into blackness which was a welcome relief. I'd spent too much time overthinking, and while I'd texted Tibbs—casually, completely not like a crazy obsessed girlfriend—and he'd texted back, there had been so much more I'd wanted to say.

It was sometime around eight when I was startled awake from a dead sleep.

"What the hell?" I looked around for my phone, wrongly thinking it was ringing before realizing it was the buzzer from my front door.

With my eyes still mostly closed, I pulled on a T-shirt and a pair of sweatpants, figuring answering the door naked wouldn't be a good look for a law enforcement officer. It wasn't until I pulled it open that it occurred to me that my early morning visitor would have probably preferred me naked.

"Ricci." Tibbs didn't wait for an invitation, stepping across my threshold and pulling me in for a hug. "Please tell me you don't sleep in that when I'm not around. I had to bribe one of your neighbors to let me into the building and now worry I've made a huge mistake. I jerked off thinking about you in a pair of lacy panties and this ensemble will totally ruin my fantasy."

"I was naked, you jerk," I scoffed, leaning my head against his chest and breathing in the comforting smell of soap and shampoo. He'd showered before he'd come over, his hair still a little damp.

"Mmmmmmm, now that I can work with." He chuckled, pulling me closer to his body. "Let's say we take you back to bed and let me experience the brilliance for myself."

My lips spread into a smile, unable to stop themselves even though I was cranky from being woken. "You get naked first." I tugged at his T-shirt pulling him toward my bedroom. "I need something to fantasize about too when I'm alone."

A low growl traveled up his throat as he pulled off his T-shirt and then went straight for his jeans. "Baby, the idea of you touching yourself and thinking about me is so unbelievably hot. Even if you don't do it, I want you to lie to me and say you do."

I laughed watching as he kicked off the rest of his clothes while I slowly stripped off mine. It didn't take long considering I wasn't wearing underwear, my sweats and T-shirt joining his pile on the floor.

"No need for lies, Justin. And maybe if you're a good boy, I'll even let you watch." I laid on the mattress, holding open the covers for Tibbs to join me.

"Fuuuuuuccck," he groaned against my neck. "Screw jerking off to you in the lace panties, I know exactly what I'll be thinking about next time I get myself off."

His lips pressed against my skin; the kisses soft as they moved from my throat to my jaw. "How was your night? Arrest many bad guys?" His hand moved down to my hip and pulled me closer. "I'm still up for being cuffed if you're into it. Just don't be an asshole and leave me hanging because that would totally not be cool."

"My night was fine. Nothing exciting. And standard issue aren't the same as what you're thinking," I chuckled, running my hand down his chest. "They hurt and leave bruising. Trust me when I tell you there is nothing remotely sexual about being cuffed with *real* handcuffs."

He kissed the top of my head and I felt his lips spread into a grin. "Sounds like that's spoken from experience. You just keep giving me more material. What else have you got to confess, dirty girl?"

"Not like *that*, moron." I nuzzled against him, loving being able to just lay with him and talk. "It was part of training. Like I said, nothing sexual, and it hurt like hell."

Even though we were both naked and in bed, it had yet to progress to sex. And while I very much wanted his hands, mouth, and cock all over me making me feel good, I liked what we were doing just as much.

"How was your shift? Miller and I were on our way back to the station when we saw you guys heading out."

He let out a long breath, and I could tell he was tired. "Day started slow and then we got slammed. I wanted to call you but there just wasn't the time. Anyway, lucky for you I decided to come over and keep you company."

"Lucky for you, I let you in," I argued back. "How pissed would you have been if I didn't answer my door?" I raised my brow knowing there wasn't a chance I'd have turned him down.

His lips moved to my mouth, kissing me slowly before pulling back and smirking. "Ricci, I'm a *fireman*. You think I don't know how to get inside a locked apartment? You really don't give me enough credit."

He kissed me again—deep and more urgent—rolling onto his back and pulling me on top of him. "Now, are you ready to see what other skills I have? Or you want to pretend a little longer you didn't miss me as much as I missed you?"

"I did miss you," I admitted, lowering my lips to his. My fingers threaded themselves into his hair as I settled between his legs.

"Good, I like that. Because I missed you too. And while I know I've only got a few hours with you before you have to go work, I'm going to take advantage of every last second." His hands moved down my back, pulling me against him.

"I only have one more question, and then you can do whatever you want." My hands reached back to his, stopping him from going any further before I got it out.

I didn't want there to be any more doubts, no chance of any misunderstandings or the possibility of conflicting ideas. Whatever it was we were doing was fine, but I had to know.

"Mmmm, whatever I want?" he groaned, his voice husky as he rocked his hard-on under me. "What's the question, baby?"

"Are you going to see other people?" I was as unemotive as I could be, trying not to hold my breath as I waited for his answer. Deep down I knew I'd be disappointed if he said yes, but I wasn't going to live in ignorance either.

He stopped, his hands stilling as his smile dropped. "You mean other women?"

I nodded, prompting him to go on.

"I don't fuck around, Tessa. Not if I'm with someone. And I'm with you. I don't even want to think about being with someone else, let alone actually doing it." His voice was devoid of his usual humor and sarcasm, his fingers lightly tracing my jaw. "I hate that you had to ask, but I'm glad you did instead of assuming."

"I'm sorry, I just . . . we just—"

"I know," he cut me off, his smile returning. "I hadn't planned any of this either, baby, so I get it. And like I said, I'm glad you asked. No one else, okay? Just you."

"No one else, just you," I repeated, dropping my mouth back to his.

"Yeah, I already knew *that*," he mumbled against my lips, chuckling. "Why would you look for a substitute when you already have the very best?"

"You are so conceited," I groaned, shaking my head as I buried it against the crook of his neck.

"And yet . . . not wrong."

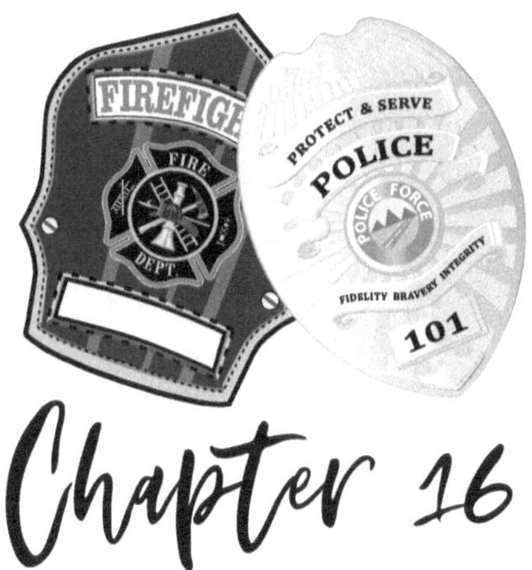

Chapter 16

Justin

TURNS OUT, OUR varying schedules weren't that big of a deal.

Yeah, it sucked our days off weren't always the same, but we made it work, using the time we did have productively.

I'd even started training with her at her old man's gym. I still wasn't sure the guy liked me, but I wasn't going to hide like a chicken shit either. And watching Tessa kick ass was not something I wanted to miss.

Seriously, she was incredible. Not only was she strong and explosive, but she was also technically good and ridiculously fast. No wonder her dad hadn't been worried about her getting into the ring with me; unless she was drunk or incapacitated, she could more than hold her own.

"Dude, you *hit* your girlfriend? And she hits you?" Evans looked horrified as we stashed our stuff in our lockers. "That is really fucking messed up."

It had been a few weeks since Tessa and I had started dating, and while we didn't make some bullshit announcement, almost everyone I worked with knew exactly where I was spending most of my free time.

It wasn't even weird hearing the word *girlfriend* anymore, me liking the way it sounded so damn much it made me smile every single time.

Leighton tapped me on the shoulder, grinning like an idiot. "Nah, he needs someone to keep him in line, Evans. Think of the public service Ricci is providing us. Make's the chief's job easier."

"I'll pay her if that helps," Mack called from the door, also wearing a smile. "We can start a collection; positive some of the guys would want in on that action."

I threw back a laugh, not even annoyed they were giving me shit. Because really, what the hell did I care? I was dating the hottest, most awesome woman ever, so they were right to be jealous.

"Whatever gets you through, Chief." I gave him a two-finger salute.

I was more excited than normal, knowing that when I got to her apartment in Brooklyn in the morning, we were going to have two uninterrupted days off together. I loved the idea of being able to wake up with her and neither of us needing to say goodbye; it was a fucking gift that I'd never take for granted.

"Hey, so Presley wants you and Tessa to come over for dinner. She's going in late to the club and thinks it would be fun to get together," Leighton coughed out, clearly tasked by my sister to pass along the invitation.

Presley rarely missed work.

As part-owner and manager of two of the hottest clubs in the city, she didn't have a lot of time for much else. We all understood, applauding her drive and determination even if sometimes she danced a little close to the line of being a workaholic. She'd been getting better about taking some time off here and there, using it to plan her wedding or spend it with Leighton. But you could guarantee she wasn't agreeing to "go in late" to the club because she thought dinner with us would be "fun."

"C'mon, brother," I chuckled shaking my head, "you're forgetting I've known Presley my entire life. She couldn't give a rat's ass about dinner, or having a good time, so why don't we call it what it is. My sister needing more intel because she's not happy with what she's getting from me."

At first, I hadn't said anything, not wanting my sister to interfere. She not only had a healthy relationship with the NYPD and welcomed them in her clubs, but she'd also gotten to know a few of them when the cocksucker she used to date was terrorizing her. Tessa had been one of the cops who'd attended when Presley's apartment was broken into. And they'd had more than just a passing professional admiration for each other. Which meant . . . she'd make it her business even if it didn't need to be.

Of course, she not only seemed to find out all the stationhouse gossip—usually from Leighton—but had a weird sixth sense when I was keeping shit from her. Which meant I had to come clean, tell her I was dating Tessa, and thanks but no thanks, we didn't require her input. Her calm "sure, just as long as you're happy" response hadn't filled me with confidence, and I'd been waiting for the blowback.

Leighton shrugged knowing he was out of his depth when it came to trying to tell Presley what to do. "I swear it's a competition as which of you two is the most stubborn. Just do it, Tibbs. If for no other reason other than she'll stop asking me. Apparently, I *suck at getting details*." He rolled his eyes, probably having heard that statement more than once.

"Tell her I'll talk to Tessa but I'm not making any promises," I agreed, selfishly not wanting to share her on the days we had together. "But even if we don't make dinner, I promise we'll swing by either *Diablo* or *Vault*, whichever she's going to be at. She can interrogate us both while we pay her for the privilege."

It had been a while since I'd been to either of Presley's clubs, and it hadn't even occurred to me until I'd mentioned it. In fact, the last time I'd graced them with my presence had been when I'd seen Tessa at the bar, not recognizing her outside of her uniform. What a night that had been, my cock twitching just at the memory of her in that hot dress. Maybe getting dressed up and taking her out wasn't such a bad idea after all, only this time around, there'd be no doubt who she'd be spending the night with.

"Sounds good. She's at *Vault* all this week. Want to help me do inventory?" His head tipped to the open doorway, most of the guys having already filed out.

"Yep, and get the rookie to help too. We've been too soft on him so far, and while Evans can be the biggest ballbuster of all mankind, he's a decent fireman. We need to do the same with Rizzo."

"Done." Leighton nodded. "I'll meet you in the bays."

I hated waking her.

The stupid buzzer from her door was loud enough to raise the dead at Holy Cross cemetery but was unavoidable. I'd managed to once again sweet talk my way into her building but unless I wanted to make good on my threat of breaking and entering, there was only one way in.

It would've been easier if I had a key. But I wasn't asking, and Tessa hadn't offered, things between us going pretty fucking awesome so far.

"Hey." She yawned, sleepily rubbing her eyes as she opened the door. "I got in late last night and need more sleep, you want to join me?"

She was wearing a rumpled T-shirt she'd obviously pulled on when she'd woken up, her bare legs hinting she'd been sleeping naked. I liked she didn't bother trying to be sexy with lingerie, it was just one more thing to take off and I preferred her bare.

"Is that even a question, Ricci?" I started to undress before she'd even closed the front door. "If there's an option to get into bed with you, I'm always going to take it."

That was absolutely the truth, and I didn't care what we did once we got in there. Whether we cuddled or fucked, it was equally rewarding, the feel of her warm skin pressed against mine, an addiction.

By the time we'd gotten back into her bedroom I was down to my boxer briefs. She smirked as she glanced over her shoulder, shimmying out of that T-shirt more seductively than was necessary. I bit my lip as I watched, my hands desperate to hook around her hips as she wiggled her ass.

"I thought you said you were tired?" I raised a brow, feeling myself get hard by her little display. "That dance isn't conducive to you getting more sleep."

"No?" she gasped, twisting around so she was on full display. She was beautiful; perfect in every single way, and I couldn't believe she was mine. "I bet I could lay right down on this pillow and go right back to sleep. Wanna see?"

Her pretty pink lips spread into a wicked grin as she shuffled onto the mattress, watching with increased interest as I pushed off my boxer briefs and dropped my hand to my cock.

"Sure." I gave myself a stroke, letting my fist glide up and down my shaft slowly as her eyes followed. "Show me."

My cock throbbed in my hand, desperate for more than what I was giving it as I moved closer. Her tongue skated across her lips, making me groan as I knelt on the bed, but she didn't move. Wide brown eyes heated as my curled fingers went from base to tip, circling the head of my dick before moving back down. I liked her watching me, loved seeing her breathing deepen as the tips of those perfect fucking tits hardened without even being touched.

"Show me," I asked again, the words almost a growl behind my caged jaw. "I know you're not all talk, Tessa, so what else have you got?"

She reached forward, her smaller hands covering mine as I continued to jerk off.

"Mmmmmm, that feels good," I groaned, fighting to keep my eyes open because the visual was so hot I didn't want to miss it. "Open your legs for me, I want to see you get wet."

Her feet dropped to the floor as her butt moved to the edge of the bed, her thighs spreading open for me as she lowered her tongue to the head of my cock and swirled around it.

"Fuuuuuck." My muscles tensed, my grip around my hard-on dropping as my fingers threaded into her hair. I loved the slick friction of her mouth, the wet pop as she pulled me from her lips, and the heat of her tongue as she teased.

It was so good.

So fucking good that I almost came right there in her mouth. I didn't though, denying myself the pleasure as I rocked my hips and continued to fuck her mouth. Her eyes widened, taking my length all the way back into her throat as she stroked me with one hand. The other hand—the one not wrapped around my dick—dropped in between her legs and did some stroking of its own.

Fuck it was hot, watching her touch herself, her fingers getting sticky as she got turned on while my cock was buried in her mouth.

A moan passed through her lips, the hum traveling down my shaft and down to my balls as she circled her clit faster. I could tell she was getting closer, the uncoordinated jerking of her hand on my hard-on getting more erratic as her tits pushed up faster with each ragged breath.

I was so fucking torn.

Wanting to come in her mouth, all over her lips, and then make her orgasm on my tongue. But I also wanted to be inside of her in the worst way, feel her pussy fist me tight and explode inside of her as we came together.

She hummed again, the vibrations making me crazy as she struggled to get her lips around me. I knew I had to make the choice, my dick so hard in her mouth that in a minute or two I'd lose the ability.

"I want to fuck you bare," I gritted out, knowing it was probably unfair to ask while my dick was in her mouth and we were both desperate to come, but needing it anyway. "I need to be in you right now, Tessa."

Every single muscle in my body was tense, with my balls so tight against me they were starting to hurt. But if she said no, I'd stop. I'd wear a condom, or I'd fuck her mouth, or I'd lick and suck her until she came on my tongue—whatever she wanted, she'd get, as long as I was the guy who got to give it to her.

"I want you, baby. I. Need. You. So. Fucking. Much." Each word broken into its own sentence, my breaths coming out faster and more desperate as my eyes locked with hers.

She nodded, the seconds between pulling my dick from her mouth to rubbing it against her core feeling like it took an eternity.

"Fuck me, Justin," she moaned, arching her back as she laid on the bed, pulling me down with her. "I need you too."

Jesus. Christ.

Hearing her say that was so hot I could barely stand it, thrusting myself into her all the way to the root. There was no way I could go slow, my hips moving whether I wanted them to or not, dragging myself in and out of her as she tightened around me.

She was soaked, so wet and needy, gripping me like a vise as I pumped deeper and harder.

"Yes, yes," she breathed, my mouth finding hers and swallowing the rest of her words as my hand wrapped around one of her tits.

Nothing had ever felt that good. No blowjob, no sex—nothing. Not a single thing I'd done with any other woman had even come close to how amazing it felt with her.

"That's it, baby, come for me," I moaned into her mouth, feeling her body tense as she got closer.

Her hips jerked, her breaths punctuated by little whimpers as they got faster and more uneven. I needed to feel her, to watch as I took her over that edge, and only then would I let myself get what I needed.

"Justin, please." Her fingernails dug into my back, the sweet sting of pain spliced with her pleas making it harder for me to hold on, driving myself deeper into her.

"Oh, God," she panted, her grip around me tightening one last time before sending tiny pulses along my shaft. She twitched under me, her legs shaking as I plunged into her again and again as her orgasm echoed through her.

I couldn't hold out any longer, the delicious vibrations on my cock sending me over the edge as I kissed her hard and exploded into her.

I'd intended to pull out, assuming she'd have told me if she wasn't on the pill but not wanting to tempt fate. But I couldn't do it, unable to do anything except pump into her as I shot my load, willing to accept any and all of the consequences.

It was such an asshole thing to do, not giving a shit if I accidentally got her pregnant because hell, her being the mother of my kids didn't scare me in the least.

Funny how shit had changed, the paranoia of me ending up someone's dad so strong that I'd literally never had sex without a condom. Not even when I'd had a steady girlfriend and I'd watched her take the fucking pill. But with Tessa, nothing felt more right. And while I was in no hurry to knock her up—and needing to make sure it was something she even wanted—the idea of getting her pregnant was something I actually liked.

"Hey." I kissed her slowly, my dick still buried inside of her as I moved my lips to her neck. "I want you to know I've never done that with anyone else."

It wasn't a matter of proving I'd been safe, or that the chances of me giving her an STD weren't high. Both those reasons super important and yet, not why I was telling her. "Only you, Tessa." I kissed her again, wanting to say more but feeling like the words were inadequate.

She nodded, seeming to understand what I assumed was a poor attempt to tell her how much she meant to me. "Only you, Justin," she echoed back, pressing her lips against mine. "I've never done that either."

It shouldn't have mattered, and if I hadn't been her first, I'd have never held it against her. Please, I was the last person who'd ever make judgments about anyone's choices. But knowing that I was—that we'd shared something with each other that no one else had—made me feel like a rock star.

"You don't have to look so pleased about it," she laughed, poking me in the ribs. "Like you aren't already conceited enough."

"How is any of this my fault?" I argued back. "I can't help being this fucking awesome."

That was a lie.

She made me feel that fucking awesome.

All of it was only because of her.

And for as cocky as I was, even I knew I was one lucky son of a bitch.

"Uhhh," she groaned, wrapping her hands around my neck as her lips spread into a grin. "What am I going to do with you?"

"You want a list?" My brow rose, only half joking. "Because I can think of at least seven things off the top of my head and all of them able to be achieved right where we are now."

She shook her head, her body shaking gently as she chuckled. "Only seven, Tibbs? Gee, someone's slipping. But fine, let's see how *awesome* you really are."

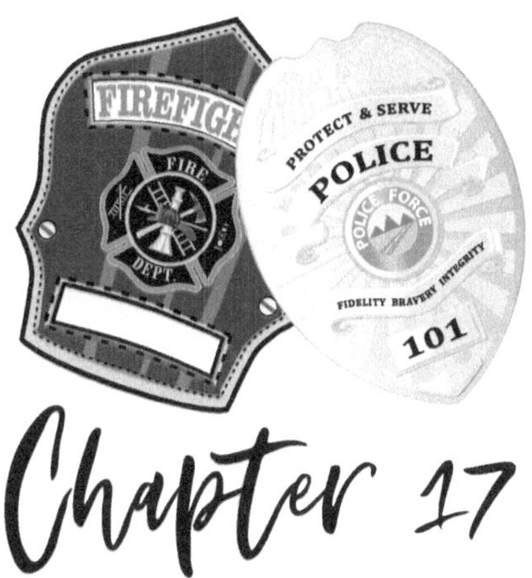

Chapter 17

Tessa

PRESLEY HAD APPARENTLY invited us to dinner, but we didn't make it.

Instead we'd spent the day in Brooklyn, ordering takeout for dinner and eating it on the couch while we sat around in our underwear. It was so nice just to be with Tibbs and not worry about whose alarm was going to go off, the two of us wasting the day doing nothing really important.

It was probably around nine when Justin mentioned we were supposed to meet Leighton and Presley for dinner. He didn't even seem sorry he'd blown off his sister and his best friend, reassuring me that the plans hadn't been solid anyway and he wouldn't have changed a thing. Part of me had been glad I hadn't known and therefore hadn't had to choose, loving the chance to have Tibbs all to myself and not share him with the rest of the world.

But when he mentioned he had promised to meet up with them at *Vault*, I didn't even hesitate. I was excited to get dressed and go out, and since the venue had extra special importance to us, I was even more enthusiastic to go.

"Fuck. Me." Justin's brows popped as I'd walked out of my bedroom, the tight black dress making me feel sexier than usual. It had been a while since I'd gone to so much effort, curling my long straight hair into glamourous waves. It made a nice change from workout wear and my uniform, my painted red lips spreading into a grin as Justin's eyes raked up and down my body. "How the hell am I supposed to keep my hands to myself? Are you trying to torture me?"

My palms pressed against his chest, lifting my head to kiss him. "Yes, I live to cause you personal pain and suffering. Which is why I'd like to take this time to let you know that I'm wearing a tiny G-string and no bra. You're welcome."

He cursed under his breath, his hands anchoring on my hips. "You're a sadist. Who knew someone as beautiful as you could be so goddamn cruel?"

"You're the sick bastard who gets off on it, Tibbs. Don't pretend to be surprised." I sighed, secretly loving how crazy I made him.

We struggled getting out of my apartment; Justin conflicted about whether we *really* needed to go out at all while testing the limits of my lipstick.

He didn't stop touching me, his fingers locked with mine while we drove into Manhattan, his lips reaching across every opportunity he got. I'd never really looked to a guy for validation before, but seeing the desperation in his eyes sure did wonders for my ego.

"Miller is meeting us?" Tibbs grabbed my hand as we were about to walk in. "I never asked him how things are going with that woman he met, does it make me a terrible person if I don't give a shit?"

He looked amazing, dressed in a pair of dark denim jeans and a black button down, and I was going to have a hard time keeping my hands to myself. His sexy smug smile wasn't helping either, his gorgeous hazel eyes lighting up with mischief as he nodded to security as they waved us on through.

"Yes, he's meeting us here. And it didn't work out." I shrugged, having already heard about Grayson's short-lived romance with the girl he'd met the same night I'd gone home with Tibbs. "He is terrible keeping things casual and she wasn't interested in a relationship with a cop. He's okay, though, I think if nothing else, it helped him get over Maxine."

Other than work—and on my days off when Justin was rostered on—I hadn't spent as much time as I used to with my best friend. Oh, he'd never made me feel bad about it, happy things were going well with Tibbs, but I could tell he missed me.

It had been Justin's suggestion to invite Grayson, pretending it would stop Presley from asking anything too personal when we both knew not even Jesus Christ himself could do that. I think it was his way of doing something nice for me and Grayson, conscious of the fact I'd spent so much of my spare time with him. It was so incredibly sweet, and while I didn't admit it out loud, it made me love him just that little bit more.

We hadn't said the words yet, but I think we both knew. For all the doubts I'd had when it started, I was absolutely positive being with him was the right thing to do.

"Wow," Leighton stood from his seat as we approached the small table, "as I live and breathe, it's Tibbs and Ricci. Such a rare sighting to see the two of you out, together, in public." He accentuated each word, making it sound so fantastical. "I'm wondering whether I should record this moment for posterity or just relish in the excitement."

"Like you can talk," Tibbs laughed, his arm wrapped around my waist as he brought me in closer. "You follow my sister around like a lost puppy. If either of us is whipped, it's you."

Leighton nodded, not even trying to deny it. "I might be whipped but people still remember what I look like."

"Yeah, yeah, we're here aren't we?" Tibbs grinned, kissing the top of my head. "We invited Miller as well. Figured if he sees us too, you can all get off our case."

"Awesome, Presley loves an audience," Leighton laughed. "You should probably sit down and relax while you can, your inquisition will start soon. Sorry, did I say inquisition? I meant evening, your *evening* will start soon."

"Oh, is this where Presley asks about my intentions with her brother?" I could barely contain my smile as I shuffled onto the bench beside Justin. "Poor innocent, Tibbs," I pouted as I stroked his cheek. "Did all those bad girls make you feel cheap and nasty?"

"Are you enjoying yourself?" he deadpanned. "And I don't know what you're talking about. I was a good boy."

"Bullshit," Leighton coughed under his breath. "Sorry, something in my throat."

Tibbs flipped him off, shaking his head as he laughed. "Whatever, asshole."

A waitress had just stopped by to get our drink order when Presley arrived. She was gorgeous as usual, her lithe body wrapped in a tight red dress. "Well, well, well," Presley's lips pursed, "I have to say I expected this from my brother, but Ricci, you have seriously disappointed me." Her dark lashes narrowed; her resting bitching face almost perfect except for her smile. "I thought we were friends."

Tibbs laughed, taking the opportunity to kiss me again. "At least I'm not the bad guy this time."

I shrugged, tipping my chin and meeting Presley's stare. "Honestly, I tried to stop myself, but he was so persistent, he wore me down. Now he's grown on me and I kind of think he's adorable. I think I'm too far gone at this point to stop and I'm not sure I want to."

"Awww, baby," Tibbs cooed. "Other than making me sound like a crack addiction, that's one of the sweetest things you've ever said."

Presley shook her head. "Uh-ah, don't try being all cute." Her finger pointed with accusation. "I'm still mad at both of you. Maybe if you give me every single detail on how it all came to be, I might consider forgiving you. Oh, and Leighton mentioned you guys first hooked up here in my club, so a public display of recognition and thanks would be great too."

Justin leaned in, pretending to whisper, "Do you want the pleasure of telling her it's none of her business or can I do it?"

"Don't even, Tibbs. Considering how much you meddled in *my* business, I get this one." Presley huffed, flicking her long brown hair off her shoulder. "You are finally dating someone decent—who I adore—and you kept it from me. I just want to put it out there that if this doesn't work out, and you break up, I'm siding with Tessa."

"Me too." Miller grinned, waving to everyone as he got closer to the table. "Sorry I'm late guys, but it looks like I got here in time for the important stuff."

The waitress returned with our drinks and took Miller's order. Presley joined us at our table, listening intently as I gave her the abridged version of how Justin and I ended up as a couple.

I'd never really liked talking about myself and my personal relationships, especially in a group. But with Tibbs, I was so freaking happy, I just wanted to share.

"You guys are too cute." Presley grinned, beaming at us like we were a pair of puppies. "Now, just keep me in the loop moving forward and no one has to get hurt."

Satisfied she had been properly briefed, she got up from the table and went back to work. Leighton excused himself soon after, suspiciously heading in the direction of Presley's office. And they thought Tibbs and I were bad.

"Sooooooo," Miller lifted his beer and took a slow drink, "guessing I'm the third wheel tonight. That's cool, I don't mind. But if you guys are going to make out and stuff, give me a head's up and I'll leave. I like you, Tibbs, but seeing you kiss my partner is still fucking weird." He shivered in his seat like he was spooked.

"We'll do our best to control ourselves." My hand slid up Justin's thigh and gave it a squeeze.

He cursed under his breath, shooting me a grin. "Miller, I tried, buddy. If you don't want to see this, you should go take a walk."

Grayson rolled his eyes, his ass lifting out of his seat. "Next time you invite me out, remind me to say no."

I laughed, leaning closer as I whispered against Justin's lips, "I think he's mad."

He captured my chin in his hands and kissed me before mumbling, "I don't care."

It felt like a coming out of sorts, Tibbs and I spending our two consecutive days off together but also with our friends and family. Not that it had originally been our plan—forty-eight hours in bed more what we'd been thinking—but after seeing Leighton, Presley, and Miller at *Vault*, I realized we'd been in a bubble.

After working out at Dad's gym, we went and visited my mom. She pretended not to be excited—me not having dated seriously in a while—but I could tell she was happy. With Emilia still away on deployment, and me being so busy with work and my new relationship, she missed having her girls at home. And of course, she loved Justin because he was charming like he usually was.

We also stopped by to visit his parents, Mr. and Mrs. Tibbs, having already met me in the past in an official capacity. They were great too, and even though I'd been hesitant about making us "public" official, I really liked having Tibbs as a boyfriend.

Boyfriend.

It was such a weird word, and not one I ever thought I'd ever be using when talking about Justin Tibbs. But even though I'd had my reservations when it came to him, his past, and the possibility of a future, I couldn't deny our connection.

We belonged together. And I was done fighting it.

Justin left early, waking me with kisses before he snuck out of his Midtown apartment and told me to call him later. I didn't start until later in the day, so had the whole morning to lounge around, not needing to worry about fighting traffic since I could literally walk to the station. It wasn't even strange being in Justin's apartment without him there, making myself at home as I made myself coffee and then took a leisurely shower.

I could barely contain my smile when I eventually got to work, Miller waving to me as he parked in the lot behind the station. "I could've picked you up on my way," he gave me a hug as he pressed the key fob locking his car, "I really miss our drives in together. No one to sing back up."

"Yeah, I miss it too. But I'm driving us in tomorrow, and I will totally murder any harmony you choose on the way," I agreed, not looking forward to spending my night alone.

It wasn't that I didn't like being by myself or even that I constantly needed to be around someone. I just *liked* having Justin in bed beside me, feeling his body pressed against mine while I slept, and waking up to sweet—and sometimes *not* so sweet—kisses.

It must be what love felt like. Knowing you were fine by yourself but wanting that special someone there anyway. For no reason other than it made you happy.

And I was.

Extremely happy.

"I need the two of you to head out to an apartment building in Hudson Yards." Cap handed us a report right after our briefing. "Developers are looking to turn it into new condos so it's empty, but the neighbors have reported seeing people coming and going. Probably some squatters or kids, but I want you guys to check it out anyway."

"Sure, Cap." I nodded, reading over the address.

Hudson Yards was turning into the sexy new place in the city, so a lot of the old buildings were sold, gutted, or torn down, and replaced with multi-million dollar reincarnations. It wasn't unusual to find either homeless people or kids using the vacated premises for shelter or venues for extracurricular activities. Not something worth calling 9-1-1 over, but we would check it out and investigate whenever we got a complaint. Half the time, just the appearance of our police cruiser was enough to scare anyone off who didn't belong there. And if that didn't do it, we'd helpfully remind them they were trespassing on private property and that they should move on. It was an easy call out, and one I was grateful to have, looking forward to easing into our shift and hoping my happy mood would continue.

"So you did the whole 'meet the parents' thing?" Grayson grinned, starting the ignition as I put on my seatbelt. "Sounds serious."

I shrugged, pretending like I wasn't giddy. "Don't even start with me, Miller. I needed to go see my mom and he just tagged along. It was no big deal."

"Oh, no big deal," he scoffed, pulling out onto the main road. "And you just happened to go see his folks too? I swear, you are in denial, girlfriend. You two are going to be shacked up with two kids and a Golden Retriever before you 'fess up to being head over heels with him. But sure, you keep living the lie if it makes you feel better."

I shook my head, refusing to admit that he was partially right. While I absolutely was more involved with Justin than I'd been with any other guy, I had yet to say the L word. It wasn't because I didn't feel it, my heart skipping a beat like I had an arrhythmia. But because I didn't want to rush into things and jinx what we had. There was no need to rush; we had all the time in the world and things were going great. And maybe, a small part of me was really enjoying the excitement of the new feelings. I wanted to feel all the things, not skip steps because we were in some stupid race to prove we weren't fucking around.

"We're not talking about my love life. I refuse to be one of those women who are unable to function outside a pair. And I am totally fine having regular discussions as well. Like, what we are going to have for dinner?"

"Denial it is. Awesome. And I'll let you choose since I led us astray with that questionable Indian food last time." He smirked, returning his eyes back to the road.

Hudson Yards wasn't far from the station, if not for the Manhattan traffic, we'd had been there a lot sooner. Still, there was no real emergency so there'd been no need for lights and sirens, the lack of hurry prompting Miller to drive around the apartment block first before he parked the squad car.

"Looks deserted." Miller looked up at the four-story building, waiting for me to join him on the sidewalk. "Let's go check the external doors and make sure there hasn't been a break-in. I know Cap has these developers up his ass trying to use us as their own security service, but I'd rather not have them accuse us of dropping the ball."

Not everyone was fond of the NYPD and the tendency to point the finger happened a lot. Sure, there were bad cops—men and women who tainted the badge and the uniform—but most of us took the oath to protect and serve seriously.

"Front door is locked." I pulled on the chained glass doors, the industrial-sized padlock still in place. "Let's check the back."

It was when we walked to the rear of the building that we found the broken window. Shards of glass lay on the concrete below, the windowpane cleared of debris with a thick piece of plastic covering it.

Ordinarily it wasn't something that we'd find overly suspicious. After all, windows got broken all the time especially when buildings were being vacated. Usually they secured the hole with a board or industrial plastic—like the one that was in place—not bothering to repair what was probably going to be replaced a few months later. But since the report had mentioned seeing a few people coming and going from a building that should be empty, it was worth a closer look.

The sheet of plastic came away easily, the tape keeping it in place stripped of its stickiness. Then all I needed to do was haul myself through the cavity and take a look. I was glad it wasn't too far off the ground, able to climb in unaided as Miller followed me inside.

It was still late afternoon so it wasn't dark. It made things easier, not needing to do the climb while holding flashlights, leaving our hands free should we need to unholster our weapons.

"What's that smell?" I coughed, a vile scent of ammonia or possibly cat pee greeting us as we stepped into the empty room. "Oh, that's fucking terrible." I covered my mouth not wanting to breathe in.

"Yeah it is. Let's check out some of the other rooms, make sure something didn't die in here." Miller covered his mouth with his hand as we cleared the bedroom we were in and moved onto the next.

The first apartment we'd searched was completely empty. There was evidence of either rats or mice—the droppings all over the place—but there didn't seem to be anything to suggest anyone else was in there.

Apartment two revealed much of the same. More rodent shit and empty rooms, but the smell was definitely getting stronger.

It was only once we got to the third and corner apartment that we began to suspect something wasn't right. Not only was the acridity in the air making my nose and throat burn, but there was a low hum permeating through the walls.

My head nodded to the closed front door, both of us pulling out our guns before my hand went to the handle.

"This is the NYPD, anyone in there?" I knocked loudly on the wood, announcing our presence as I slowly opened the door.

Miller covered me, his weapon drawn as I pushed open the door, the odor so pungent I wanted to vomit.

"Got to be some kind of lab," I coughed out, the hum louder with the door open. "We should call it in and get backup."

Miller nodded, keeping his gun pointed as we took a small tentative step inside. There was a chance we'd scared off whoever was there when we'd knocked but someone had definitely been cooking. A large generator powerful enough to run an entire house was sitting in the middle of the living room still on, the gas fumes alone enough to make me gag.

"NYPD," I shouted above the drone of the generator, my arms locked as I kept my gun drawn. "If there is anyone in here, come out with your hands above your head."

Nothing.

Not even the slightest disturbance to hint that there was anyone there.

"They've probably gone." Miller's eyes scanned the room. "This place looks like the same layout as the others. One bedroom, one bath, and I assume a window that backs out into the alley we walked around."

He was probably right, but we weren't taking chances, and we should have already called it in. "Let's go outside and wait for backup. Check the exterior again." I nodded to the front door.

We backed out slowly, staying alert as we moved from the living room into the hall. Miller reached for his radio, contacting dispatch while I glanced down the hall. Last thing we needed was some tweeker jumping us, and I already had a bad feeling.

"I told them to call FD as well just in case." He winked. "Maybe your boyfriend will show up."

The sound of a window breaking had us both snapping our heads up, the shattering coming from the apartment we'd just left.

"Outside," Miller shouted, running back to the original apartment we'd entered from hoping we'd be able to catch them on the street. "Watch my six."

It was probably too late, whoever had broken the window probably already sprinting up the street. But there was always a chance they weren't so savvy, Miller jumping out of the window first and landing back on the sidewalk.

A white male who was at least two hundred pounds had fallen and was bleeding on the ground, the asshole groaning as he stood, limping as he attempted to run. Miller took off after him as I braced against the frame, my body halfway out when I heard noises coming from behind me.

I should have gotten out, followed Miller and the perp, or waited for backup, but instinct made me turn and head in the direction of the noise. Other than the generator, it had been dead quiet in that apartment when we entered. And unless they were the stealthiest crew of all time, it was probably just a one-to-two person operation. One of them sacrificing themselves—or chickening out—while the other tried to save some inventory.

Calling in my location, I let dispatch know Miller was in pursuit on foot while I was still inside. I didn't wait for the reply, turning and sprinting back up the hall promising myself I wouldn't reenter the apartment without backup.

I didn't get the chance.

Not even making it to the doorway when I heard the click of the trigger, a bullet piercing the drywall.

"Shots fired," I called back into the radio. "Second suspect is armed."

"Get the fuck out, pig, or I'll shoot you where you stand," the gruff voice shouted into the hall.

I didn't hesitate, maintaining my position with my arms locked as I used the open door as cover. "This place will be surrounded in a few minutes and you're going to have no way out. Toss out your weapon and come out with your hands raised above your head, or it's going to be you who will be shot."

The use of deadly force wasn't something I took lightly. But if it was going to be him or me, I knew which choice I was going to make.

"Fuck you," he tossed out as he fired another shot.

He was either high or had an incredibly bad aim, both bullets lodging themselves in the wall nowhere near my position. I'd seen guys like him before—desperate, scared, possibly already on parole or with outstanding warrants—and they figured they had nothing more to lose. It made them unpredictable and dangerous, and it didn't matter how good an officer you were, there was no way to know how it was going to go.

"Suspect is cornered," I radioed back as dispatch asked for an update, letting me know units were moments away. "Possibly under the influence. Highly erratic. Armed with at least one handgun, possibly 9mm, and is actively firing."

"Fuck," he called out again, emptying two more rounds as the sound of smashing glass spilled out into the hall. "I am not going back to jail, whore. You and all the other pigs can suck my dick."

Such a charmer. No wonder his friend had bailed. If I was riding shotgun with that shitshow, I'd take my chances on a foot pursuit too. But he was not doing himself any favors, and if there'd been any chance of working out some kind of plea, he'd burnt that bridge.

I didn't bother trying to engage, holding my position as I maintained cover. Any minute officers would be here to assist, and unless he legged it out the window like his buddy, there was nowhere for him to go.

The shooting had stopped, but I knew it wasn't because he was out of bullets. Even if all he had was a nine, he'd only fired four, maybe five rounds. There would be more left in the clip, and that was assuming he wasn't packing something else.

Just a little longer, Ricci, I whispered to myself, straining to hear if sirens were approaching. *They'll be here any minute.*

And then everything went black.

Chapter 18

Justin

SUSPECTED METH LAB.

We'd been called out to Hudson Yards to assist PD with a lab situation. Nothing had been on fire when the two engines rolled out—us and the hazmat team—heading to what was apparently an abandoned apartment building. Chemicals had a tendency to get dicey, so it was always better to have us onsite.

Last thing you wanted was things to go *boom* and then call for an assist. The time wasted literally the difference between saving the building and surrounding property to watching the shit burn to its foundations.

We had almost arrived when the call came over the radio.

Our suspected lab situation had turned into an explosion.

"Fuck," North cursed as the building came into view, the flames already licking the outside bricks. "We're going to need two more units and a ladder. Rev, call it in."

I'll admit, when the call first came through, I was excited about the possibility of seeing Tessa. There were no guarantees she was one of the officers on scene, but in the past, we'd attended more than one emergency together. It was only a matter of time before it happened again.

"Which officers?" I glanced over at the squad cars joining us as we pulled up in front, none of the uniforms getting out, Tessa. "Any idea if Ricci and Miller are here?"

But there wasn't enough time for anyone to answer the question, all of us piling out of the engine and getting ready to attack the flames.

"Tibbs and Leighton, east side lines," Cap barked out as he met us at the front. "Maintain maximum distance and protect surrounding properties. We have an active shooter and the scene hasn't been secured yet by PD. No one gets close, understood?"

"Yes, Cap."

"Sure thing, Cap."

We both answered, my eyes doing a quick survey of the scene.

No Tessa.

And while I'd been initially hoping to see her, I was glad she wasn't around given the change of the sitch. Not that any cops seemed to be hurt or injured, all of them wearing their vests as they maintained a perimeter.

"If the shooter is still inside, they're not going to be happy for long." Leighton shook his head. "Guess we should be thankful the place was empty."

He was right about that.

Apartment buildings presented a number of challenges. And even if smoke alarms did their jobs and residents evac'd, there was still a chance someone was left behind. Door-to-doors were necessary unless it became too dangerous to enter, which definitely would have been the case when there was a shooter. Luckily for us, the one we were standing next to was a tear-down, which meant no one had been in it for months.

"Hey, is that Miller?" Leighton asked, the mention of Tessa's partner making my head snap up. "Who knows, you might get to see your girl after all."

Grayson Miller wasn't known for having a temper, but if the way he was waving his hands was any indication, he could fire up just like the rest of us.

"Where is she?" I asked more to myself than to Leighton, not seeing her near him. "They'd have come together surely."

I wasn't sure if it was the desperation on Miller's face or the churning of my gut that made me come to the realization. They *absolutely* would have come together, they were partners. So if she wasn't with him, that could only mean bad things.

"Fuck, fuck, fuck," I cursed under my breath, the chance that she was inside that hellhole not a possibility I wanted to entertain. "Evans," I called out, "get on this hose, now."

"Where are you going?" Leighton looked back at me in surprise. "Dude, what—" He didn't need to finish, the answer coming to him without any assistance from me. "Fuck."

I didn't wait around to hear what he had to say, making for Miller with the single focus of proving myself wrong. "Where is she?" I demanded, grabbing him by the vest as the bile rose in my stomach. "Where the fuck is Tessa?"

His face said what his mouth was struggling to do, shaking his head as his fists balled at his side.

"I'm going in."

It had leaped out of my mouth before I'd finished formulating the thought, grabbing an axe from the engine as my feet moved of their own accord.

Cap blocked my path, his hands hitting the front of my turnouts with enough force to make me take a step back. "Stand down, Tibbs. No one goes in there until SWAT secures the scene. They're five minutes out."

"Five minutes?" I pointed to the smoke pouring out of the broken glass. "Tessa is in there, and her exit is going to be cut off in two."

He tried to push me back, getting more up in my face than he ever had before. "Tibbs, I'm giving you a direct order, do you hear me? I will not risk one of my men—"

"Then fucking fire me, Cap," I yelled back, telling him exactly what he could do with his order. "Or better yet, get SWAT to shoot me. Because the only way I am not walking inside that building right now is if I'm not breathing."

"Hey," Leighton was at my side, Rev having taken over on his hose. "I'll go with you."

I shook my head, not willing to risk anyone else's safety but my own. "I can't ask—"

"That's right, you didn't ask. So let's fucking do this." He pushed against my chest and tipped his head to the door.

"Yeah, figure I might join you boys," North piped in. "You might need an extra pair of hands and let's face it, mine are the best ones here."

I wanted to argue, to tell them that not only was it too dangerous but fucking stupid as well. The paperwork alone was going to be ugly, the chances one of them not making it home too much for my conscience to bear. But there was no time, and honestly I could use the help, and I wasn't going to waste one more second with a conversation.

North already had bolt cutters in his hands and Leighton was grabbing a hose. The plan was to run it right inside the front fucking door. And if the shithead with a gun was still breathing, he was going to have a hard time staying vertical with 290 psi hitting him dead on.

Cap swore under his breath, yelling at us to be careful as he turned on the hose. Our actions might not have been sanctioned, but not one of the badges on their side or ours tried to stop us as we hit the front of the building like a missile strike.

We barely had time to put on our SCBAs, North popping the chain on the external doors, Leighton pointing the hose at the entrance as North swung open the glass.

An avalanche of water exploded from the nozzle, clearing a path at least in the short term as I was able to squeeze in beside it. There wasn't much room, keeping myself parallel to the blast so I didn't end up on the floor.

"Tessa," I called out, knowing for the most part she wouldn't have heard shit over the water and the masks. "Ricci, where the fuck are you?"

"Last contact was made outside apartment 1C," Cap's voice came over the radio. "Third door from the left as you enter."

I pointed to the left, making sure Leighton and North swung the hose in that direction as I jogged alongside it. We didn't get very far, the place of Tessa's last radio contact also what seemed to be ground zero for the fucking fire.

"Shit," I pulled up short, 1C no longer resembling anything close to a structure with its side walls blown completely out. The blast had also removed the door from its hinges, the piece of wood laying like a corpse on the floor a few feet away.

"Tessa," I screamed, unwilling to believe she'd been inside. There was no way it ended like that, no fucking way. She was one of the strongest people I knew, and if anyone was fucking capable of walking away from this, it would be her.

Like a madman, I dropped my axe, yanking up pieces of sheetrock with my hands and refusing to accept any other outcome where she didn't walk out of there with me. We didn't have much time, the flames closing on us as we tried to push them back. We had maybe single minutes left, and even that was being optimistic, my hands grabbing whatever they could as I called out her name.

It was North who pointed back to the blown-out door, the wood having shifted just slightly and not from any assistance from me or the hose. Like a fucking demon I tore the thing off the floor, Tessa's curled up body revealed underneath.

THANK. FUCKING. GOD.

There wasn't time to celebrate or even check if she was conscious, my hands hauling her off the floor as we retreated back the way we'd come in. She didn't look good, a cut on her forehead bleeding down her face as I pulled her close to my chest. Leighton and North used the hose to shield us from the flames, the roof starting to cave in as we made it back to the exterior doors.

"Tessa," I pulled off my mask while maneuvering her in my arms, needing her to respond. "Ricci, you need to fucking wake up."

If there was a possibility of waking a person with will alone, I'd have been the guy to do it. I'd cleared us just enough from the entrance for me to safely lower her to the ground, my fingers pressing against her neck and checking her carotid pulse before the EMTs had even gotten close.

She coughed, my hand on her—or maybe it was my fingers digging into her neck—making her splutter as she breathed in a mouthful of air. It was the single most beautiful thing I'd ever seen, her chest rising and falling as she took another breath, and then one more right after.

"Tibbs?" she squeezed out, her eyes fluttering open. "What are you—"

"Shhhh, save your throat," I warned her, knowing the smoke inhalation alone was going to make talking unbearable. "I've got you, and you're safe."

"We need to check her, Tibbs." Darcy one of the EMTs was at my side with a stretcher. "You can stay, but just give us room to work."

The permission to stay had meant jack shit, because there was no other way it was going. And if they thought I was leaving her side, they were fucking delusional.

Darcy put an oxygen mask on Tessa, checking her vitals while my hand stayed locked around Ricci's fingers. I was positive I wasn't giving them as much room as they wanted. But considering Tessa's injuries didn't seem fatal, they were going to be hard pressed to convince me they couldn't work around me.

I hadn't even noticed what was going on, only realizing Leighton and North had kept the line on the entrance while other crews provided further support. The ladder had arrived too, the aerial line going a long way at keeping the fire contained and sparing the neighboring buildings.

Guess the tear-down was going to happen a lot sooner than anyone thought, one of the side walls crumbling under the weight of the water being blasted at it.

"How is she?" Miller's voice came from behind me, taking a tentative step closer. "Jesus, Ricci." He shook his head as he looked down at her on the stretcher. "I don't know who I'm madder at right now, me or you."

"We're moving," Darcy barked out. "You both can meet us at Mont Sinai West, but we're leaving now."

For all the patience she'd shown before, she was fresh out, muscling me out the way as her and Cole—the other EMT—got ready to put Ricci in the ambulance.

"You want a ride?" Miller asked. "I'm assuming you came here in an engine and unless you want to add grand theft auto to your rap sheet, coming with me will probably be easier." He shoved his hands into his pockets as his mouth thinned into a line. "And before you even fucking say it, I thought she was right behind me or I never would have fucking left."

"You think I'm going to try and pin this on you?" My brows knitted, genuinely surprised he'd go there with me. "You remember I'm dating her, right? So I *know* that whatever decisions she makes—good, bad, or indifferent—are hers alone. And to be quite honest, I don't give a fuck. As long as she's okay, that is all I need."

I got it.

Really, I did.

There was a responsibility you had to the man—or woman—on your left and right. And unless you wore the uniform, it wasn't easily understood. When we said we'd die for each other, that was literally what was on the line.

"Dude, guilt is a waste of fucking time and emotion. No one—especially not Tessa—blames you. Not for this. So you need to get right with yourself, talk to your shrink or your God if that's what you need, or it will eat you alive. But I will say this, if you don't take me to the hospital so I can see my girl, we're going to need another ambulance for you."

I'd only been partially joking, mentally counting the minutes since the EMTs left with Tessa. I wasn't even worried about leaving when I was still technically on duty, the chances of me still having a job after my rogue mission probably not looking good.

Miller tried to laugh but came up short. "You really are perfect for each other, you know that. Okay, let's get out of here."

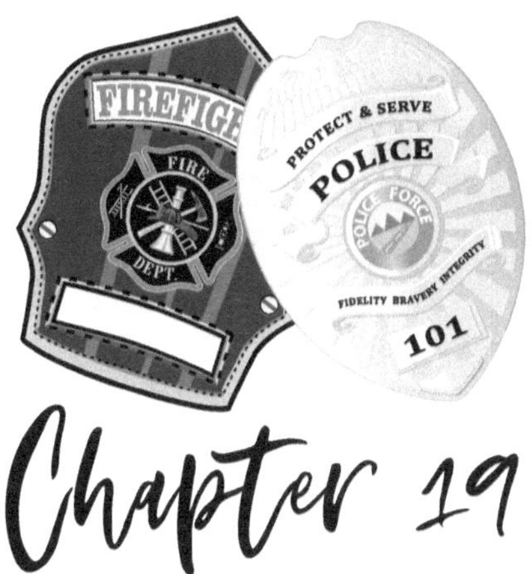

Chapter 19

Justin

CAP DIDN'T SAY a word to me as I left the scene, but that was no surprise. He was probably saving it all up for the shitstorm that was going to rain down on me when I finally got back to the stationhouse. And if I thought Cap was mad, the chief was going to be worse. Not that it would've changed a thing, my choices and decisions would have been exactly the same given the situation over, and my only regret was that Leighton and North were involved. Still, I'd deal with all of that once I was positive Tessa was okay, and I'd be sure that both Cap and Chief knew the only person who should be facing repercussions was me.

Miller got us to the hospital quicker than expected. Guess a pair of flashing lights and some solid defensive driving moves helped. But even though we weren't stuck riding taillights like regular civilians, I was still going out of my mind until we got to Mont Sinai.

"Tessa Ricci." Her name the only greeting given to the nurse at the ER.

"Hey, Carole," Miller added, tapping my shoulder and trying to make me step aside. "Tessa was just brought in, any idea of her status?"

He might have sounded calm, but I knew better, the tight smile on his face giving away he was just as anxious as I was.

"Hey, Grayson," Carole smiled, not giving me the same warmth when she turned in my direction, "let me check the system and see where she is."

She tapped on her keyboard with a lot less urgency than I would've liked before pausing. "She is in exam 3, you both can go back there if you like."

We'd barely waited for her to finish the sentence, pushing through the doors and heading into the main part of the ER. It didn't take long to find her, Miller seeming to have a pretty good idea of the layout and walking us directly to the curtained-off area.

"Hey Grayson," another nurse pushed apart the curtains as she walked out, "they've taken her for a CT, she should be back soon."

"Was she conscious?" I asked, ignoring I hadn't been the one addressed. "How were her vitals? Are they running a chest x-ray as well? She was in that smoke longer than she should've been. And—"

"Slow down there, FD." She shot me a smile that I wasn't feeling. "She is with Dr. Camden, who is one of the best ER doctors in the city, and I'm pretty sure he knows what he's doing. But if it helps put your mind at ease, she was conscious and responsive. Tessa Ricci is a tough cookie. I am positive she is going to be fine."

While I appreciated her assessment, I really didn't give a shit what she *thought*. What I wanted was a fucking guarantee and a visual confirmation that Tessa was going to be all right, not willing to settle for anything less.

"Hey, you want to take a seat and wait until she gets back?" Grayson rubbed the back of his neck. "I'm going to call her parents. I'm sure our captain is going to call, but I want them to hear it from me. I owe them that."

"Yeah, fine." I shoved myself into a chair, my turnouts taking up more room than I would have liked. I wasn't sure if he'd meant out in the waiting room, but he was delusional if he thought I was going to be anywhere other than her bedside.

He nodded, taking his phone out of his pocket and pointing to the direction we'd come. "I'm just outside, come get me as soon as she gets back."

After assuring him I would, he left to make his call. I didn't envy him, the phone conversation with a next of kin when something went bad, the worst thing ever. It was while I was waiting that the nurse from before came back.

"Justin Tibbs?"

"Yeah, that's me." I stood, wondering if she had any more news.

"Chief McPherson is out front for you."

FUCK.

I shouldn't have been surprised; Mack wasn't the kind of guy—or chief—to sit around and wait. And while I absolutely expected—and deserved—whatever punishment was coming my way, I was hoping it could wait until after I'd seen Tessa.

Swearing under my breath, I begrudgingly followed the nurse into the hall. It would only be worse if I kept the man waiting, and considering I was fairly positive I was going to be suspended or worse, it was just better to get it over with.

Chief was eerily calm as he waited by the triage desk, his face devoid of the anger I was expecting as he watched me approach. "Tibbs."

"Chief." I tipped my chin, wondering if that was the calm before the storm.

His head pointed to the exit. "Let's take a walk," and it didn't sound like a suggestion.

"I know what you're going to say, and I'm fine with it. I understand you have to do what you have to do. But Tessa is getting back from CT soon and I want to be waiting for her when she does. I know you get it, Mack. When Hayden was lying in a hospital bed not even Jesus Christ could've moved you until you saw she was okay. So give me that, and then I'll talk, walk, or do whatever you need me to do."

It wasn't like me not to follow orders, especially when they came from the big guy. But when it came to Tessa, protocol went out the window and I wasn't apologizing.

Chief cleared his throat, looking around before he lowered his voice. "Oh, you know what I'm going to say? You become a mind reader at some point when I wasn't aware?"

"No, but—"

"But nothing." Mack cut me off, raising his hand. "I know you want to be with her. If you didn't after that stunt you pulled, I'd have some pretty serious questions. But there is something I need to say and I'm not doing it here. So give me two minutes outside and then I'll leave you the hell alone."

Since arguing with him wasn't going to get me anywhere, I followed him out the door. He wanted two minutes, so that was what I was giving him, exactly one hundred and twenty seconds, and then I was back beside that bed whether he was done or not.

It was only after we'd cleared the main doors, away from the crowd, that Mack started to speak. "First things first, are you okay? And I'm not just talking physically, Tibbs."

"Chief, I'm fine. Things got toasty, but I had my SCBA on the whole time and North and Leighton were on hose support. Other than going off script, we did everything textbook. As for my head, I'll be solid once I see Tessa and know she's okay." It was the best I could give him, knowing if I told him I was all good that I would be lying.

He nodded, understanding probably better than anyone what I was going through. "Good, and I need an assurance from you that if anything changes you will tell me."

"Promise, Chief," I agreed, having no intentions of hiding anything. "We good?"

"No. We're not." He shoved his hands into his pockets. "What you did was not only a direct violation of your captain's orders but incredibly reckless as well. There's a reason we don't go into an unsecured scene, Tibbs, turnouts aren't bullet proof and you can't fight a fire with a hole in your chest."

I huffed out a breath, his sermon one hundred percent what I was expecting. "Yeah, I got it. But—"

"Let me fucking finish." He cut me off again. "It was also one of the bravest things I've ever seen you do. Cap said you didn't even hesitate, took point on Leighton and North. And if it weren't for you, Ricci would've come out of there in a body bag instead of in your arms."

I swallowed hard. It was one thing to know her chances wouldn't have been great but hearing it out loud made it feel more real.

"We won't know everything until we read the police report and get our investigator down there, but from what PD said, the guy was cornered and probably lit a fire out of desperation. Asshole probably hadn't passed high school chemistry or he'd know that just the vapors of what he was cooking were enough to cause an explosion. I'm guessing they'll find him somewhere in the rubble, and Ricci was shielded by the door. In any case, while I can't officially approve of what could've been a suicide mission, I want you to know that PD are incredibly grateful. I've also never been prouder of you in my life."

Praise didn't usually make me emotional, but hearing those words from Chief choked me up in a way where I was glad we didn't have an audience. "Thanks, Chief. But I wasn't going to let her die in there."

"I know. So, here's what we're going to do." He slapped me across the back. "You'll get paperwork, because there's nothing I can do to avoid that. But it will come with an addendum that you acted with exceptional bravery and therefore will not be a mark on your record. You'll also take a few days off because while I am not suspending you, I have a feeling your head isn't going to be in the game, and I won't have that on my crew."

I nodded, not trusting myself to talk while he basically gave me the biggest free pass ever. It wasn't what I was expecting, and sure as hell not what I'd been ready for, willing to have lost my career if that's what it came down to. But knowing I got to go back, that I got to work alongside my brothers and do what I loved to do. Fuck, that was a gift I hadn't even hoped for.

"Okay, I'd say I've exceeded my two minutes and I know you want to get back." His head tipped toward the hospital doors. "North and Leighton will drive your car over and get any personal items from your locker. You might also want to get out of your turnouts before they get here. I'll email you later tonight or tomorrow morning and we'll discuss your return date. I'm sure that will probably be contingent on what the doc says anyway."

"Thanks, Chief." I put out my hand, unable to fully convey my gratitude. "I don't know what else to say."

Mack returned the shake, his shoulders lifting as he gave me a slight grin. "Well, that works for me because usually I can't shut you up. Go on, get out of here. And I want status reports, let Ricci know we're all pulling for her."

"Will do." I waved goodbye before sprinting back to the emergency room.

"Hey," the relief flooded me when I pulled back the curtain and saw she was back in the bed, "was beginning to think you ran away with the X-ray tech. And yeah, I wouldn't put it past you to try and make me jealous."

I could barely contain my grin, willing to put up with anything she wanted to dish out if it meant she was okay.

Her hand reached out, clasping mine. "He's not my type," she wheezed out. "Looks like a nice guy but probably has like ten bodies buried in his backyard. I won't even consider dating someone who doesn't commit to proper disposal."

I laughed, because if there were any doubts at all she was going to be fine, they were firmly put to bed. That was exactly the kind of response I'd expected if she hadn't been pulled out of a burning building unconscious, so hearing it gave me more assurances than any doctor ever would. "That's what I love about you, Ricci. More integrity than you know what to do with."

It was supposed to be flippant, the kind of thing we said to each other when we were being smart asses. But saying those words didn't feel like a joke, and I didn't want her to think they were either. "Actually," I sat beside her, gripping her fingers tighter, "there's a lot that I love about you."

Her eyes got wider, like she couldn't decide if I was baiting her or it was for real. "Tibbs—"

"Tessa, I love you." I leaned in, kissing her. "You scared the fuck out of me, so I don't want to waste any more time by not telling you how I feel."

Blinking, her beautiful brown irises turned glassy. And I couldn't tell if it had been from the smoke or what I'd said. "Justin, life-threatening experiences can make you say things you don't mean. If you're worried that it's what I need to hear right now, please know I'm okay. You don't have to rush it."

I shook my head, swallowing back the laugh. "Would it kill you to not argue with me for one fucking second? I'm telling you I love you because that's the way I feel. Not because of a life-threatening experience or to fill some quota. I LOVE YOU. Love. You. And I don't care if you're ready to hear it or not, I'm still going to say it."

"I love you too." The words hitched on a sob, her hand reaching up to brush my cheek. "So much."

Man, I hadn't known how much I'd wanted to hear those words, convinced that if she didn't say them back, I'd be fine. And I would've been. But knowing she loved me too made me feel like I had superpowers, my heart feeling like it was going to bust through my ribs.

"Good, but I want it on record I said it first." I pointed out, not willing to let her go yet.

She rolled her eyes, her voice still hoarse as she spoke. "It's not a competition, Tibbs."

"C'mon, Ricci, everything with you is a competition." I lowered my lips to hers doing my best to not crowd her but needing to kiss her.

"Guys, this is a public place." Miller walked in, shielding his eyes. "You couldn't wait until you got out of here? There are *kids* out there."

I'd almost forgotten Miller was still around, his phone call having taken him longer than I'd expected. Between the visit from the chief and my newly confessed feelings, I'd barely cared if he even came back.

"Relax, Miller. The kids can't see anything unless you open the curtain." I chuckled, settling back into the chair beside Tessa. "And even if they did, one look at my turnouts and mention of an engine, and I've got them eating out of the palm of my hand."

"Firemen." Miller yawned. "No wonder your vehicles are so large, only a truck is big enough to fit your egos."

Tessa coughed out a laugh. "Miller, I've said the exact same thing. And you know I'll always have your back, but I'm going to side with Tibbs on this one. The uniform is pretty impressive."

Miller shook his head. "Just remember which side of the line you stand on, Ricci."

"Wouldn't forget it," she looked at me and smiled, "but I can appreciate being between the lines as well."

My head lowered, risking traumatizing kids, or Miller, or whoever else was watching, as I kissed her again. "That's exactly where we need to be."

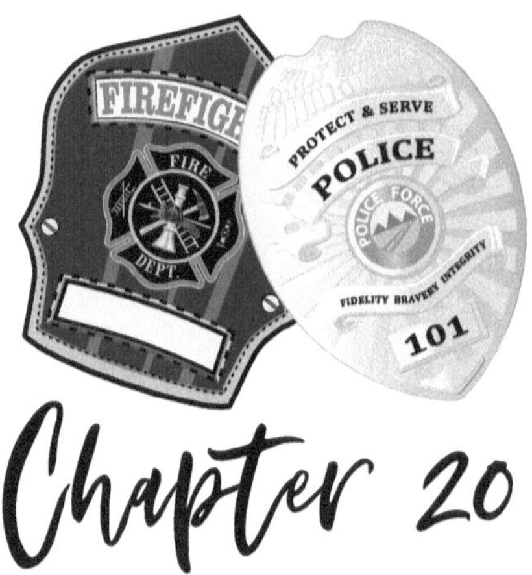

Chapter 20

Tessa

I WAS DISCHARGED the next day, still feeling like shit. I'd suffered a concussion, smoke inhalation, and some pretty impressive bruising from being tossed across a hallway while body surfing on a door. It wasn't anything I couldn't handle though, years of taking a beating in my dad's gym had given me a high pain tolerance. And being grateful just to be alive was an excellent motivator to improve my mood.

And then there was Justin, the man who'd literally run into a burning building to save me, and then went all in by telling me he loved me. Honestly, saving my life was probably enough, but he had to go one step further. Talk about overkill. And I couldn't even pretend I didn't love it.

"I didn't think you were the *sweep you off your feet* kind of girl, Ricci. All those feminists would be shaking their heads if they could see you now." Tibbs laughed as he carried me into my apartment.

"I can walk, asshole." I rolled my eyes. "You're the one who insisted that you needed to carry me up the goddamn stairs."

He didn't let up his grip, grinning as he hugged me closer to his chest. "You're concussed. You get dizzy or skip a step, and you'll end up with a double concussion or broken ribs. Besides, how else am I going to prove how strong and awesome I am? Just shut up and let me alpha here."

It was ridiculous how much I loved his smart mouth and enjoyed how cocky he was. The very two things I once loathed about him were fast becoming my favorite things. He was also beyond adorable, lowering me so carefully onto my bed that I couldn't help but marvel at his ridiculously strong core control. I was so incredibly lucky, and I wasn't even going to pretend I didn't love him being with me.

"How long are you going to be off?" I asked, shuffling up the bed onto the pillow. The movement made me wince, Tibbs immediately looking concerned as he joined me on the bed.

"Well, considering it's being classed as vacation time and not administrative leave, I can really go back whenever I want. But Mack doesn't want me in the stationhouse until I can give him a hundred percent. And I know I can't do that until I'm sure you're not going to pass out on the way to the bathroom."

"I can go stay with my parents, Tibbs. You don't have to stay," I offered, my parents having already hounded me at least five times to come home while I convalesced.

"Please, you think I'm doing this for you?" he scoffed, screwing his face into fake horror. "We both know I'm not *that* good. Nope, this is all for appearances, so when *The Times* wants to interview me for my heroic efforts, I have something else to add to their piece. I come up a little short in the bleeding heart bullshit, so you're just going to have to grin and bear it while I improve my image. Jesus, stop being so selfish."

It hurt to laugh, my hand wrapping around my sides while I tried to stop the chuckle. I was glad he was with me, preferring my own apartment than my childhood bedroom, and my amazing boyfriend rather than my wonderful—but probably overanxious—parents. You'd think the military would have desensitized them, but apparently when your kid got hurt, it didn't matter.

"I'll do my best, Tibbs. But fair warning, you're going to end up my sex slave. And I don't want to hear any complaints from you when you're rocking Stockholm Syndrome and can't function without me."

He kicked off his shoes, nuzzling closer. "Ricci, I already can't function without you, and being your sex slave would be an honor and a privilege. Just don't use regulation cuffs." He winked. "A pervert I know told me they hurt, and I want to keep myself looking pretty."

I just couldn't with him.

Could.

Not.

Every single time I thought he couldn't get any sweeter, funnier, or sexier, he pushed the boundary a little further, making me fall even more in love with him.

Next time I saw Maxine I was going to hug her and thank her for breaking Grayson's heart. If it hadn't been for that horrible bitch's inability to be faithful, I might never have been at the club that night and seen Justin. And for as much as I'd originally hated it, I had become so incredibly thankful.

"Hold me," I asked, not caring if it made me sound needy and weak. I didn't have to pretend with Justin, he knew exactly who I was, and wouldn't think less of my vulnerability.

"Anything you want, baby." He wrapped his arms around me without question. "I'll hold you for as long as you want."

Justin and I had been playing house for about a week. My parents had checked in a few times but knew better than to hover. It wasn't the first time I'd had a concussion so I knew the drill, and they only had themselves to blame for me being so fiercely independent. Emilia was no different, and as much as I knew they were pleased they'd raised two strong—both mentally and physically—daughters, they were glad I'd let Tibbs be around.

I was less dizzy, and my vision was getting better, and my bruising was starting to clear as well. It had also been a week since Tibbs had touched me sexually. Every single time we got a little heated with kissing or it looked like we were getting too close to crossing the line, he'd pull back. And while I knew why he was doing it, loving how considerate he was being, it was driving me slightly crazy.

My boyfriend was insanely hot.

Ridiculously sexy.

And while my head and body had undergone some trauma, my hormones hadn't.

I wanted to touch him, to feel him, and to have him touch me. And my god, could I use an orgasm, the desperation for release making me irritable. There wasn't any medical reason why we couldn't have sex, so if my body wanted it, I couldn't understand why he was turning me down.

"Are you no longer attracted to me?" I asked casually over lunch, fairly positive it wasn't the right way to bring up the conversation but needing to know either way.

Tibbs coughed, grabbing a glass of water as he tried to swallow the mouthful of food he'd been chewing. "Jesus, Ricci, did you OD on the pain meds? What kind of question is that?"

I dropped my fork, no longer interested in the chicken salad I'd been eating. "I just want to know if maybe you're not as turned on as you used to be since you've seen me using the bathroom. I know that sometimes happens."

Intellectually, I knew *that* wasn't the reason. I'd felt his hard-on against me whenever we got too close in bed, then heard him quietly go jerk off in the bathroom when he thought I was asleep. I wasn't even upset that he did it, part of me turned on he needed the release too, loving the sounds he made as he got himself off. I wanted to watch, to be part of it, wanting nothing more than to open the door and take his cock in my hand and help him finish.

But I also didn't want to hear he was scared of hurting me, almost believing it was easier to accept he'd become less attracted to me than think I was no longer strong.

"It happens sometimes?" he repeated, asking me the question like he couldn't quite believe it. "Guys see their hot girlfriends doing normal life things and they suddenly forget how sexy they are? Really? And where did you get this fascinating information from? Because I've been a guy my whole life and I can tell you *that* is bullshit."

"It's not bullshit," I argued. "There's definitely a chance some of that sex appeal disappears when all the intrigue is gone. It's like knowing the secret behind a magic trick, it's not as impressive if you know how it's done."

He held up his hand, shaking his head. "I'm not sure I agree but for the sake of the argument, let's say it's possible. That a guy saw you pee and suffered some kind of aneurysm, no longer finding you attractive. I'm not *that* guy," he pointed to himself. "Tessa, you're gorgeous. You could grow horns and have your skin turn into animal fur, and I'd be the sick bastard who'd be into it."

"Then why won't you sleep with me?" I tried not to make it sound like an accusation, not wanting for it to dissolve into an argument. I'd seen it happen too many times before, something stupid getting blown way out of proportion, and then people saying things they didn't mean. I didn't want that with Tibbs, not wanting for the first relationship where I honestly felt like an equal to end because of stupidity.

"It's only been a week, baby. A concussion can take months to heal, and brain injuries are serious." He reached for me, touching my hand. "I'm trying to be the good guy here and you know how much I suck at it."

I shook my head, having heard his excuse about not being a "good guy" too many times. "You are so wrong. You pretend like you're an asshole, but you've been faking it the whole time, Justin. I *see* you and the only man I've seen has been caring and considerate. He's been kind and loyal. He has integrity and does the right thing even if it means risking his own life. You can pretend all you want, baby, but you are absolutely a good guy and I want you to touch me."

I rose out of my seat and walked the short distance to his. He swallowed hard as I lowered myself onto his lap, straddling him as I wrapped my arms around his neck and kissed him. "We don't have to have sex, Justin, if you don't want to. But just like the day you got in that ring with me and trusted me not to get hurt, I need you to do this. I won't break and I will tell you if it doesn't feel good. But I need you so badly, Justin, and more than anything, I need you to see how strong I still am."

His mouth was on mine so fast I'd barely taken a breath, his hands wrapping around my ass in a way that wasn't PG. "You think I don't think you're strong?" he moaned against my mouth, lifting me in his arms as he stood. "That's almost as bad as you thinking I don't find you hot anymore."

"I just needed to know." I breathed between kisses, the ache between my legs almost unbearable. I'd been so turned on with no release, it wasn't going to take long before I came. "I just missed you touching me like this so much."

"Fuck, Tessa." My name came out in a guttural growl. "I've been going crazy not touching you. I think about fucking you so much it's borderline perverted, I just don't want to fuck this up."

"You won't, I promise. But *please* take me to bed. Because if I don't come soon, I will probably go insane."

He made it to my bedroom carrying me with such confident strides I'd have been impressed if I wasn't already so turned on. But I didn't care how we got there, willing to have crawled on my hands and knees if it meant we were going to get naked.

I'd never felt so desperate, my skin tingling as he carefully—he hadn't totally eased off the brakes—lowered me to the bed and started pulling off his clothes. I was mesmerized, my eyes glued to his perfect body as he stripped himself bare for me while I watched. His mouth twitched into a grin hinting that he liked it, standing in front of me naked so I could get a better look.

"Your turn," he leaned down and whispered, his hands moving to my clothes.

I didn't even try to help, pulling him down as he wrestled first with my T-shirt and then with my jeans. He didn't complain either, proving how talented he was peeling each item off my body despite me hindering his effort. With a flick of his wrist he removed my bra, replacing the lace with his hands and mouth as he tossed it to the floor.

"Will this convince you how attractive I still find you?" he groaned, grinding against me with his hard-on. "The minute I get these panties off you, I'm going to be in you, Tessa. So let's make sure you're ready before I do that."

Just hearing him say those words made me wet, the need biting at each syllable as he breathed them out. I was just about to tell him I was ready, when his hand sunk into my underwear, my body exploding when the tips of his fingers hit my clit.

"Oh my God, oh my God," I panted against his neck, feeling myself shake as he continued to circle. I'd never come that quick, my body feeling like it had been primed for days and teetering on the edge. "Justin, that feels so good."

"Jesus, Tessa." He pumped a finger in me as his thumb continued to swirl. "I had no idea, baby. I'm going to give you everything, but you have to promise you'll tell me if it gets too much."

"I promise," I nodded, still feeling my body twitch, "just don't stop. Please, don't stop."

He pulled down my panties, yanking them down my legs roughly before returning his hand to my center. Even though he'd threatened to be in me the minute they'd come off, he was doing his best to slow himself down, teasing me before sucking on his fingers.

"Condom or not?" he asked, reaching down to his cock and giving himself a stroke. "Just tell me fast because I'm beyond making the choice."

"No condom," I heaved out, watching him jerk off turned me on so much I wasn't sure I wouldn't come again purely from that. "I want to feel you."

His head lowered, bringing his mouth to mine as he kissed me. It was rough and intense, the gentle kisses he'd given me the last few days forgotten and replaced by desperation and heat. "Lay back for me," he growled against my mouth, kissing me between each word as he crawled over me, spreading my legs and teasing me with the blunt head of his cock.

It was so good, the pressure building with the anticipation. "I need you, Justin." My hands slid up his chest, touching him all over. "I need this."

He cursed out a breath, pushing into me barely an inch as we both moaned. His dick throbbed, my hips tilting off the bed wanting more contact. "Fuuuuuucccccccck," he gritted out, burying himself to the hilt in one swift thrust.

We didn't move, both of us staring at each other with ragged breaths as I felt him inside of me. I was already so close to coming and my body tingled all over.

God, I loved him, loved this, loved the way we fit, and how amazing sex felt with him.

"Baby, I need to move," he kissed up my neck, "and even though I jerked off earlier, I haven't been in you in over a week, so this is probably going to be quick."

"I don't care, just do it." I kissed back, needing to move too. I wasn't going to last either, and more than anything, I wanted him to stop being careful. "I will not break," I reminded him. "Fuck. Me."

He didn't flinch, grabbing my hips with his hands and thrusting deep into me given the permission. Our eyes locked, his heated stare burning me up inside as he plunged into me again and again.

It was so good.

So.

Good.

His hard cock teasing me with each long stroke in and out, taking me closer until I was right on the edge.

My body started to shake as I struggled to keep my eyes open, overwhelmed by so many feelings there was a real danger I was going to start crying. It wasn't just about the sex—which make no mistake, felt fucking amazing—but gratitude as well.

That I had him.

That I had us.

That he trusted me when I told him I wouldn't break.

"Oh my God," I cried out, every nerve in my body feeling like it been lit on fire. "I'm so close."

His hand slid from my hip, flicking my clit just once as I came in a heated rush. Everything shook, tears leaking out of my eyes as muscles contorted and released in waves of pleasure. I couldn't even stop, wrapping my arms around his neck and rocking my hips as he swelled inside of me and then finally exploded.

"Tessa, Tessa."

He repeated my name over and over again, the tight cords of his abs completely engaged as he spilled into me. He didn't stop either, pumping into me again and again until we were reduced to a sweaty mess.

His lips returned to my mouth, kissing me gently as he pulled out and rolled to his side. "At the risk of pissing you off, I still need to ask." His hand brushed along my jaw. "Are you okay?"

I grinned, feeling more okay than I had in days as I rolled toward him and snuggled against his chest. "You thought it might piss me off and you *still* asked?" I chuckled against his skin. "Wow, you really *are* brave."

"Oh baby, make no mistake, part of me is still terrified when it comes to you. But I wouldn't have it any other way." He laughed kissing the top of my head.

"Justin," I tilted my chin, looking into his beautiful hazel eyes, "I am better than okay. Thank you."

He threw back his head and laughed. "You're thanking *me* for sex, Ricci? Jesus, how hard did you hit your head? You don't *ever* have to thank me, baby. Seriously. Any time. Any place. Any circumstances. No thanks necessary."

"Annnnnnnd your transition into my sex slave has commenced." I grabbed his chin and squeezed it. "I know this obedience is going to be short-lived, Tibbs, so I'm going to take it while I can."

"Well, you knew what you signed up for, Ricci. You can't claim buyer's remorse now." His hand wrapped around me, pulling me closer. "You want to go finish lunch? Or do you have other duties you'd like me to perform?" His brow rose suggestively, and I loved it.

He was back.

My crazy, dirty, and insane boyfriend was back, and I was so in love with him it was ridiculous.

"Why does it have to be either/or, Tibbs? I thought firemen were good lateral thinkers," I teased, biting my lip. "We can feed each other lunch, in bed."

He barked out a laugh. "Trust a cop to find a workaround. Fine, stay right there. I'm going to feed you and fuck you until you can't see straight."

I moaned, the idea of both of those things sounding so delicious I didn't know which one I wanted first. "Make it so, Tibbs, because I'm hungry for both."

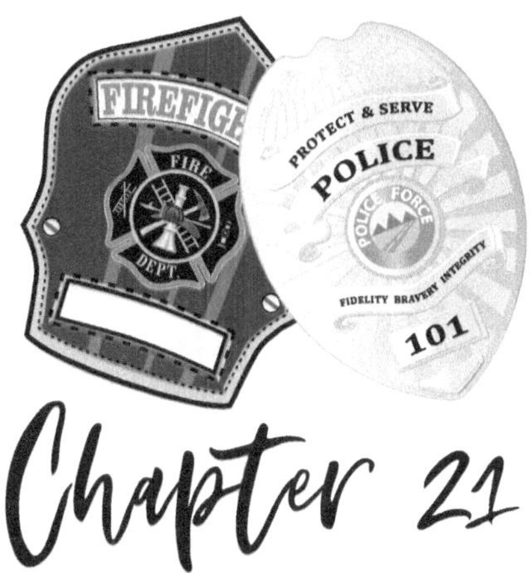

Chapter 21

Justin

STRUCTURE FIRE.

It was my first day back and our first call out was an abandoned warehouse.

Not going to lie, it was good to be back even though the week and a half I'd had with Tessa had been amazing. She still hadn't returned to duty yet, the doctor refusing to sign off because of her headaches. I could tell she was ready to climb the walls, not being able to work or train, but I did my best to make sure she stayed in shape with homebased workouts.

Two engines and a ladder had responded to the call, and being back with my team had never felt so good. I could barely wipe the smile from my face, grinning like an idiot as we tackled the burning warehouse.

"Tibbs, you look deranged." Rev, laughed, shaking his head. "People are going to start thinking you lit this baby."

Leighton chuckled, working alongside of us. "He's in looooooove, Rev. We should probably get used to that stupid look on his face."

I shrugged, not giving a shit what they had to say. "Laugh all you want. My girlfriend is fucking awesome and I'm not going to pretend not to be ecstatic about it."

North slapped me on the back as he came up behind me. "Speaking of ecstatic, it's been a whole month since you've stolen my deodorant from my locker. Good for you sacking up like a big boy and using your own."

There were other jabs, each of the team taking their turn in giving me shit. Not because they didn't love Tessa—hell, everyone at the stationhouse thought she was too good for me—but because I'd always said I didn't want a long-term relationship.

Yet there I was, spending every available second with a woman I couldn't get enough of, and wondering when it was too soon to ask her to move in with me. It was only a matter of time, alternating between apartments and neither of us spending nights alone unless we absolutely had to.

The warehouse hadn't stood a chance. We'd had the blaze under control in record time, working like the well-oiled machine that we were. It was the one place I'd never doubted myself, knowing when I had that uniform on, I was the best I could ever be.

As for the guys I worked alongside, there wasn't one who could've been replaced. I trusted them with everything. So being back with them, feeling that spike of adrenaline, yeah, it was pretty fucking good. Which was why I understood why Ricci hated being away from Miller, her need to be with her partner kicking ass and taking names as much a part of her as anything else.

We were packing up the trucks when Rockefeller arrived. He was a detective from Tessa's precinct, and we knew him pretty well. "Gentlemen, what have we got?"

While Cap filled him in on the details, I couldn't help but watch the interaction. With Tessa's dedication and drive, it wouldn't take long before she made rank, and there wasn't a doubt in my mind she was going to be one of the best detectives on the force.

"Tibbs, you ready to roll?" Leighton asked as he closed the last of the equipment doors on the engine.

"Yep, all good. Let's get back to the station."

We piled into the engine and started back to base, the thought of Tessa with a shiny gold badge still dominating my thoughts.

I wanted that for her.

Wanted her to succeed more than I did myself, which was saying something. Guess it was true what they said about being in love and it changing your perspective.

It was when we got back to the stationhouse that I decided to check in on the chief. He had gone above and beyond for me since the incident, making sure that not only my record stayed clean, but Tessa and I got any support we needed. He'd even cooked us dinner a couple of times, the man just as talented in a kitchen as he was wearing a uniform.

"Hey, Chief," I rapped my knuckles on the open doorway, "you got a minute?"

Mack looked up from his desk, giving me a smile as he waved me in. "Tibbs, was almost starting to miss your face around here."

"Yeah, not as much as I missed being here, Mack. Not sure what I would've done if my leave of absence had been permanent." I shuffled into a chair opposite him.

He nodded, dropping the pen in his hand, and gave me his full attention. "Yeah, well I don't like losing good men so that wasn't happening on my watch. That isn't an invitation to push your luck, though. I will bench you if that's what's best for the team."

I didn't doubt that for a second.

If there was one man who lived the *duty before self* mentality, it was the guy sitting in that chair. He'd taken an eighteen-year-old North and raised him as his own. Didn't care he didn't know the kid or that he'd been a pain in the ass. Nope, just took the responsibility and didn't look back. And it wasn't just Riley he treated like family, each and every one of us feeling like that too. It didn't matter that he'd recently had his own biological son, Mack not once making us feel like we were any less important than the little boy who shared his last name.

"You won't get any trouble from me, Mack, I swear." The promise made not just because I didn't want to lose my job but because I wanted to be better. Not just for the crew and for the chief, but for Tessa as well. "But while we're discussing futures, I wanted to talk to you about Ricci."

Mack laughed, leaning back in his chair as he stretched his arms behind his head. "Tibbs, a little late in the game to be asking permission, isn't it? But if it makes you feel any better, I approve. She's a fine officer—respected and hardworking—and will have no problem keeping you in line."

He was right on all accounts, but I wasn't looking for his blessing. "No, I meant she's probably going to make detective soon. She has her criminology degree and it's been a few years. That's how it works, right?"

Mack nodded as he took me in. "Yeah depending on which department, she would be up for rank soon. I know the Cap speaks highly of her so it wouldn't be a performance issue, but I'd say it will happen sooner than later. Why? You worried about her because of the fire?"

"No." I shrugged. "I mean, of course I'm worried she might get hurt or something, but that's the job. And I can't ask her to stop any more than I can walk away. It's what I love about her, Chief. She's fucking fearless. And I want to make sure I do everything I can not to screw things up for her."

Mack chuckled, shaking his head. "Tibbs, unless you turn into a felon and make her an accomplice, there isn't a lot you can do to screw up her chances. But as anyone who's put on extra stripes will tell you, she'll need support and understanding. You give her that, and she's already ahead of the curve. I will say that you being concerned says a hell of a lot about you too. You know, Tessa isn't the only one who can make rank."

"Yeah, I know." My lips spread into a grin, not having given it much thought before. "Can you imagine?" I laughed, thinking I'd probably give the guy a heart attack.

"Yeah, I can actually. I can imagine it very easily," he responded with no humor in his voice.

"Well then, guess I better go out there and do some work." I cleared my throat, rubbing my palms down the front of my pants. "Thanks for . . . everything."

"All good, Tibbs. Again, welcome back." He nodded and then went back to his work.

That was the other thing I loved about the chief; he never made a big deal out of shit like that. He let you have your moment without crowding you, and along with his other talents, it was something I hoped to learn.

It was around dinner time when I finally got the chance to talk to Tessa. There'd been some messages back and forth throughout the day, but there hadn't been time for anything more. So unless we got another call out, we were going to be sitting down to some chicken fettuccini cooked by North, and I was going to call my girlfriend.

"What are you doing?" I asked when she answered the phone. "And more importantly, are you naked?"

Tessa laughed, the sound warming my chest. "Miller stopped by. Still want me to be naked?"

"Yeah, that's a negative, Ricci. But if after he leaves you want to take off your clothes and send me photographic evidence, I won't complain." I grinned, just thinking about her naked getting me hard.

"Don't hold your breath, Tibbs. Phones get hacked all the time and I'm not interested in being the next scandal."

She had a point, something I needed to remember. "Fine, disappoint me," I groaned, pretending to be annoyed. "I'll have to make up for it tomorrow morning. I'll call you when I'm on my way over in case you sleep in," I offered, accepting we were going to be spending the night apart, but not willing for it to extend to the morning.

"Soooooooo, about that."

"What?" I asked, wondering what she was going to say.

Her voice was muffled like she was covering the phone, the words spoken to Miller inaudible before I heard footsteps taking her out of the room.

"Tessa, you're killing me right now. What were you going to say?"

I honestly had no idea. Things had been great between us and she'd given me no indication when I left that she didn't want to see me after my first shift back. In fact, it was the opposite, telling me she'd be waiting for me when I got back and that she wanted to hear all about it after I made love to her. So if she'd suddenly had a change of heart, and didn't want to see me, I was going to need an explanation.

"Tessa," I barked again, shaking my head as I heard a door close. "Baby, tell me."

"Jesus, you're impatient, Tibbs." She laughed, the carefree sound of her voice making me feel better, but not by much. "I just wanted some privacy when I told you, so I came to the bedroom."

"Told me what?" I asked, a million scenarios going through my mind and not all of them good.

"When you were in the shower this morning, I slipped my spare keys into your backpack. I figured you might want them." Her voice was like liquid, smooth and calm with no hesitation.

"You gave me a key, baby?" My ass lifted from my seat, heading to my locker like the room was on fire. Sure enough, there in the front pocket was a cheesy *I heart New York* keyring with a set of keys.

My fingers closed around them, squeezing the metal tight in my hand as I brought it to my chest. "I've got them."

"Good, the brass one is for the external door, the silver for mine. You might want to use them in the morning, saves you making a phone call or harassing my neighbors." Her voice lowered. "I'll be naked."

Jesus.

Christ.

"You really expect me to be able to work after that?" I cursed out. "You are a cruel woman, Tessa Ricci."

"Yet, you're still hanging around. Says more about you than it does about me, Tibbs. Might want to check that," she chuckled. "Now I'm going back into the living room before Miller assumes we're having phone sex. Call if you get time later *or* just come wake me up in the morning."

How could any man resist an offer like that? "Will do, Ricci. Have a goodnight, baby. I'll see you in the morning." And without really wanting to, I ended the call.

Man, I had it bad. Turning the keys over to look at them in my hand again, in case I'd imagined it. Nope. Still there. And I was not going to be giving them back anytime soon. Instead, I was going to be giving her a set of mine and then suggesting maybe we downgrade to just *one* set of keys.

I'd assumed it was too soon. Worried she would think it was a knee-jerk reaction to the fire, her injury, and everything else. But she'd made the first move without hesitation, so that was how I'd make the second. And I wanted to move in with her, willing to move to Brooklyn if that was what I had to do. Of course, I really, *really* hoped she preferred Midtown since I had an extra bedroom, my rent was fixed, and we could literally walk to work. But whatever, it didn't matter the location, so long as we were together.

"Hey, you ready to eat?" Leighton's head popped around the corner. "North is done and the rest of us are starving."

I shoved the keys in my pocket, plastering a grin to my face. "Yeah, I'm more than ready."

It was early morning when my twenty-four hours were done. I hadn't slept much in my bunk, glad we'd been kept busy most of the night with call outs. And even though I wanted nothing more than to get into my car and drive to Brooklyn, I took a quick shower before leaving the stationhouse. I didn't want to waste time taking one when I got to Tessa's, anxious to use the keys she'd given me and then slip in naked between her sheets. Man, I was a lucky son of a bitch.

"Hey, Justin." A blonde I had "dated" casually was waiting for me outside, looking nervous as hell as she shoved her hands into the pockets of her hoodie. "I know it looks creepy me waiting for you out here like this, but I didn't want to corner you at your apartment."

"May." Her name finally flashed in my mind. We'd met at Presley's club *Diablo* and seen each other a couple of times. Nothing serious, of course, but she'd been kinda sweet. "Hey, no, that's okay. Was there something you needed?"

I really hoped she didn't respond with "*your cock,*" because as appealing as that proposition might have been a couple months ago, she was going to be shit out of luck. There wasn't a chance I'd cheat on Tessa, and I wasn't even tempted.

She looked around, the other guys leaving and waving goodbye as we stood out front. "Is there somewhere we could go talk? Privately?"

Yeah, that wasn't going to work.

And considering we hadn't done a lot of talking when we had been together in the past, I was sure "talking" was code for something else. Besides, while there had never been an emotional connection between us, I didn't want to be an asshole either. And I had zero interest in leading her on.

"I'm actually on my way to my girlfriend's house." *A bit of a dick move sliding it in there instead of just telling her outright, but I didn't want to be a total jerk.* "So I'd rather just talk here if that's okay."

"You have a girlfriend? Oh, I didn't know." She shifted uncomfortably on her feet.

"May, what is it? You obviously came here to say something, so whatever it is, just say it. It's okay. I don't bite." I tried to laugh but was starting to get nervous.

She wasn't a psychopath, right? Sure, we'd had a casual relationship, but it hadn't ended badly. I hadn't ghosted her or fucked her over, and as I'd mentioned before, she'd seemed really sweet. So If I'd misjudged the situation and ended up with a knife wound, it was going to suck.

"Okay." She let out a long breath, her eyes flicking nervously to mine. "I just wanted to tell you that I'm pregnant. And it's yours."

What.

The.

Actual.

Fuck.

"What?" I wheezed out, barely able to get the word out on account of it felt like I couldn't breathe. "But we used condoms."

I didn't imagine wrapping my dick before having sex, the habit one I had never broken before Tessa. And hold on a fucking minute, I hadn't seen May in . . .

"I'm twelve weeks, Justin. And yes, it's yours. I know you probably don't believe me, but other than you, I didn't sleep with anyone else. But I'm prepared—and expect—to take a paternity test, so you won't have to take my word for it. Guess the condom didn't work because, here we are."

It felt like I was dying; my chest so tight it was possible I was having a heart attack. I'd been careful, how the hell could it happen? It *couldn't* be happening, desperate for it to be some crazy weird nightmare I was going to wake up from.

"Twelve weeks?" I was reduced to broken sentences, unable to process the information, speak, and breathe all at the same time. And if it was okay with everyone, I'd prefer to keep respirating. "Twelve weeks?" I repeated like a parrot.

She nodded, the apology clear in her eyes. "I know, I know, I should've told you earlier, but I honestly didn't know what I wanted to do. I mean, how the hell am I going to be someone's mom? And I didn't want you to pressure me into making a decision when I couldn't make one myself. But, Justin, I'm keeping this baby. And you deserved to know."

It wasn't happening.

It just wasn't.

I'd assumed I'd have kids some day and since being with Tessa, that hypothetical point in the future had seemed a lot closer. Hell, I'd even tempted fate, the idea of knocking Tessa up something I'd probably welcome. But having a baby with a woman I barely knew and didn't love hadn't been part of the plan.

"Okay," I nodded, still not doing real well with finding the right words. "There's a coffee shop around the corner. Let's go there."

Clearly it wasn't going to be a two-minute conversation, and considering we were out in the street where anyone could hear us, I wanted to manage the fallout as best I could.

I had no fucking idea what was going to happen. But what I didn't want was some asshole hearing half of it, and then running and telling Tessa. Whatever she heard would be the truth, and it would be from me. And only *after* I knew what the fuck was going on. Because even though May had made it clear she was twelve weeks pregnant with my kid, I was still grappling with it.

"Sounds good," she agreed, her feet moving in the direction of the corner. "All I want is to talk."

We walked in silence to the coffee shop not far from the stationhouse and it felt like someone had died. I guess in a way they had, because if what May was saying was true, my life as I knew it was done.

I ordered myself a double shot espresso—because they didn't serve vodka—and May wanted a herbal tea. Then with our drinks in our hand we found a quiet booth toward the back and took a seat.

She was the first to speak. "I know this isn't ideal, and you are probably freaking out. And the reason I know that is because that was exactly what I went through. I was terrified, I was angry, I was in denial—and so much more. But when I really thought about my choices, I just couldn't face a termination. And I am fully prepared to have this baby on my own. I'm not trying to trick or trap you, or force you into something."

I held up my hand, not wanting to accuse her of anything. "May, I never said—"

"You didn't have to," she shrugged, "it's written all over your face, Justin. I know there are women who weaponize their uterus, but I'm not one of them." Her hand dropped to her stomach, the bump still MIA. "I want this baby, Justin. And as unplanned and messed up as this situation is, I refuse to think of any child of mine as a mistake."

She was surprisingly calm and well-adjusted, but then she'd been given weeks to digest all the information and I'd had it dropped in my lap like a grenade a few minutes before.

"You're right." I prayed the next words I said were decent and didn't make me sound like a complete asshole. "And you're wrong, May. It *isn't* the baby's fault. And whether the condom failed, or we fucked up, I don't want him or her growing up with that kind of emotional baggage. But you also can't tell me that you're having my kid and that you're just going to do it solo. Firstly, you didn't get knocked up on your own, that was a two-person activity. I also can't pretend I don't have a child and just go on with my life."

Even though my lungs were struggling to inflate and function as normal—and my instinct was to run—it was unfathomable I would abandon my son or daughter.

My dad had been amazing, the best a kid could ever ask for. And I'd become the man I was today because of him, helped along by the chief. So the idea that I could say *fuck it*, and walk away without giving my kid a similar chance, honestly made me want to throw up. How would I ever look at myself in the mirror?

Nope, wasn't happening.

So, while I had no idea how it was all going to work, or what I needed to do, there was one thing that was certain. If the paternity test—because as much as I wanted to trust her, I needed the proof—came back, and I was the dad, I was going to be a part of that baby's life.

"What are you saying?" May asked, stirring her tea as she looked at me cautiously. "I think it's probably best for both of us if we say exactly what we mean. I don't have time for games, and I know you don't either."

I took a breath, the air pushing past my lips in a rush. "I mean I'm going to be there, May. Financially, emotionally and physically. I'm not going to let my kid grow up without a dad."

My kid.

Dad.

The words sounded so foreign coming out of my mouth I wasn't even sure I'd been the one to say them.

Fuck.

Fuck.

Fuck.

"You're freaking out again." May pointed to my face.

I nodded, figuring there was no point lying. "Yeah, I am. But I'm going to get my shit together so you don't need to worry. I just need a little time."

She lifted the cup to her lips, blowing across the surface of the drink before taking a slow sip. "Well you've got roughly six months. You've got time."

Funny, hearing that didn't give me any reassurance.

I was so fucked.

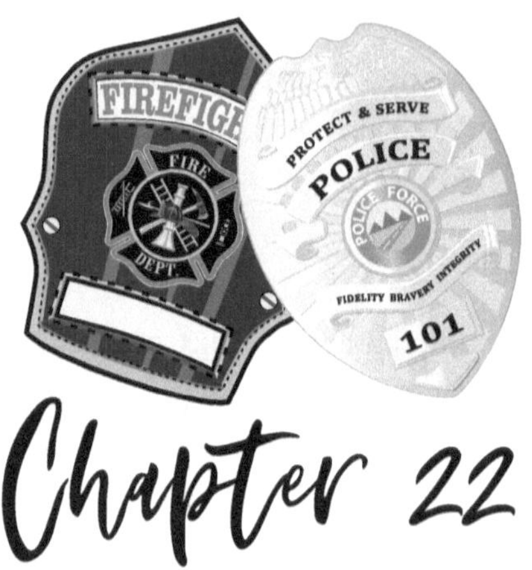

Chapter 22

Tessa

WHEN I WOKE to an empty bed, I assumed it was still early. My head was still cloudy and sleep was a little erratic, so it wasn't unusual for me to wake at varying times of the night and day.

But when I got up and went to the bathroom, I noticed the light pooling in from the gap in my drapes, my phone confirming it was well past nine.

Huh, I guess Tibbs got caught up.

While he usually finished around seven, he might have headed to his place before coming to mine. Traffic across town wasn't exactly favorable any time after seven, and there was always the possibility he'd decided to have breakfast first. He hadn't been at the station in over a week and had probably decided to catch up with Leighton or North. Or maybe he figured I'd probably sleep in since I knew he had a key so was running a few errands before coming over. In any case, it wasn't like he'd gone missing, and an hour or two late when we'd had no real plans was nothing to get excited about.

Debating whether I should crawl back into bed and wait for him, I decided to go shower first. I figured it would not only help pass the time, but if he came home while I was still in there, he could join me for shower sex. I was glad he seemed to have lost the earlier concerns he'd had. And while he seemed worried about the headaches I still couldn't shake, he was letting me take the lead on my own recovery.

I'd showered, dried my hair, changed the sheets and had coffee by the time I started to be concerned. All the earlier possibilities were still valid, but I'd have thought he'd have at least called me. It was when I picked up my phone ready to text him that I saw that I had an unread message.

Something came up.
Going to have to take a raincheck.
I love you,
Tibbs x

Something came up?
What the hell could have come up that he couldn't just say what it was?

No, *hey, babe, I got a blow-out and need to go get a new tire.*

Or *Leighton needed me to move furniture and it's going to be a few hours.*

Or even, *I didn't realize how exhausting my first day back was going to be, and I just want to sleep by myself.*

I'd have been good with all of those excuses. Would've happily told him to do whatever he needed to do, and I'd be waiting when he was done. And why the hell did he need a raincheck? Was he going to be busy the whole day? Something just didn't add up. It wasn't like Tibbs to blow me off, especially when things had been so good between us.

I'd even given him a key—

Shit.

The key.

Maybe because I'd given him a key to my apartment that he thought he had to give me one to his. Or maybe he felt pressured, thinking the key symbolized something else, and I was trying to muscle him into something he wasn't ready for. And while I had no hesitation or doubts on where we were headed—even hoping that sometime in the near future we might even move in together—I wasn't in any rush. Funny, I'd assumed he'd felt that way too.

"Okay, do NOT freak out," I told myself as I wandered around my apartment. "We have no idea if he thinks any of that, and if he was feeling pressured or overwhelmed surely he would have just told me."

Great, now I was talking to myself and acting like a lunatic.

My stomach churned with unease as I reread his message again. He'd said he loved me, something he surely wouldn't say if he was having second thoughts. Unless he was trying to give me the gentle brush off, placating me without raising too much suspicion. Thoughts and scenarios swirled in my mind, and most of them weren't great, mentally already building a case for a crime that hadn't been committed.

Sometimes I honestly hated being a cop, wishing I could shut down that part of my brain and live in blissful ignorance like other people. But noooooooo, not only was I seriously contemplating mapping it all out on a dry easel like Detective Rockefeller did with a case, but I was also turning into one of those hysterical girlfriends we saw in the precinct. You know the kind, all doe-eyed and sweet looking, but slashed all four tires and then took a Louisville slugger to the front end of a car because they suspected their boyfriend was cheating. I promised myself I'd never be one of those women, yet there I was, spinning out of control.

Disregarding the text—which told me nothing—I hit the call button instead and was promptly sent to voicemail. Which meant either his phone was turned off or he was avoiding me, my hand gripping the phone tighter as I waited for the obligatory "I'm busy, leave a message," bullshit that was prerecorded.

"Hey, it's me." I breathed out, trying to not think the worst. "Look, I know you said something came up—which is cool—but the text just didn't sound like you. So if you could call me back and let me know you're okay, that would be great. We don't have to hang out if you're busy or . . ." I paused, hesitating before adding, "or if you don't want to. It's fine. But call me so I don't think you've been kidnapped and some asshole is sending fake messages so we can't pinpoint the time of your disappearance. I will hate myself forever if you're lying in a ditch somewhere. Okay. I love you. Bye."

It was a terrible message, and not half of what I wanted to say. And if I could be sure the next one I recorded would be an improvement, I'd have deleted it. But hopefully he'd call me soon and we'd just be able to talk. We could laugh about how stupid I was for being paranoid, and how he absolutely wasn't freaking out about the key. Then he'd come over after whatever he had to do and we'd spend the night together. After all, it's not like I was headed back to work in the next few days, and he was off for forty-eight hours.

So I waited.

And waited.

Annnnnnnnnnnnnd waited.

But after two hours with zero response, I was beyond sitting around and pretending like I wasn't worried. While I hadn't left any more messages, I had attempted to call his phone a couple—fine, six—times and every single one went straight to voicemail. It didn't even ring, which suggested his phone was off rather than him deliberately avoiding me. But that didn't give me much comfort, which was why I got into my car and drove to Manhattan.

Technically I wasn't supposed to get behind the wheel. I still had some blurry vision and spontaneous headaches, which was the reason I'd yet to be cleared to go back to work. But it was the middle of the afternoon and I'd be careful, and I was starting to reach a level of concern that made me uncomfortable. I just had to know he was fine. Willing to postpone my wrath for making me worry like an idiot for later, if everything checked out.

I didn't even have my stereo on, letting my phone connect to the in-car system so if he called or texted, I'd be able to answer it immediately. But he didn't, my arrival at his Midtown apartment happening with zero communication.

Finding parking in the lot at the rear of his building, I walked back around to the main doors and buzzed. There was no answer, just like the other three times I pressed the damn thing.

Where the hell was he?

His Impala hadn't been parked in the usual spot, but it was fucking Manhattan and even resident parking had a tendency to be sketchy. Maybe whatever it was that had kept him had happened at work? My feet already walking the short distance to the stationhouse before I could change my mind.

"Ricci!" James—one of the other guys who worked alternating shifts—greeted me at the door. "How's the head? When are they going to let you go back? We saw Miller the other day and the dude looked like someone kicked his puppy. Safe to say, you're missed."

"Hi, James." I tried to sound normal, considering we were supposed to be having a normal conversation. If someone could tell that to my adrenal glands that would be great too. "Yeah, I'm still on medical leave. I'm fine, but you know what doctors are like. Got to be sure." I rolled my eyes, pretending to look annoyed. "Hey, any chance Tibbs is still around? I got a weird message from him earlier. Like weirder than usual," I clarified, since *Tibbs* and *weird* weren't exactly mutually exclusive.

James laughed. "Nah, he left hours ago. He was talking to some girl at the front last time I saw, but I had to get to the briefing before Cap chewed me a new one, so I didn't see much after that."

"Some girl? His sister, Presley?" I asked hopefully, refusing to accept the clichéd overreaction that he was cheating.

"Ricci, come on, we all know what Presley looks like. Leighton is one lucky bastard." His lips spread into a grin. "This was someone else. Haven't seen her around so can't say I know who she was."

"Okay, okay," I nodded, remembering I was a cop and jumping to conclusions wasn't helpful. "Blond? Brunette? Estimation of height and weight?"

James shrugged, scratching his chin. "Blond, about five-four, five-five? Maybe one hundred and fifty? She was wearing a running suit so I didn't get a really good look. She wasn't smiling if that helps."

Not really, but it was more than I'd had an hour ago. "And Tibbs? Anything about the conversation that looked unusual? Did he seem upset? Or agitated?"

"Jesus, Ricci, you launching an investigation?" James laughed. "He seemed . . ." He paused, hopefully trying to recall. "Normal, I guess. There wasn't any hostility or anything. And before you ask—because I know you two are dating—they weren't kissing, or hugging, or anything like that. They were just talking."

The relief I felt he wasn't kissing or hugging some random girl was instant, the tension in my shoulders easing as I took the information and decided what to do with it. "Thanks, James. I appreciate it. Any chance I can grab Leighton's number before I go? I know I'm probably being over cautious, but Tibbs isn't answering his phone. Hard to turn off being a cop."

He nodded, giving me a sympathetic smile. "Oh, I get it. I'm the same way. Can't go to a family BBQ without checking the connections on the gas tank and making sure everyone is the required distance away from the flame. And yeah, I can give you Leighton's number. Let me just grab my phone."

James went back inside, returning with his cell and the number I needed. Then after thanking him and promising they'd be seeing me in uniform soon, I walked around the corner to a nearby coffee shop and called Leighton.

"Hello," Leighton answered as I swallowed a silent thank you I didn't have to leave another awkward message.

"Hey, Leighton, it's Ricci. I got your number from James, I hope you don't mind," I explained trying to not sound like a bumbling moron.

"Ricci! Of course I don't mind, but you probably could've just asked Tibbs instead of James. How's the head?"

"The head is fine," I lied, already sick of talking about my recovery. "And Tibbs is the reason I'm calling." I took a deep breath, reassuring myself that I wasn't behaving like a jealous bitch.

The message was odd, and it would have given me pause if it had been *any* one of my friends. Hell, if it had been Miller, I'd have done exactly the same thing. The fact that it was Tibbs— and I was more emotionally invested—didn't mean I wasn't right to be concerned.

"He was supposed to meet me, but he canceled with a weird text. And I know he's going to have a field day with this later, but I checked his apartment, and work, and he isn't at either of those places. His phone keeps going to voicemail as well. He was also last seen talking to a blond, around five-four, five-five that weighs approximately one hundred and fifty pounds just outside your stationhouse."

"Ricci, he would *not* cheat on you," Leighton responded without hesitation. "I'll agree, all of that sounds strange. But I can tell you that whatever he is busy doing, it's *not* with that girl."

"I know he isn't cheating." *But did I?*

Who the hell was she?

Why wasn't he answering his goddamn phone?

And where the fuck was he?

"Look, I know he's your friend, and I'm not asking you to betray any confidences here. But if you know anything—either where he could be or go, or if he might've been upset—I'd really appreciate you telling me."

If the key I'd given him—and what it could potentially symbolize—was messing with Justin's head, he would've absolutely told his best friend. And while I knew Leighton would die before giving up anything they discussed privately, I hoped he'd be able to give me enough of a clue so I could work it out myself.

"Ricci, he was far from upset when I saw him. He was glad to be back at work, grinning like an idiot on our first call out. And he was looking forward to coming home to you. It's not a secret the guy is crazy in love. So whatever his reason is for being MIA, it's not because of you."

I wished I could believe it, but my gut was telling me different. And while he might not be cheating on me, the blond was definitely connected to Tibbs and his disappearance.

"Look, why don't I call around and see if I can find him," Leighton offered. "Tibbs is a great guy, and I love him like a brother, but he can be absent-minded sometimes. Chances are someone asked him to do something and he just got tied up. Let me see what I can find out, but I'm positive you'll probably hear back from him before I do."

I squeezed the phone, unable to express my gratitude. "Thanks, Leighton. I owe you."

"Nah, you'd do the same for me. Talk soon, Ricci."

With the call ended, I decided to get a coffee and head back to my car, which was still parked near Justin's apartment. He would eventually have to talk to me. And hopefully Leighton would have better luck than I did locating him, so I could just be mad at him for making me act like a psycho. He was going to be punished for sure.

I was still thinking of ways of exacting restitution when I got back to my car, his black Impala driving in before I even unlocked my door.

Thank.

Fuck.

His eyes flicked to me, but there was no happiness in them. He looked exhausted, like a shell of a human being, and whether it was me or something else, he was definitely miserable.

Shit.

The pep talk I'd given myself on the way back from the coffee shop was toast. And every and all bad scenarios presented themselves front and center as I waited for him to get out of his car. I could barely breathe, watching as he ambled out slowly, hesitating before walking toward me.

It was so not good.

"Tibbs, you're really starting to freak me out." I reached for him, pulling him closer and wrapping my arms around him. "You look like you've seen a ghost."

He didn't talk, just kissed the top of my head gently and hugged me tighter.

"Justin," I lifted my chin, desperate to know what the hell was going on, "please talk to me. I can count the number of times I've been really scared, and this is one of them. Whatever is going on, it will be okay, I promise."

"You can't promise that," he whispered, dropping his lips to mine. "I'm sorry."

I had no idea what the apology was for, or what it meant, but it was breaking my heart. And not because I was worried about what he'd done, and why he'd felt I needed to hear it. But because whatever it was, he'd obviously given up. And that was the most terrifying thing of all.

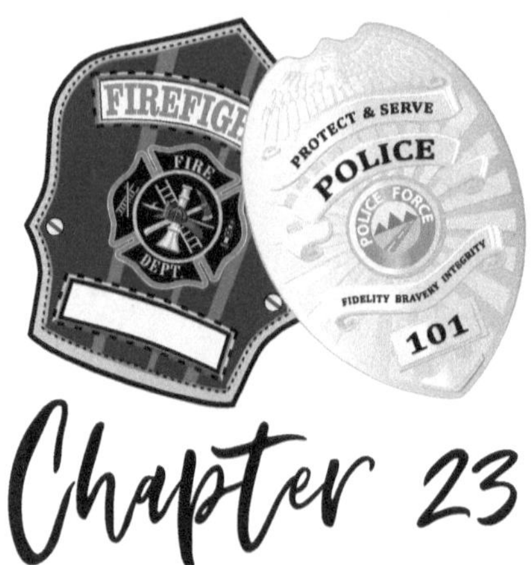

Chapter 23

Justin

SEEING TESSA AT my apartment wasn't a surprise.

Even a regular girlfriend would have been suspicious by a sudden change of plans, and Tessa was far from regular. But even though I'd expected it—and knew we had to have a conversation—it didn't make it any easier.

Honestly, it just made things a million times worse. Seeing that love and concern in her eyes, and knowing it was probably going to be for the last time.

Fuck.

Things had been epically screwed up. And it wasn't just my life that was about to be changed, but Tessa's as well. As for May, she'd had time to adjust, but was far from skating on easy street. The pregnancy, the birth, and everything that came after was a LOT to take on. And even though I promised I was going to be there every step of the way, it still didn't change that she was carrying the bigger burden.

"Tibbs, please," Tessa begged as I led her to my apartment.

I'd barely said two words since I'd hugged her in the parking lot, trying to formulate sentences that could adequately express how fucking sorry I was. And while I knew I hadn't intentionally gotten May pregnant, and sometimes shit just happened, it was really no one's fault.

But my actions—intentional or otherwise—were going to be responsible for hurting the woman I loved, and no matter which way you sliced it, that shit was on me.

"I just need to kiss you right now, Tessa." I lowered my mouth knowing I wasn't being fair. It was entirely possible that if she knew the whole truth, the last thing she'd want is my kiss and touch, which was why I needed to take it while I still could.

I was going to miss this.

Miss her.

And I wasn't willing to mourn the loss until I absolutely had to.

Her lips hesitated, the unasked questions just simmering below the surface, but she did me that favor. She kissed me back, holding me tightly as I backed her against the wall and felt every inch of her body pressed against mine.

I wanted to take her right there, to strip her naked and make love to her slowly, telling her how much I loved her. I wanted to make a memory for her that she'd never forget, something that would soften the blow. And maybe part of me wanted it for selfish reasons, to have her one last time without the baggage, and make her come so hard I'd ruin her for other men.

Other men.

Yeah, that was something I wasn't ready to fucking face, the thought alone making me want to kill something with my bare hands.

She pulled her lips from mine, resting her hands on my chest. "Justin, if you're dying, I'm going to kill you."

I laughed, my beautiful Tessa saying possibly the most Ricci thing ever. "I'm not dying, baby. But we definitely need to talk."

Taking a deep breath, I pulled away from her and moved toward the couch. I kept my fingers laced with hers, needing whatever contact I could get as we sat down and got comfortable. I had no idea where to even start, looking at those beautiful brown eyes as I opened my mouth.

"So, I had a visitor today after I finished work."

"The five-five, five-four blond who's approximately one hundred and fifty pounds?" she interrupted, looking to me for confirmation.

"Umm, yeah," I coughed out not expecting she'd already done recon. Although I wasn't really shocked either, and wouldn't have been surprised if she produced a composite drawing she had prepared. "*May*, her name is May."

"Who is May, Justin?" she asked, her tone tempered.

She was probably assuming the worst, which, to be fair, wasn't far from the truth. While I hadn't done anything with May in a really long time, it wasn't going to matter.

Nodding and knowing prolonging it wasn't doing me any favors, I got my mouth moving again. "She's a girl I saw casually. Not really a girlfriend, but it was more than a one-night stand. I need you to know that while I think she's a great person, it is not like what I have with you. I *never* loved her, Tessa. I've only ever loved you."

"Tibbs, please. I can already tell this is bad and what I'm imagining is probably worse than it is. But you need to tell me straight. Did you fuck her? Is she blackmailing you?"

I shook my head, knowing that would be her immediate go-to. "I haven't had sex with her in three months. Way before we got together, and I haven't had sex with *anyone* else since that night I saw you in the bar. I am not cheating on you, Tessa. I wouldn't do that. And she's not trying to extort me either. But she's—"

"Pregnant," Tessa finished for me, a million emotions flashing through her eyes. "She's pregnant, right?"

She was going to make one hell of a detective, barely having any of the puzzle pieces and putting it together all the same.

"A girl, you didn't share a deep connection with, shows up after three months looking miserable and wearing sweats. I spoke to James at the station, he saw you two talking and said she didn't look happy. And now you look like your world has ended. I'm right, aren't I?" Those eyes were begging me to prove her wrong, wanting for me to provide any other explanation other than the one she so expertly put together herself. But wishful thinking wasn't going to change shit, no matter who was thinking it.

"Twelve weeks," I confirmed. "She just had her scan."

The sharp intake of air cut me to the core as she visibly moved back. I wasn't sure if she'd meant to create the distance or if it had been unconsciously, but that one movement confirmed everything I'd thought about on the drive home.

"Twelve weeks. Wow." Her breaths were shallow and uneven. "*Twelve* weeks."

I knew she'd have questions, probably some of the same ones I'd asked May. We'd started at the coffee shop, and then when she told me she'd had her scan we went back to her apartment. It felt like a conversation we needed to have in private, and for better or worse, I wanted to look at a photo of what potentially was my son or daughter.

You could see the baby as clear as day, a perfectly formed little person surrounded by a shadowy bubble. And as I held those black and white images in my hand, deep down I knew it was mine. "Obviously I'm getting a paternity test, but the math adds up and I don't think she's lying. She just isn't the kind of girl who would do that."

A humorless laugh made its way up her throat. "Isn't the kind of girl? Tibbs, how would you fucking know? You said it yourself, you didn't really know her that well, that it was just sex. And what happened to the condom?"

Anger bit at her tone, and I knew she had every right. But lashing out at May wasn't going to help either, because she hadn't exactly done it to herself.

"Tessa, when I said I've always worn one, I meant it. I'd never lie to you. But sometimes—and I know it's shitty—they don't work for whatever reason. And I know this is a lot to deal with. But you have to trust me on this. May isn't the enemy. The situation is fucked up, and I don't blame you for being pissed off and hurt. But it won't change anything."

"Great, so now you're defending *her* and I'm the bad guy." She got to her feet, pushing me away. "Look, I think I should go. I really need to get some air because I feel like I can't breathe."

That was a feeling I could relate to, understanding the need to get out. But I didn't want to leave it the way it was.

"Baby, I'm not defending her. And if anyone is the bad guy, it's me. I know this hurts and I'm responsible, but please don't walk out of here like this. You shouldn't even be driving yet."

"I was worried, Justin," she hissed out, pushing me away. "Of course I got in my car. When you didn't answer your phone, I thought something bad had happened to you."

"I know, and I know I should've called. But I didn't know what to say, and May and I had a lot to talk about. I'm not going to let a child of mine grow up without a dad, Tessa." It was a shitty excuse, but it was the only one I had. Having silenced my phone because instinctively I knew she'd call, and I wouldn't have been able to lie to her.

She held out her hands, stopping me from getting any closer. "Justin, I know that I probably sound like a raving bitch right now, but I just found out my boyfriend is having a baby with someone else. And I know it was before we got together and that it was in the past, but it feels very much in the present to me. And maybe some other woman would be totally cool with it, but I can't pretend that it doesn't hurt. So what I'm going to do is leave and clear my head before I say something hurtful, because they seem to be the only words I have."

It wasn't easy to hear, but at least she was being honest. And as much as I knew she was probably right, and distance was probably what we needed, it felt so wrong.

I was completely torn, not knowing what the hell was the right thing to do. I wanted to fight for her and beg on my hands and knees if that's what it took. Or did I let her walk away and hope she came back? It was a gamble that had a buy-in well above what I was willing to pay, worried there was a better-than-average chance she wouldn't return.

"Ricci . . .Tessa, you don't sound like a raving bitch. Please don't go."

Her body gave me the answer without her needing to say a word. She'd wrapped her arms around her middle protectively, standing as far as she could from me without being out in the hall. Nothing I said was going to change her mind, and I understood that. Hell, her reaction was exactly what I'd expected, what I'd prepared myself for, and even then, it still fucking stung.

"Okay." I nodded, defeated and unwilling to add to any more of her pain. "As much as I don't want you to leave, I know I have to let you go. But please be safe. And if you feel dizzy or sick, promise me you'll pull over. Call Miller if you don't want to call me, I just need to be sure you get home safe."

"I'll be fine." Her voice flat as she reached for the door. "Bye, Tibbs."

"Bye, Tessa," the words almost choking me on the way out, "I love you."

And when she didn't say it back, I knew that goodbye was probably for good.

Fuck.

Tessa hadn't been the only person looking for me, Leighton letting himself into my apartment with his spare set of keys sometime after she'd left. "Jesus, Tibbs, Tessa's been looking for you and no one else had seen you since you left work. Even I was starting to get worried."

Fortunately—or maybe it was unfortunately, I couldn't be sure which—for Leighton, I'd used the time since Tessa walked out productively. Jack Daniels and I were having ourselves a little party on the floor, half the bottle already consumed. Because as dumb as it was to get drunk—and knowing it solved nothing—it had seemed like a really attractive option.

"What the fuck?" He looked to me and then to the bottle. "Are you trying to fuck up your liver?"

"My liver is fine," I slurred, doing my best to stay upright. "It's the rest of me that's fucked up."

Taking the bottle—my ability to stop him hindered by gravity and a blood alcohol level that was probably close to my buddy Jack's—he screwed the cap back on and put it on the table.

"Here's what we're going to do." He reached down, yanking me off the floor and helping me on to the couch. *I hadn't wanted to sit there, remembering it was where I'd hurt Tessa.* "I'm going to make coffee, and you're going to start talking."

I groaned, tossing my head back and closing my eyes. "Uhhhhhhhhhhh, I don't want to talk. Talking isn't going to change shit. What I want is for you to hand me back the bottle and leave me to my misery."

"Wow, dramatic much." Leighton laughed, the bastard still having the ability since his life hadn't gone nuclear. "And I'm not doing either, *Justin*. Giving you back the bottle or leaving. So start talking or we're going to sit here in an awkward silence. I'll call Presley if I have to."

"Do *not* call my sister," I warned, not even having thought about what my family was going to say. "And in case you've forgotten, you were my friend before anything ever happened with her, so your loyalty should be to me."

He shook his head, giving up on the coffee idea and taking a seat beside me. "Now I know you're fucking drunk. Because as much as I love your sister—and can't wait to make her my wife—I have always and will always have your back. Now stop acting like a prick and tell me what the hell is going on. I assume it has something to do with Tessa?"

I laughed, because it was funny he could be so wrong and so right at the same time. "Yeah, so I'm going to be a daddy."

"Tessa's pregnant?" He blinked back in surprise.

"Nope." My lips popped on the P as I jabbed him in the ribs. "Try again. I mean, it really could be anyone. I'm pretty sure I fucked half the city—at least that's what Tessa probably thinks— it's a miracle there's only one baby. Maybe there's more. Maybe," I leaned in closer, pushing out a breath, "there's a whole fucking basketball team of little Tibbs I don't even know about."

"Tibbs, what? Who? How?"

"May." I groaned, my head pounding from either the Jack or the situation. "The blond I met like four months ago. We used condoms, but clearly we're in that *lucky* two percent where it didn't work. I found out this afternoon. She's due in six months. And astonishingly my girlfriend isn't excited by the news. Who would have guessed it?"

"Fuck," Leighton cursed out, reaching for the bottle on the coffee table, unscrewing the lid and taking a swig himself. "Okay, so she knows?"

My head bobbed forward, attempting a nod but being unable to complete the action. "Yeah, she knows. And fairly sure when she said goodbye it was for good too. I can't even blame her, because why the hell would she even want to stick around?

So that's where I'm at. Now give me back the bottle." I tossed out my hand, hoping I'd feel the cool reassuring glass against it.

"Nope, no more drinking. We're going to figure this out."

"Figure it out?" I laughed. With the level of optimism he had, I had to wonder if he wasn't the one who was drunk. "Brother, did you not hear me? I'm going to be a father, and not with the woman I'm in love with. You think that's something we can *figure out*?"

No.

It wasn't.

I could save him the time, and the effort, and tell him right now that there wasn't a fix. Because I'd ran every fucking scenario in my head at least a dozen times and ended up with the same fucking result.

Assuming Tessa got over it—and that was a *huge* fucking *if*—she'd end up resenting me. There were going to be times where I would need to sack up and be a dad because that kid didn't choose to be born, and I was going to have to put him or her first. How was that going to fly when you were trying to tell a woman she was the most important thing in your world?

Or even, if by some miracle, we tried to fucking work it out and Tessa and I stayed together. And she didn't hate me for having a baby with someone else. How the fuck was I going to give her the support and love she fucking deserved? She wanted to be a detective, and already dealt with my weird hours, how could I ask her to accept even less of my time while I tried to work, be a half-way decent dad annnnnnd be a boyfriend to her? Even if she didn't hate me, I'd hate myself, knowing I was shortchanging her and stopping her from having better. And fuck did it kill me to even consider the possibility of her being with someone else. But if I loved her like I said I did, then I had to do what was right for her too.

And then there was May.

She also deserved better. And while I was not ready to fucking drop to a knee and marry her just because we were going to be sharing DNA, she needed to be able to count on me. I would *not* be one of those assholes who didn't own his responsibilities.

"As hard as it is to say, Leighton, I can't be with her." It was the first time I'd admitted it out loud. Hating the way the words felt in my mouth even though I knew they were the right ones. "It's not fair to her, and I won't put her through that. I'd be selfish to even ask, and she deserves better. I fucking love her enough to see that being with me will only hold her back. And I'd rather her hate me now than later when I've completely fucked up her life."

"Tibbs, don't you think she should get a say?" Leighton offered, clinging to hope like I was to my sobriety.

"No, because for once in my life I'm going to do the right thing and put someone else first."

And even if she couldn't see it—or maybe would never even know—I loved her that much.

Enough to break my own heart worse than I could ever break hers.

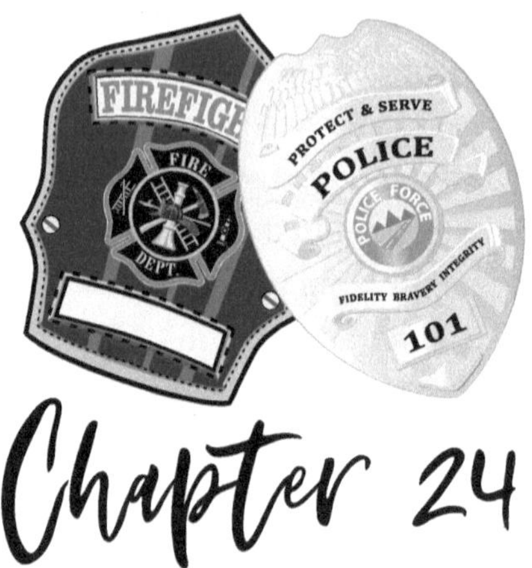

Chapter 24

Tessa

I DIDN'T REMEMBER driving back to Brooklyn, sitting outside my apartment in my still-running car wondering how the hell I'd gotten there. It probably wasn't a good thing either, knowing I was taking chances I'd usually yell at someone else for, and switching off my ignition as I wiped my eyes.

Crying wasn't something I did often. Not because I thought it showed weakness or anything like that, but because I'd usually kept my eyes firmly fixed on the future. You couldn't change the past, so why live in real estate you didn't want to pay rent for? But every once in a while—whenever I'd wonder if I'd lost the capacity—something or someone would make me cry.

Justin Tibbs was the latest in a very short list.

Intellectually I *knew* he hadn't intentionally gotten someone else pregnant, and it had happened way before we'd even started dating. But the thought of him fathering a baby with someone else—sharing that special moment with someone else—just broke my heart into so many pieces I wasn't sure it would ever be put back together.

I'd wanted it to be me.

Not right now. Hell, we hadn't even moved in together yet. But I'd hoped—sometime in the future—that there might be a little person that was part me and part him. And it was stupid irony that I'd never ever considered having a baby until I'd met him.

He was going to make an amazing father, the thought making me cry even harder because I felt like it was so unfair. And I knew I was being unfair too, my feelings so scattered and fractured that I didn't even want to consider what he was going through.

I hated him.

I hated her.

And I hated myself.

Everything felt like it was too much as I sucked in desperate breaths while I continued to sob.

We'd been in such a good place.

And just like that . . . it was gone.

Forcing myself to get out of the car, I made my way back to my apartment. The last thing I needed was for one of my neighbors coming to investigate, or worse, calling the cops. Because *that* would be a fun conversation to have with people who knew my boss. I could already imagine the station gossip.

Fuck!

It was already going to be bad, almost everyone knowing Tibbs and I were together. And that was why you shouldn't date anyone you might see or have to deal with at work.

I was such a fucking idiot.

When I was in the safety of my apartment, I crumbled to the floor. I knew crying wasn't going to solve anything, but I couldn't do much else, grabbing my phone and dialing the one man—other than my father—who would never hurt me.

Grayson Miller.

"Ricci, what's happening? I know you can't do much to hurry along your recovery, but I'm kinda lonely without you so I'm really glad you called."

I could hear the smile in his voice, could picture his amazingly kind eyes, and it just made me cry harder.

"Grayson," his name torn out between sobs, "I need you."

Miller hadn't asked questions.

Just got in his car and drove the couple of blocks to my apartment, letting himself in with a spare key I kept at his house, and picked me up off the floor. He didn't even ask why I was there, just scooped me up, carried me to my bedroom, and laid me on the bed.

Then he held me. Letting me wet the front of his T-shirt with tears that didn't seem to stop, stroking my hair in such a calming way that I eventually closed my eyes.

It was only after I woke up still hugging him that I realized I'd fallen asleep.

"Miller?" I croaked out, my throat feeling dry and scratchy.

He stirred, also having fallen asleep and opened his eyes. "Hey Ricci." His hand rubbed against my shoulder as he gave me a sad smile. "You need me to get you some water?"

I nodded, watching as he threw his legs over the bed and padded out to my kitchen. He'd taken off his shoes, mine also having been removed, and I couldn't remember if he'd done it for me or if I'd been responsible. Everything felt like a blur, like it had been a week since I'd left Justin's apartment, when I knew it had only been hours.

Miller returned with a tumbler of ice water, sitting on the edge of the bed as I swallowed it down. I knew I had a lot of explaining to do, comforted by the fact that Miller would never rush me. It's why our friendship had always worked, both of us innately knowing what each other needed. And I couldn't have asked for a better best friend and partner if I tried.

"Tibbs and I—" I started, stalling out just from saying his name.

Miller shook his head. "He called me while you were asleep. He was worried you didn't make it home and wanted me to check on you. Then he told me the whole thing. You don't have to say anything, Tessa, unless you want to."

I breathed out a sigh of relief, thankful I was saved from recounting it. "I don't really want to talk about it."

"Then we won't." Miller shrugged. "What we *are* going to do is get you hydrated and get some dinner. I haven't eaten yet and I'm guessing you haven't either."

I shook my head, unable to remember the last time I ate something. Breakfast? I didn't have lunch, too busy trying to track down a missing Tibbs when he hadn't been missing at all. "Yeah, okay. But can you order in, I'm not up to going out."

He tapped my leg, giving me a small smile. "Ricci, we can absolutely order in. I'm thinking pizza because carbs cure everything."

I nodded in agreement. "Carbs are definitely our friend. Order a large."

While Miller organized dinner, I went to the bathroom and took a shower. It felt good to just wash everything away, feeling better after I dried off and slipped on my pajamas. And by the time I'd walked back into the living room, the pizza had arrived, both of us sitting on my couch and eating straight from the box.

"So, when's your next assessment?" Miller asked, avoiding the topic of me and Tibbs entirely. "I wasn't kidding when I said I was lonely. They've got me partnered up with Davis, and while I think the guy is okay, he's no Tessa Ricci."

It was good to feel missed. The concern about being away so long that I'd somehow be replaced, something I'd actually considered. "Next week. Other than having a headache now—which I'm positive is from all the crying—I've been good the last few days. I know they're just being cautious, but the sooner I can get back to active duty, the better." *Especially now.*

"Good, well fingers crossed the doc says you can come back." He took another bite. "Are you okay if I spend the night? I don't feel like driving all the way back."

"Grayson, *all the way back*? You live like five miles away." I laughed, the idea that he couldn't drive home, ridiculous. "If you're worried about me, you don't need to be. I'm fine now. I've gotten it out of my system."

Miller dropped the slice he was eating and shook his head. "Look, I wasn't going to bring it up because you said you didn't want to talk about it, and I can respect that. But Tessa, you didn't see yourself when I walked in. In all the years we've known each other, I have never seen you that devastated."

"It was just a shock, okay," I protested, knowing I had been a mess, but I was since doing better. "I hadn't been expecting to find out my boyfriend had fathered someone else's baby. But I've accepted it now. I mean, it's not like a have a lot of choice. And really, it doesn't have anything to do with me, does it?"

"What does that mean?" Miller asked.

My brows furrowed, confused by the question. "What do you mean, what does it mean? Two people are having a child, and I'm not one of them. What I want, doesn't matter."

"So you and Tibbs broke up?"

I laughed, and then stopped, because honestly, I didn't know. *Had we broken up?* I'd been pretty mad when I stormed out, so I had no idea where it had all been left. I guess I assumed we did, or that I did, or at least, that it was what I wanted. But I hated to admit, I was no longer sure.

If we had broken up.

And if that was what I wanted.

"I think . . . I guess I don't really know." I shrugged, shaking my head.

What the hell was wrong with me? He was going to have a baby with his ex-girlfriend. Where would I even fit in that equation? They'd be a team—because hello, baby—and I'd be the third wheel. Who knows, maybe they'd get married and be a family, and I'd be the home wrecker, standing in the way.

"He's going to be a really good dad, you know." I sighed, feeling my chest get tight. "And he's going to want to do the right thing."

Miller reached out and grabbed my hand. "But what do *you* want? And don't tell me it doesn't matter. Because I don't give a fuck about Tibbs or his ex-girlfriend."

My lip trembled, but I promised myself I was done crying. "I love him, Miller. I wish I didn't, and I just can't turn it off. But I also know that right now, I hate the thoughts in my own head. I can't be happy for him. I can't be happy for her. And I can't be happy for this innocent life they created that has done nothing to me other than ruin my life by its very existence. Did you hear what I just said? I am blaming a *baby*, for ruining my life. What kind of monster thinks those things?" I shook my head, hearing myself and being disgusted. "Am I a terrible person, Grayson? Because right now, I feel like one."

Miller slung his arm around me and brought me in for a hug. "Tessa, you aren't even close to being a terrible person. All those feelings are valid. And yeah, I even understand hating the baby, however irrational it is. Not only do I not judge you, but I can't say my reaction would be any different. Do you not remember how crazy I was when I found out Maxine was cheating?" He reared back, pulling his mouth into a grimace. "You got a long way to go before you hit the big leagues, sister."

I snuggled in closer, so thankful he was with me. "Hey, Miller."

"Yeah, Ricci."

"Maybe you should spend the night. I don't really want to be alone."

It was a big step for me to admit it, but I needed his comfort and support.

He chuckled, rubbing my arm gently. "I wasn't planning on going anywhere."

Chapter 25

Justin

MILLER HAD ASSURED me Tessa was home and safe, but I still fought the urge to go see for myself. I should never have let her get into a car, cursing myself for not taking her keys and calling her a fucking cab. If something had happened to her, or if she—I couldn't even finish the thought, swallowing hard and glad she'd called Miller when she'd gotten home.

I'd barely been able to sleep, constantly checking my phone for a message from her that didn't come. And it was totally wrong to even want it. Because what the hell was I going to say back? That I loved her and that I wanted her? None of that would be helpful and only prolonged what I promised myself I'd do.

End it.

It was the only way.

And maybe it was already over, saving me from having to be a bigger asshole than I already was. It wasn't even funny how much I toggled between wishing for it—because I was a coward and couldn't be trusted to pull the pin—and praying she wasn't done yet.

Fuck, I'd really made a mess. Finally met a girl I couldn't live without and was going to have to say goodbye.

Poetic justice.

Guess that was what I got for believing love was for suckers and relationships weren't my thing. They really showed me.

As maxed out as I felt on disappointing people, I decided to go and see my parents. They were going to be grandparents and had a right to know. And honestly, I needed someone else to yell at me awhile and drown out the voices in my head.

They were predictably stunned, both Mom and Dad sitting silently at the kitchen table as they heard the news. No yelling— which was a disappointment—and finally asking a few questions once the initial shock had worn off.

"I'm glad you are doing the right thing, Son," my dad breathed out. "I know it's not going to be easy, but you're not a kid anymore, either. And we raised you to take responsibility for your actions."

"I know, and I'm going to do everything I can to be a decent dad. I know I've got a long way to go before I'm close to your level, but I don't want my son or daughter thinking they weren't wanted." It was hard to look at a man I'd idolized and admit I'd fallen short. But between him and the chief, I'd had some pretty fucking awesome role models and the benchmark was set high. So I was going to do everything I could not to screw it up.

My dad slapped me on the shoulder, his heavy hand giving me a squeeze. "You're a good man, Justin. Don't doubt that. You don't have to try to be on some level, just be yourself. That is more than good enough."

Trust my dad to say something nice and make me feel even worse. So much for getting yelled at. And to think you used to be able to count on your parents for that.

"Where does Tessa fit into all of this?" my mom asked, giving me a look that was beyond serious. "Have you told her?"

I rubbed the back of my neck, knowing she'd be curious. My mom loved Tessa, and I think secretly harbored fantasies that I'd be next down the aisle after Presley. So it was unsurprising that she was asking.

"She knows, but we broke up, and it's for the best. It would be unfair to Tessa to ask her to be a part of this, and I want her to be happy." The words felt bitter in my mouth and I wasn't sure I believed them, but I said them anyway. Because as much as I wanted them to be bullshit, every single one of them was true.

"Oh, okay." My mom knotted her hands in her lap, and I knew she had more to say. But she didn't say it, the acknowledgement feeling more like an accusation.

"I know you both loved Tessa." I decided it was easier just to get it over with. "But not even close to how much I do. And that's *why* I'm doing this. This will kill her, and I won't have it. May and the baby need me right now, and like Dad said, I'm doing the right thing."

"You're not going to marry May, are you?" My mother looked panicked. "Because, Justin, that is an antiquated tradition, and marrying someone you aren't in love with is a very bad idea."

"I don't know," I admitted. The thought had crossed my mind at some point in the early morning, and it wasn't like I was going to be marrying anyone else. The only woman I'd ever *wanted* to marry was Tessa, and that was no longer on the table. "I'm not rushing into anything, but who knows what will happen in the future. Anyway, it doesn't matter. I'm going to be there for both of them, with or without the ring."

"You want to do right by May, you be honest with her," my dad warned. "It would be easy to pretend and make promises right now, but all that is going to do is hurt her in the long run."

"I know, I know." I shook my head, the pressure of trying to keep everyone's feelings straight making me feel like I was drowning. "Trust me, the last thing I'm going to do is lead her on."

My mom stood, walking around and giving me a hug. "We know, Justin. And we want you to know how much we love and support you. Dad and I will do everything we can to help you in any way. We're proud of you, baby. And when you're both ready, we'd like to meet May too."

Hearing they were proud was hard, mostly because I felt so undeserving. But that's what you got when you had awesome parents. Even when you fucked up, they loved you unconditionally.

"Well, I'm going to head back to Midtown. I promised Leighton I'd tell Presley. He is incapable of keeping a secret from her, so I should go see them." I got to my feet, grabbing my keys. "And thanks for being so cool about all of this."

"Awww, baby, you don't ever have to thank us," my mother cooed. "Make sure you keep us updated."

Saying goodbye to both of them, I headed back over the bridge. I really wasn't in the mood to see either Presley or Leighton, deciding to go home first. What did it matter if I waited another hour or two? And to be honest, if I didn't take a minute just for myself, it was possible my head was going to explode from the pressure.

It was déjà vu when I got back to my apartment.

Tessa leaning against her Toyota, waiting for me in the parking lot.

I had to fight the urge not to run and kiss her, just *seeing* her simultaneously the best and worst thing ever.

It was never going to get easier.

For as long as I lived, I was never going to be able to look at her and not love her.

Cursing under my breath, I got out of my car. If she'd come to yell at me—or hell, even hit me—then I was going to give her that chance.

"Hey." It was all I allowed myself to say, knowing if I said anything else it wouldn't be good for either of us.

"Hey," she responded, folding her arms across her chest.

Her body told me everything I needed to know. She was wounded, her arms wrapped around her chest, protecting her from a hurt I'd put there. And knowing how strong she was—both inside and out—it cut me in ways I doubted I'd ever be able to recover from.

"I know I'm the last person you want to hear this from, but I really wish you wouldn't drive." I looked at the car, my private hell from the night before being re-lived all over again. "I'd have come to you if you wanted to talk."

"Miller drove. He's taking a walk." Her admission making me breathe a sigh of relief. "And I wasn't sure if you'd come, so I figured it was just easier if I did."

There was so much in that, I didn't even know where to start. She could ask almost anything, and I'd fucking do it, traveling to Brooklyn, the least of it. But I had to remind myself making that confession wouldn't be helping anyone, so I kept my mouth shut and I nodded for her to continue.

"Justin—" she stopped, swallowing hard before going on, "I just wanted to say that I think you're going to make a great dad. This baby is lucky to have you."

Every single word cut me, the underlying pain in her voice, even worse. She was trying to be the bigger person, and I hated that she felt she needed to.

"Tessa, you don't have to do this." *Please don't do this.* "You are absolutely entitled to be angry and hurt. No one expects you—"

"Well thanks for the permission, Tibbs, but I'm not here for that." She cut me off, a new wave of hurt flashing through her eyes. "And I don't care what anyone expects." She swore under her breath, moving her lips silently like she was having a separate conversation with herself. "Anyway, that's why I came." Her tone had artificially brightened, and I hated it. "Because I couldn't say it yesterday, and it needed to be said."

I wasn't sure it *was* needed, but I wasn't going to argue with her. "Thanks, was there anything else?"

It was a landmine, and so fucking stupid I already regretted it. Because what I wanted to hear was not what I needed her to say, the tug-of-war in my head and my heart so fucking brutal I wish she'd just fucking hit me.

"Yeah, that's it." She balled her hands at her sides, trying to manage a fake smile. "Well, I should let you go."

And wasn't that the statement of the century. Because that's exactly what I was doing, letting *her* go. "Okay, and thanks again," I mumbled awkwardly, shoving my hands in my pockets. "I'll let you go find Miller."

Even though it needed to be said, I couldn't do another goodbye. Instead, deciding to carry through with the theme and be an asshole as I turned and walked away.

"Bye, Tibbs."

I stopped, hearing her call out to me, but I didn't turn around.

I couldn't.

There was some shit I just wasn't capable of, and that was at the top of the list.

And without looking back, I took a deep breath.

"See ya, Ricci."

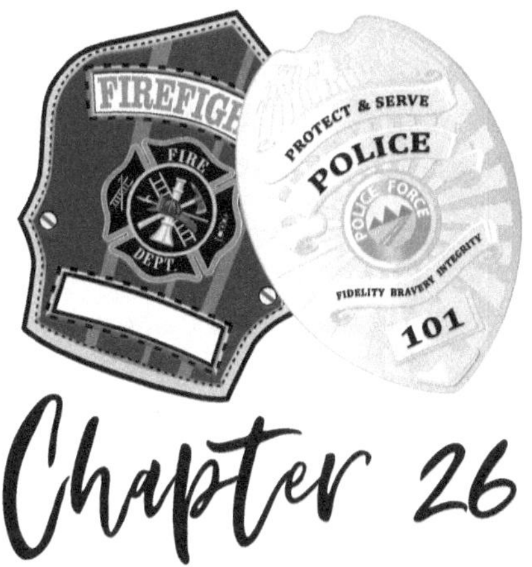

Chapter 26

Justin

IT HAD BEEN four weeks since I'd last seen Tessa, only hearing about her returning to duty from North. I was positive he was looking for a reaction, mentioning it casually after we'd gotten back from a call out. I wasn't sure if I'd passed the test, doing my best to look impassive when he said her name, and wishing I could call her to see how she was doing.

There'd been zero communication between us.

No text messages, no calls, not even a fucking like on her social media. It was like we didn't even know each other—our earlier friendship dissolving as well. And I guess it was for the best.

I'd told myself I would be cool running into her, assuming now she was back, I might see her in the field like before. But honestly, I was glad I hadn't, thanking my lucky stars it always seemed to be someone else from the NYPD who showed up.

Not sure if that was by fate or design, and really it didn't fucking matter.

"Hey, you want to grab some breakfast?" Leighton offered, doing his best to pull me from my funk. "Presley got in late last night, so I'm going to let her sleep. I've got a couple of hours to kill."

"Nah, May has a doctor's appointment. They're going to do another scan and hopefully we get to see if it's a boy or a girl. The baby was uncooperative last time." I tried to smile but wasn't really feeling it, fatigue weighing me down.

"Imagine a kid of yours being uncooperative," Leighton laughed. "Guess some genetics you just can't outrun."

He was right, and it wasn't like I needed any more proof. But since the paternity test had already proclaimed me the daddy, I guess it was fitting that the kid already started displaying Tibbs-like traits.

"All right, well, make sure you let us know when you find out, Presley and I are excited for you." He slapped me on the back and closed his locker. "And if there's anything you need, make sure you ask."

I had to hand it to the guy, he was *really* trying.

Presley had flown completely off the handle when she'd found out. Not about the baby of course. She was weirdly excited about being an aunt again, already filling that role a couple of times over on Leighton's side. But she made it crystal fucking clear that she thought I was a stupid moron for letting Tessa go. And I couldn't even argue with her, knowing she was right. But *being* right and *doing* right were two very different things, so even though I had to endure the stink eye from my sister, nothing was changing.

"Thanks, brother, we're all good. I'll call you when I know." I grabbed my backpack and headed out the door.

May lived in a small apartment in the Village with her sister, and usually I'd have offered to pick her up. But since our appointment was in Midtown and I was getting off work, she'd insisted we meet there, saving me from doubling back.

She was already waiting for me in the coffee shop when I arrived, sipping her herbal tea. She smiled as I got closer to the table, pushing a cup toward me. "Double espresso, and I got you a breakfast wrap as well."

"Thanks, May, you're the best." I took off my backpack and joined her at the table. "How are you feeling?"

Things were surprisingly great between us. She hadn't fought my decision to be in her and the baby's life, and actively welcomed my involvement. But despite me offering my spare bedroom to her at least a dozen times, she kept turning me down. I'd assumed she'd have jumped at the chance, considering we'd agreed to raise the baby together, it made sense to live in the same place. Not to mention saving her a buttload in rent, and access to my car whenever she needed it, but she insisted she wanted to keep living with her sister.

"How was work? You look tired." She lowered her cup and gave me her full attention. "You know I could've gone to the appointment on my own if you needed to sleep. I could've FaceTime'd you for the big reveal."

I shook my head, not willing to miss any more than I already had. It was bad enough she'd gone the first twelve weeks without me by her side, moving forward I was going to be there each and every time. "I *want* to be there, May. It's important to me. And work was a little crazy, but I can sleep when I get back."

Ironically—even though we'd obviously had sex and our DNA had mingled—our relationship wasn't even close to romantic. There were no accidental kisses or inappropriate touches, with it feeling so fucking platonic I was confused how we'd gotten together in the first place.

But whether it made sense or not, we'd settled into an easy existence. And out of all the casual relationships I'd had, I was glad that if I'd had to accidentally knock someone up, it had been her.

She reached across giving my hand a little squeeze before returning to her tea. We drank, sitting in a comfortable silence together before heading to our appointment.

May gave her name to the receptionist, both of us taking a seat as we waited our turn. There were other couples throughout the room, varying stages of bumps on display as were the diverse looks on their faces.

Before I could try and stop it, my mind took a little detour, wondering what Tessa would look like pregnant. It wasn't hard to imagine, the idea of her with a swollen belly making heat crawl up my neck.

Not fucking helpful, Tibbs, I reminded myself, shaking loose the mental picture and trying to not feel like a fucking prick for thinking it in the first place.

I'd been so involved in trying to scrub all thoughts of Tessa from my brain, I almost missed it when we'd been called. May had needed to give my hand a jerk, prompting me out of my chair before we walked toward the exam room.

"Okay, let's see if baby will let us take a peek." The woman with the ultrasound wand grinned as May laid on the table. "We didn't have any luck last time."

I chuckled, holding May's hand as the gel was squeezed onto her belly. "That's probably my fault. I've been known to be stubborn."

The swishing noises of the ultrasound filled the room, and then came the steady rhythm of the heartbeat. Boy or girl, our baby was strong, my fingers gripping May's a little tighter as we listened.

Then there he or she was. A perfectly formed little human moving in her belly with little legs, feet and hands, as clear as day on the monitor. It was nothing like the photos, the sight of the little person making me choke up.

"Well, we are definitely having better luck this time. Either of you want to take a guess?" She looked at us excitedly, pausing on a frame.

"Is that a . . ." May squinted, looking at the screen.

"A penis," I finished. "We're having a boy."

"Yep, definitely a boy." The ultrasound tech nodded. "Let me print some pictures off for you. Everything else looks great. No concerns at all."

The pictures were printed and handed to me as May wiped off the gel. It wasn't until we were walking outside that the full realization hit me that I was going to have a son.

"Holy shit," I grabbed May, hugging her before planting a kiss on her lips. "We're having a boy."

But as awesome as that moment felt, the kiss was all wrong, both of us pulling away from each other in a hurry.

"Sorry, got caught up in the moment." I tried to smile.

May reached for my hand and threaded it with hers. "You don't have to be sorry. Honestly, I'd been wondering, and the kiss pretty much confirmed it."

"Nothing, huh?" I chuckled, unbelievably relieved it hadn't been just me.

She shook her head as she laughed. "Nope. So weird. I still think you're hot though."

"Jesus, May, don't do me any favors." I shook my head, suddenly feeling a little lighter. "Well, I guess we know now."

"Yeah, we do." She grabbed my hand as we walked back to my car. "But just because there's no attraction, doesn't mean I'm not happy that this is your baby. You're going to make a great dad, Justin."

I'd heard those exact words before, except she hadn't been the one to say them. That day, in the parking lot—one of the hardest of my life. And I guess it was written on my face, May looking at me concerned. "What is it? What did I say?"

"Nothing, May, honestly it's not you. Just that . . ." I debated being honest, wondering what made me a bigger prick. To lie, or tell her about Tessa. "Someone else said a similar thing to me a while ago, and I wasn't sure whether or not to believe them."

It was a compromise, but considering how amazing things were with me and May, I didn't want to screw it up. Instead I helped her into my Impala before getting into the driver's seat beside her.

Her hand reached out, stopping me from hitting the ignition. "You can say her name, Justin. I know you loved her."

Just talking about Tessa made it harder to breathe, the pressure in my chest returning. But it had been weeks, and it was for the best, and I had to get my head in the game and not screw it up for everyone else involved.

"It doesn't matter, and I don't want to hurt you by bringing up the past."

"Justin," May laughed, "you aren't hurting me. You've been nothing but great throughout this whole thing. You've gone above and beyond, and I count myself lucky to have you. But I know you're not in love with me. That you were *never* in love with me. And it's okay, because I wasn't in love with you either."

It wasn't earth-shattering news to hear she hadn't loved me, or that she knew I hadn't loved her, but I felt guilty all the same. Because surely no woman wanted to hear about the one you *did* love, even I knew that.

"Look, it doesn't matter. We didn't and don't love each other, that's fine. I'm good with it, May. I'm still going to be there for you and the baby, and that's what is important."

"Wait a minute." She held up her hand, turning in her seat to face me. "The other girl, the one you *were* in love with. Did she break up with you, or did you break up with her?"

I shrugged, positive I was entering dangerous territory and wishing I'd paid more attention to tempering my reaction. Fuck me, couldn't I just be normal for a change. Tessa was gone, why the hell did I have to keep thinking about her? "What difference does it make? We're not together. And honestly, I don't think we should be talking about this."

My hand moved to the ignition, but May pulled it back. "Why can't we talk about it? If you're worried about sparing my feelings, it's incredibly sweet but unnecessary. I'm not jealous over something I never had with you. And the circumstances of your breakup matters a lot, actually."

I heaved out a heavy breath, feeling so incredibly tired that I wasn't sure I had the energy to even pretend anymore. "You really want to talk about this?" I asked, giving her a chance to call timeout and we could go on our merry way. "Because you don't have to. I'm fine with the way things are."

May shook her head, a humorless laugh making its way up her throat. "You are not fine, Justin. You're miserable. And I can see it. Now, answer my question. Why are you not with her?"

What the hell could I say to that?

Because the truth was brutal and whether she thought she could handle it or not, I wasn't going to risk inflicting it. "We just decided—"

"Decided?" She interrupted me with a laugh. "You had a discussion and thought it was better to leave someone you obviously still care about? Was it her? Was it because of me? There has to be a reason. You don't just turn your back on someone you love."

It was too much.

The strain of it all wearing me down while I felt pulled in a million directions. Why couldn't everyone see I was fucking trying to do the right thing? Why the hell did it feel like I was forced to live in a perpetual state of purgatory with no chance of parole?

"Tessa," I hissed out her name on a breath, probably a little harsher than I'd intended. "Tessa," I said it again, the heat rising up my neck as my tone hardened and got louder. "And yes, I loved her, and yes, I still love her. But I'm here with you."

May sat in silence, my little outburst probably taking her by surprise considering I hadn't so much as raised my voice in her presence. But it was just too much, and I needed a fucking break, and fuck me, I was so fucking tired.

"I'm sorry." I shook my head, squeezing the bridge of my nose. "I just need to get some sleep. I didn't mean to lash out at you. It's just . . . it's not easy talking about her."

"It was you, wasn't it?" she said quietly. "You thought that in order to be a father to our baby, you had to let her go."

Bingo.

And why the hell were all the women in my life so fucking smart? Couldn't someone just pretend to know less than me? That would be a big help, thanks.

"May, this isn't your fault," I started to explain, not wanting her to think she was responsible.

"You're damn right it's not my fault," she scoffed, not letting me finish. "I'm not the one who blew up your life, Justin. Lots of people raise kids together but not *together*. And those kids thrive. What did you think was going to happen? We'd magically become a couple just because we're having a baby? Because I don't want to be with a man I'm not in love with and doesn't love me. So what? We don't date anyone else for as long as we live? That's the stupidest thing ever."

I was ready to argue, and then stopped, shutting my mouth because, well, she was sorta right. It was clear that May and I were never going to be a couple. And as unrealistic as it was that neither of us had a relationship with anyone else, I guess I hadn't given it much thought.

"What?" She smiled. "Trying to tell me I'm wrong, but realizing that I'm not? Well, well, today has given us more reason to celebrate than just finding out we're having a boy."

I laughed, because once again, she was right. "Okay, wiseass, give me a break here. But even if I admit you have a valid argument, there's still the big problem that being with someone is a two-person deal. She didn't exactly say she wanted to be with me either."

"Oh really? She gave you *no* indication that she cared and wanted to be with you?" she argued, not having any clue what Tessa was like.

"No, she didn't. If Tessa wanted to stay together, she would have said so." Hell, Ricci wasn't exactly shy in asking for what she wanted. So unless there'd been some magical sign that I'd missed, she was pretty clear she wanted it over too. "And can we just take a minute, because I still think this is weird, talking about it with you."

"No, it's not weird, so get over it. We are going to be having a lot of conversations in the future, and some of them might involve the women and men in our lives. This little boy," she reached down and stroked her small but growing bump, "is going to tie us together for the rest of our lives. And if you're being an idiot for giving up on the woman you love, then I'm going to tell you. Now, really think. There was nothing?"

I scrubbed my face with my hands, wondering if all the women in my life weren't only smart but liked to bust my balls. Presley, May, Tessa. Definitely a theme. "No."

"Did you *not* just tell me she'd said you were going to be a great dad?"

Awesome, me and my big mouth.

"And? She was being polite, trying to be the bigger person," I argued.

"Please." May laughed. "If she didn't want anything to do with you, she wouldn't have bothered. Why would she feel the need to bolster your ego? I'm fairly sure you know this already, but I'm going to tell you, anyway. You're extremely cocky, you don't need the encouragement. No, she told you *because* she cares about you. It was an opening, dumbass."

I waved my hands, refusing to believe I'd misread it. "No, no, no. She came over for closure, for one last goodbye—"

"Wait, she came *back* to see you, and then dropped these pearls of wisdom? Are you kidding me?" May looked horrified, punching me in the arm. "Seriously, I really hope our son inherits his ability to read cues from me because his father hasn't got a clue."

"Hey! Why don't we rewind to how awesome a dad I'm going to be instead of calling me a dumbass." I shook my head, glad it had been May's right hook instead of Ricci's. That wouldn't be as easy to shake off.

"*Tibbs.*" She rarely called me that, saying she thought it was weird to use my last name. "She came BACK. She wanted you to fight for her, goddamn it. I don't even know this girl, but I know that."

"But—"

"Really?" She laughed. "Look, it's obvious you are trying to do the right thing. And I appreciate it. But it doesn't work like that. And if she was willing to give it a chance—even with us in the picture—then you should have tried too. I want to teach our little boy that love comes in all different ways. And we can love each other and not be *in* love, and not love him any less. But I also want him to see *both* his parents happy, and his daddy needs to be with the woman he loves for that to happen."

Jesus.

Christ.

I could barely speak, wondering if everything I'd been thinking and doing had really been wrong.

"It's probably too late," I sighed, unable to take back the lost time and distance. "There's no guarantee she'd even talk to me again, let alone still want to be with me."

May leaned in closer. "Nope, no guarantees. But isn't something so important worth trying for anyway?"

And once again, she was fucking right.

"Yeah, yeah it is."

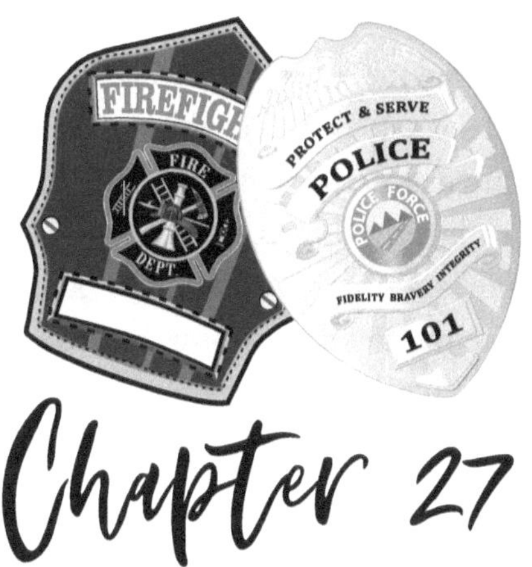

Chapter 27

Tessa

"TESSA, OUT OF the ring!" my father yelled from the other side of the ropes. "Now."

"Just give me someone else," I huffed, the guy I'd been going rounds with limping to the corner. "Where's Terenzio?"

My dad entered the ring and pulled at my gloves. "I said, get out of the ring. Your technique is sloppy and you're taking cheap shots. And either you're going to hurt yourself or someone else. That shit doesn't fly in my gym, and you know better."

The concussion meant training had been sidelined. But I'd been cleared weeks ago, and I was anxious to get back, and more than anything I really missed hitting things.

"I wasn't taking cheap shots," I argued, annoyed he'd stopped me. "If Gary would stop fighting like a little boy and grow a pair, he wouldn't be so beat up."

"Out," my father yelled, his face turning red. "This is the last time I'm fucking asking."

"Fine," I cursed under my breath, so pissed off I could barely see straight. "Looked like I was fucking done anyway." I walked past Gary who visibly flinched as I pulled up the rope and yanked myself out.

My dad followed me, watching as I stormed to the lockers to get my bag. "Not so fast, Tessa. You're not leaving just yet."

I huffed out a breath of frustration, seriously wishing I could go back to hitting things. "First you want me out, now I can't leave, which is it, Dad?" Agitation bit at my tone.

It wasn't like me to snap at him, but my temper had been short. Sometimes that happened after a head injury, the brain taking longer to heal than most people thought. And sometimes it happened when you were still angry about losing the man you loved, feeling like a stupid idiot for wanting what you couldn't have.

Honestly, I wasn't sure we would've made it, but something inside of me was really willing to try. And even though I was hurt, mad and confused, I went over to his apartment the next day, looking for a thread just to hold on to.

Something.

Anything.

Just one tiny reason to try.

But all I'd done was look like a fool, Tibbs turning around and leaving me in that parking lot like he didn't give a shit.

I shouldn't have bothered.

Should've stuck to my original plan and let him and his baby momma sail into the sunset, while I went in the opposite direction. But I couldn't stop loving him, the stupid, gorgeous asshole stuck in my fucking heart like a virus. Which is why I went there in the first place.

Damn it.

"You want to watch your tone, Baby doll," my dad warned. "I'm giving you a lot of rope at the moment because I know you've been through a rough patch, but I will not tolerate disrespect. I raised you better than that."

My head snapped up, sobered by my dad's words.

He was right on every level.

Not only had both he and my mom supported me through my injury and returning to work, but through my broken heart as well. I'd gone home and confessed the whole thing, crying like a freaking toddler and allowing them to comfort me. They didn't even hate Tibbs, which was exactly what I'd been expecting. Instead they commiserated it was a tough situation for all involved, and they just wanted me to be happy. Ironic that what would make me happy was to be with Tibbs. But that wasn't possible because he didn't want me.

So considering how incredible my dad and mom had been the last few weeks, he didn't deserve to deal with me when I was acting like a brat.

"I'm sorry, Dad. I'm just frustrated." There was no point pretending because he knew me well enough to see though my lies and call me on my bullshit. Out of my parents, he was the one I was most like, so he got it better than anyone.

"Still no word from Tibbs, huh?" He helped me shuck my gloves. "Given any thought to calling him?"

I shook my head, unwilling to humiliate myself again. "I should've stuck with my original plan and let them be a family. Showing up that day was stupid and desperate, and all it did was hurt me all over again. I know it doesn't seem like it, but I'll be okay."

"Of course you'll be okay, sweetheart." My dad held out his hands waiting for mine. He gave them a squeeze, gently unwrapping the gauze over my knuckles as he continued to speak. "But *okay* is a low bar, and I want better for you."

Excellence wasn't just a buzz word in my household; it was expected. Not like overbearing stage parents who beat their kids if they didn't get straight A's or letter in track. No, we were expected to find our passion and never settle for less.

And there I was—in front of a man who had more medals and commendations than I could count—settling.

"I know, and I love you for it. Even if you are kicking me out of your gym." I tried to smile.

"Hey, rules are rules, killer. And I don't need you beating the living shit out of everyone unless you're on a ticket. It's bad for business." He winked. "But for what it's worth—and you can tell me to keep out of it—you've never been a quitter. So, if Tibbs is someone you want, then maybe you should see if there's something there."

It had to be hard for him. Championing the virtues of a man he knew had broken his daughter's heart, because ultimately it was the only thing that would mend it. That was why I had the best dad in the world. Because he was tough, but my God, was he fair. And he loved me unconditionally.

"Dad, they're probably together now. I don't want to be responsible for breaking up a home." It was something I'd never do, willing to live with my own unhappiness rather than ruin a family. I just couldn't, especially when there was a baby involved.

"Maybe they are, maybe they aren't. It isn't like when me and your mom got together. People are having kids and timesharing them like condos in Florida. You did the right thing and gave them time, sweetheart. But there's no harm in at least exploring the option, right? You're a cop, for Christ's sake, poke around and see what you find out."

He was so right.

I *was* a cop.

And with any luck I'd be a detective soon, so it should've been fucking obvious. But I had been going out of my way to avoid all things Tibbs, deliberately dodging any information about him or the baby.

News had obviously filtered through to the station, Justin's impending fatherhood something a lot of people wanted to talk about since he'd previously dated me. I was glad I'd still been on medical leave, spared the hushed whispers and pained glances. And by the time I got back, well, everyone had already moved on. It was Midtown after all, and Tibbs knocking someone up was a three-paragraph story even on a slow news day. It was clear cheating hadn't been involved, so other than a couple of sympathetic nods from the ladies in dispatch, I'd come through it relatively unscathed.

But since we worked in the same precinct, finding out information wasn't going to be hard. Hell, all I had to do was show up at *Vault* or *Diablo*—either of his sister's clubs—and one of the bar staff would probably tell me everything. And I'll admit, part of me was curious.

"Thanks, Dad." I threw my arms around him, hugging him tight. "And I really am sorry about before. I promise I'll take it easier on your guys next time."

"You're sweaty and you stink." He laughed as he caressed my hair. "And you'll do no such thing. I expect you to always go hard, and never apologize for that. But no more cheap shots," he warned. "You get it honestly, or not at all. There's no honor in a cheated victory."

I nodded solemnly, admitting I hadn't been fighting fair. "Promise."

"Good, now hit the shower. And have a good shift tonight, tell Miller I said hi." He gave me a quick kiss on the cheek and turned back to the gym. "Jesus, Gary, get off the floor already. If you vomit on the canvas, you're the one mopping it up."

And then he was gone, leaving me with a decision to make and a heart that was still very much in love with a man I'd said goodbye to.

Man, love really sucked.

"So any ideas on dinner?" Miller's brows lifted. "I was thinking maybe that new place near Bryant Park?"

I laughed, wondering how someone I adored had such shitty taste in restaurants. "You mean the tourist trap? Miller, are you sure you're actually *from* New York? You're not secretly from Alabama and just pretending to be a local, are you?"

He flipped me off, shaking his head. "I like to sample what the city has to offer." He spread his arms wide, inhaling deeply to prove his point. "It's called appreciation, Ricci, don't be such a snob."

My morning had given me a lot to think about, and if I hadn't needed to go into work, I'd have picked up the phone and called Tibbs. But our conversation wasn't something that could be rushed, and I still had no idea if he and May were together. And as much as it would kill me to know for sure, there was no way I'd even attempt to talk to him if they were trying to build a family. I just wouldn't do it.

So, as my dad suggested, I decided good old fashion police work was the way to go. And since it was a slow crime day on the streets of New York, I thought Miller and I could stop by one of Presley's clubs. Sure, technically I wasn't supposed to be taking care of personal business on company time, but we were still entitled to a meal break. And how I chose to spend that break was entirely on me. I could be chowing down on overpriced food from that place in Bryant Park orrrrrrrr I could head to *Vault*.

"I have a confession to make," I turned to Miller as we both got into the squad car, "I need to make a little pit stop and it's not of an official nature."

"Are we going to visit Vinnie and his cousins?" Miller grinned. "Because I'm telling you, anyone you want to make disappear, they can do it."

I punched him in the arm. "Will you quit with Vinnie and his cousins. They aren't the mob. And need I remind you, you're a fucking cop."

"First I can't eat where the tourists eat, now you're shitting on my mob fantasies." He threw his hands in the air. "Jesus, Ricci, why am I still friends with you?"

"Just start the car and head to *Vault*, Tony Soprano." I pointed to the road ahead of us.

"*Vault*?" His head whipped around. "Exactly what are we doing at this pit stop? And don't tell me we're checking for violations, because Presley runs a tight ship."

I bit my lip, knowing if there was anyone who would understand it would be Miller. He'd seen his once unshakeable partner crumble like a house of cards, not once judging me and my moment of weakness. "I'm thinking of talking to Tibbs, but I need some information first. Raelle will give me what I need and not run and tell him. Or at least I hope she won't. It's a risk I'm willing to take."

There was a possibility that Raelle's loyalties would be to Presley and Tibbs, and wouldn't say shit. There was also the possibility—more than likely—that Raelle would like nothing more than to gossip, especially when I'd been prepared to be transparent about my motives. She could think of it as a community service, sparing me from making a bigger fool of myself and saving Tibbs the drama of an ex who apparently wasn't over him. Unless he wasn't over me either, in which case . . . we'd just have to wait and see.

Miller shrugged, starting the car and putting it in drive. "Guess we're going to *Vault*."

He could've easily said no. That he didn't want to be involved in my shenanigans, and that he was going to use our break time constructively and go eat dinner. But Miller was loyal to a fault, which meant if I was up for making questionable decisions, he was joining right alongside me. And it helped knowing I'd have backup, because it was actually terrifying.

I'd thought about Justin so much that my brain was starting to hurt, and it all came back to me being unable to get over him. I knew that he was going to be a father, and that the child and his or her mother would forever be part of his life. But maybe, maybe I could still be part of it too. People got married and divorced and then found love again, and sometimes there were kids involved, and they *still* made it work. And maybe the time since finding all of it out had put things into perspective, and I wasn't really mad at him; it had just been a shitty situation.

He really was a *good* guy—kind, thoughtful, and gentle—who I loved with every fiber of my being. And he hadn't intentionally done anything to me, all of it just repercussions from before we were even together. And I just didn't want to be angry anymore and punish him for something he didn't deserve.

Except for not fighting for me, and for us. I would punish him for that. Assuming there was still an "us" worth fighting for.

Fresh nerves jangled in my stomach as we parked at the rear of *Vault*. Presley split her time between clubs, and I was hoping it was a night she was at *Diablo*. Not that I didn't love Presley, but the last thing I wanted to do was put her in the middle. Enlisting Raelle's help was one thing, using Tibbs' sister was a low blow.

"We got a plan, Ricci?" Miller asked as we exited the car. "Because we're both in uniform so we're going to get attention whether you want it or not."

My lungs expanded, taking a deep breath as I filled them with air and tried to find a smile. "I figure I'll wing it. Not like I've ever had a plan when it came to Tibbs, no point starting now."

"Sounds fucking awesome." Miller chuckled. "Let's go see if Raelle gives up the goods. Just putting it out there, if you need me to seduce her, I'll take one for the team."

I shoved Miller's shoulder as we headed to the front of the club. "She'd eat you alive, Grayson."

"Miller, Ricci," Marcus, the head of *Vault's* security team met us out front, "something I should know about?"

My eyes met his, doing my best not to look as terrified as I felt. "This is more a social visit; we just wanted a quick word with Raelle if we could."

"Social or off-the-record, Ricci?" Marcus clarified, the man smart enough to know the difference. "Because if you're questioning one of my team members—officially or otherwise—I'd appreciate a head's up. And I'll be sitting in on it too."

"She's here to pump Raelle for information about Tibbs," Miller answered before I could. "Trust me, you're not going to want to be involved."

I turned, horrified he'd caved so easily. Sure, Marcus could be intimidating, but Jesus, we had fucking guns. "Miller, seriously?"

"Just trying to hurry this along, and Marcus doesn't care, do you, Marcus?" His head tipped to the mountain of a man who was still blocking the entrance.

Marcus lowered his head, looking at Miller and then back to me. "Is that a fact, Ricci?"

"Yes, yes." I held my hands up, figuring there was no point trying to hide it. "That's exactly what I'm here for. Can we just go in already, or do I have to cite some bullshit about needing to check your liquor license or something?"

Marcus laughed, something I'd never seen before considering the man barely smiled. "I like you, Ricci, so I'm going to give you a freebie."

"Oh yeah?" I asked, knowing there was no such thing as a free lunch especially with someone like him. "And what's that?"

"Skip Raelle and the bar, and head to the booth closest to the VIP section. Tibbs is there with North and Leighton, strategizing on how to win you back."

"I'm sorry, what?" The words fell out of my mouth, not fully understanding what I was hearing.

"I said I liked you, Ricci, don't make me repeat myself." He lifted the red velvet rope and ushered us through. "Just because I don't talk a lot, doesn't mean I don't listen. And he's been a miserable shit for weeks; it's starting to really mess with the décor."

If I could've hugged the guy and it not been seen as totally unprofessional, I'd have done it. But I knew it would be pushing it too far, and Marcus had already done more than he needed.

"Thanks Marcus, I know you said it was a freebie, but I'll owe you one any way," I offered, nodding as we walked in.

He shrugged, seeming unperturbed either way. "Suit yourself, have a nice night."

My heartbeat was so loud and fast, I was positive everyone else could hear it. I had planned recon—a chance to gather intel—but my mission had been changed.

Marcus was a reliable source; one I would absolutely stake my reputation on if he was a witness and we were heading to court. So, if he said Tibbs was there with his two best friends, thinking up ways to win me back, that was *exactly* what was happening. Which meant—and yes, I was speculating, but again, something I'd stake my reputation on—that he was not with May.

He just wouldn't do that.

To her or to me.

"You ready, Ricci?" Miller grinned, stretching his arm out indicating I go first.

I took a deep breath, my eyes flicking to the club full of people and knowing somewhere in there was a man I couldn't live without. "So ready."

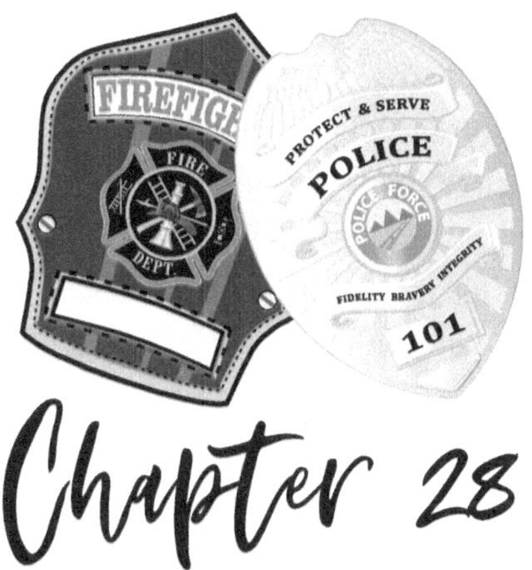

Chapter 28

Justin

NEVER IN A million years did I think the woman carrying my child would be actively trying to get me to reconcile with Tessa.

It was like a reality show, and not something I'd been initially comfortable with.

I didn't care how much May said she was cool with it; you just didn't talk about other women with the woman you were with. And while, yes, technically May and I weren't "together," it just felt wrong. I didn't want to disrespect her like that, or cheapen what I had with Ricci by talking about her behind her back.

But as it turned out, May was pretty fucking awesome when it came to perspective. And she'd been right in pointing out that unless we planned on giving up dating all together, eventually we'd both have significant others in our lives. And as weird as it was to think—let alone say—I really hoped May found a guy who would love her in a way I couldn't. Of course, he better be fucking awesome or he'd have to answer to me, but other than that, I wanted her to be happy.

As for me, there was only one woman I wanted, and that wasn't going to change in a few weeks or even in a lifetime. So I either found a way to win her back, or I joined a fucking convent or something. Because I'd rather be celibate, miserable, and single for the rest of my life, than be with anyone else.

"You know we've been telling you the exact same thing for weeks." North took a long pull on his beer. "Take it from me. If you love a girl, you don't just get over her. Maybe you should start wearing my deodorant again, it might knock some sense into you."

Leighton lifted his bottle and pressed it against his grin. "I've been saying the same thing too, North. Mack too. He even took Tibbs aside in the bays and threatened to beat some sense into him. Told him that he was being a moron and that wasn't what taking responsibility looked like. And that being a father didn't mean he had to give up on the woman he loved. But I guess baby mommas have more pull."

"Can you guys stop bitching about who said it first and think of something constructive?" I shook my head, thinking I should've just asked Presley. "I have some major ground to cover, and I can't waste any more time."

Going to her apartment had been my first instinct, but considering we hadn't spoken in almost a month, I wasn't sure she wouldn't call the cops. And being locked up would *not* help my cause. Not to mention I'd promised Mack that he wasn't going to get any more problems from me, and being hauled in for trespassing felt like a big ass problem.

So I'd—stupidly—gone to the two people who I not only trusted with my life, but who I figured would know what the hell to do. One, because they were both in relationships that had weathered their own storms. And two, because they knew both me and Ricci, and hopefully had a fucking clue.

But as we sat there drinking our beers, no one had come up with a better idea than "just go and talk to her." Which clearly illustrated that I'd been wrong, and they didn't know Ricci at all.

It was going to take an act of God for her to forgive me. Some kind of Old Testament shit where I disemboweled myself on a sacrificial altar and then admitted what a moron I'd been. Not for getting May pregnant, which as unfortunate as it was, had been beyond my control. And as much as I hated that it had hurt Tessa, I couldn't be sorry for what essentially created my son.

No, my stupidity—and required apology—was for things that she was going to have a harder time getting over.

For giving up on us.

For not fighting for her.

And for not giving her a choice as to whether we had a future.

Then there was the whole other fucking mess when she came to see me the next day. Me, stupidly believing she was coming to get closure, and not seeing it for the opening May promised me it was.

Fuck.

"Fuck," I said out loud because as far as ideas, I was all out. "Maybe I should go talk to her dad? Or to Miller? I'm positive they both hate my guts and will probably want to kill me. But at this point, I'll take whatever punishment they want to dish out if it gives me a chance." Hell, I was willing to do anything if I thought it would help, even if it meant putting my own personal safety on the line.

"Well, this just got interesting," North laughed, tipping his chin as he raised a brow. "Batter up, Tibbs."

My head snapped up in time to lock eyes with Tessa, her steady confident strides toward me making me forget how to fucking breathe. She looked amazing, her beautiful brown hair tied back and tucked under her hat, while that ridiculous body of hers was hidden by her cop blues. She was obviously on duty and the look on her face meant business, and I'd never been more in love with her than I was at that moment.

Fuck me, she was gorgeous. So beautiful and sexy that I couldn't even see straight. And either I'd somehow forgotten, or she'd found a way to get even hotter, because as inappropriate as it was, I was so turned on my dick hurt.

"Please don't disembowel yourself here though, your sister will kill you if you get blood on the floor." Leighton chuckled as she got closer.

"Gentlemen," Miller greeted us. "How's everyone doing?"

I hadn't even noticed him, unable to take my eyes off Tessa as she stopped in front of me. Honestly, I didn't give a fuck what Miller said, because as far as I was concerned, there was only one person I needed to talk to, and he wasn't it.

"Tibbs." She said my name with no emotion. And if I didn't admit to being a tiny bit terrified, I'd be lying. "Can you please stand up."

My ass rose from my seat like she'd commanded it herself, unable to say anything as I watched her. I had no fucking idea where any of it was going. But I'd been stupid enough not to read between the lines once, and I wasn't making that mistake again.

"Hey, is everything okay?" Presley rushed over looking at me and then to Tessa. "Tessa? What's going on here?"

"Police business," Tessa responded curtly, then turned back to me. "Place your hands on your head and turn around, Tibbs."

What.

The.

Fuck.

I was both turned on and confused, but I did what she said, putting my hands on the back of my head and turning around so I could no longer see her.

One hand was yanked down and cuffed, and then the other, the metal biting into my skin as she secured them extra tight. She wasn't kidding when she said they hurt, feeling the unforgiving bite of the cuffs every time I moved.

I'd still argue it was hot.

But considering I was unsure if she was going to slice my dick off and force me to eat it, I thought I should reserve my judgment.

Her hands gripped the cuffs, pulling me back toward her with a tug. "You have somewhere I can interrogate him?" I heard her ask. "Because he isn't getting out of custody until we get some things straight."

"My office," Presley responded, her giggle hinting she was enjoying it. "And this is some really kinky shit, so I hope you guys are getting back together."

"Let's go, Tibbs." She yanked again. "If you know what's good for you, you won't give me any trouble."

I was going to come.

I was literally going to jizz in my pants from being cuffed by the woman I loved, telling me she was going to interrogate me. I didn't care how fucking perverted it sounded, or what sick, sadistic shit she had planned.

Tessa was not only talking to me, but had her hands on me. And I didn't give a fuck what the circumstances were.

Jesus, I loved her.

I loved her so fucking much, and I'd do whatever she wanted if it meant she wouldn't leave.

Clubbers turned to watch me grinning like a lunatic as Tessa led me to Presley's office. It only held their interest for about five seconds before they went back to their business, probably relieved *they* hadn't caught the attention of the NYPD.

Marcus was standing beside Presley's door, his mouth barely twitching as he opened it for Tessa without asking any questions. Either they had an understanding, or he really didn't give a shit, no words exchanged by anyone until Tessa and I were safely inside and the door was closed.

"Tessa—"

"Not now, Tibbs." She shoved me into an office chair and switched on the light. "I need to ask you some questions first. Then, if you have anything to say, you can say it."

My hands were starting to hurt, my body contorted from being tossed into the chair, but I didn't move, watching as she came to stand in front of me and took off her hat.

"Do you understand, Justin?" she asked, her eyes locked with mine.

I nodded, giving her a verbal, "Yes," in case there was any doubt.

She took a breath, visibly steadying herself before starting. "Do you love me?"

"Yes," I answered without hesitation. "I never stopped."

She nodded, but didn't respond, moving on to the next question.

"What is the nature of your relationship with May? And don't tell me what you think I want to hear. I need the truth."

"We're just friends." I leaned closer, needing to touch her but being unable to. "I swear to you, there is nothing romantic with me and May, and there hasn't been. We're having this baby, but that's it. Neither of us are interested in each other in that way."

"Have you kissed or slept with her?" she clarified, too smart to leave any loopholes due to semantics.

And fuck, I couldn't lie.

I wouldn't lie.

Even though I knew it would probably hurt my case, I would never tell her anything other than the truth. "I kissed her this afternoon. Once, for like a second. It was the first and only time. It wasn't even a proper kiss and was over so quickly that it almost didn't happen. We'd just found out we were having a boy, and I got caught up in the moment. But it was like I was kissing Presley, and I was sorry a moment after I'd done it."

Her eyes flashed to mine, tears starting to form, and I hated myself all over again. "Baby, I'm sorry. I swear, it didn't mean anything. I was just—"

She raised her hand stopping me. "You're having a little boy?"

"Yeah, I'm going to have a son," I answered, a lump forming in my throat. "He's so strong too. I can't believe how much he moves."

Her hands moved to my shoulders, shuffling me so I was sitting straight before bringing her body closer. "Is there room in there for me, Tibbs? With May and your son?"

My heart seized, the muscles that kept it pumping giving me the finger as it felt like I was about to have a heart attack. I couldn't breathe either, the air feeling too thick as I tried to suck it in.

"Yes," I croaked out. "I need you, Tessa. I should never have let you go."

She lowered herself into my lap, straddling me as she brought her lips closer. "I love you, Justin. And I know that little boy is going to need you. But I need you as well. I tried to walk away. First, because I didn't think there was a place for me, and then because I thought it was the right thing to do. And when you didn't fight for me, I assumed that was what you wanted too." Her lips brushed against mine, not enough to kiss me, just barely letting their softness register. "But I want you, and I want to be with you, and if there's a place for me—"

"Yes." I leaned forward, straining against the cuffs and kissing her anyway. "There will always be a place for you," I murmured between kisses. "Please come back to me, baby. Please. I love you so much and I can't do this without you."

I didn't care if I sounded like a pussy, or if a better man would be able to walk away. She'd said she loved me, and I was hanging on to the second chance like my life depended on it. Because it did.

My life was *with* Tessa. No matter what else happened, or where either of us went. I just knew if she was with me, I'd be able to get through.

And I'd never stop fighting for her.

Never.

"I love you, dumbass." She laughed, kissing me between each word. "And I'm so fucking in love with you, I can't even think straight."

I kissed her too, my hands rocking against my back in desperation to get loose. "I love you too, baby. But you think we can uncuff me? These are really starting to fucking hurt and if I don't touch you, I'm going to explode."

Her mouth moved to my neck, teasing me a little before licking the shell of my ear. If she was trying to slowly drive me crazy, she was succeeding. My body confused by the pain of being restrained and being ridiculously aroused.

"Ricci," I moaned, my mouth trying to find hers. "Uncuff me."

"I thought this was what you wanted?" she teased, panting against my ear.

She was going to kill me.

Kill me.

And I would happily go. But if she didn't let me touch her, I was going to dislocate my own fucking shoulders.

"Tessa, take them off. Now," I warned, unable to wait any longer. "I need to kiss you properly."

"Fine, Tibbs," she chuckled, climbing out of my lap and then reaching to where my hands pressed against the chair. Finally I felt the slack, first one wrist and then the other, the metal coming loose and then removed all together.

With my hands free, I moved toward her, grabbing her face and bringing it closer. I couldn't stop kissing her, my fingers tracing the curves of her body like they were trying to remember every inch of it.

"I need you. I love you," I repeated, over and over again. "I'm never going to let you go."

It was a promise, a fucking vow, and one I intended to keep until my dying breath.

"Good." Her arms wrapped around me as she tilted her lips to mine. "Because I won't be letting you go either. And I have handcuffs."

"You're a fucking deviant." I laughed against her mouth. "But I'm *really* into it."

I'd almost forgotten where we were when there was a knock at the door.

"Guys, you better not be defiling my desk." It was Presley, and if she was trying to sound mad, she was failing. "But I am opening this door and you both better be decent."

Noise from the club flooded the room as Presley, Miller, Leighton and North huddled in the doorway. North swore, handing over some cash to Leighton who nodded in our direction. "I told you they'd be back together."

North shook his head, rolling his eyes. "Ricci, you couldn't have made him sweat it out a little longer? Jesus, you cuffed the guy. You didn't even rough him up a little?"

Ricci shot a glare at North. "You bet that we *wouldn't* be back together?"

"Noooooooo," he scoffed, looking horrified, "I bet that he'd have a black eye first," pointing accusingly at my unmarked face.

"Thanks for the support, North." I flipped him off.

Miller cleared his throat. "I hate to be the asshole and ruin this touching reunion. But we're still on duty and I haven't had dinner."

I knew she had to go, but I kissed her one last time even though everyone was watching. "I'll be waiting for you when you get off work," I whispered against her mouth. "In your bed. Naked."

She chuckled, lowering her voice. "You going to break in? You've already been cuffed once tonight, Tibbs, you want to make it two?"

I shook my head, holding her against me. "You seem to have forgotten you gave me a key. I never gave it back, and now I never will."

Recognition flared on her face, remembering that just before everything imploded, she'd given me her spare keys. I never got a chance to use them but couldn't bear to give them back. I guess some sick part of me wanted to hold on to whatever little shred of hope I had, even if they were made of brass and metal.

"Good," her hand pressed against my chest, "because I don't ever want to be without you."

"You won't have to," I promised.

And while I knew it wouldn't be easy, there wasn't a doubt in my mind she was the one for me.

She was my ride or die.

And I was hers.

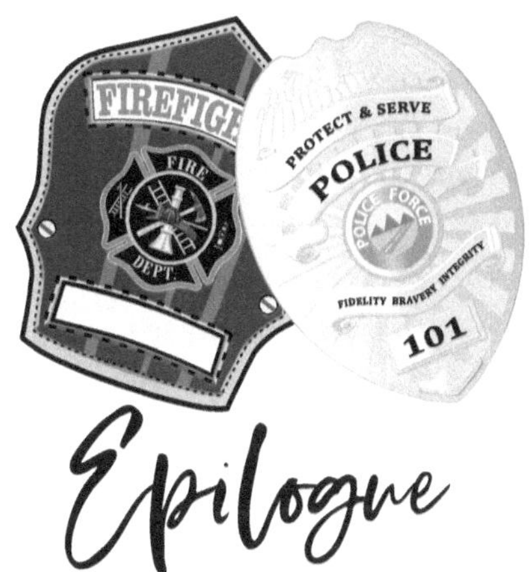

Epilogue

Justin

"**P**LEASE JOIN ME in welcoming the newest addition to the homicide department, Detective Tessa Ricci."

Everyone applauded, but none louder than me. The pride made me feel like I was literally going to burst out of my skin as I watched her accept her new badge. She'd worked her ass off, and there was no one who deserved it more. And there wasn't a doubt in my mind she was going to make one hell of a detective.

"You know, she's keeping *Ricci* for the force." Miller leaned in, grinning. "We don't need the *Tibbs* name coming up in here and sullying the NYPD."

I laughed, not giving a rat's ass what Miller had to say. "Her badge might say Ricci but she's still my wife."

We'd only been married a month, and I still couldn't believe it, the day she said she'd marry me one of the best days of my life. The other had been when my son was born, but Tessa had been there for that too. And I couldn't imagine my life without either of them.

"Shit, we missed it," May whispered, cradling Finn in her arms. "I'm sorry, Justin."

I hugged May, taking Finn and nuzzling him against my chest. "No need to apologize. She just got her badge and they're still doing photos, you're here and that's all that matters."

If you had told me twelve months ago, I'd be standing in a room with my wife and the mother of my child, I'd have told you, you were crazy. If you went a step further and told me they weren't the same woman, I'd have probably had you committed. But as it turned out, that was exactly what happened.

Tessa had moved into my Midtown apartment shortly after that night she handcuffed me in Presley's club. I didn't wait much longer to add an engagement ring.

And because May was one of the sweetest, most understanding humans I'd ever met, she welcomed Tessa into our son's world too.

Both women had been amazing. Tentative at first, neither of them wanting to overstep any boundaries and trying to be respectful. But that didn't last long, coming home after a shift to find both of them in a sugar coma after demolishing a chocolate cake. Apparently, they'd worked it all out, and they'd been friends ever since.

There was no fighting, no asking me to choose sides, and when Finn was born, Tessa was the first person to hold him after me and his mom. She knew May would always be part of our lives, and didn't punish me for it. And May believed that our baby boy had won the jackpot, getting three parents instead of just two.

So yeah, it was a little unconventional, but it worked, and that was all that mattered. Besides, who the hell was going to say anything when I was married to one of the toughest homicide detectives in the city. Ha! I'd say that would be a pretty short list.

"Heeeeeey, you made it!" Tessa gave May a hug before turning to Finn and kissing his little head. "How are my favorite boys doing?" She grinned as she reached down and grabbed my ass.

"You should be ashamed." I shook my head, pretending to shield Finn's eyes even though he was sleeping. "Not only is your boss and parents right over there, but I'm holding my poor innocent kid. You are such a pervert, Ricci."

"What are you going to do, Tibbs? Call the cops?" She laughed. "Now hand over the baby and no one gets hurt." She held out her hands, waiting for me to fill them with Finn.

I sighed, falling more in love with her every single day. "That badge has already gone to your head."

"Get a room already," Miller coughed under his breath. "Everyone knows these insults are like foreplay. And while Finn has no idea what's going on, May and I aren't so lucky."

May grinned, nodding in agreement. "Why don't you let me take Finn," she whisked him out of my arms and back into hers, "and Miller and I will go check out the refreshment table."

"Mmmmmmm, I like this plan." Miller rubbed his hands together in excitement. "Peace out, deviants."

We watched as the two of them strolled to the refreshment table; Finn sleeping peacefully through the whole thing. And even though I loved my son with everything I had, I was grateful to have a moment just with Tessa.

"Have I told you how much I love you?" I pulled her closer to me, brushing my lips against hers.

Unlike her, I respected the brass even if it wasn't mine. Keeping the PDAs to an acceptable level that wouldn't get us flagged by HR. Plus her dad was watching, and even though both he and Tessa's mom were supportive, I was positive he didn't want to see us making out.

She nodded, the happiness in her beautiful brown eyes making me feel like a rock star. "You did, but you can tell me again. I like hearing it."

"I love you, Tessa Tibbs. I am so fucking proud of you and I will never take for granted how lucky I am."

It was the mantra I repeated every single day. Sometimes whispered to her as she slept, sometimes while she was awake, but I'd never stop saying it.

"And I love you, Justin Tibbs. I'm proud of you too, and I will never take for granted how lucky *I* am."

She kissed me. And as much as I was trying to be respectful, my wife had a badge and a gun, and I wasn't stupid enough to deny her.

And truth be told, I didn't want to deny her.

Because I'd only be denying myself as well.

"You want to go back to our apartment and interrogate me?" I whispered in her ear. "Don't worry, I bought suitable handcuffs off the internet because we know you can't be trusted."

She mock gasped, the smile spreading across her lips. "Miller is right, we are deviants."

I laughed, lacing my fingers with hers as I pulled her toward the door. "Yeah, but I wouldn't have it any other way."

And lucky for me, I didn't have to.

Tessa

Loving Justin had never been hard.

Even when I'd wanted to hate him, my heart had always known he'd been my person. And as much as it had initially hurt that he had this deep shared connection—a child—with someone else, I couldn't walk away. In the end, I was glad I hadn't, because he was the best man I'd ever met. Hell, even my parents adored him, and they had a pretty high standard when it came to the men their daughters ended up with.

Mom and Dad had hugged us both before we'd left, telling me again how proud they were. Emilia hadn't been able to make my presentation but promised we'd catch up later. I was glad she was back from her latest duty tour and was hoping we'd get more time together. But more than anything, I was happier than I'd ever been.

"God, I love seeing that smile." Justin pulled me in for a kiss as we reached his car. "Even though sometimes it makes me nervous."

I chuckled, loving the feel of him pressed against me. "You worried, Tibbs? I mean, I get it. Your wife cannot only kick your ass but made rank before you did. Not all guys would be okay with that."

"Ricci, please," he scoffed, using my old last name as he reached down and squeezed my ass. "You know none of that shit matters to me. I'm *big* where it counts."

My eyes rolled, shaking my head because as much as he'd humbled since becoming a father, he was still as cocky as hell. "Just get in the car, wiseass."

"Oh, I'll get in the car." He popped open the door, holding it for me as I slid in. "But even you can't tell me I'm wrong."

And he was right.

I couldn't and I wouldn't, trying to hide my grin as he closed the door and went around to the driver's seat.

"Hmm," I looked around the inside of his Impala, thinking back to the first time I'd ridden in it, "you know, I was right too."

"About what, sweetheart?" he asked, slipping on his seatbelt before hitting the ignition.

"I told you this was a *dad* car." I laughed, pointing to Finn's car seat in the back.

He didn't even blink, taking his hands off the steering wheel and pulling me in for a kiss. "I thought we agreed it was *Daddy*?"

I laughed against his lips. "I didn't agree to shit, Tibbs. But just so we're clear, you *are* one sexy daddy, and one I fully intend to do dirty, dirty things to when we get home."

He swore under his breath. "Never *ever* selling this car."

"Good." I grinned. "Because if you even think about buying a minivan, I'm divorcing you."

But that was a lie.

He could get a minivan, start wearing socks and sandals, and embrace every "dad" stereotype there was, and I'd never love him any less.

I kissed him again, because I couldn't help myself. "Get me home, deviant. I want to check out these new cuffs you got."

THE END

To keep up-to-date with all T Gephart's news, appearances, and releases, please subscribe to her mailing list (http://eepurl.com/bws5Av).

Also please consider leaving a review on your retailer of choice. They help the author and future readers and we're all eternally grateful.

Acknowledgements

Thank you so much to my amazing family who never read these acknowledgements but hopefully know how much they mean to me. Gep, Jenna, Liam and Woodley, I love you. I'd say I'm sorry you don't have a "regular" wife and mother, but we all know I'd be lying. I wouldn't be sorry, and you guys aren't regular either.

Thanks to my extended family and friends, who I mostly haven't seen during this lockdown. 2020, right? Who knew it would be such a shitshow? I will never take for granted the ability to get in my car—or plane for those of you across the pond—and see you. I miss you beyond words. Thank you for your love and support, and we will see each other on the other side.

Thanks to Kelly Elliott who has been with me—usually daily—sending me encouragement throughout this entire series. It started because of you, and now it's done. What a ride! I adore you.

Thank you so much to Gayle Williams, who despite her own trial and tribulations, is never too busy to check in on me. I'm more grateful for our friendship than you'll ever know, and hope you will one day see what a gift you are. Thanks for all your help, love and support. You're truly a beautiful human, and I am grateful and blessed to have you in my life both personally and professionally.

Thanks Kimberly, Aimee, and Caroline and everyone at Brower Literary and Management. Sending hugs, guys. I'm totally bringing celebratory Tim Tams to you next time I'm in NYC.

Thanks so much, Nichole Strauss from Insight Editing. I know this year has been a challenge—as have been my manuscripts—but we got there. Another one is wrapped, and Lord, I think we're both relieved. Thanks for sticking with me.

Massive thanks to MK who isn't sick of me yet and whose initial read throughs give me so much value, I'm not sure what I'd do without it. Gah, I'll be sending more soon so hang in there LOL.

Thank you Elaine York from Allusion Graphics LLC, Publishing and Book Formatting. Not only do you make my books look pretty but your ability to deal with my changing schedule is amazing. Girl, I'm a hot mess, and you're awesome.

And LORDY, how could I ever release a book unless it has a Hang Le cover! You not only produce the most beautiful work—often under ridiculous conditions—but do it with so much patience and grace. Thank you for everything, the covers being the least of it. I adore you.

Thank you so much for finding all those pesky typos and proofreading, Rebecca from Rebecca Fairest Reviews Editing Services. Hopefully this time around it was a little easier!!

Much love, thanks, hugs and inappropriate kisses to all my author friends both near and far. I haven't seen you at all this year—except for online—and I miss you all desperately. Your words, messages, texts, FaceTimes, Marcos, and of course, your books have kept me going this year. I love you guys so much, thanks for everything.

Thank you, thank you, THANK YOU to all the bloggers, reviewers, bookstagrammers, group admins and promoters who read, promote, review, and share my work. I will never take any of it for granted and am so thankful for all your LOVE and SUPPORT.

Thanks so much to Mary Dubé from Grey's Promotions. I have LOVED working with you and so excited to be part of the family. Thanks for your love and support and dedication when it comes to my babies.

Thank you, Liz, MJ, and Jillian at 1001 Dark Nights.

THANK YOU TO THE T GEPHART REVIEW CREW AND ENTOURAGE. Thanks for your love, support, messages, and general bad-ass-ary. I love our little group, and your participation means everything to me.

And lastly, as always, thank YOU. Yes, you, the person who has this book in their hands and spent some time with me, allowing me the pleasure to entertain you. It's an honor, and I will never take it for granted. PS your hair looks amazing!

About the Author

T Gephart is a *USA Today* and International bestselling author from Melbourne, Australia.

With an approach to life that is somewhat unconventional, she prefers to fly by the seat of her pants rather than adhere to some rigid roadmap. Her lack of "plan" has resulted in a rather interesting and eclectic resume, which reads more like the fiction she writes than an actual employment history. She'd tell you all about it, but the statute of limitations hasn't expired yet. But all those crazy twists and turns have led her to a career she loves—writing romantic comedy.

When she isn't filling pages with sassy and sexy characters with attitude, she's living her own reality show in the 'burbs of Melbourne with her American husband, two teenage children, and her fur child—Woodley.

She loves adventure, to laugh, travel, and strives to live her life to the fullest.

Connect with T

tgephart.com
Facebook (https://www.facebook.com/tgephartauthor)
Goodreads
Twitter (https://twitter.com/tinagephart)

Books by this Author
The Lexi Series
Lexi
A Twist of Fate
Twisted Views: Fate's Companion
A Leap of Faith
A Time for Hope

The Power Station Series
High Strung
Crash Ride
Back Stage

The Black Addiction Series
Slide
Sticks
Stand